The Mysterious Fluid

The Mysterious Fluid

by
Paul Vibert

translated, annotated and introduced by
Brian Stableford

A Black Coat Press Book

ISBN 978-1-61227-020-3. First Printing. June 2011. Published by Black Coat Press, an imprint of Hollywood Comics.com, LLC, P.O. Box 17270, Encino, CA 91416. All rights reserved. Except for review purposes, no part of this book may be reproduced or transmitted in any form or by any means, electronic or mechanical, including photocopying, recording, or by any information storage and retrieval system, without permission in writing from the publisher. The stories and characters depicted in this novel are entirely fictional. Printed in the United States of America.

Table of Contents

Introduction

"There are unforeseeable things," wrote Pierre Versins in his *Encyclopédie de l'utopie et de la science-fiction* (1972), in his article on Paul Vibert. "You open a book and *paf!* there is an unexpected amazement, a richness, that nothing—neither the title, nor the author, nor the appearance—gave any grounds to expect." He goes on to list the fantastic ideas broached in the items contained in the book in question, *Pour lire en automobile, nouvelles fantastiques* [For Reading in an Automobile; fantastic short stories] (1901), with considerable approval, but does not seem to have taken his research any further. He cites the year of Vibert's birth (1851) but not that of his death (1918), and only mentions one of the several further collections that Vibert issued in the same series of books, merely to record that he has not seen it. He asserts, mistakenly, that all the items in *Pour lire en automobile* were originally published in a obscure periodical called *L'Ouest républicain* between 1895 and 1899—although the author admittedly does not give him much help in that respect, offering no detailed credits and mingling numerous items clearly written in 1900 and 1901 with earlier pieces in a somewhat hectic fashion.

Versins was undoubtedly right to identify *Pour lire en automobile*—here translated in its entirety as *The Mysterious Fluid* (that being one of its four subheadings)—as a book that contains, among other things, some significant contributions to the early development of French speculative fiction, but was also entirely justified in being somewhat confused by it. It is a deeply eccentric work by a man who seems always to have worn his eccentricities flamboyantly and provocatively, alongside his deeply-felt convictions—and seems, in that respect, to have been consciously and conscientiously carrying forward a tradition initiated by his father. Versins inevitably and quite rightly, likens the items assembled in *Pour lire en automobile* to the work of the popular humorous journalist Alphonse Allais,[1] but Allais was always a complacent absurdist, playing everything for laughs in an essentially amiable and risk-free manner. Vibert's range is considerably greater, and the satirical aspect of his work often takes on a much sharper edge; his fascinations were considerably more intense as well as more various.

Allais, in company with his sometime associates Charles Cros and Gabriel de Lautrec,[2] took a consistent interest in contemporary scientific controversies and discoveries, which is off-handedly reflected in his published work, but Vibert seems to have developed a real bee in his bonnet with regard to "the mysterious fluid" (electricity) and the possible consequences of its development. Although all the items dealing with that subject reproduced in *Pour lire en automobile* are blatantly farcical, their remarkable repetitiveness—which becomes a trifle tedious in the relevant section—betrays a strange fascination. One of the advantages of farce as a medium is that it liberates the imagination and conscience from restraint, and allows thoughts and expressions that might otherwise be censored to find gaudy depiction, and one cannot help suspecting that Vibert took his theory that electricity was "the unique motive force of the universe" quite seriously, choosing to express it in a farcical manner as a manner of shielding it from criticism. It is certainly the case that the scathing sarcasm in some of the other items in the collection—most notably the fake legend accounting (falsely) for the nomenclature of the *Grotte des dames* in "How People Die in the Colonies" and the supposed letter from a survivor of electrocution in "How People Die in America"—is as determinedly malicious as it is admirably intemperate.

---

[1] Two examples of Allais' work in this vein can be found in the Black Coat Press anthology *The Germans on Venus*, ISBN 9781934543566.
[2] All of Cros's proto-sf can be found in the Black Coat Press anthology *The Supreme Progress*, ISBN 9781935558828. A Black Coat Press sampler of Lautrec's work, including some proto-sf, is *The Vengeance of the Oval Portrait*, ISBN 9781612270098.

There are several reasons why Pierre Versins had to stumble across Paul Vibert by accident. By 1972, Vibert and his father were forgotten men, although Versins' advocacy did result in *Pour lire en automobile* being reprinted in 1981 by Slatkine, and the Bibliothèque Nationale's *gallica* website has at least laid the groundwork for the resurrection of their work by making some of it available on line. It did not help that some of the ideas they tried so hard to promote—including the notion that electricity is the unique motive force of the universe—turned out to be false, but many other promoters of mistaken ideas have survived more visibly, mostly because they were better at what they did, but also because they did not put so many people's backs up. The fact that Vibert was less polite than Alphonse Allais might seem a recommendation today, but it did not when he was alive or recently dead, and he was never good enough to mount any serious competition to Alfred Jarry as a satirist, proto-surrealist or pataphysicist. The best of his work does, however, reward reading—and when Vibert set out to collect the cream of his periodical publications in book form, *Pour lire en automobile* was his initial selection.

In spite of the prompting of Versins' enthusiasm, few historians of proto-science fiction have paid any attention to Vibert, perhaps because his work does not much resemble conventional fiction. It was all written for newspapers, to very strict word limits, and although he occasionally produced short serials—the one translated here as "The Submarine World" seems to have been his most sustained attempt to write something more like a story than a mere anecdote, and might well have been initially envisaged as a novel—he restricted himself almost entirely to the fictional formats that can easily be crammed into a thousand words; those items that are not straightforwardly anecdotal are almost all conversation-pieces, and many of the speculative pieces seem more closely akin to non-fiction than fiction.

Early writers interested in speculative endeavors had, of course, discovered that any attempt to import scientific argument and extrapolation into fictional frameworks caused problems of length, because of the sheer quantity of explanation required. Given that newspapers were such a vital part of the literary marketplace—having expanded much more broadly and rapidly in France than anywhere else in the world, because of the early advent there of widespread literacy—writers of speculative fiction had acute marketing problems, compounded by the reluctance of *feuilleton* novel-lovers to stray too far into such esoteric realms. The development of anecdotes, conversation-pieces and character studies as fictional devices was a natural response to this predicament.

The use of formats uneasily suspended between fiction and non-fiction was commonplace among the popularizers of science of the 1860s, including Camille Flammarion, Henri de Parville[3] and S. Henry Berthoud—Berthoud's *"fantaisies scientifiques"* would be an obvious ancestor of Vibert's work were they not so earnest—and had also been taken up in the 1870s by such humorists as Eugène Mouton.[4] It was, however, Alphonse Allais and Alfred Jarry who popularized the practice of condensing speculative themes into very short and wildly flippant formats, thus routinizing farce as a medium for calculatedly-unserious scientific speculation. Vibert undoubtedly took his cue from them, probably adding a tangible supplement to their influence on later writers in a similar vein, most notably Gaston de Pawlowski[5]. This entire tradition now seems something of a sideline to the history of the *roman scientifique*, but it is not without importance and certainly not without interest.

As Versins points out, Paul Vibert's forenames were officially registered as Edmond-Célestin-Paul, but he preferred

---

[3] cf the Black Coat Press translation of Parville's *An Inhabitant of the Planet Mars*, ISBN 9781934543450.

[4] Two of Mouton's stories of this kind are featured in the *The Germans on Venus* and *The Supreme Progress*, q.v.

[5] cf the Black Coat Press translation of Pawkowski's *Journey to the Land of the Fourth Dimension*, ISBN 9781934543375.

to sign himself Paul Théodore Vibert, and it is under that designation that he is catalogued in the Bibliothèque Nationale. His father, Théodore Vibert (1825-1885)—not to be confused with the printer of the same name (1816-1850)—was educated in law and practiced as an advocate in Paris, but, like many lawyers of the time, also had literary ambitions. Whether or not he was successful in that career, he must have had a considerable private income, because he was able to maintain a country residence in Verneuil-sur-Seine as well as a house in the Boulevard de Montparnasse—the latter in close proximity to the residence of Charles-Augustin Sainte-Beuve—and he seems always to have felt free to indulge his whims.

According to one of Paul Vibert's numerous brief memoirs, his father invited numerous literary men to Verneuil, in an attempt to develop that residence as a center of literary society; Alfred de Musset visited, as did Charles Nodier's daughter, although the other names Paul cites have now lapsed into relative obscurity. Paul also records that his father "virtually retired" from the bar at a relatively young age in order to concentrate on his literary endeavors—further evidence that he had independent means and no need to earn a living. At any rate, Paul recalled being brought up "in an exclusively intellectual atmosphere" and seems to have been drawn into his father's literary endeavors, as well as his political agitations, at an early age. Théodore was a fervent Republican, which presumably did not help him thrive under the Second Empire, although he was doubtless deeply distressed by the way that Empire eventually came to an end in the Franco-Prussian War in 1870. The helpful suggestions that he occasionally addressed by letter thereafter to Adolphe Thiers—the Third Republic's first President—might not have been as welcome as he hoped, but he was doubtless recognized in the last decade of his life as a man who had made a contribution to the great cause in darker times.

Théodore Vibert's first publication was the novel *Edmond Reille* (1856), an epistolary melodrama with philosophical pretensions, very obviously affiliated to the Romantic

11

Movement. He followed it up with several volumes of poetry, most significantly *Les Quatre morts, poésies* [The Four Dead Men, poems] (1864), *Rimes d'un vrai libre-penseur* [Rhymes of a Genuine Freethinker] (1876) and *Rimes plébéiennes* [Plebeian Rhymes] (1881), and one further novel of a similar stripe to his first. He thought the earlier fraction of this work sufficient significant to offer himself as a candidate for the Academy in 1877, with the support of another obscure poet, Arsène Thevenot,[6] and reacted badly to his rejection, publishing *Les Quarante, ou la grandeur et décadence de l'Académie Française* [The Forty, or the Grandeur and Decadence of the Academy] (1879), whose comments on the forty current members of the Academy were supplemented by further examples of his own poetry, a bibliography of works by himself and his son, and a list of all the favorable reviews those works had obtained. He also charged one of the Academy's members, Victorien Sardou, with plagiarism, on rather dodgy grounds. Thevenot went on to publish a study of the works of Vibert senior and junior in 1881, and they reciprocated by publishing an equally complimentary study of his work

Théodore's sense of unjust neglect and his resentment against his literary contemporaries are further reflected in the non-fiction book that was to become his most significant work, at least in terms of modern citation: *La Race sémitique* [The Semitic Race] (1883). The text begins, rather oddly, as a scathing attack on a historical novel by Marius Fontane, which had attributed a longer history to humankind than the one contained in Biblical chronology (as famously calculated by Archbishop James Ussher), but soon branches out into a general attack on all religious traditions and scientific works alleging that the human story must go back far beyond the supposed date of Noah's flood. Having dismissed everyone else's evidence—whether historical, geological, paleontological or

---

[6] Thevenot is nowadays remembered primarily as one of Louise Colet's lovers, and thus gets a passing mention in biographies of Gustave Flaubert.

archaeological—in a cavalier fashion, as false or corrupt, Théodore builds his own case based on a curious linguistic argument supposedly proving that Greek, Sanskrit and all other languages are, in fact, derivatives of Hebrew.

This project, far outgrowing its apparent origin as an intemperate book review, eventually became a projected four-volume *Histoire universelle* [History of the World], but only two volumes were published during Théodore's lifetime; Paul published a third, confusingly entitled *La Race chamitique* [The Hamitic Race—i.e. the black race supposedly descended from Ham], posthumously in 1916, but the fourth was never completed. Although the fundamental argument of the history is based on Biblical chronology, Théodore was a committed atheist, and brought his son up the same way. In that respect, at least, he was a "genuine freethinker," although he might more accurately be described as an "independent thinker." Paul presumably discovered later in life that his father had been wrong about many things, and that Théodore's mulish defense of anything in which he happened to believe, carried forward with all the rhetorical skill and dedicated partiality expectable in a skilled advocate, was a trifle absurd in itself, but that did not prevent Paul from remaining a staunch defender of the man who had carefully nurtured his own talents and ambitions.

Paul Vibert's first book was *La Démocratie impériale* (1874), one of numerous works that he was later to categorize in bibliographies of his work as "social propaganda." His next publications were, however, poetry; he published three sets of *Dizaine de sonnets* [Ten Sonnets] in 1875, 1878 and 1879, then the longer *Sonnets parisiens* [Parisian Sonnets] in 1880. He published *Le Péché de la baronne, idylles normandes* [The Sin of the Baroness; Norman idylls] in 1885, which he placed under the heading *Romans* [Fiction] in his bibliographies, and a collection of reprinted *Poésies, contes et nouvelles* [Poetry, Tales and Short Stories], appeared in 1889, but he appears to have given up on his literary ambitions by then. All his publications in the 1890s, and most of those thereafter, were non-fiction; those he did not categorize as "social propaganda" were classified in his bibliographies as works on "political economics," although they include such essays as *L'Électricité à la portée des gens du monde* [Electricity within the range of ordinary people] (1895).

Like many men of his era whose literary ambitions were frustrated, Paul Vibert eventually settled for a career in journalism, but he seems to have spent a good deal of time traveling, presumably financing his expeditions with his own money, and his colleagues probably regarded him as an amateur dabbler rather than a dedicated professional throughout the 1880s and early 1890s, although he does seem to have worked very assiduously. He visited both North and South America, and published an account of *La République d'Haïti* in 1895, but most of his observations and conclusions were decanted into articles for periodicals. His public profile was, however, dramatically raised when he became embroiled in the Dreyfus affair, as one of the unfortunate captain's staunchest defenders. He became closely associated with Georges Clemenceau's campaigning newspaper *L'Aurore*, which published Émile Zola's famous article headlined "J'Accuse."

When the most strident of Dreyfus' attackers, Édouard Drumont—the obnoxious founder of the Anti-Semitic League, who had earlier called or the expulsion of all Jews from France—set out to boost his virulent influence by standing as a candidate for the *Chambre des deputés* in Algiers in the spring of 1898, Vibert set off for Algiers to stand for election and campaign against him. Drumont not only won the election to the French parliament, but also succeeded in getting his equally-repulsive sidekick Max Régis elected as mayor of Algiers (with eventually disastrous consequences), but Vibert returned to Paris a hero of sorts, defeated but valiant.

In 1899, he signed the preface of a book vilifying Drumont and all he stood for, entitled *L'Anti-Pape Drumont-démon*, whose authorship was credited to "Montmartre l'Ermite"—almost certainly Vibert himself, although the Bibliothèque Nationale refrains from cataloguing it under his name. It was at that point in time that his journalistic career went into overdrive, and for the next decade, articles and books poured from his pen in amazing quantity.

Many of the books Vibert published in this period were collections of reprints of newspaper articles, loosely organized according to subject-matter. The first was a serious of *Silhouettes contemporaines* [Contemporary Sketches] (1900), but the most interesting, from a modern viewpoint, are the elements of a series launched with *Pour lire en automobile* in the following year. In that collection he deliberately grouped together the majority of his fantastic and scientifically-inspired pieces, those evidently being his first priority. Although his preface to the book is as assertively tongue-in-cheek as the items reprinted therein, there is probably no reason to doubt his assertion that he had conceived the ambition to write fantastic stories in the various veins of E. T. A. Hoffmann, Edgar Poe and Jules Verne back in the 1860s, but had never quite got around to it until he was finally encouraged by a friendly newspaper-editor to re-launch himself as a rival to Alphonse Allais—which gave him the opportunity to make up the deficit somewhat, albeit in a calculatedly clownish fashion. There is also no reason to doubt the allegation made in one of the items in the book that he often gave public lectures at La Bodinière—the exhibition hall of the Théâtre d'Application in the Rue St. Lazare—in the mid-1890s, and that one of the topics that went down well with the audience was interplanetary communication, with the citation of such fictional precedents as Cyrano de Bergerac and Poe; his interest in such subjects was evidently longstanding.

The other books in the *Pour lire* sequence are *Pour lire en bateau-mouche, nouvelles surprenantes* [For Reading in a Motor-Boat; surprising short stories] (1905), *Pour lire en ballon, nouvelles sentimentales* [For Reading in a Balloon; sentimental short stories] (1907), *Pour lire en traîneau, nouvelles entraînantes* [For Reading in a Sleigh; stirring short stories] (1908), *Pour lire en sous-marin, nouvelles énivrantes* [For Reading in a Submarine; intoxicating short stories] (1914) and

15

Pour lire en aéroplane [For Reading in an Airplane] (1915), although the last-named is not really part of the series, being entirely non-fictional and ostensibly offering "bird's eye views" of various parts of France. The contents of the third volume, as partially listed—unfortunately in garbled form—in Google Books, reveal that it continues several themes broached in the first, including animal intelligence, and has items on such philosophical topics as the nature of life and spontaneous generation, as well as material on neurasthenia and other forms of mental illness. The only volume fully available on line at the time of writing, however—the fourth in the series—consists almost entirely of nostalgic pieces about Paris and its inhabitants. The last two items were his final books, appearing after a five-year gap in his production, perhaps occasioned by ill-health.

Most of the "stories" contained in *Pour lire en automobile* require no further comment (although many of them do require a certain amount of explanatory footnoting), but it is worth making a few further points in advance with respect to their literary background.

There is one very obvious debt in one of the stories relevant to the history of scientific romance that Vibert is curiously reluctant to acknowledge. Just as he never mentions Alphonse Allais, he never mentions Allais' friend Charles Cros, although he must have been aware that the method of communicating with the inhabitants of Mars for which he takes the credit in the opening item in his section on "The Mysterious Fluid" was initially described by Cros in an article reprinted as a pamphlet in 1869. Although the topic became hot again in 1900, for reasons touched on in Vibert's footnotes to his own piece, it had never really gone away in the interim, and Cros's suggestions, properly credited in several proto-sf works of the period, were still being discussed in connection with the theme. Even the eccentric supplement about the long-range photography of a young Martian woman is oddly reminiscent of Cros's first proto-sf story, "An Interastral Drama" (1872) which was reprinted in *Le Chat Noir* in 1886.

Another author that Vibert does not mention, but who might well have been a significant precursor of his work, is Albert Robida,[7] whose pacifism he shares, although his own brief piece on war in the future, "The Art of Killing People," is a pale shadow of Robida's speculations on that subject. Robida, of course, took the opposite tack to Allais in solving the problem of how to incorporate speculative elements into his work, mostly writing long novels rather than anecdotal pieces, although his works often string together series of absurd anecdotal incidents in a fashion not dissimilar to Vibert's composite exercises. Vibert also shares with Robida an abiding fascination with the *Expositions Universelles* [Great Exhibitions] held in Paris in 1889 and 1900, and, in particular, with the changing face of Paris as celebrated in those exhibitions— with the extensive aid, in the latter case, of Robida's illustrative models.

Two further items in the present collection had previously trailed extensively by others writers of proto-sf. The fundamental motif of "Divine Prescience," first popularized by Camille Flammarion in the 1860s, had been employed in stories by Eugène Mouton and Louis Mullem,[8] among others. The idea of chemical nutrition, featured in "The Chemical Life of the Future" had been popularized by the chemist Marcellin Berthelot and previously developed in fiction by Charles Nodier and Jules Lermina,[9] among others. The most

---

[7] Black Coat Press has issued three volumes of Robida's work: *The Adventures of Saturnin Farandoul*, ISBN 9781934543610, *The Clock of the Centuries*, ISBN 9781934543139, and *Chalet in the Sky*, ISBN 9781935558873.

[8] Cf "The Historioscope" in *News from the Moon*, ISBN 9781932983890 and the title story of *The Supreme Progress*, q.v.

[9] cf their respective stories in *The Germans on Venus*, q.v. Black Coat Press has issued four volumes of Lermina's work: *Panic in Paris*, ISBN 9781934543832, *Mysteryville*, ISBN 97881935558279, *To-Ho*

straightforward reproduction of an earlier work is, however, the plot of "The Monster Telescope." The notion that tiny creatures—a mouse and a number of insects—caught in the view-field of a telescope might be mistaken for huge inhabitants on another world was previously the basis of Samuel Butler's satirical poem "The Elephant in the Moon," written *circa* 1676 but not published until 1759. It is, however, possible that Vibert might not have known that, and that he came up with the idea independently.

One significant writer of proto-sf that Vibert must have known personally is Louis Mullem, who also worked for *L'Aurore* and became one of Georges Clemenceau's closest political allies after an initial period of rivalry. As the stories by Mullem reprinted in *The Supreme Progress* show, Vibert and Mullem did have certain speculative ideas in common, especially related to the fluid nature of the soul, but Mullem's stories were almost certainly written before Vibert's prolific phase began and were only published, posthumously, after it had finished, so the probability of any direct influence in either direction is extremely slim, and entirely dependent on the possibility of the ideas being broached in conversation. Indeed, the great majority of all these connections and similarities mainly serve to demonstrate the extent to which these ideas were "in the air" during the relevant period, and the extent to which, in spite of its manifest eccentricities, Vibert's work slots very neatly, and interestingly, into the developmental pattern of the *roman scientifique* genre at the end of the 19th century.

The following translation is taken from the 1981 Slatkine reprint of *Pour lire en automobile*, which is a photographic reproduction of the first edition published by Berger-Levrault in 1901. The original contains numerous typos, misspelled names and errors in punctuation, and sometimes gives the im-

and the Gold Destroyers, ISBN 9781935558347, and *The Secret of Zippelius*, ISBN 9781935558880.

pression that text has been accidentally omitted or garbled; I have done my best to get through these difficulties, usually correcting misspelled names without comment, although I have probably allowed some to survive unwittingly. The author's abundant use of puns caused inevitable difficulties in translation, but I have tried to limit my footnotes to the most significant examples. Inevitably, some of the flavor of the original has been lost, but I hope that enough survives in English to render the reading experience pleasurable.

Brian Stableford

Preface

This has no pretention to being a preface, properly speaking, but simply a small notelet—and if I add a qualification to a word that has no need of it, already being a diminutive in the Italian manner, it is because I want to emphasize its unimportance.

Many years ago—let us say, if you wish, before the war,[10] that fateful date—I thought of writing a number of fantastic stories, all (or very nearly) resting on some scientific premise, thus continuing, pleasantly—for me, at least—the tradition of Hoffmann, Edgar Poe and sometimes even the more modern Jules Verne.

Since then, the years have gone by, the need for scientific precision has made itself felt more imperiously with every passing day, the quotidian occupations and preoccupations of the life of a journalist have enveloped me—bogged me down, I was going to say—a little more each day, and I scarcely had time to scatter a few occasional chronicles approximately corresponding to the plan originally conceived.

Two or three years ago, however, a Breton periodical, the *Ouest Républicain*, which had heard talk of the odious and imbecilic fashion in which I had been pursued by EIGHT HUNDRED AND NINE Breton priests, and the even more ridiculous and monstrous fashion in which I had been condemned for telling the truth, offered me hospitality, by inviting me precisely, and very amiably, via the intermediary of its editor-in-chief, my excellent colleague Adolphe Henry, finally to bring the project so long-cherished—I do not say ripe, for it might better be described as over-ripe—to completion.

I was still hesitating somewhat, increasingly absorbed by the multiple travails of my journalistic life, writing a little eve-

---

[10] The Franco-Prussian War of 1870.

rywhere, always embattled, when an altogether unexpected external circumstance convinced me to pursue the realization, partial if not integral, of my old project. There was a place—more than one, if I am not mistaken—vacant in the general history and philosophy section of the Académie des Sciences Morales et Politiques, and I decided to offer myself as a candidate. Having published at least twenty volumes in my life and having written the equivalent of more than two hundred in the press, I confess that I modestly believed myself qualified.

Naturally, I made the traditional, if not obligatory, visits; the majority of the members of the learned assembly received me with the amiable but coldly sphinx-like courtesy that is intended to frighten timid souls, but some, less self-controlled, could not hide their surprise.

"But Monsieur, you're no philosopher. A historian, perhaps, but no philosopher at all."

I confess that, in my turn, I could not hide my profound amazement.

"What, no ten-centime philosopher! (I don't say *two sous* out of respect for the metric system, which is one of the glories of my homeland.) But that's all I am, and it seems to me, my dear future colleague, that we're the victims of the most abominable of misunderstandings.

"Come on, let's explain ourselves better. Everyone knows that in the Middle Ages, Theology held philosophy in humiliating servitude—*ancilla theologiae*—and that it was only much later, with the encyclopedists, if you wish, that it finally succeeded if freeing itself completely. But everyone also knows that pure philosophy, that of the school, is soon bound to disappear forever, with Cousin, Jouffroy and Royer-Collard,[11] its last representatives—unless one has both the

---

[11] Victor Cousin (1792-1867), Théodore Jouffroy (1796-1842) and Pierre-Paul Royer-Collard (1763-1845) were all what the terminology of the day would have called *spiritualiste* philosophers—philosophers of mind, in today's parlance—who were interested in the study of consciousness *per se* rather than its perceptions of the external world.

naivety and audacity to consider oneself a philosopher because one spends one's time raking over the schools of yesteryear, writing pretty rhetorical essays on Kant, Hegel or Descartes.

"Does that mean that philosophy has disappeared with them? Not at all; only that, the outdated formulae having had their day and modern chemists, electrical theorists, naturalists, botanists, sociologists, as well as economists—scientists of every sort—having arrived, with the experimental method as their means and the discovery of the truth and the application of justice as their goal, are the only real philosophers of modern times, before whom the members of the crowd ought to take off their hats respectfully, because it is by virtue of their endeavors that every great democracy must hope to reach an ideal of relative happiness in the future....

"Thus, from that viewpoint, I confess that, with my work on economic and colonial affairs, I had the great naivety if believing myself an arch-philosopher."

"Well, Monsieur, that's your error; here, on the other side of the water, we regret to inform you that we still hold to the old formulae of eclecticism."

As I have always been full of deference—in my youth by virtue of generosity, and now by virtue of egotism—for old age, being almost in the antechamber of the respectable body, and not being stubborn by nature, I emerged from my visits firmly resolved to *obtemperate* with the aforementioned advice (as the famous colonel[12] said), and that is why I finally decided to write the present volume, which is, this time, entirely philosophical—at least, I hope so.

Perhaps it will be found to be a little too scientific; that is because I have not been able entirely to dispose of the man of old: a touch of the fantastic is the indispensable condiment of the present era, and if the salt is not always Attic,[13] that is

---

[12] The reference is to a character in Rabelais' Pantagruel, who was fond of using such words as *obtempérer* [to comply] and *equipollent* [of equal value or significance]

[13] "Attic salt" (*sel attique* in French) is a fancy expression for lively wit, as credited to the Athenians of the Classical era.

simply because I was born in the heart of Paris, on the Butte-aux-Moulins, between Molière's house and the Opéra, and not in the shadow of the Acropolis.

These explanations being given with the sole aim of passing conclusively for a serious philosopher, according to the consecrated formulae, and to obtain my pardon, I ought to say why these stories have almost all been reduced to the compendious form of simple chronicles. I repeat that it is that my crude trade as a journalist, conducting an ardent battle of ideas for justice and liberty from one day to the next in twenty newspapers, that leaves me little time lovingly to sculpt long stories in the manner of the author of *Contes Fantastiques*.[14] Then again, I thought that in our era, when everything is hurried, active, ardent and urgent, it is perhaps best to write short stories in order to be widely read and to popularize one's ideas, one's philosophical system.

"What? So you have a philosophical system!"

"Certainly, and this is it, in brief: to arrive at justice and liberty, by virtue of generosity and tolerance, with the integral application of Human Rights and the great principles of the Revolution, which ought to be the honor of the Republic, the glory of France, the very patrimony of humankind in its entirety, reconciled in peace and in universal labor…"

"Utopia, people will say."

"That's possible, but in the matter of human perfectibility, so dear to my father, I want to die with my generous illusions—which, it seems to me, always ought to soothe the placid demise of a philosopher…for let's not forget that I'm a philosopher, at present.

"Finally (why should I not admit it?) I also wanted to leave something of myself, akin to a sincerely affectionate visiting-card—not the last, if possible—to my relatives and

---

[14] By the time Vibert wrote this preface, this title had been applied to collections by numerous writers, but he means the pioneering collection of translated tales by E. T. A. Hoffmann that became an enormous influence of French fantastic fiction in the 19th century.

old friends. On that point, to translate the whole of my thought, I cannot do better than to recall here these eloquent and dolorous passages of Guy de Maupassant, which my excellent friend and colleague Pol Neveux[15] evoked so aptly in May of last year, in Rouen, if my memory can be trusted:

"'In his appetite for oblivion, Maupassant went as far as to deny his own effort. I found these lines in an unpublished letter: 'I am incapable of loving my art truly. I judge it too harshly, I analyze it too thoroughly. I know how relative the value of ideas, words and the most powerful intelligence is. I cannot help being scornful of thought, so feeble as it is, and form, so incomplete as it is. I have a genuine sense, in a sharp, incurable fashion, of human impotence and a scorn for efforts that can only lead to poor results...

"'If I were ever able to talk to a person rather than to a barrier, I might perhaps let out all the unexplored, repressed, inconsolable thoughts that I sense in the depths of my being. I feel them inflating and poisoning me, as bile does to the bilious. But if I can spit them out one day, perhaps they will evaporate, and I shall no longer find anything within me but a light and joyful heart—who knows? Thought becomes an abominable torment when the entire brain is nothing but a wound. I have so many bruises in my head that my ideas cannot stir without making me want to shout: *Why? Why?* Dumas would say that I have a bad stomach. I think it's more that I have a poor shameful and prideful heart, a human heart, that old human heart at which people laugh, but which becomes emotional and also makes one's head ache. I have a Latin soul, which is exceedingly worn-out. Then again, there are days when I don't think like that, but I suffer all the same, because I belong to the family of the flayed. But that, I don't say and I don't show—I even think that I hide it very well. I am un-

---

[15] Goncourt Academy member Pol Neveux (1865-1939) became better known for his study of Guy de Maupassant, which was used as a preface to both French and English editions of Maupassant's collected short stories, than for any of his own works.

doubtedly thought to be one of the most indifferent men in the world. I'm a skeptic, which isn't the same thing—a skeptic, because I see clearly. And my eyes say to my heart: *Hide yourself away, old chap, you're grotesque.* And it hides itself away…'"

He was also afraid of death:

"He would soon die in his turn. He would disappear, and it would be over…how frightful! Other people would live, laugh, love one another…. Isn't it strange that one can laugh, amuse oneself and be joyful under the eternal certainty of death!

"No one ever comes back. Millions and billions of near-identical people will be born, with eyes, a nose, a mouth, a skull, with thoughts inside, without the person who had lain down in this bed reappearing. It was finished for him, finished forever. A life! A few days, then nothing more! And yet everyone has a furious and unrealizable desire for eternity within him; everyone is a sort of universe-within-the-universe and everyone is soon annihilated completely in the compost-heap of new seed-germs. Plants, animals, humans, stars worlds— everything is animate, and then dies, in order to be transformed. And no individual, human or planet, ever comes back again!"

Thus he expressed himself, tragically, in *Bel Ami.* It is the eternal story of all men of letters, of all thinkers, who always have the desire to survive—and I don't think that I can make my own confession with such a persuasive and poignant sincerity…

One more thing. It is for the public, as indulgent as it is benevolent, to determine the fate of this volume and subsequent ones. If there is a fine welcome reserved for it, I warn the public that there are four more of them ready, similar and *equipollent*, as the amiable colonel would say, without prejudice to what may come after.

If, therefore, these stories amuse you—as the song says—we can begin again…sorry, continue them…which certainly proves that their fate and mine depend on your verdict, and I would like to think, dear readers, that you will take pity, for once, on a poor devil of a philosopher—doubtless the last, in the official sense, if he has succeeded in retaining the secret of it—who is, above all, always full of good will!

Paul Vibert.

LIFE

The Rabid Elephant

In the reign of Louis-Philippe. Along the Boulevard du Crime.
A bloody adventure.

> The great white elephant of the Indies
> Fell, broke its leg, and died.
> It was buried near the Madeleine
> With imposing ceremony.
> Only the captain of the firemen
> Retreating to a corner,
> Wept into his helmet.
> When the ceremony was over
> The captain of the firemen
> Made a speech and said:
> "The great white elephant of the Indies
> "Fell, etc…"

It is extraordinary how quickly everything is forgotten. Thus, the perfectly true story that I am about to tell you today unfolded in the early years of the reign of Louis-Philippe, in the very heart of Paris, in the open air of the boulevards, and yet no one today has any memory it, except perhaps for a handful of long-lived individuals who were once resident in the Boulevard Beaumarchais, or that part of the Marais bordering the old boulevards.

It was during the festival held every year in the Place du Trône, at the top of the Faubourg Saint-Antoine, under the benevolent gaze of Charlemagne and Saint Louis, if I'm not

29

mistaken—the festival popularly known as the Gingerbread Fair.

On one side of the immense circle formed by the plaza stood a long series of vehicles forming a sort of internal gallery. It was a famous menagerie belonging to some ancestor of Pezon[16] whose name I have forgotten. The incontestable ornament of this interesting family of ferocious beasts was an enormous and superb white elephant, as white as the King of Siam's—which indicated that he was very old, for the hair of pachyderms turns white, exactly like that of humans. As he was sober and philosophical, however, he had conserved all its strength.

Several years before, a pretty little spaniel bitch had served as his companion, and they had loved one another tenderly. One day, the little dog had disappeared, without anyone being able to find her. The menagerie's owner thought no more about it, after having mourned appropriately for a week with his dear proboscidian—which was, as I said, the glory of the menagerie, and was named Alfred, although no one had ever known why. Alfred, however, had conserved a great depth of melancholy since the disappearance of the little dog, which answered to the affectionate name of Aglaea. It was evident that the old philosopher had taken a blow to the heart.

One Sunday, when the joyful and densely-packed crowd entirely covered the Place du Trône, Alfred was in the process of performing with his mahout in front of the spectators, dancing an up-tempo polka, when he suddenly stopped. He took three steps back, braced himself forcefully, and, displacing a few planks with his rear end, found himself in the plaza, in the midst of the crowd, whose members stampeded, howling with fear, as the animal came straight toward them.

Knocking over everything in his path, the beast went down the Faubourg Saint-Antoine at top speed, followed by all the menagerie staff, who were saying: "He's gone off in search of Aglaea, for sure."

---

[16] The famous lion-tamer Jean-Baptiste Pezon (1827-1897).

Arriving at the location of the Colonne de Juillet, Alfred saw the huge elephant of stone and plaster and prepared to hurl himself upon it—but, recognizing his error, he turned round, murmuring internally, a long time before the song: "For he's made of stone, of stone…" And he continued his mad race along the sequence of great boulevards: Beaumarchais, Filles-du-Calvaire, etc.

Two minutes later, he was in the Boulevard du Crime, where all the theaters in Paris seem to be holding a meeting. The event had taken on enormous proportions, however; a hundred thousand people were following Alfred at a distance, exciting him further with their racket. National Guardsmen, mounted and on foot, had been sent to alert the Prefect of Police, the King, his august family and the Place Vendôme, who were in mortal dread.

Finally, in haste, at the corner of the Boulevard Poissonnière and the Boulevard Montmartre, the generalissimo of the National Guard himself ordered half a dozen *citadines*—the omnibuses of the day—to be overturned, along with two *gondoles*, a *Batignollaise* and three *écossaises*, if I'm correctly informed, as well as a certain number of *cabriolets*, to form an improvised barricade.

It was just in time. Ten minutes later, Alfred—still in search of Aglaea, raced forward, trunk forward and tail raised, with a provocative little white tuft, and fiery eyes! Confronted by the unexpected obstacle, however, he unleashed a formidable trumpeting, which caused the dormant brass instruments of the Opéra in the Rue Le Pelletier to resonate—and his little eyes became bloodshot.

After a momentary hesitation, alone in the middle of the deserted boulevard—the crowd was far behind him and the National Guardsmen were massed on the other side of the barricade, weapons in hand—Alfred began furiously uprooting all the trees and gaslights in the boulevard with his trunk, along with the oil-lamps hanging from poles outside the houses, and hurling them pell-mell at the barricade, which seemed to grow proportionately. In the blink of an eye, for a hundred meters around, the boulevard was laid bare, as bald as the skull of the late Siraudin.[17]

Proudly raising his head, his trunk stabbing the sky, trumpeting with such violence that the windows in the quarter shattered into smithereens, he saw a beauty of the day—a *little darling*—in the forecourt of a fashionable restaurant. He bounded forward and, stretched out his trunk, seized her round the waist and launched her furiously at the barricade.

White foam was beginning to fleck the edges of his trunk, and a horrible clamor suddenly went up throughout the heart of Paris, only comparable to that raised during the Deluge.

"He's rabid! He's rabid! Alfred is rabid!"

And the cry reverberated from one echo to the next, beyond the future fortifications, throwing all of France into terror, while the Chappe telegraph[18] waved its long arms everywhere, from Montmartre to Belleville to Monthléry, demanding the immediate dispatch of artillery from every province, all the way to Marseilles.

Meanwhile, the firemen were arriving—quite impotent, poor fellows! The situation was becoming increasingly grave. Paris was breathless, and a million voices were moaning: "Alfred is rabid! Alfred is rabid!"

And the situation was, in fact, grave, for hydrophobia multiplied the pachyderm's strength ten- or a hundred-fold.

After having darted a circular glance around him, establishing that he had made the boulevard a desert, Alfred had launched himself at the barricade, caused it to collapse and passed over it in a single bund.

---

[17] The dramatist and librettist Paul Siraudin (1813-1883)

[18] A semaphore system invented by Claude Chappe (1763-1805), whose establishment began in 1792; it became a vitally important carrier of information during the Napoleonic War and remained in use until it was displaced by electric telegraph systems. Chappe committed suicide because he felt (rightly) that his invention had been stolen.

Paris was doomed, and I would require the pen of a Victor Hugo to describe the anguish that gripped a million hearts at that moment within the capital and its suburbs, not to mention Robinson and the Lilas. Even Paul de Kock[19] had no further desire to make his co-citizens laugh.

It was a supreme and solemn moment—a moment ineradicable from the soul of a race!

The director of the menagerie remembered that Aglaea had bitten Alfred lightly on the trunk. There was no doubt about it: Aglaea had died of rabies!

Alfred was rabid! The Cardinal-Archbishop of Paris had sent a telegram to Rome asking the Pope to bless France.

It was, however, the governor of the Invalides who saved the situation; hastily, with his fittest men—which is to say, the least invalid[20]—had set up his cannons in a battery in the Place de la Concorde, lined up in front of the Rue Royale.

When Alfred, handsome and terrible in his horror, with foam dripping from his mouth and blood in his eyes, emerged opposite the Église de la Madeleine, he hesitated for a second—the time of a lightning-flash—and threw himself recklessly into the Rue Royale.

The old governor of the Invalides uttered a cry of victory, which made his silver nose fall off. He waited five seconds—five centuries! The sun itself seemed to pause to contemplate the scene, and the fountains in the Place de la Concorde spontaneously stilled their crystalline song...

When the elephant reached the corner of the Rue Saint-Honoré, the old governor of the Invalides shouted: "Fire!"—and a frightful discharge of grapeshot scythed Alfred, cutting him in two, causing the steps of the Madeleine to explode into shards through the closed gates.

---

[19] Paul de Kock (1794-1871) was an enormously popular writer of light romantic fiction.

[20] There is an untranslatable pun here; the term I have translated as "fittest" is *plus valides*.

Paris was saved, but it counted thirty-seven dead, crushed in the crowd, and nine hundred and eighty-one wounded. As for the *darling* hurled at the barricade, she got away with a broken leg.

It was from that day on that, in anticipation of another rabid elephant, the Prefect of the Seine had the trees surrounded by protective iron grilles. Bureaucracy never surrenders its rights!

People who fall ill are legion, numbered in thousands, and that is why I have undertaken to tell you this true and terrifying history of an already distant epoch today.

Mammonth and Behemoth

How I saw a living mammoth. Curious experiments.

I had come to dinner one evening at the home of a young attaché in the Ministry of Foreign Affairs in St. Petersburg, Prince D***, and we were chatting in a desultory fashion in the abandoned and ecstatic pose of boa-constrictors digesting their meal, when, after a pause during which we had watched the bluer wisps of or cigar-smoke rise up, he spoke to me, suddenly but slowly, as if to make sure I understood what he was saying.

"There's a legend here, you know, which says that the Mammonth—which is mistakenly called the Mammoth, without the N[21]—is simply the contemporary, or rather the same animal, as the famous Behemoth of scripture."

"I know."

"Do you also know that layers and mountains of the bones and tusks—fossilized ivory—of these animals have been found on the innumerable islands that extend into the Arctic Ocean like a long chaplet, along the coast of Siberia?"

"Yes."

"Finally, you're not unaware that a certain number of Mammonths have even been found intact, in the ice, with their fur and their impressive manes, reminiscent of those of majestic lions—irrefutable witnesses of those remote times?"

"Indeed."

---

[21] The French for mammoth is *mammouth*, so the original substitutes the N for a U. "Mammonth" is, in fact, an alternative spelling, still used in some place names in North America. As in English, the Biblical "Mammon" is used in French as a synonym for wealth or its worship.

35

"And perhaps you know that one day, at the great banquet held for the entire European scientific community by the Imperial Geographical Society of Tobolsk, it was possible to serve excellent Mammonth fillet-steaks, perfectly conserved, fresh and exquisite, which might have been twenty, thirty or forty thousand years old, perhaps more."

"I was there."

Prince D*** looked at me, suddenly interested in his own words, on finding that he had listener already initiated into all these mysteries. It was in an earnest tone that he went on: You've eaten one, but have you seen a living one?"

"That's madness!"

"Madness, you say! Well, I have a living one, very much alive, at home on my country estate—except that, as the Emperor would certainly want it, no one knows that I possess such a treasure.

"And it's forty thousand years old?"

"No, it's only three years old, and if you'll promise to be discreet, we can take the express tomorrow—it's only a day's journey from here—and I'll let you see it."

I looked at the Prince, convinced that he was mad. He was very calm, though, and smiling, enjoying my amazement and bewilderment.

"You're wondering whether I have a spider in the ceiling, as you say in France, eh?" Suddenly gripping my hands affectionately, he added: "No, my friend, I only have a living Mammonth, very much alive, in my stables."

"A male?" I asked, with an involuntary hint of mockery.

"No, a female."

The Prince's features then contracted so violently with pain that I thought I had offended him, and offered him all my apologies.

"It's not that—no, no, you'll understand in two days, when we get to my country house."

We left the next day, and two days later, overwhelmed with emotion, ready to faint in confrontation with that sudden evocation of the earliest days of terrestrial fauna, I was contemplating with my own eyes and touching with my fingers the fantastic rump of the Mammonth.

I thought I was dreaming; I could no longer pronounce a single word. The Prince patiently enjoyed my nervousness.

Finally, when I was able to speak, I said: "Indeed, one can see by the coat alone that it's a female; the fur is beautiful and thick, but the mane isn't as imposing as those I've seen in your Natural History Museum, which belonged to males.

"Evidently," he said, bitterly.

"But tell me, please, how you come to have this fabulous beast in your home."

"It's quite simple, and I'll explain it to you in a few words. Have you heard mention of artificial fertilization? There's a physician who specializes in it."

"Of course."

"Well, about twelve years ago, a Mammonth was found in a perfect state of conservation. I took the frozen fecund material—you understand—and melted it in a basin over a little fire, and by virtue of ordinary procedures that there is no need to go into, I put a female elephant that I had ordered by for that purpose from India, on the off chance, in an interesting condition. You can see that the spermatozoa returned to life after thousands of years—an admirable operation, chemical rather than vital—and after nine years, my female elephant delivered into the world the young Mammonth that you have before your eyes. Unfortunately, this one is also female, and when she dies, probably in a hundred and fifty or two hundred years, or more, it will be over; I will not have been able to resuscitate and perpetuate the species entirely."[22]

Prince D***'s eyes moistened with tears as he told me that.

---

[22] Even as late as the end of the 19th century it was widely believed that the characteristics of animal offspring were entirely determined by their sire, the dam merely providing a sort of incubator; this why Vibert assumes that "mammonth" sperm impregnating a female elephant would produce a mammonth, while a female mammonth would be useless for breeding purposes in the absence of a male.

"But why not recommence the operation that succeeded so well the first time?"

"I tried to conserve the material taken from the parts of the Mammonth, but it did not take long to decay, in spite of my precautions, and since, in spite of the millions I have spent financing searches, no one has been able to find a single intact Mammonth in the ice. Save for a chance impossible even to anticipate, I've lost all hope. And who knows, even if the condition were met, whether a second attempt would succeed?"

I left the Prince plunged in his reflections—and that's how I was able to see, twenty years ago, in the depths of Russia, a living Mammonth of flesh and bone. It is very probable, though, that it will never be possible to produce another specimen, nor to revive and recreate the species—and that, it must be admitted, is exactly what caused the despair of Prince D***, attaché to the Ministry of Foreign Affairs of the Empire of all the Russias.

Author's Note: Like the majority of the stories comprising this volume, this story was published in the press several years ago, and since then, almost every day, events have occurred that prove me right and confirm my theories.

In this respect, once and for all, I quote the Aurore *of May 23, 1901:*

"The Russian Academy of Science has taken responsibility for bringing to St. Petersburg a mammoth that has been found in a state of perfect conservation in Siberia.

"Measures have been taken to prevent the decomposition of the flesh, especially the internal organs, as well as the vegetables contained in the mammal's stomach.

"The body of the mammoth was discovered in the canton of Kolymsk, three thousand versts *from Sredny-Kolymsk, after a landslide that occurred on the bank of the Beresovaya, a tributary of the Kolyma. Participants in the expedition include Messieurs O. Herz, fulfilling the functions of the principal*

zoologist of the Imperial Academy of Sciences, and E. Pfitz-meyer, chief curator at the same Academy's Museum."[23]

Followed by this, from July 12 of the same year:

"We have reported that an extraordinary mammoth has recently been found in Siberia. The Petersburg Academy had received a telegram from the leader of the mission charged with transporting it, sent from Yakutsk, announcing that the expedition arrived in that town on 14 June, that it will travel up the river Aldan by steamboat and will then travel three thousand versts overland to reach Kolymsk, where it expects to arrive in two and a half months.

"The mammoth in question is a unique specimen of its kind; the hair, skin and flesh are conserved entirely, and there are residues of undigested nourishment in its stomach."

No need for comment, is there?

---

[23] Alfred Otto Herz was an entomologist, but he took part in mammoth-hunting expeditions financed by the Grand-Duke Nicholas Romanoff, perhaps the model for Prince D*** in the story. Pfitzmeyer is a more obscure figure, but his paper on mammoth morphology is widely cited. These two newspaper excerpts are accurately cited, although many of the supposed quotes contained in the bodies of the stories are paraphrases seemingly rendered from memory.

Animal Longevity

Fish and birds. Surprising memory.
A curious scientific inquiry.

Some time ago, the majority of well-informed newspapers published the following surprising information:

"The longevity of pike.

"Extraordinary as it may seem, this fact in confirmed by a scientist.

"According to him, one of the pike that can be seen in the Imperial Aquarium of St. Petersburg was born toward the end of the fifteenth century and is in relatively good health in spite of being four hundred years old and in captivity.

"The professor adds that the fact is not as improbable as one might be inclined to believe, and that various other fish in the same aquarium are several hundred years old."

Struck by the truly mysterious and exciting nature of this dispatch, I immediately got in contact with the illustrious Petersburgian scientist, who desires to remain anonymous out of modesty, and took the liberty of sending him a program for an entire series of scientific experiments that I implored him to carry out, asking him to keep me up to date with the results obtained.

With a sagacity and flair that exceeds the range of the most renowned artillerymen by a hundred yards, the illustrious scientist consented to follow my instructions to the letter, and the results have far surpassed his hopes and mine, as may be judged from the following letter, which he has just done me the honor of addressing to me:

Monsieur, and honored colleague,
On receiving your instructions I immediately realized that I was dealing with a distinguished naturalist (thank you)

and, your instructions being, for me, the stroke of genius that lit my lantern (*sic*), I hastened to execute scrupulously the program that you wanted me to follow, and which was to prove so fecund, since it has permitted me to establish in a definitive manner the longevity and memory of fish and birds—brothers in nature, since they each swim in a fluid of different density.

I began by seeking information as to the location where the venerable pike that has lived for more than four centuries was captured; it did not take long to discover that it had been caught in a lake not far from the capital.

With the permission of the authorities, I returned it with a thousand precautions to its ancestral lake, and as the water therein is very clear, I followed its initial maneuvers with poignant excitement and a little boat.

At first it was a little out of its element—which is understandable after such long captivity. Soon, though, I saw it dart like an arrow beneath the surface to find another pike as large as itself, and they both delivered themselves immediately to unequivocal manifestations of joy and leaps that proved to me that *they recognized one another*.

Immediately, with a much-improved apparatus of my own invention, I captured the four-hundred-year-old pike from the aquarium again, and the other. After an attentive examination I realized that the latter was a female and bore a particular mark on its head, just as the pike from the aquarium bears a slight mark on its tail—and, by virtue of a very curious phenomenon, the majority of the young pike that are presently in the lake posses the two revealing signs, albeit considerably attenuated. Go on, then—after that, deny the power of atavism across the centuries. There was no longer any possible doubt; those two venerable representatives of the pike species really were the father and mother of all the pike in the lake today, and the aquarium pike had spontaneously recognized the companion of his youth, which he had loved four centuries ago, the mother of his children. O prodigy of animal memory!

But that was not all that I obtained from the truly marvelous aspect of my experiments. Still in conformity with your instructions, I replaced my pike in the lake, this time keeping its female companion captive.

As on the first occasion, when it was put in the water, I follow it in my boat. Slowly, it traversed the entire lake, but suddenly, as it was passing the lock-keeper's house, it stopped, leapt out of the water several times and began uttering little cries of joy—which is very rare in fish—while a parrot that was in a cage outside the lock-keeper's house began flapping its wings gaily, crying out several times in the old Russian manner: "Cuckoo! There he is!"

I confess that I was amazed, astounded, overwhelmed; in my long career as a scientist, I had never been privileged to witness such a spectacle. There was no possible doubt: the fish and the bird, the pike and the parrot, recognized one another!

I made feverish enquiries and learned that the lock was no more than a hundred years old, but that it had been attended by the same family, from father to son, and that the parrot had been given to the first lock-keeper by a poor family of fisherfolk resident there for centuries.

I immediately examined the parrot, and by means of attentive study of its tongue and teeth was able to acquire the conviction that it had been born in 1460—which is to say, seven years after the fall of Constantinople!

Everything then became as clear as day to me. The pike and the parrot, old contemporaries, had definitely recognized one another, and the memory of birds and fish could no longer be put in doubt.

That, Monsieur and most honored colleague, is the result of my inquiry. You have been its inspiration. I believe that it will constitute a considerable advance in natural history, and I beg you to believer in my eternal gratitude.

Deign to accept, etc.

I have nothing to add to this interesting missive, only too glad to have been able, in my modest fashion, to assist in the definitive scientific determination of the surprising longevity, and even more surprising memory, of fish and birds.

Animal Intelligence

How I was able to reconstitute a language dead for centuries.
On the banks of the Amazon. Informative parrots.
A feathered Philemon and Baucis.

Thirty years ago, my father was able to demonstrate that a certain primitive language of the Redskins of North America was almost identical, word for word, to the Basque language, or at least its twin sister—which I shall publish one day, it the necessities of daily life should ever permit it.

Today, I simply wish to tell the story, briefly, of how I was able to reconstitute a language that had been absolutely dead for centuries on the banks, as enchanting as they are malarial, of the Amazon—which is, as everyone knows, in South America.

I had been there for more than six weeks, studying the whole range of the local hummingbirds—which, beneath their dazzling plumage, are merely ambulant carrion, and fall into decomposition as soon as they are caught—when I was taken by surprise one day by a terrible storm in the heart of the forest, still virgin in spite of its advanced age.

I and my faithful escort were about to be drenched to the skin when we discovered a crack in a rock that gave access to a veritable grotto. After having explored it with circumspection and several lanterns, we began by building a large fire at the opening, and warmed ourselves voluptuously, while smoking a pipe.

We had scarcely been resting in this fashion for a quarter of an hour when two superb large green parrots with rosy breasts, like those of little cockatoos, came to settle on branches close by, and began uttering a number of amicable cries—*hum! hum!*—as if to say: *here we are, hello; it's a long time since we've seen a human.*

Surprised, naturally, I began speaking to them politely, and, while watching them, saw that they were a male and a female, certainly very old.

In a friendly fashion, but without allowing themselves to be caught, the two peculiar parrots started talking, pronouncing entire sentences—which, of course, I did not understand. From that moment on, though, keenly interested, I resolved to stay in the grotto in order to clarify the mystery, as strange as it was philological, that I scented there.

In no time at all, I had the grotto papered with a few rolls of colored wallpaper that I had brought for an entirely different purpose. Installed in relative comfort, I made haste to try to tame the two parrots—which, it seemed, wanted nothing more, to the extent that, a week later, they came to perch in a familiar fashion on my wrist. Then we held long conversations—without understanding one another, of course—although, for a lump of sugar, I was able to get my parrots to dictate hundred of phrases to me, slowly and methodically, with admirable articulation. By that means, I discovered that they knew more than three hundred sentences, which I wrote down religiously.

My parrots—which, according to an examination of their teeth and feet, had to be at least eight hundred years old—were definitely much superior to a phonograph.

Once in possession of three hundred and eleven sentences, I set compiling a dictionary, in alphabetical order, of all the words pronounced—postponing the grammar until a later date, when I would be in possession of further elements of information. As a result, I had more than five hundred completely unknown words, in a language absolutely dead for centuries, of which the two parrots were assuredly the last custodians.

Then an idea of genius occurred to me. I started pronouncing words in their language while touching the objects around me: trees, water, rocks, items of furniture, my companions, etc., etc. Admirably, the parrots understood, and, with a marvelous lucidity, were able to give me the meaning of at least four-fifths of the words they were pronouncing.

That was enough for me, and by that means, all their sentences were admirably clarified.

From then on, I got down to work, simultaneously writing a great dictionary and national grammar of that vanished language, in which I was fortunate enough to find many points of contact with Phoenician and, in consequence, Hebrew. This offers further proof that the two Americas were colonized in remotest antiquity by the Phoenicians—which is to say, the trading branch of the Jewish people.

You might now be wondering how I managed to reconstitute an entire language with 1500 words, even knowing what they meant—their exact significance.

Nothing simpler, and my dictionary—still in manuscript, because I have not yet found a serious publisher—includes exactly 91,007 words, including the technical terminology of those distant and primitive eras.

I have—this was my second idea of genius—applied to linguistics the quasi-divinatory methods of reconstitution devised by the immortal Cuvier.[24] It's as simple as saying hello, you see, except that it was necessary to think of it. Even then, setting modesty aside, it undoubtedly requires a certain skill and a good deal of flair to make use of that method, as instructive as it is experimental, successfully—which did not prevent me being able, by that means, not only to reconstitute a language but also to shed new light on ancient Phoenician colonization.

But all that doesn't make one's fortune; so, at the time of writing, I am happy to inform my numerous readers that I am

---

[24] The pioneering paleontologist Georges Cuvier (1772-1838) proposed two principles (the law of organic subordination and the law of formal correlation) that allowed him—or so he claimed—to deduce the entire form of a prehistoric animal from a small number of fossil bones. There has always been a certain account of skepticism regarding the reliability of the method, but modern paleontologists still engage in similar extrapolation.

still in search of a publisher for my dictionary and my grammar—for I forgot to say that, also thanks to me two parrots, who led me to a few tombstones, I have discovered the characters, which are merely phonetic Hebrew letters, scarcely altered by their distant transplantation centuries ago.

That should be worth a million or two.

Finally, my two faithful parrots—Philemon and Baucis, as I call them—did not want to leave me. They are in Paris with me, quite healthy but very sensitive to the cold. According to my calculations, they cannot be far off a thousand years old—a fine age.[25]

The three of us—including myself, the pen-holder—are in the process of setting up an open course in this beautiful language, dead for more than four centuries, at the Collège de France or the École des Langues Orientales. I might be mistake, but it seems to me that on the day the course begins, I and my two companions will have a famous success, and it must be admitted that, owing to the rarity of the event, the persistence invested in it, and the collaboration of a philologist with two birds, we shall not be undeserving of it.

That will be one in the eye for the Dutch canaries that play cards on the boulevards during the New Year's festivities.

Oh. I forgot to say that Baucis can sing the songs of prehistoric times admirably; one might think it were plainsong.

Strange!

Author's Note: It is evident that the intelligence and memory of animals is quite extraordinary; to convince yourself of it, first read this curious note by Henri de Parville:

---

[25] The narrator inserts a footnote here: "I believe that they are, in fact, merely the great-grandchildren of ancestral climbers, contemporaries of the vanished races, and, in consequence, the simple and faithful custodians of philological traditions dead for centuries."

What a brave beast a dog is, and how intelligent! Read the following story told by Professor Forel of Morges, Switzerland.[26] *He calls our attention to an act of reflective intelligence that guided two poor dogs to seek help for their master and indicates as particularly worthy of admiration the collaboration of the two animals, which must have deliberated and reached agreement on what to do in the grave predicament that was tormenting them:*

"Several days ago, the caretaker of the hotel at Z'meiden, above Tourtemagne, in the Valaisian district of Loèche, came out of the house to chop wood. He had spent the winter alone with two dogs, his two brave and faithful companions in solitude, a wolf-hound and a griffon, smaller in size but clever and intelligent. As the master was chopping his wood at the foot of a little wall, not far from the large roof covering the hotel, the layer of snow accumulated on the roof unexpectedly slid off. It hit the man, plastering him against the wall and imprisoning him up to the shoulders, only his head projecting above the avalanche. The snow was moist, heavy and ice-cold. It was impossible for the unfortunate fellow to move his arms or legs. The dogs saw their master in this predicament. They drew near and tried to scrape away the snow to free him. A vain attempt! Then they conferred. Suddenly, as rapidly as an arrow, they launched themselves down into the valley. Their master's brother lived down there, in Ems. They would tell him about the accident that had occurred and begged him to come to the aid of their friend, who was about to die.

"Flat out, they ran through the snow. The journey takes a good walker four hours; they covered the distance in less than an hour. The avalanche had fallen at about midday. Within an hour they were yapping, barking, wailing and howling in front of the house from which salvation ought to emerge. The chalet door was opened and the two dogs, cov-

---

[26] The psychologist Auguste-Henri Forel (1848-1931), father of the artist after whom the present-day Forel Museum in Morges is named.

ered in sweat and fuming, were invited in. They refused. That generated anxiety. Why were the brave animals wailing like that? Had the brother suffered some misfortune up there at the hotel? The peasant quickly put on his coat and leggings and equipped himself with a spade and a rope. He went to ask his friends to make up a rescue party. The dogs took the lead; their barking, sinister a little while before, when they were announcing the fatal news, had changed its nature. They were now cries of summons and encouragement. They ran ahead, indicating the route and wagging their tails.

"It took seven hours for the rescuers to reach the hotel. When they arrived, it was nine o'clock at night. The dogs had preceded them. The caretaker, still trapped in the snow, had lost consciousness. The two dogs, crouched near the dying man's head, were licking his face to warm him up and bring him back to life. He was dug out. The unfortunate fellow was half-frozen. Without his intelligent four-legged friends, he would have perished."

Ems is at an altitude of 1330 meters, Z'meiden at 1847 meters. The distance between the two stations, as the crow flies, is nine kilometers.

This happened in July or August 1900, and in February 1901 Scaramouche confirmed my excellent opinion of animals in the following note:

"A reader in the Aube tells us about a curious manifestation of intelligence in a dog. A peasant took a flock of fourteen sheep on foot to the principal town of the canton. The flock was sold to a buyer who left the same evening, going home in a hurry to his village, which was a good way off, with a population of about five hundred.

"It had been agreed that the dog, which was accustomed to accompanying the fourteen sheep and answered to the name of Parisian, would be ceded to the buyer at a bargain price. Night having fallen during the journey, however, he found a means of separating the fourteen animals with which he was *familiar from the larger flock without anyone noticing, retracing their steps and bringing them back to the accustomed fold.*

"One can imagine the bewilderment of the worthy countryman, who had sold his lock for a good price, on finding them back home the following day. He returned the sheep—but he kept Parisian."

One could multiply these examples infinitely; these seem conclusive enough to me, and I shall leave it there—for now!

The Human Microbe

I. The Hummingbirds. The selection of smallness.
Lilliput surpassed.
Curious endeavors.

There was a recent exhibition—as the English say—in Paris of a truly curious company of dwarfs, to which the *Petit Journal* devoted a long article, from which I have extracted the following lines, with the sole aim of showing them to my readers right away:

"For several, the *Cirque Nouveau* has been presenting, among other exhibits, a company of dwarfs, 'the Hummingbirds,' the tallest of whom measures 92 centimeters, and weighs 17 kilograms.

"Although not very heavy, this individual, M. Henry, weighs more than any other member of the company, and is the strongest—its Hercules. The athletic feats that he accomplishes every evening are truly surprising.

"The other individuals, of lesser height, juggle, dance and sing under the supervision of and after introduction by M. Piccolomini, the head man of the company, the writer on behalf of them all, the reason and the common sense: a blond-haired man of twenty-nine with a face that is both energetic and gentle, an honest gaze and a proud mouth ornamented with a fine moustache, but only 90 centimeters tall.

"One of Piccolomini's brothers is an officer in the Italian navy.

"We should also mention another of these heroes, or, rather, the heroine of the drama that has so profoundly disturbed the company of the Hummingbirds: Mlle. Thérèse, a graceful dancer, blonde and flirtatious—very flirtatious, as we shall see—standing all of 81 centimeters tall.

"For two years, Mlle. Thérèse has been the intimate friend of M. Piccolomini. A daughter—a little doll—was born to them fourteen months ago. The child is in Ugra in Hungary, in the home of her father's mother.

"Three months ago, one the banks of the beautiful blue Danube, before coming to Paris, Piccolomini and Thérèse made plans for the future, of which marriage was to be the first step. The ceremony was to take place without delay.

"Little man proposes, however, and little god disposes. Dazzled and fascinated by M. Henry's Herculean feats of strength, the inconstant blonde allowed herself to be led up the garden path and elope with her new lover..."

Having read these lines, I said to myself one fine evening—which is only a manner of speaking, for it was raining torrentially—that I ought to go to see the Hummingbirds with my own eyes. (I say *own* because I wash every morning.[27])

Incontinently, I hired—I say hired because it was pouring down, as I've already observed—a *sapin*, so-called because it was made of maple-wood, and had myself taken to the Cirque Nouveau in the Rue Saint-Honoré, which is called after a famous cream-cake, thinking all the while about Gulliver in the charming city of Lilliput, and Swift's humor, so keen, so naturally witty and so argumentative.

Once comfortably seated, I chanced to find myself next to an old and most distinguished gentleman, who began talking to me about the Hummingbirds we would shortly be seeing, in a knowledgeable manner.

"Are you by chance Monsieur," I asked him, laughing, "an impresario yourself—a *manager* of dwarfs?"

"Not at all," he said, laughing in his turn. "It's my accent that has deceived you. I am indeed a Yankee, but not of the Barnum family; I'm simply a physician and physiologist, seriously occupied with science—which is, in fact, quite rare in my country, still too new to have taken its scientific investigations very far."

---

[27] This joke does not translate; the French *propre* [own] also means "decent" or "clean."

Once the ice was broken, I told him that I had been to America myself, and it did not take us long to become the best friends in the world.

While young ballerinas, as thin as half a hundred nails, broke through paper disks in front of us with the gauche and clumsy elegance of ill-dressed errand-girls, the young American—for he was still young—brought me up to date with his endeavors.

"The whole world is making ingenious use of selection, to obtain enormous cattle, swine and poultry. It's the fable of the frog, put into action in all the agricultural competitions in the entire world, and when someone succeeds in showing you a rabbit as big as a calf, he's sure to carry off the gold medal.

"Well, after long study—or, rather, after meditations as profound as the coal mines of Hainault—I arrived at the very simple observation that, since the beginning of the world, its fauna has been continually getting smaller...as witness the disappearance of mastodons, mammoths, plesiosaurs, ichthyosaurs, megalosaurs, etc. etc., which have already disappeared from the surface of the globe thousands of years ago.

"To put it another way, one might believe that the great architect of the universe wanted to imitate humans, unless it is the latter who are imitating him, and that after the cyclopean and megalithic animals—if I might express myself thus with respect to fauna—he wanted to revert to the doubtless modest but divinely harmonious proportions of Greek temples, the Venus de Milo..."

"Bravo!" I said, enthusiastically.

"Yes, and in trying to makes things larger, with these agricultural competitions, humans are going against the wishes of nature, which is marching slowly but surely toward the city of Lilliput, by making the methods of the Colas Reduction its own.[28]

---

[28] Colas Reduction was an application of a mechanical technique devised by the artist Alphonse Colas (1818-1887) for copying statues,

"That's why Swift was a great man, a true prophet who has had a pure and overwhelming vision of the future, across the centuries…"

Increasingly carried away by the grandiosity of the American's vision, I interrupted him again, involuntarily, and said: "But morally speaking, look at our little men, our petty passions, our petty ambitions for petty goals and petty ribbons, our petty ministers—we're already there!"

He smiled bitterly, and slowly replied: "I never pay any heed to politics…but I'll continue, if you'll permit?"

"Pray do."

"Thus, instead of opposing the laws of nature, after having discovered them, I have simply given myself the mission of supporting them, and if I can only live for another thirty or forty years—which is possible, for I'm only thirty-seven—I shall have found…but what good does it do to sell the bear's skin before having killed it? I'll stop there, for not only won't you believe me, but you'll mock me…."

"Never. Go on."

"No, the Hummingbirds are leaving the stage now—and those Hummingbirds are giants compared with the race of true dwarfs that I've already obtained…." As if speaking to himself, he added: "Oh yes, if I live another thirty years, I'll have found…."

"What?"

"The *human microbe*, Monsieur."

I started so violently that he exclaimed: "You see—you take me for a lunatic. Well, come to dinner tomorrow at the Café de la Paix, at seven o'clock, and I'll explain to you how I was finally put on the right track, almost certain of success."

And because he noticed my amazement, as we were going down the circus stairway, he showed me a perforated gold locket on his watch-chain, as large as a two-franc coin, and said, gravely: "That's to let them breathe."

---

which could produce reduced-scale versions as well as identical copies; it was a great boon to the souvenir industry.

This time, I thought him entirely mad—but he opened the locket, and said: "Look, here's a husband and wife, very much alive, no more than a centimeter in height, the pair of them weighing seventeen grams. This is what I've already obtained by the methodical and scientific regressive selection, from which I've never deviated in the fourteen years that I've been pursuing this research and endeavor."

Defeated, afflicted by the vertigo of the very tiny, I parted company with him, without being able to say a word.

He shook my hand, saying: "Tomorrow, we shall see how the human microbe might be attained…"

And he disappeared.

II. From Aztecs to dwarfs. Microbial dwarfs.
The regressive or descending scale.
The conquest of the Earth. Return to the primitive cell.
The cycle of worlds.

After installing myself comfortably in a good armchair, smoking a cigar, my eyes fell upon his desk. In the middle, in a Japanese porcelain ash-tray on his blotting-pad, which was as large as the palm of my hand, the young couple he had shown me the previous evening in his locket were sitting on a sofa whose surface area was a quarter the size of an ordinary postage stamp. As I leaned forward, to contemplate the human fly and his wife at closer range, I said to the American scientist;

"Can they talk?"

"English and French, like you and me."

"But we wouldn't be able to hear them?"

The doctor smiled, and held out a piece of wire about two meters long, terminating in a tiny receiver, just like those in telephones.

"Put that in your ear—it's an ordinary telephone, whose power is multiplied a hundredfold by an invisible little microphone of my own invention."

Indeed, I was put in communication with the human fly and his amiable companion, and the conversation might have continued indefinitely, so great was the charm and surprise for me, if the doctor had not torn me away from it.

"Now look at them through this powerful microscope, and you will see that these individuals—whom it is necessary not to call midges, because it offends them—are as well-formed as you and me."

I uttered a cry of surprise and admiration on thinking that I recognized the man and his wife as well-known young deputé who had got married in America—the resemblance was striking.

"And how old are they?"

"He is 25 and she 21 months," replied the doctor, "but set aside amusement Monsieur, for I must now give you a brief explanation of the method I have employed and the goal that I am pursuing. The method I've employed is quite simple. I began by making crosses between the last representatives of the Aztecs, whom I was able to find, although they were believed to be lost in the virgin forests of Mexico, and all the dwarfs that I was able to procure throughout the world. I proceeded by always mating the smallest individuals together..."

"Pardon me, but that represents several human lifetimes, for it's necessary to await the age of puberty."

"Of course—but as one descends the scale of living beings, formation is more rapid and life shorter; thus, this young couple of 25 and 21 months are already old—practically centenarians—and have been great-great-great grandparents for some time."

"I'm truly amazed."

"No, it's logical. What am I doing, if not following the regressive or descendant scale—admittedly by artificial and hasty means—just as nature, in the beginning, followed the progressive and ascendant scale of beings as far as the vanished monsters we spoke about earlier? For you, who have so brilliantly discovered the secret of the geological life of worlds and have explained so perfectly, in your lectures, how worlds are born, live and die, ought to find it perfectly natural, since I am only doing the same for the zoological cycle of worlds."

"You fill me with admiration."

"You're too kind. But let's get on; the point I have now reached, with passionate attention, is the logical, fatal, ineluctable moment when, by continually obtaining smaller individuals, I shall pass from vertebrate humans to invertebrate humans, like insects.

"What will the transition be like? I don't know, but today, I shall be very close to the final triumph of my theories and their experimental demonstration. I shall rapidly reach the stage of the human microbe conquering the entire Earth, killing all the other harmful microbes and reproducing themselves instantaneously by the billion—as you know.

"Then I shall be very close to attaining the primitive cell, the very one that swam with the spirit of God on the surface of the waters, according to all theogonies and *Genesis* itself, and I will have provided, in miniature, a living and palpable demonstration of the zoological cycle of worlds. That final conquest of the Earth by microbial humankind is not lacking in a certain grandeur, is it?"

"Certainly not."

"Except, I should tell you, that there is another, even more exciting problem in my experiments, which grips my utterly. The human soul, mind or intelligence, is an impalpable fluid that has no location—but how long, as Cicero said,[29] could I contrive to enclose it in the bodies of my human flies, and then my human microbes? At the present moment the one-centimeter individuals you have before your eyes are still vertebrates; their bones are like taut spider-silk, but they still exist. But will intelligence be maintained when the transition to invertebrates occurs? That's the big question, and I will admit frankly that I don't believe so, that I shall soon be able to formulate this law: *It is not location that intelligence lacks, but*

---

[29] The Roman orator Cicero famously complained "How long, Catiline, will you abuse our patience?"

what it requires are sophisticated organs—which is to say, instruments enabling it to manifest itself and maintain contact with the external world."

"Bravo!" I said, involuntarily, seized by the luminous evidence of the demonstration.

"Yes, of course. I'm convinced that microbes have a fraction of the great universal intelligence, just like us, but they do not have the organs, the instruments, to manifest it and make use of it." Suddenly becoming thoughtful, he continued: "Who knows? Perhaps microbes suffer in consequence. For the time being, I shall set my problem aside—and if I arrive thus as an experimental demonstration of the zoological cycle of the universe, I shall deem myself very fortunate."

"Certainly—and you will be recognized as the greatest scientist of the twentieth century. But as one is insatiable, can you not invert your hypothesis—or, rather, your experiments—to depart once again from the gelatinous cell and return via the microbe, invertebrates, vertebrates, humans and large animals to the culminating point of the huge monsters of yesteryear?"

"No, for the higher one remounts, the longer the generation-time becomes, after a puberty that only arrives as twelve, fifteen or even twenty years."

"You're right."

"I would be dead before then—although the inversion of the proposition would obviously be interesting. That will be the work of my successors...if I thought it possible, for the geological conditions on the Earth are not the same. One can't recommence the same cycle twice, and we're heading for the death of the globe...slowly, oh, very slowly!"

"Fortunately."

My cigar went out. The doctor was mute and pensive. In the quasi-religious silence, my eyes happened to fall on the couple of the human fly and his wife, and I uttered a cry. They had fallen off their sofa on to the cold porcelain of the ashtray.

Imperturbably, the doctor said: "They've just died of old age."

"At 21 and 25 months?"

"Of course—arch-centenarians."

"Well, I prefer still having my natural human size."

The American scientist picked them up and threw them in the fire. "The ceremony of cremation." And, as I was painfully distressed, he took me by the arm and said: "Let's go out and have an aperitif."

Since then, I've lost sight of him; he has returned to the United States. Has he recovered the primitive cell? I don't know. But I thought it my duty to report here the extraordinary experiments that I witnessed in his home and the marvelous results that he has already attained in this order of research, so exciting for the future of humankind.

The Submarine World

I. In the Ocean depths. A strange population.
The revealing missive.

Most of the newspapers recently published the following small item of information:

"It is well-known that the depth of the seas surpasses the height of the largest mountains. The most accentuated terrestrial relief is the summit of Gauri-Sankar in Asia. The greatest depression beneath the Ocean had been found in the South Pacific; it was measured at 9425 meters.

"A captain in the United States navy has just discovered, in the North Pacific, a trench whose depth surpasses all those previously known. This depression is between the islands of Midway and Guam (one of the Marianas). It was found in the course of reconnaissance for the laying of a cable between the two archipelagos. The soundings carried out by the commander of the American ship have given a mean result of 9635.76 meters.[30] Here, at approximately 400 meters, we are ten kilometers above the greatest known depth of the ocean."

For its part, the *Bulletin de la Societé des Etudes coloniales et maritimes*, in the issue dated June 30, 1900, published a very complete note on ocean depth and temperature:

"In his presidential address to the geographical section of the British Association, Sir John Murray[31] summarizes as follows the results furnished by the soundings carried out at various points in the Ocean:

---

[30] The ship in question was the *USS Nemo*, which recorded that depth-sounding in what is now called the Mariana Trench (Vibert refers to it as the Aldrich Trench) in 1899.

[31] After the oceanographer Sir John Murray (1841-1914) took part in the *Challenger* expedition of 1872-76 he published 56 volumes of scientific results derived therefrom.

Percentage of the total surface
Depths less than 180 meters............7
180-1800 meters.........................10
1800-3600 meters.......................21
3600-5400 meters.......................55
Above 5400 meters......................7

"More than half of the surface of the sea therefore offers a depth in excess of 3600 meters. On the *Challenger* charts, all depths in excess of 5400 meters have been indicated and have been given distinct names. 43 depressions of this kind are currently known, 34 in the Pacific Ocean, 3 in the Indian Ocean, 15 in the Atlantic Ocean and one in Antarctic waters. The surface occupied by these 43 trenches is estimated at 7,152,000 square miles, which is about seven per cent of the total surface of the waters. Of 250 soundings taken in these regions, 24 have surpassed 7200 meters, including five in excess of 9000 meters.

"Depths of more than 7200 meters have been found in eight of the aforementioned trenches; depths of more than 9000 meters have only been found, thus far, in the Aldrich Trench (South Pacific) east of the Kermadec islands and the Friendly Isles, where the greatest depth recorded was 9429 meters.

"Sir John Murray then observed that all temperature measurements thus far made in the seas indicated that, at a depth of 180 meters, the water temperature remains almost invariable in all seasons. It is estimated that 92% of the mass of the oceans has a temperature less than 4.4°C, while the proportion in the superficial waters is only 16%.

"Almost all of the deep waters of the Indian Ocean have a temperature below 1.7°C; the same is true of a large proportion of the South Atlantic and certain parts of the Pacific. In the North Atlantic, however, and a very large part of the Pacific, the temperature is higher. For depths in excess of 3600 meters, the mean temperature of Atlantic waters is about one degree above the mean temperature of the Atlantic sea-bed; the mean temperature in the Pacific has an intermediate value.

"The depths of the seas are an obscure region, which solar radiation does not reach, so vegetable life is absent from 93% of the ocean bed. The abundant fauna of the great deeps thus lives on organic matter assimilated by plants growing close to the surface, in water or on the coast."

This reminds me of an extraordinary adventure that happened to one of my friends, a long-haul captain, on that very same celebrated Aldrich Trench in the South Pacific, which was once the deepest known, since—as we have just seen—it reaches 9429 meters.

This perfectly true adventure is so extraordinary that I don't know how to make a start in order to relate it simply and clearly, without omitting any element or essential detail.

I don't believe in the fatalism of the Muslims, the Destiny of the ancients or the Providence of believers, but I'm forced to recognize there really is an extraordinary coincidence in the chain of events that I am about to report here, for if my friend had not been a very erudite Israelite who had studied to be a rabbi in his youth, before becoming a long-haul captain, having been disappointed in love. I wonder fearfully whether he could have made a discovery so interesting for human science, especially for ethnography and anthropology.

So, one day, when my friend Jacob Laquedem[32] paused over the trench with a heavy cargo of cinnamon that he had picked up in the Moluccas, he began very conscientiously to take soundings of the great depths, at the request of a great scientist, a famous sounding-father whose name I shall not disclose here, because he has since gone to the bad.

As the cable ceased sliding, stopping exactly at the depth, since verified, of 9429.11 meters, according to the cus-

---

[32] Laquedem is one of the surnames conventionally attributed to the Wandering Jew, normally coupled with the forename Isaac. In chapter V of the story Vibert appears to forget that he has substituted the forename Jacob and starts referring to his own character as Isaac Laquedem, but I have used Jacob throughout.

tom of a cable that "skids" on contact, he thought that he felt—after an appeal by his men and after careful examination—a sort of rhythmic movement, very gentle and almost imperceptible, but regular and determined.

"Damn it," he said to himself. "The claws of my probe have closed on some unknown fish or crab, which is struggling—but it seems to be struggling in step, which is odd. Well, let's see." And he gave orders to his men to bring the 9429.11 meters of cable in question back up on to the winch, very slowly and carefully.

The operation took a long time, and when it was finally terminated, it was with a veritable anxiety that Jacob Laquedem fell upon the probe to see what monstrous fish or strange crustacean had made the cable oscillate thus. But the steel teeth had closed, and nothing projected from them or betrayed the presence of a living creature inside.

Increasingly intrigued, the captain raced to the automatic trigger, and when he had activated it, he was greatly surprised to see, not a fish of an unknown species, but a pretty little wooden box fall at his feet.

"Look," he said to his sailors. "Here's a box that must go back at least to the Queen of Sheba's time, and has been on the sea-bed since some prehistoric shipwreck."

"I beg your pardon, captain," said his first mate, who was an equally fine Parisian, educated and intelligent, "but how can a box made of wood, and light in consequence, have rested thus on the ocean bed without drifting to the surface?"

"My word, that's true—but in the meantime, let my open it to see whether it contains the treasures of the aforementioned Queen of Sheba."

The casket was closed by a hermetically-sealed lid, which was secured by a buckle, and it contained nothing but a piece of paper folded in four, which looked like a piece of strong parchment, or rather tanned fish-skin.

Once unfolded, the sheet was covered with characters that seemed strange at first sight—but after examining them at

63

length, Jacob Laquedem suddenly declared, as if choked by astonishment and stupefaction:

"Two things amaze me in the attentive and summary examination of this mysterious parchment, which appears to have been fabricated from shark-skin: firstly, that its characters bear a strange resemblance to Hebrew and Sanskrit characters—more so to Hebrew—and secondly, that they do not seem to date from the remotest antiquity, but to have been written only a few hours ago…"

And as the captain scratched his head furiously, staring at those strange characters, suddenly, as if emerging from a dream, he said abruptly to his first mate: "In my time you know, I had some skill in the art of cryptography; I could solve the most conventional secret scripts and the most mysterious ciphers in less than an hour.. This language seems to me to be a germane cousin of Hebrew. If I find the key, we're saved, and I'll bring you the translation within an hour—for I still know my Hebrew, thank God, and it isn't very long. We're at rest, the weather is calm; I leave you in command of the ship. Look after her, old chap, and I'll see you soon…."

And the captain, feverish with impatience, went to shut himself up in his cabin.

II. In the Ocean depths. A strange population.
The revealing missive.

After an hour and forty-five minutes, his features utterly convulsed by emotion, Captain Jacob Laquedem emerged, with the piece of paper in his hand. When he had joined his first mate, however, and had beckoned to a few sailors, he spent some time feverishly shaking the piece of paper without being able to pronounce a single word.

Finally, gradually regaining his self-composure, he was able to articulate, slowly: "Well, my friends, indeed, as I suspected at first glance, these characters really are half-Hebrew and half-Syriac, profoundly altered and modified by time, but with a little groping and a certain amount of time—because the vowels are naturally lacking, since this is a primitive language, I've had to consider the alternatives—I've arrived at the following translation, and you'll be as amazed as I am:

"We are poor folk who have been living on the sea-bed since the famous Deluge of Noah—which is to say, about 4900 years. If you still understand our ancient patriarchal language, which was spoken by Tubalcain and Methuselah, whose traditions and primitive mores we pride ourselves on having conserved in the depths of our maritime grottoes, O men of the land, find a means of communicating with us.

"By virtue of shipwrecks that sometimes bring us boxes of books, we have contrived an approximate understanding of your modern languages, which all derive from ours, and are fairly familiar with what is happening on the land surface, but we would be glad to be able to communicate with you, thanks to your modern scientific means, and to tell you the history of a branch of your family of which you are certainly unaware."

The captain was only just able to pronounce the last lines, and it is only fair to add that his very legitimate emotion had gripped all the surrounding crewmen. The adventure was so extraordinary and so unexpected that it made a strong impact on the crude and primitive imagination of the seamen.

"Well, captain, what are you going to do?" said the first mate, thus formulating the question that was on everyone's lips.

"It's quite simple. I'll try to draft a clear reply in this primitive patriarchal language, as they call it. Fortunately, I nearly became a rabbi and I have a thorough knowledge of Hebrew, without which we would be f...".[33]

And Jacob Laquedem went to shut himself in his cabin again—but the drafting of the reply must have been laborious, for it was not until the following morning, having spent much

---

[33] The word Vibert has in mind in leaving this word unfinished—a device he will repeat in other stories—is presumably *"fichu"* [done for] but English readers will doubtless be able to think of a suitable alternative that an old sea-dog might well employ.

of the sleepless night going over it repeatedly, that he was finally able to read it to his second-in-command—translating the meaning, of course.

This is what the laconic note said:

Those aboard my ship—specifically me, Jacob Laquedem, long-haul captain, in command, in my capacity as an Israelite—are glad to be able to understand you, or very nearly, and thus to be the first to enter into communication with the submarine people who inhabit the sea-bed.

You will find on the claw of the probe, along with the ball enclosing this note, an instrument with which you are doubtless unfamiliar. Speak into it softly and clearly; I will write under your dictation, and when I return to France, I shall carefully translate your story with my old friend Vibert, who is very interested in such matters and will then inform the world of your existence and revelations, if you think it appropriate. Every time you hear an electric bell, stop speaking into the mouth of the tube and place your ear to the receiver instead, for I will then speak to you.

With that, be patient, and accept the compliments of the people of the land to the people of the sea, while waiting for me to find a means of paying you a visit, if scientific progress ever permits me to do so. In the meantime, I shall send down the probe with this note and the telephone, which will still constitute a procedure as long as it is delicate.

"Well, my lads, that's the little morsel I'm sending to these porpoises—do you like it?"

"It's perfect."

"I found it very difficult to write—in my trade, literary talent takes flight...hang on, that rhymes! Let's move quickly. Get everything ready to send the probe down as soon as possible, with the telephonic apparatus. Don't hurry, though—we don't want any snags."

The instruction was unnecessary; all the members of the crew, naturally devoted to their captain, were impassioned by this strange affair. I shall pass over in silence the vicissitudes of sending down the probe, which was successfully accomplished in the end, in order to get on with the long and curious story that the citizen living at a depths of 9429 meters on the bed of the Pacific, at the very bottom of the Aldrich Trench, told my excellent friend Jacob Laquedem.

As the voice was clear and the diction perfect, once the telephone receiver was attached to his head, in order to avoid any inconvenience, he was able to transcribe the following story very accurately.

We have both retranslated it and checked it with extreme care, so, without further commentary, here is the truly novel and curious narrative.

III. In the Ocean depths. A strange population.
The revealing missive continued.

"You are not unaware that when Noah retreated with his entire family and the animals fleeing the waters, not in the symbolic Ark but simply to the summit of Mount Ararat, what is conventionally called the Deluge did not last for forty days, but for many years.

"Thus, after some years, Noah and his wife had numerous grandchildren, and when the waters began to retreat to the level of the plain, the most audacious wanted to go forth and explore the mountain's surroundings.

"The family, however, ever prudent, decided to wait longer. What your Biblical history of the Earth does not relate, however, is that in addition to them, there was a poor devil of a servant, with his wife and children, who might be thought of as Noah's concierge—and when there were too many mouths to feed on the mountain, he decided to take his family away in order to try to establish them on the plain, in spite of all the prayers and objurgations of his master's family.

"Noah's wife then put some provisions in a basket for him and his family, and they went down into the plain.

"At first, all went well, and after having built a raft, they were able to sail from one dry place to another, and finally to cultivate the ground on hillocks of a sort, for three generations. Little by little, however, the waters rose again, and his descendants lived for another three generations, at first spending three-quarters of their time and then almost all of it in the water, thus becoming, albeit reluctantly, almost amphibious.

"One day, however, the waters rose and all our villages—populated by six prolific generations, as in the virtuous times of the patriarchs, when no one yet knew how to give short weight—were swallowed up.

"Miraculously, though, as they had been long accustomed to spending most of their time in the water, everyone perished except for one young couple who had been married for exactly three weeks. They were able to adapt themselves to that new way of life, and did not take long to constitute, after four generations, a true city in the depths of the mysterious grottoes of the sea-bed.

"They did not take long to spread out via the Red Sea over the bed of all the Oceans and to populate them. They were our venerable ancestors..."

At this point, the electric ball rang, for the worthy Captain Jacob Laquedem had been unable to prevent himself interrupting the man of the sea's story, to exclaim in his turn: "That's wonderful!"—in aquatic Hebrew, of course.

He did not have to wait long for the response.

"Not as wonderful as all that, for according to what we have read in your books, collected from the wrecks that reach us, we believe that your first historians—including Sanchuniathon,[34] for example—declared that the first humans, and the Egyptians themselves, were descended from fish."

"That's true. Buy why don't you come to see us as the earth's surface?"

"Simply because it's impossible for us to do so. Firstly, we have no means of coming up to the surface of the waters,

---

[34] Sanchuniathon was a supposed Phoenician author of great antiquity, credited with three lost works, whose contents are cited by the early Christian writer Eusebius, allegedly summarizing a second-hand account by Philo of Byblos that was also lost. The suggestion that he believed humans to be descended from fish is highly dubious.

and even if one of us wanted to hoist himself up by means of your probe—the first that we have seen in the depths of our 9429.11-meter valley—he would not take long, not merely to perish, but to leap like a rabbit, as your novels put it.

"In the approximately 4900 years that our arch-white race has been living in the Ocean depths it has been gradually modified, according to the great universal law of adaptation, and—although we aren't hunchbacks, believe me—in order to live and breathe we each have a little pouch on our back, containing air compressed to three or four hundred atmospheres, according to the depth. If we were in the air above the water, or even before then, our pouches would burst with a thunderous noise and we would be blasted into little pieces.

"But you, with a heavy weight and an abundant provision of compressed air in an apparatus that you could bring down with you, could come to see us. Then, for sure, there would be a great celebration in our submarine dwellings to welcome you."

"That's worth investigation—but first, I'll have to return to Paris in France..."

"We know your country by reputation; we have a little bronze Eiffel Tower here, which was found inside a shipwrecked trunk..."

"That's marvelous. Yes, when I return to France to translate this conversation exactly with my friend Vibert, afterwards, if he wishes, we'll come back here and try to come down to you together."

"Agreed. We'll wait for you with keen impatience."

The following year, almost to the day, Captain Jacob and I were on our ship in the middle of the Pacific, above the Aldrich Trench, getting ready to make our descent—and it's the story of our voyage of 9429.113 meters to the Ocean bed that I shall have the honor of telling you in the next chapter.

IV. Our descent into the Pacific depths. A new race.

Our preparations for the descent were neither long nor complicated, because we had spent a long time planning our attempt and preparing for its execution.

We did not hide the fact that we had a considerable chance of losing our lives in the endeavor. If the cable were to break or the air-supply to be interrupted for five minutes, we would be well and truly dead. But what do you expect? Although we were no braver than anyone else, we were carried away by curiosity.

We had, therefore, prepared two solid steel cables, coated with a thick layer of Surinam quassia[35] to deter whales desirous of cutting our communications while playing with them. Each of us also had, instead of large cannonballs on our feet, an enormous, exceedingly heavy and resistant tube, similarly made of fine steel, coiled to boot, to retain and to equalize the pressure on the walls of air molecules obedient to centrifugal force, simply enclosing air compressed to 500 atmospheres, with the appropriate dose of sodium peroxide.[36] Each of us had two of these, one on each foot, which would provide us with air for a fortnight. We did not expect to remain with our new friends for as long as that. Finally, by means of a set of valves, appropriately combined and graduated, we only had to put a little tube around our heads to our mouths, when necessary, in order to breathe freely. It had been necessary to organize this system because there was no possibility of sending air down to such depths from our boat by means of a pump.

---

[35] A pharmaceutical extract of the plant *Quassia amara*, renowned for being the most bitter substance known, fifty times as bitter as quinine.

[36] At this point Vibert adds an exceedingly long footnote, inspired by his delight in having anticipated the use of sodium peroxide in diving apparatus; I have moved it to the end of the chapter for the sake of convenience, as he usually does with his more substantial addenda.

We were warmly dressed in furs within our diving-suits, to avoid the cold and damp, although our excellent unknown friend that it was neither cold not hot, but only cool, in the eternal night of the profound depths. It is true that the submarine humans possessed electricity and phosphorescent light, but in the meantime, we attached wires for the telephone and an electric lamp to each of our cables, to unroll solely as we descended.

Thus ballasted, when the great moment arrived, after having embraced all our sailors, who were weeping like calves, we sealed ourselves in our diving-suits and our tube-feet, and the immersion commenced, slowly at first.

Curious as we were, we must confess that at first we experienced a series of sensations singularly reminiscent of bad stage-fright. Gradually, however, we got used to it, and after half an hour, we telephoned to ask for the descent to be accelerated slightly.

Strangely enough, at that moment some kind of seal passed close to us, pronouncing very distinctly: *Papa.* Who could have taught it to do that? It's a mystery that we were never able to solve, although we formulated a considerable number of hypotheses.

We continue to descend vertically into the black darkness, sweating, but not too badly, without skidding. We had an acoustic trumpet with which to talk to one another, and we were, as they say, beginning to get a grip on the hair of the beast.

At one moment, a powerful shock made Captain Jacob Laquedem afraid that he might lose his precious tubes; fortunately, that did not happen.

Curiously enough, the further we descended the lighter we felt. Evidently, the pressure between the inferior and superior layers was beginning to equilibrate.

Finally, after four hours twenty-two minutes of descent—a century!—we touched the bottom of the famous trench, more than 9429 meters beneath the surface of the water and, in consequence, our ship.

Our unknown friends were there to greet us, and at first we were dazzled by all the lights surrounding us.

One problem had occurred to us on the way: how would we be able to live on the sea-bed? It would be impossible for us to come out of our diving-suits. Our friends, however, forewarned in advance of our descent and our visit, had thought of everything. We had hardly set foot on the fine sand with our tubes when our cables, detached by expert hands, were solidly attached to a crampon fixed in a granite wall, and we were drawn gently through a series of corridors that were closed off by means of automatic doors, into a vast grotto, superbly lit and absolutely watertight.

For us that was salvation, and we were able to emerge from our diving-suits while retaining our respiratory tubes.

When our hosts could see us and touch us, they uttered cries of joy and astonishment, and when we looked at them, we were no more able to hide our surprise, so different from us did these kindred, separated from us since the Deluge—which is to say, for about 4900 years—and living nearly ten thousand meters deep on the Ocean bed, appear.

Imagine...

Author's note: Since our descent, the problem of air-purification has finally been solved. This is what the Suni *for September 27, 1900 said:*

"The recent experiments of Messieurs Desgresz and Balthazard[37] regarding chemical means of purifying an atmosphere in a hermetically sealed environment are of 'vital' interest to the innumerable victims of 'investment properties.' Divers who explore the ocean bed and the future crews of submarine boats will have reason to bless this regenerative chemistry.

---

[37] A. Desgresz and V. Balthazard, as they signed the relevant report, seem to have no other claim to celebrity, although Charles Bouchard (1837-1915), in whose lab they carried out their experiments, was much better-known

"The problem is simple: it is necessary to get rid of the carbon dioxide emitted by the breathing lungs and to restore the oxygen that pulmonary consumption removes.

"A providential substance has been found that enjoys this double virtue: it is sodium peroxide—or, if you prefer, superoxygenated soda. Take a piece of sodium peroxide and put it in contact with water, without heating it, at room temperature; oxygen will be given off, leaving a sodium oxide residue that is capable of absorbing carbon dioxide and combining with it to form a carbonate. The exhausted air is reconstituted.

"In Professor Bouchard's laboratory at the Faculty of Medicine, Messieurs Desgresz and Balthazard have succeeded in keeping animals alive in a sealed jar for hours, by deploying appropriate quantities of sodium peroxide. The substance is a powerful oxidant which, moreover, burns and destroys the poisons with which the expired gas is impregnated.

"Our experimenters wanted to apply the method to human respiration, and addressed themselves for that purpose to users of driving-suits. Present users of diving-suits are only provided with the air necessary to their underwater excursions with considerable difficulty, by means of a special pumps operated from a boat. With sodium peroxide, pumps are no longer necessary.

Messieurs Desgresz and Balthazard's diver will carry with him, so to speak, air-tablets, which will be contained in an ad hoc apparatus and will 'react' as necessary.

"This is the principle of the apparatus:

"A prismatic steel box is divided into compartments by superimposed horizontal shelves, each of which carries a supply of sodium peroxide. A clockwork mechanism, tips up the successive shelves at regular intervals, calculated according to the respiratory activity. At each stroke, the peroxide falls into another box containing water, and the chemical reaction proceeds, bringing about the absorption of carbon dioxide and the exhalation of 'new' oxygen.

"A little ventilator, activated by the electricity of a bat-tery, provokes a continuous circulation of the vitiated air and the regenerated air within the apparatus and in the enclosed space that constitutes the diver's 'armature.' The good air is incessantly delivered within range of his mouth.

"The upper part of the body is isolated in a hermetically-sealed garment with the regenerative apparatus. The entire system only weights twelve kilos, and the volume of circulating air is scarcely five liters, but five liters constantly renewed, like the Wandering Jew's five sous, *with only two hundred grams of peroxide for an hour's work."*

For its part, the Aurore *published the following note on November 3 of the same year:*

"It is well-known that an animal enclosed in a confined space ends up dying of asphyxia after a certain time by virtue of the disappearance from the atmosphere of the oxygen used in respiration and replaced by carbon dioxide. This phenome-non is even more rapid in humans. Thus, one must ensure the renewal of air in every instance in which a human is enclosed in a sealed environment—which are numerous.

"Scientists have been searching for some time for a sub-stance capable of regenerating vitiated air by destroying the carbon dioxide it contains and restoring the oxygen.

"A few weeks ago, the Académie des Science received a note from two French scientists, which announced that they had solved the problem. The substance that they used was sodium peroxide.

"Monsieur Jobert[38] has claimed priority of the invention, which he described in a sealed submission deposited on April 28, 1898. Sodium peroxide fixes atmospheric carbon dioxide and replaces it with oxygen. In a new note, Monsieur Jobert

---

[38] I have retained the spelling in Vibert's text, as it is presumably taken from the *Aurore*'s pages, but the reference is to Georges Jau-bert.

announces that he has found industrial applications for his discovery."

Finally, the Chronique Industrielle *adds, in its turn:*

"Following the presentation at the Académie des Science of the apparatus devised by Messrs. Desgresz and Balthazard, which permits a restricted volume of confined air to be renewed indefinitely, producing by means of sodium peroxide the absorption of carbon dioxide and its replacement by an equal volume of oxygen, Monsieur E. Derennes has informed that assembly of the use of sodium peroxide for the cleansing of wells polluted by carbon dioxide.

"Such invasions are extremely frequent, and to remedy them, ventilators are employed; they give satisfactory results, but they require special apparatus and the employment of motive force. Use is also made of wooden tubes or pipes, inside which a little fire is sent down to provoke the renewal of the air, etc. Recourse has also been made to chalk solutions that absorb carbon dioxide in a short time. Most frequently, however, the vitiated air that pollutes wells is a mixture of carbon dioxide and nitrogen, representing air in which the oxygen has been replaced by a equal volume of carbon dioxide; if one absorbs the carbon dioxide by means of chalk, the nitrogen remains; the solution thus seems incomplete.

"Now that the properties of industrial sodium peroxide are known, it seems that the employment of this substance solves the problem completely. The carbon dioxide is absorbed; the air resumes its normal composition. The only objection that can be raised is the difficulty of widely distributing supplies of a compound like sodium peroxide."

Thus, the issue is resolved, and our little submarine exploration, which was original and rather courageous a few years ago, would be mere child's play today!

Who's for a diving-suit?

V. How the submarine humans are formed.
Customs full of wisdom.

The human beings of both sexes that we had before us—
for it was certainly a matter of ancestral kin—were entirely
nude, but there was nothing immodest or shocking about that,
for, having lived at the bottom of the sea for nearly five thousand years, their bodies were covered with delicate silvery
scales, like those of sardines or trout—which gave them a
bright and sparkling gleam in the glare of the electric and
phosphorescent lights, utterly incomparable and charming.

Above the eyes, they all possessed enormous luminous
balls, which lit the way far ahead like two searchlights, exactly
like the fireflies of the Antilles. Between the two shoulders,
finally, a slight protuberance drew the gaze without being a
deformity or a disgrace; it was there that the air was enclosed,
at several thousand atmospheres, which permitted them to live
and breathe as freely at the bottom of the sea as we do on land.

Such were, at first glance, the three visible transformations that they had been imprinted upon them, across the centuries, but the great law of adaptation to the environment, according to the theories of Lamarck, the famous creator of
transformism.

As we exchanged handshakes, however, we did not take
long to perceive that they all had hands and feet lightly
webbed for swimming, not like the feet of a duck, but more
reminiscent of fishes' fins.

As they all had beautiful flavescent hair, complexions as
white as immaculate snow, with a slight hint of pink by virtue
of the impression of joy or curiosity, with no scales at all,
however imperceptible, on the face, we were seized with admiration for the surprising beauty of the young women and the
imposing majesty of the old men, as handsome as the most
clear-skinned of aged Arabs.

After the first exchange of greetings, Jacob Laquedem
soon embarked upon a conversation, as best he could, in Hebrew, with our new submarine friends. Fortunately, they un-

derstood one another better and more easily in speech that in writing, provided that they spoke very slowly. As a result, I was able, with a little effort, to follow the gist of the captain's conversation.

At first the lighting intrigued us; we could see well enough that the phosphorescent light, soft and bright at the same time, was produced by the luminous headlights that they all had above their eyes in the middle of the forehead, but we asked how it was came about that they also possessed so many electric lamps, strongly resembling ours. They told us that the bulbs in question had been suggested to the by those they had found in the hold of a wrecked ship. As for the production of electricity, they obtained it very easily, thanks to the submarine mountains, entirely magnetic, by which they were surrounded.

I do not want to spin this story out immeasurably, but I ought to add that they explained to us how they came to have veritable palaces, watertight grottoes perfectly lit, thanks to a system of successive doors, diminishing the force of pressure and resistance, capable of making Berlier[39] himself jealous, and that they showed us the marvelous illustrated newspapers that they printed on the skins of large sharks, prepared as needed, with extreme delicacy, as solid and supple as Japanese paper.

When we asked them what their political system was, the replied that they were governed by patriarchs, the oldest and wisest, in an absolutely democratic and egalitarian republic, without a president, and that their government was much wiser than ours—which seemed to us to be the exact truth.

Apart from hunting—which is to say, fishing—they live very much like us, modeling themselves on us and educated by the incessant fall of the ships that sometimes slid gently to the sea-bed. Like us they have balls, fêtes, dinners, theatres

---

[39] Jean-Baptiste Berlier (1841-1911), the inventor of the Parisian pneumatic tube postal system, inaugurated in 1866, and a pioneer of the Paris Metro.

and superb promenades, with immense pathways, in the midst of forests of coral.

By means of our cable we had all the books that they wanted sent down, and all the objects that they desired—and their joy, like ours, was unconfined.

On the fifth day, however, we thought that we ought to go back up, having learned from our friends' own mouths that in the Pacific and the Atlantic alone there were seven great submarine states, which certainly represented more than three hundred thousand inhabitants, of whose existence we had, until that day, been absolutely unaware.

Finally, progressing from lone surprise to the next, we got ready to go back up, and decided that our submarine friend, who was the first to have spoken to Captain Jacob Laquedem, would go with us.

VI. How a submarine man came up to the surface.
Necessary precautions.

"But I'll explode, with the compressed air that I have between my shoulders, when I reach the superior layers where the pressure is weaker!" exclaimed the man we shall call, for the sake of the clarity of our story's conclusion, by his true name, Tubalcain Souleau.

"Definitely not," the captain relied, for we're going to enclose your protuberance, containing the air you need, in a strong cap of fine steel, capable of resisting any explosion. Is that practical enough?"

"Not at all, my dear captain, for then the explosion would be produced in the opposite direction, internally—and it's my breast that would be blasted to pulp."

"That's true."

"So you see that I am condemned, like all my companions, never to follow you to the surface of the waters, much less on to land."

"That remains to be seen," I said, in my turn, "so much so that I'll give you the real solution."

"You're joking!" cried the brave Captain Jacob Laqudem.

"Joking? Listen for a moment—luckily, you have very skilful surgeons here?"

"For that, yes," said Tubalcain Souleau, emphatically.

"Well, you're going to have a small incision made between your shoulders, to which a tube made of silver and rubber will be attached, with a suitably-arranged system of automatic valves, and as you rise up toward the surface of the sea, you—or rather your pouch—will gradually deflate, and you'll be safe."

"In my arms!" cried the captain, who hugged me forcefully, adding, in a whisper: "You surprise me, old chap."

"Keep up appearances, not forgetting that a submarine population is listening to you and watching you, ten thousand meters beneath the waves—in round numbers."

"Why exaggerate?" the terrible captain went on. "We're only at a *bassitude* of 9429.17 meters."

"Go on—the Academy will give you five *sous*."

"That's all very well," Souleau put in, but here's my sister in tears at the idea of this operation and my departure. Will you answer for my life?"

"Let your sister, the charming Coral Flower, be consoled; the surgeon and I will answer for your life."

And the operation was carried out forthwith—but it was scarcely over when Tubalcain Souleau cried out again.

"What is it?"

"I'm doomed."

"Why's that?"

"It's quite simple: once on the surface of the sea, I'll be deflated…"

"But you'll be breathing our ambient air."

"Exactly, but when I come back down, my provision of air will be empty; I'll be done for. You can see that I can't go with you."

"Yes you can," I said, authoritatively, "for these tubes of compressed air that you see at our feet"—I addressed him as *tu* in my delirious joy (cf Doumer)[40] at having found the solution—"We'll also put on your feet when you come back."

"And then…?"

"Then, being in communication with your compressed-air pouch, as you descend along the cable, with the aid of a little pneumatic pump working in reverse, you'll store the air that you need just as one charges a bottle of soda-water. Do you understand?"

"So well that I'm at your disposal, to leave whenever you wish."

Soon, the seductive Coral Flower had dried her tears, and after touching farewells and promise to return, three parallel cables slowly pulled Captain Jacob Laquedem, Tubalcain Souleau and your humble servant up to the surface of the sea, which we had quit nearly a week earlier.

I shall not linger over the vicissitudes of our return voyage, which was relatively undramatic. Suffice it to say that our air-supply tubes were only half-empty and that the brave Souleau's apparatus functioned very well. He was very glad not to explode and to be able to breathe freely, like you or me, on the deck of the boat—with a slight dizziness at first, as when one has mountain fever.

Having ascertained exactly where we were, we set off rapidly to allow Souleau to see the Kermadu archipelago and the Friendly Isles, but heavy seas prevented us from disembarking, with the result that the poor fellow, whom we had dressed like ourselves, to protect him from the cold of the ambient air and from the curiosity of our sailors, said to me, half-sadly and half-cheerfully: "Like Moses, I must content myself with seeing the Promised Land from afar; I ought to count myself fortunate, since I'm the only man of my submarine race who has ever come to the surface of the waves, thanks to your tranquil audacity and ingenuity.

---

[40] Paul Doumer (1857-1932) was the Governor-General of French Indochina when this story was written, involved in continual negotiation with the Emperor Tu Duc.

Strangely enough, through contact with him, and re-membering lessons taught my father, who had learned Hebrew from Père La Touche,[41] I had reached the point of understanding him as well as the captain.

After a week, as he seemed to be getting a little anemic, we prepared for his descent with the same care and precaution. As he left us, he gave me a manuscript: his impressions during his sojourn aboard our ship, which I might publish some day, when I have found a generous publisher who is also prepared to publish the 173 slides that I brought back from my voyage to the bottom of the Pacific.

A few hours later, a telephone call and a short conversation informed us that the brave Tubalcain Souleau had returned to the bosom of his family, at a *bassitude* of 9429 meters under the sea, as the captain put it, in the South Pacific east of the Kermadu isles.

And now it is with tears in my eyes once again that I think of that double and strange adventure, which ranks among the best and happiest of my life—which is already long, alas!

---

[41] i.e., not via formal education.

DEATH

How People Die in the Colonies

I. Strange deaths. The surprising revelations of explorers.

As I was coming back from Algiers at the end of May last year, after my candidature and my campaign against Drumont, I was invited while passing through Marseilles to give a lecture on electoral practices in Algeria by the *Club Nautico-Agricole de la Colonisation Pratique.*

I did so with good grace, and after having spoken for an hour and forty-five minutes on the cannibal mores of Drumont's companions and exhibited the dark traces of several horizons, we set out, according to the custom of the province, in search of an opportunity to have a good time, legitimate in wifely eyes, by swilling champagne.

For myself, I will remark in passing that I drank mine, refusing forcefully to swill it, thinking that it is very unpleasant to find sand and pebbles at the bottom of one's glass.[42] How droll customs are, all the same! One of my neighbors told me that it was metaphorical, and that I didn't understand it at all—but let's pass on.

One of the joyful guests at the little improvised party turned to me abruptly and said, amiably: "We have read with pleasure your *Morts étranges,* which is every bit as curious as, and considerably more amusing than, Richepin's *Morts bi-*

---

[42] This pun, based on the contrast between the metaphorical use of *sabler* [to drink avidly] and its literal meaning [to sprinkle with sand], does not translate.

zarres[43]—but what you have forgotten are colonial deaths, which are both strange and bizarre. We're not, of course, talking about stupid deaths caused by the plague, cholera or *vomito negro*,[44] but beautiful deaths—*flavorsome* deaths, as one says today, which occur s frequently in hot tropical countries, to the delight of the observer who thus finds a way of occupying—or, if you prefer, breaking—the monotony of life."

Becoming more animated by degrees, he went on: "Look, here we have here a gathering of serious men, shipowners, retired colonists, explorers, old soldiers in the marine infantry, who have all been globe-trotters, and if you wish, we can, while swilling this last bottle, tell you about the most curious deaths that we have seen in the colonies with our own eyes—for, mark me, old chap, you're not in a company of liars here, you know."

I made a sign of assent, and he pointed at a fat man with a face as red as a tomato and hair as white as a swan—a head *signed* by twenty years in Africa—and exclaimed: "Over to you, Marius!"

The mouth belonging to that head opened slowly, in response, and the following emerged:

"I won't recall for you the hundreds of strange, bizarre or marvelous deaths that I've seen in the colonies, for our guest would still be here next week, nor shall I recall the death of poor Kunckel d'Herculay, so thoroughly eaten by ants that his skeleton was as white and polished as ivory within an hour and he was only recognized by his esparto-grass cravat, respected by the voracious hymenoptera because it appears that the knot was properly contrived. I propose to cite only one truly amazing colonial death."

"Adopted!" cried twenty voices.

---

[43] Jean Richepin's story-collection *Morts bizarres* was published in 1877. Vibert did not publish a volume entitled *Morts étranges* but might have contributed a series with that title to a periodical.
[44] Yellow fever.

"Perfect," said Marius. "I'll continue. It was one day when I had set off with a column toward El Goléa, beyond Ouargla. I went hunting outside the encampment, in midmorning, with a young adjutant, a great pal who was a native of the Mouffetard quarter in Paris—while I myself was born in the Rue de Pierre-qui-Rage in Marseilles. Enough—I'll go on. My weary friend told me that he was going to rest for a quarter of an hour in a clump of palm trees. When I came back fifteen minutes later, he was dead of a fractured skull. An ostrich had arrived from the desert in that interval, and having seen my poor friend's prematurely bald head, had doubtless mistaken it for an egg. So it had crouched down over him and laid an egg—and that egg had split his skull in two. I ran to the camp, and my friend was swiftly buried under three large stone slabs in a ruined Marabout shrine, for fear of jackals and hyenas. And what an omelet we made from the egg of the unwittingly murderous ostrich! I'll say no more than that—but for want of truffles, it was sprinkled with tears."

"If it had only been the egg of a moa or an aepyornis!" said an explorer, who wanted to show off his science.

But Marius caught the ball on the volley: "I've seen eggs of the former in Melbourne or Sydney Museum, I can't remember exactly. If one of those birds had laid an egg—if it were a female, of course—on a sleeping patrol, it would have crushed at least three men!"

I burst into loud laughter. "I beg your pardon, gentlemen, but it's two forty-one in the morning. Let's go to bed—and if you want to do me the honor of coming to lunch with me tomorrow at seventeen minutes past noon at Roubion's, we can continue listening to accounts of how people die in the colonies while we eat a nice bouillabaisse—for Monsieur Marius has already delighted me,"

"You're too kind. Tomorrow, the floor will be given to my friend Castagnat, who explored Madagascar at almost the same time as Grandidier himself."[45]

And we separated, in order to get a few hours sleep.

II. Strange deaths. The surprising revelations of explorers. The giant clam's bite.

As has been agreed during the night, all the members of the Club Nautico-Agricole de la Colonisation Pratique met again at the appointed time in the Restaurant du Chemin de la Corniche, owned by Vincent Roubien, as well as your servant. By twelve thirty-three—just time to strangle a small parrot— we were at table, confronting an excellent bouillabaisse, according to the program.

As soon as the coffee was served, the president cried: "The floor's yours, Castagnat.

And, having extracted a powerful puff from his cigar, Castagnat began in these terms:

"As I've had the honor of telling you, I was one of the fist explorers of Madagascar, since I was one of the companions of the celebrated Grandidier. You know that he's been a member of the Institut for a long time, in recompense for that little voyage, and if the same thing didn't come my way, it's only because I received a less distinguished education than him."

"That's very true," said Marius.

"Shut up. Everyone knows how one is cut in two by sharks in Madagascar, from its busiest harbors to the mouths of its rivers, as in all tropical regions.

"In the aforementioned river-mouths one even finds alligators and caimans, to complete the feast...for people here, who only know the mouth of their trombone, can't have any idea how it is."

---

[45] Alfred Grandidier (1836-1921) made his first voyage to Madagascar in 1865, returning in 1866 and 1868.

"Apologize!" howled the members of the Club Nautico-Agricole, "We're all familiar with the mouth of the Rhône—you're the one with the bad mouth."

"All right—I'll give you that and continue. It's also in the strange land of Madagascar that eels are put in shafts of bamboo, between two knots; to fatten them up, three little holes are pierced on the bamboo, it's dropped down to the river-bed with a stone attached, and after three months the bamboo is broken—for the eel, deformed like a bit of black pudding, is fitted exactly to the interior of the bamboo. You have to take care not to be bitten then, for it's not pleased by its imprisonment, especially if it has been separated from its intimate friend, and its bite is dangerous."

"You're joking," Marius opined.

"I'm telling the exact truth, but I'll get to the main point of my story. Early one morning, a friend and I had set out for a stroll along the sea shore, on the Fort Dauphin coast."

"I can see that from here," Marius opined, again.

"You can't see anything at all. We spent some time collecting marine algae for the boss's collection; the sun rose rapidly to the zenith without the aid of a funicular railway, and we had a diabolical thirst. Suddenly, my companion stopped dead and uttered a cry of joy. I ran over; he was in front of a superb specimen of the acephalous conchifera, a *Tridacna gigas*—as Monsieur Grandidier later informed us—resting gently on the sandy beach.

"I ought to tell you that these very strange animals are better known by the common name of *giant clams*, and that it was two of that species that the Republic of Venice once gave, in the times of its splendor, to François I, which can still be admired at the Église Saint-Sulpice in Paris."

"You're boring us with your erudition."

"I'll continue. The bivalve's two valves were wide open; one could see that the bird was inhaling the warm air, the salty breeze and the perfume of the sea. It was all pink, nacreous, shiny and pretty inside, with its soft, flaccid flesh—and as the sea had only just retreated from the shore, it was full of admirably transparent water.

"'There's an oyster unknown in Batignolles,' said my friend, a Paris lad. And before I could even make a gesture, he was on his knees in front of the giant tridacna, sticking his head out in order to drink that water...'"

Here Castagnat stopped to mop his brow, breathlessly. Two large tears slowly escaped his eyes. He drank a small glass of chartreuse, feverishly, and continued:

"At that moment, the beast abruptly reclosed its two valves, its colossal nutcrackers, and my friend uttered a scream—just one, which I shall never forget as long as I live. I hurled myself forward and, without thinking about the anger, I slipped my two hands into the gap in order to open the upper valve. It continued closing, automatically, and ten seconds later, I had the middle fingers of each hand—except for the thumb and the little finger—cut off at the first knuckle...'"

A frisson of horror gripped the assembly, in which there was no more laughter when Castagnat displayed his six severed fingers. He resumed as follows:

"Having left my phalanges in the giant clam, I ran to get help. When we came back, the bivalve was open again, and my friend's head was only attached to his torso by a shred of bloody flesh, A Malagasy went forward, and, with an accurate blow of his machete, cut the tendon permitting the beast to contract and close at will, like a large powerful rubber spring. It was dead. We took it away; it weighed no less than 240 kilos 353 grams.

"Well, that's an unholy font[46] that's stuck in my memory. We gave my friend an appropriate funeral and sent the terrible murderous giant tridacna, well wrapped-up, to his family in the Passage Hélène, in Batignolles."

Everyone, profoundly shaken and emotional, declared that Castagnat was well worthy of the Club Nautico-Agricole,

---

[46] An untranslatable pun: the French call giant clams *bénitiers*, after the vessels containing holy water provided in churches.

and it was decided that we would spend the evening at Frioul, in order to listen to the story of the celebrated Capdediou, a distant cousin of Tartarin of Tarascon[47] and a former long-haul captain in the Austral seas.

III. Strange deaths. The surprising revelations of explorers. The fatal knot.

Ever faithful to *rendezvous*, and moved by the hope of hearing some more interesting stories, we were all sitting tranquilly in a perfumed arbor at Frioul's, inhaling the gently and warm sea-breeze, which seemed to be bringing us the heady scents of Africa, at nine o'clock on the dot.

The night was radiant, and each of us had a glass of beer in front of us; without further ado, we gave the floor to Capdediou of Tarascon.

"Indeed, gentlemen, I've spent a lot of time sailing the South Seas and the Pacific in my long career as an old sea-dog—on long hauls, it's necessary to add—although today, if you please, we won't go as far and we'll stop on the way, on the enchanted island of Ceylon.

"One morning, about thirty years ago, I had arrived with my old tub to make a stopover in Colombo, in order to drop off some rice and pick up a little coffee. I settled all my business in the town during the morning, and in the afternoon, while my matelots—as the admirals say—were finishing off unloading and loading the cargo, I slipped away in order to get a little air, through the outlying districts of the town, which I used to know like the back of my hand, by virtue of having frequented them at every shore-leave.

"So, without a care in the world, I headed for a hospitable house well known to mariners, and was very glad to run

---

[47] The eponymous hero of Alphonse Daudet's comic novel *Tartarin de Tarascon* (1872) is supposed to be an archetypal Provençal, whose adventures as a big-game hunter have a certain Munchhausenesque quality about them. In two sequels to the novel he becomes a mountaineer and an explorer of the South Seas.

into a young Englishwoman there, not long disembarked, still unfamiliar with the country, who spoke French well enough. Now, as I jabber English like a Spanish heifer raised in Russia, I was delighted to encounter a quasi-compatriot, at least in linguistic terms.

"Having fulfilled the customary formalities, we went out together to take a stroll. After half an hour we were in a paradisal forest, and, suddenly reverting to childhood under the influence of the intoxicating effluvia of the tropical forest, I started dancing around among the trees, collecting a bunch of orchids—those marvelous parasites which, in Marseilles, would have been worth at least ten louis—and joyously putting them in her arms. While she struggled beneath the avalanche of strange flowers, I took out my pipe—an old seadog's habit—stuffed it and lit it; that was her ruination.

"Without me noticing it, that crazy daughter of Albion, ignorant of the terrible dangers of Ceylon, had picked up a red filament from the middle of the road to tie up her bouquet of flowers. She fell down, struck dead, without uttering a scream.

"The red ribbon was a little coral snake, which had bitten her—and, as you know, it kills instantly…"

The captain fell silent, and we remained pensive momentarily, for these tales of strange deaths were causing us to experience, involuntarily, the *petite mort*, as the immortal marquis puts it.[48]

"A week later," Capdediou went on, "I found myself in the harbor of a little independent Sultanate not far from Katmandu, in Nepal, when…but I've finished, for each of us only ought to tell one story.

"Go on, yes, go on—there's no need to make us salivate…"

"I was invited to witness and execution the following day. At the appointed hour, in the square in front of the Sultan's palace, the condemned man knelt down of his own ac-

---

[48] Vibert means a "shiver down the spine," although that is not exactly what the Marquis de Sade meant by *petite mort*.

cord, with typical Asiatic resignation, and put his own head on the block. Grave and solemn, sure of his strength and skill, the executioner put a foot on his head, laid on, and squashed it instantaneously, like a cooked apple. The man died of it, without even saying *oof!*"

"Well, he was reliable, your executioner."

"I believe so—it was an elephant performing the noble function of executioner."

"It's curious," Castagnat interjected, sententiously, "how it has been necessary, in every country in the world, for man to make it a duty to corrupt animals in his own image, and render them as cruel as him."

"That's true," we said—and the floor was given to the celebrated inventor of the galvanized steel mosquito-net, who had also travelled extensively in the Pacific isles selling his incomparable product."

"Over to you, Lagriffoul—let's go!"

And Onésime Lagriffoul began forthwith, in these terms...

But first, my dear readers, I request a ten-minute interval, which you have certainly deserved.

IV. Strange deaths. The surprising revelations of explorers.
The golden cyst.
A new decoration.

All the members of the Club Nautico-Agricole de la Colonisation Pratique being very impatient to hear another marvelous story, the President, without further delay, gave the floor of Onésime Lagriffoul, a former long-haul captain celebrated throughout the Cannebière,[49] as I've already said, for his voyages to the South Seas.

"Well," said the latter, "you're going to be robbed again, poor chaps, for I shan't take you to the Antipodes, but merely

---

[49] The Cannebière [literally "hemp-field"] is the central dock area of Marseilles, named after its main street.

to the kingdom of Annam, but as I don't want to be *booed* by you..."

"Bravo!" cried the assembly.

Without having noticed the excellent pun he had made,[50] Lagriffoul continued: "I promise you that the tall lanky chap at the far end to the table, to the left, by the name of Isidore Phétu, who lives in the Rue Pavé d'Amour nor far from the Rue de la Pierre-qui-Rage—my first mate, in a word—will take you there in a little while.

"Now, one day when I was in Annam to purchase a cargo of tea and rice, not to mention castor-oil..."

"Bravo!"

"I knew that a mandarin—a fat vegetable—had just been condemned to death by the king for forgetting to snuff out the candles for the ceremony celebrating Confucius' birthday in a timely manner.

"He could have argued in his defense that he was fat and impotent, and that his immense belly on his thin legs—more voluminous than late of the late Renan[51]—had prevented him from getting up in time to snuff out the sacred scented candles, but he preferred to die in carrying out the order of his most gracious overlord, and, as the thing was to be done in secret, the French authorities would be unable to intervene in time. As for me, I had been kept up to date by my quartermaster, whose girl-friend was a servant of the mandarin's wife—you follow?

"Yes."

"All right. On the appointed day, he took his long sword of honor, curved and damascened, and *bang!*—with a single stroke, he plunged it resolutely into his belly, thrusting it vio-

---

[50] Which, inevitably, doesn't translate; *hué* [booed] is phonetically identical to Hué, the name given by its French conquerors to the capital of Annam, now part of Vietnam.

[51] The historian Ernest Renan (1823-1892) was considered unorthodox by many, brilliant by some, but his unorthodoxy did not match that of Théodore Vibert, who loathed him.

92

lently upwards, in such a way as to cleave the abdomen in two.

"That done, he closed his eyes and waited, saying to himself: *I'm dead.* But some time passed and, utterly astonished at not being dead, he doubtless felt very weak, but also much better, and much lighter in front, for having delivered his great sword-thrust—and as he began a series of serious philosophical reflections on that subject, his wife, followed by her maid, who was my quartermaster's girl-friend, from whom…but that's enough…came in, all in tears, to see whether her poor potsherd of a mandarin had killed himself without overmuch pain, and was most astonished to find him tranquil on the sofa, a smile on his lips.

"'You're not dead?'

"'I'm quite well—but it's necessary to obey my master, the king, so finish me off.'

"'No need—you've obeyed your lord and master, so death doesn't want you; you've simply burst your cyst, and here you are, saved.'

"And right away, without losing a moment, she emptied the sac, washed it out with tea, as a substitute for carbolic acid, and sewed the belly up—as per Rollin—or stitched it up—as per Amyot—(the grammatical difference is indifferent to me)[52] with a long silver needle.

A fortnight later, the mandarin was back on his feet, with a figure as slim and elegant as a young man's, the mandarin's wife was wearing a cherubic smile and her maid was in an interesting condition…of joy.

The king, amazed by the adventure, having convened a supreme council of physicians, pharmacists, apothecaries and veterinary surgeons of Hué and several suburbs, granted a pardon to the mandarin, and, in memory of the marvelous cure, made him a Grand Commander of a new Order, the Gol-

---

[52] The references are to Charles Rollin (1661-1741) and Jacques Amyot (1513-1593). The pedantic point at issue would have been quite irrelevant to Vibert's readers.

den Cyst. Comprising a simple sharkskin pouch, the decoration is worn on the belly, and serves to carry all the utensils—bowl, pipe, seeds and Japanese matches—necessary to opium smokers.

"And that's how I was able, in Annam, in our beautiful Indo-Chinese empire, to witness the surprising cure of a brave mandarin, thanks to my quartermaster and his girl-friend, who was the maid of the aforementioned…enough said."

"Pardon! Forfeit! Forfeit!"

"What?"

"It's not the story a death that you recounted there, damn it, since your mandarin came back to life," said Marius.

"That's true—waiter, four bottles of champagne. He died twenty-seven years later, but I'm a good sportsman. Come on, my old Isidore Phétus, it's your turn to talk—and, most of all, to do honor to your former captain!"

V. Strange deaths. The surprising revelations of explorers.
The magic herbal.
A meteor strike.

Without making him repeat it, with good grace and with the tranquil assurance of an old sea-dog, Isidore Phétu started speaking in these terms:

"We had set out on a long-haul voyage to northern Polynesia, going from the Palaus to the Carolines and from there to the Marianas to buy up all the copra we could find from the natives before the Germans came to outbid us.

"As you can see, we were good businessmen aboard our old tub, which made good headway under full sail—I'll say no more than that.

"It's true," opined Onésime Lagriffoul.

"However, the captain had taken aboard a sort of eccentric, a middle-aged scientist…"

"More than middle," said Lagriffoul.

"That doesn't make sense," said Marius.

"…Who, without an official commission from the government, nevertheless claimed to have been sent to observe a transit of Venus, or some other peculiarity of the firmament."

"Pardon me," said Capdediou. "Venus went to India—perhaps it was the same year."[53]

"Well, that was another one—enough said. As well as astronomy, this singular beanpole was interested in all the sciences—geology, for which he had collected so many stones that there were enough to ballast the ship, botany, etc., even though he had the most beautiful herbals in the world, and had one true marvel, a big one, for conserving plants and flowers with their original colors. I emphasize the herbals because you'll see, later, that they were called upon to play a considerable role in our story.

"Now, one morning we had landed on one of the largest Palaus to pick up copra, and also a little tortoiseshell, and we were calmly in the process of negotiation while our astronomer, whom we jokingly called Father Comet, had gone into the interior with a cabin-boy who was carrying his specimen-box and two or three young savages native to the island—for the inhabitants were very peaceful and liked us a great deal.

"Suddenly—it was nine fifty-seven in the morning, I'll never forget it—there was a terrible explosion in the sky no more than half a league away from us.

"The natives dropped the sacks of copra, and we had a real fright ourselves, which didn't last long—but twenty-five minutes later, covered in sweat, our cabin-boy and the young Polynesians came running crazily, with all the marks of terror on their faces.

"Over there," the cabin-boy finally articulated, "on a rocky plateau, a big stone has fallen from the sky—a black stone that smells of sulfur. It plunged down on the rocks, and it's crushed Father Comet!"

---

[53] The veiled reference is to a celebrated pornographic novel, *Venus in India* (1889) published in Brussels and signed "Charles Devereaux."

"We immediately launched ourselves on his track, and soon found the place, where we saw that an enormous bolide of more than two cubic meters, which had fallen on the rock—which was flat and smooth at that location—had made a sort of splash in the aforementioned rock, sending shards in every direction....and our poor astronomer was underneath it."

"In all the time I was selling my galvanized steel mosquito-nets and picking up copra in the Pacific," Lagriffoul put in, "I'd never seen anything like it."

"With a winch and a capstan brought from the boat and hastily set up, the bolide was carefully lifted up, and we pulled Father Comet's corpse out from underneath it—as flat as a bug and absolutely desiccated already. As we were looking at one another, mournfully, the young cabin-boy had an impulse of sublime pity. 'We shouldn't throw him in the sea, but stick him between two sheets of silk paper in one of his herbals, fixing him there with three or four drawing-pins.'

"Which is what we did—and when we got back to France we delivered him intact to his widow, who had him well and truly encased in glass and placed in the dining-room. Although the chap looked as if he had been put through a mangle, he was still perfectly recognizable—except that his nose was a trifle elongated, like Cyrano's. All in all, he made another nice *still life* in his widow's dining-room."

Everyone was ill with laughter and emotion at the same time.

"It's three o'clock in the morning," Marius remarked. "It's time for the Club Nautico-Agricole de la Colonisation Pratique to let Monsieur Vibert rest; come on, let's be off—we'll escort him back to his hotel."

And we left the Frioul, bathed by the radiant glow of that Tarascon moon, which gives the young women of Marseilles sunstroke.

"And tomorrow, all hands on deck to see Monsieur off on the Paris express, and offer him a stirrup-cup!"

"Hurrah! Until tomorrow!"

VI. Strange deaths. The surprising revelations of explorers.
A minute in mid-air.

All hands on deck for the stirrup cup! Absolutely. I had to take the Paris express at seven forty in the evening, and everyone was at the Hôtel Terminus at five sharp, responding to my final invitation promptly.

Without wasting any time, therefore—drinking Madeira, because it was early, as I said—I gave the floor to young Gardanne, who had said nothing so far and had been to Paraguay—Para*gwoy*, as poseurs say—with a trader in quest of rubber, if I remember correctly, and other Republics in South America. Flattered that I had remembered, young Gardanne began thus:

"By virtue of going further, no longer in Paraguay but into the heart of Bolivia, in a large or small *chazot*—questions of military headgear are unimportant to me..."

"Oh, shut up, darling," said Castagnat, Capdediou, Marius, Onésime Lagriffoul and Isidore Phétu, in chorus.

"...We had ended up almost at the heart of one of the large branches of the Andean Cordilleras. We had been in a half-Spanish, half-Indian village for three weeks. The poor peasant with whom we were lodging—half-planter and half-trapper, as they say in Canada—had married and Indian woman who had given him three superb *midges*, as we say in the Cannebière, and the youngest child was a pretty little she-midge, two years old, who was always getting under our feet when we came in to dinner, after which we would rest, smoking not the pipe of peace but the pipe of amity.

"I remember that the children in question had a coppery complexion and an inexpressible charm.

"One day, as we—the boss, our host, me and the dogs—were coming back for dinner at a late hour, beneath a leaden sun, after seven hours marching through the undergrowth in search of precious lianas or even simple tree-trunks producing the sought-after gum, we heard our hostess, the worthy Indian woman, uttering heart-rending cries. In two bounds we were in front of the hut, and this is what we saw three meters over our heads: an enormous eagle, which was carrying the youngest child—Magdalena, my poor little favorite she-midge—into the air.

The mother was wringing her hands in despair. "My daughter! My poor daughter!"

With a rapid glance the father had seen everything and understood everything—and as he was carrying his rifle, he shouldered it with lighting speed.

"You're going to kill her," said the mother.

"No,"

"But she'll be killed by the fall when it lets her go."

"Rather death than knowing that she's been devoured by those cruel beasts—and then, the eagle's going to pass over the lake—there's no danger..."

He took aim with a sure eye—not the eagle's, his—but as a father in despair, and the beast fell, its head shattered, along with the child, whom it dropped, in the middle of the lake.

There was perhaps a hundred meters of water to cross, but the banks were full of grass and mud, and one couldn't just jump in and swim. The dogs set off like the wind, but didn't take long to get bogged down and caught in the grass. We unhitched a boat and started paddling feverishly. Well over three minutes had passed, and the child was still floating, with her red dress like a bloodstain on the blue lake, but head down. When her father grabbed her and held to his bosom, rather than in his arms, she was barely breathing.

"Half an hour later she was undressed and rubbed energetically with a little camphorated alcohol; I carried out a rhythmic traction of the tongue, but nothing came of it, and it didn't take her long to die in her parents' arms, before our eyes, without a spasm. We knew that she was dead because of the corpse-like coldness and stiffness of her poor little body..."

At that moment, all the members of the Club Nautico-Agricole de la Colonisation Pratique, gripped by the story and very emotional, started at the sound of a heart-rending sob, and turned round. It was the wife of the owner of the Hôtel Terminus de Marseilles, who said: "Forgive me, gentlemen—I overheard, and I'm a mother…"

On that declaration, so simple and poignant, the worthy Marius and I both shed a tear.

"I'll continue," said Gardanne, simply, as if in a dream, hypnotized by that distant vision of the past. "Suddenly, the father, snapping out of his torpor and seizing little Magdalena's frail body with a frenetic movement, cried: 'At least she's here—the filthy mountain beasts won't have her.' And, the trigger having been pulled, the poor parents wept for a long time over the body of the she-midge, my dear little friend."

"Your story's very touching," said Lagriffoul, "but it isn't set in a colony—pay the forfeit."

"Bah—it's a former Spanish colony."

"Pay the forfeit, all the same—but as there are extenuating circumstances, we'll let you choose it."

Immediately, Gardanne shouted: "Waiter, a round of toothpicks for these gentlemen!"

Everyone burst out laughing, and as soon as the oysters had been opened and an odorous Marseillaise sauce had been prepared, on the wing, the floor was given to Fimbel, a former tax-collector in Cochin-China.

VII. Strange deaths. The surprising revelations of explorers.
From strength to strength, as at Nicolet's.[54]
Twenty minutes in mid-air.

Without preamble, Fimbel, the former tax-collector in Cochin-China, a short white-haired old man, but with a searching eye and a ferrety face, began as follows:

"Our friend Gardanne has just related a drama of a minute in mid-air; well, I'll tell you one that lasted twenty

---

[54] The slogan of a famous mid-century *cabaretier*, which became a popular saying.

minutes. That's no small beer, as they say in the damnable North, where there are neither olives nor Arlesian women."

"Come on, no insults," said the President of the Club Nautico-Agricole de la Colonisation Pratique of the Bouches-du-Rhône."

"On the Cours Belsunce[55] there's what they call a hydraulic shooting-gallery—because you see an empty egg suspended on top of a powerful jet of water—and you can often see me lost in contemplation for half an hour in front of that egg. Well, I'm going to tell you why!

"Before I was a tax-collector in the Colonies, when I was a young officer, I found myself in that situation for twenty minutes..."

"You?"

"Yes, me—and a hundred meters up in the air as well. I was on a little transport vessel, with a number of marine soldiers as well as the crew, in we were in the middle of the China Sea. It was during the war, if you remember, when we took the Emperor's summer palace—in 1860, I think..."

"That's right—go on."

"So, one afternoon, suddenly, in the distance, in the sky above the horizon, a little black dot appeared that the captain—a worthy fellow—had just noticed. After looking at it for a minute or so through his telescope, he said to us: 'I think we're in trouble, lads.'

"'Why's that, Captain?'

"'Because that black dot will be on us in forty minutes—it's impossible to flee. That black dot is a typhoon—a *tornado*, as the Spaniards call it; a cyclone, as we say in Europe, and these diabolical corkscrews, in their gyratory form, dance a waltz from which one rarely emerges alive in the China Seas...or elsewhere. It's too late to run away; in half an hour we'll be inside that accursed typhoon's attractive corkscrew.'

---

[55] The Cours Belsunce is the main street of a district in Marseilles adjacent to the Cannebière.

"An old topman said: 'Damn—it'll be every man for himself.'

"After shaking his head as a sign of incredulity, the captain said: 'Haul in the sails and close the hatches'—and with admirable self-composure, everyone set to it.

"We passengers watched the sailors at work. Twenty minutes later, everything was ready, and as the captain had said, the typhoon was tracking us.

"'Dead center,' said the captain, deducing that from the form of the waterspout. 'We're well and truly f...' He didn't finish; the corkscrew, emptying the sea to a crazy depth as it passed, grabbed us amidships. The ship cracked and made a tremendous leap; we thought we were all doomed. That lasted ten seconds, and when we opened our eyes again we were looking down at the sea, the waves, the giant spindrift, everything. We were a hundred meters up in the air, at the top of the waterspout, the ship waltzing around in a rapid but smooth movement, almost horizontal. We all looked at one another at that supreme moment, and I don't know what fear or admiration for the power of nature overwhelmed us. You see, my friends, we were exactly like that egg on top of the water jet at the hydraulic shooting-gallery on the Cours Belsunce."

"Go on," said Maius. "Don't leave us in suspense."

"'So far so good,' said the captain, 'but when the waterspout breaks up for some reason, we're going to fall into the abyss, with the gyratory movement of the typhoon—and then we're *f...lambé...*quite a dish, my friends!'[56]

"The first mate wanted us to fire our guns, because three or four cannon-shots, according to him, would break the column and cause us to fall outside the focal point of the ty-

---

[56] The gist of this complex play on words is evident, since *flambé* has been translocated into English culinary parlance, but if f... is read in the same way as before, "*lambé*" recalls *lambeau* [shred], so the term could be read as something like "[expletive] torn to shreds," while the term that I have rendered as "dish" is actually "*plat-c...*"—which might be the beginning of *plat-chaud* [hot dish] but might also be suggestive of an unspecified expletive.

phoon—which is to say the gyratory gulf that might be two hundred meters deep beneath us, since we were already a hundred meters above sea-level.

"'That's true,' said the captain, calmly, "perhaps it's the last rotten spar that represents salvation...let's try it.' And he had all the cannons aboard loaded to the muzzle.

"'All or nothing,' he said, 'I've never given the order to fire in such circumstances and at such a height. Light up.'

"I took out my watch, we had been dancing madly on top of the giant column of water for exactly twenty minutes, a hundred meters up in the air. There was a frightful discharge, a similar fall, and that was all. I felt as if I were falling into the depths of the sea, and I fainted.

"When I came round, how long after I don't know, I was alone in the open sea and the tempest was easing. The typhoon was far away. Thanks to the instinct of self-preservation—for I was no longer thinking rationally, being brutalized and a little crazy—I grabbed a wooden beam that was fortunately close at hand.

"An hour later I was picked up by a Spanish collier that was returning to the Philippines with a cargo of Japanese coal. I was finally able to produce a few swords, and told my story. The boat searched the locale for an hour but didn't find anything. The ship had completely disappeared into the depths of the sea, with more than a hundred men aboard.

"How I came to be saved, I don't know, but I still can't look at an empty egg on a jet of water at a hydraulic shooting-gallery without shivering and crying like a baby."

"Bravo, Fimbel!" cried the assembly.

"And now, to conclude," said the president, "the floor is given to Fougasse, former owner and trainer of wooden horses[57] in Sidi-Bel-Abbès...and I the meantime, let's drink to the health of our last story-teller!"

"Hurrah!"

---

[57] I have translated this phrase literally, to conserve the joke, but what it really means is that Fougasse manufactured carousels.

VIII. Strange deaths. The Surprising revelations of explorers.
The ill-protected woman... in the tent.

Without wasting any time, Fougasse began:

"The day after the fall of the Commune, in which I had taken part as a lieutenant—me, a simple machine-fitter!—I was obliged to flee to escape the fire of the Versailles platoon. Once I had arrived in Canada, a country still French in terms of language, having accumulated a some savings, I fitted out and equipped a modest carousel factory; it made a fortune, for I soon had savings of fifty thousand francs, but when the amnesty was declared I hastened to abandon my Canadian friends and their excellent county, which was too cold for me, and came to set up my business, on a slightly larger scale, in Sidi-Bel-Abbès, in a sunny climate, in the midst of Arab poetry.

"There, I didn't take long to forge ties with many children of the desert. They knew that I liked them, and that I respected their liberty above all else, and that was enough to make me many devoted lifelong friends. Do the members of that loyal race not consider hospitality sacred, whether you eat at their table or they at yours?

"Thus, one day when I had been able to travel to a considerable distance to an Arab's tent, in order to stay there for a week and hunt amid the surrounding clumps of esparto-grass, and he offered to tell me something about the customs of his country, I accepted gladly.

"'That's agreed, then—this evening, when the women have retired to their own quarters in the tent and gone to bed, I'll come to fetch you...'

"At the appointed hour, while smoking placidly with the smiling calm of the Arab, in front of his little cup of coffee, half-recumbent on the carpet, he began thus:

"'You Europeans, who only see the superficial lives of Arabs, and the way we protect our women, who only go out into the street veiled and in numbers, naively suppose that there are no passionate dramas among us, and that husbands here are never deceived. You are certainly mistaken. Most of our women are faithful, as much out of love as fear; that does not, however, prevent dramas of jealousy, love and passion occurring from time to time—more terrible violent and more colorful than among you, permit me to tell you.

"'Firstly, among us, in tents in the desert, an amorous man is certainly much more audacious than in Europe, at least according to everything I have heard. So, if he loves a young woman who is lodged in another tent, with her husband, it's a matter of penetrating by night and getting into bed with her, next to her old husband, without waking him—and that's the delicate part of the enterprise.

"'The dogs know him, though, and don't stir. Then, he penetrates silently, a knife between his teeth with which to defend himself, but without clothes—stark naked—in order not to offer any purchase and not to be recognized. Thus, in the most absolute silence, stifling their sighs, the lovers succeed in deceiving the sleeping husband in the same tent.

"'Wives are funny creatures, you know—but things don't always go that way; the lover isn't always as brave and the husband isn't always old. Then, to achieve their end, when a wife is absolutely determined to betray her husband and pledge her love to her good friend, this is how she goes about it: by night, at an agreed hour, on the side of the tent where she lies—in consequence, on the side opposite her husband, she evades the surveillance of the latter and deceives him by only putting half of her body outside the tent.

"'Look through the open door of your tent—do you see that other tent over there, limned in the moonlight? Well, a horrible drama of his sort happened there. Five years ago, the chief's wife, young and ardent, betrayed her husband in that fashion. The latter, seeing himself so brutally deceived, understood everything, and, as quick as lightning, seized the long curved sword that was by his side and, seizing a handful of his wife's black hair, which was streaming over the carpet, while her body, up to the hips, was outside the tent, and cut off her head. There was no scream, scarcely a stifled moan, and the husband scarcely understood that the spasm of love had just changed into that of death, at the exact psychological moment.

"'The chief let go of his wife's head, and the following morning, he stuck it on a pike in front of the tent, to serve as an example. Half of the women of the tribe, on seeing that, fainted with horror, feeling pangs of conscience…for the most part.

"'As for the lover, it was only the next morning, on seeing his lover's head suspended on the end of a pike, that he understood what had occurred, without his being aware of it.

"'You see, comrade, that love is sometimes tragic under our beautiful African sky.'

"And he fell silent.

"I respected that silence, but asked, abruptly: 'Was that lover you?'

"'Yes,' he said, simply."

IX. Strange deaths. Surprising revelations of explorers. How the Spaniards transformed Carib women into salted herrings. Horrible details!

We were still feeling the impact of that terrifying story of love in an Arab tent when, suddenly looking at my watch, I exclaimed: "It's seven thirty-five—the Paris express leaves at seven forty. I only have five minutes to get away, while thanking you for your cordial welcome and your excellent banquet of friendship…"

"Not in this life," said Marius. "You're going to tell your own little story, and catch the next express at three minutes past eight. You'll have plenty of time, I think, in twenty minutes, old chap. Get on with it!"

Thus amicably cornered, there was nothing to do but comply, so, without further delay, I began:

"Since you're absolutely forcing me, I'll tell you how someone died in the Colonies, a long time ago, in America, shortly after its discovery by the Spaniards.

"I'm going to talk about events whose setting I know well, having visited it and traveled it in every direction—if one can travel a setting—not so very long ago.

"So, one day, we left Cap Haitien, in Haiti, the former San Domingue, a dozen friends on horseback—as one does in these new lands—to undertake a little expedition of three or four days into the interior.

"We began by going to call on the widow of the former president,[58] killed so tragically the day after the sacking of Salomon, a large town in the interior on the Grande-Rivière, and to stay overnight there. The next day, at four o'clock in the morning, we left for Dondon, and after a summary meal and a further night's sleep, we headed on a bright morning toward the *Grotte à Minguette*,[59] a cave especially noted for its thick layers of bat-droppings and the curious heads and faces sculpted in raw stone and granite, disposed by the Caribs, and, trust me, very well preserved.

"Having made an excellent meal at the entrance to the cave, at the bottom of a wild ravine, which we had reached by making our horses swim—with us on top, of course—we took the same route back to Dondon. This time, near the town, we visited an even more curious cave, with regard to historical memories: the *Grotte des dames*.[60]

We tethered our horses on trees at the foot of the mountain and gained access to the entrance to the cave by means of machetes. This is what happened: we went into the first cave, then, with a ladder, we got into a second on the same level; at the back of that one, by sliding sideways through a narrow opening, gazing our backs and bellies, we penetrated into a third cave.

---

[58] Presumably Lysius Salomon (1815-1888), President from 1879-88, who attempted to modernize Haiti.

[59] The cave in question is better known as La Voute de Minguet.

[60] The *Grotte des dames* is so-called because of two large stalagmites that allegedly resemble saints, not because of any legend remotely similar to the parody of European travelers' tales that Vibert is about to develop.

"At that very moment, perpetually in the midst of flying bats, with guano and coffee-grains brought by night-birds on the floor, I couldn't help thinking that the slightest earthquake—so frequent in those Antillean isles—might close that narrow opening forever. Eventually, we came out without difficulty. As all the walls were blackened, as if charred by fire, I asked the brave local general who was showing us around the historical highland caves, why that was. I knew, but I wanted to hear it again and without being begged, he began thus:

"'Those charred black rocks have been like that since the country's conquest by the Spanish. You know that it was here, in *Nuova Espanola*, that Christopher Columbus landed, and, as he had found a great deal of gold in the region, he demanded enormous masses of it from the Caciques—and as soon as there was a delay in the delivery, he and his companions massacred the poor Caribs in large numbers.

"'One day, when they had massacred thousands in this fashion, the Caciques had hidden the women, children and old men of the region in this *Grotte des dames*, but they were soon massacred in their turn and the Spaniards discovered the grotto. They rapidly walled them in with a mountain of green wood, in order to obtain more smoke, set fire to it, and waited. The heart-rending screams of the women and children reached them, and, excited by the priests—very Catholic, Apostolic and Roman—they danced, uttering cries of savage joy.

"'Two old men launched themselves through the flames to implore mercy for the women and children, and we cut down on the spot...and the Spaniards were still laughing, excited by their priests—ferocious and cruel laughter—and shouting: *They'll be well-cured, the lovely Carib women!*

"'When it was all over, a few Spaniards, in accordance with tradition, rushed forward to eat the flesh of the Carib women cooked to perfection as a substitute for salted herring!'

"And after that," I said, "Are you astonished that Cuba has had enough of the cruel and fanatical domination of Spanish *padres*?

"But damn it—this time it's two minutes past eight..."

107

X. Strange Deaths. Surprising revelations of explorers.
How people perished in the infernal circle of optical illusion.
Across the South American pampas.

But as I launched myself toward the express, a member
of the Club Nautico-Agricole de la Colonisation Pratique de
Marseilles who had not yet spoken, the likeable Boucairol, a
manufacturer of maggots from galvanized bread-crumbs in the
aforementioned Rue de la Pierre-qui-Rage, shouted; "We'll go
with you as far as Tarascon."

"But the train doesn't stop until Avignon."

"Well, we'll go as far as Avignon, old man—we owe
that to our guest Monsieur Vibert—come on, let's all go up to
the restaurant car, and while we have a glass of beer—I won't
use the horrible word *bock*[61]—I'll also tell mine, for I have
one to tell...."

"Go ahead, Boucairol, my old pal," Marius put in.

"Obviously, my adventure is less poignant that those nar-
rated by these gentlemen, but it's so true, so authentic..."

"That it's not to be laughed at," said the incorrigible Isidore Phétu.

"And it happened in the middle of South America, which
was already been mentioned. One day, we all left in a caravan
for a long expedition in search of asbestos mines, for the chief
had received a big order for the manufacture of tutus for the
ladies of the *corps de ballet* of the Grand Opera of Carcassonne.[62]

"We'd already been crossing the pampas, which alter-
nated with forest, for a week and were heading toward the
foothills of the Andean Cordillera—it's necessary not to confuse Andeans with undines—when all of a sudden, one morn-

---

[61] Because a *bock* is a small glass of beer, and Boucairol obviously
intends to have a large one.
[62] Carcassonne was the heart of the region where the "Cathar cru-
sade" took place in the 13th century and thousands of alleged heretics
were burned.

ing at daybreak, we saw a cloud of flames and smoke coming toward us, in the middle of the boundless grassland in which we had camped.

"Without wasting any time, uttering piercing screams, the three natives—Redskins, more or less—who were serving as our guides hurled themselves towards the matches, which were fortunately still on the ground, because we'd just struck the tents and were methodically wrapping things up, and set fire to the grass on the opposite side to the flames coming toward us. In the blink of an eye, the immense grassland was in flames in front of us.

"'Very well, now let's run after the retreating fire,' said our guides, with a good deal of logic, and it was thus that five minutes later, caught between two fires—one coming at us and the other dying—we were saved a from roasting.

We would have been glad of asbestos garments then...but we lacked the mines..."

"Bravo!" cried Onésime Lagriffoul, "you sound like a child of the Cannebière."[63]

"No," said Castagnat, "he reasons like a drum-beater"—and everyone laughed, in that dry and staccato fashion that one always has on an express train.

"Don't interrupt me, by Brest's thunder!"

"Marseilles' thunder."

"If you like. Two days later, by some unknown fatality, the expedition leader noticed that our compasses were going crazy—which is to say that they were shaky, and we could no longer count on them to guide us through the quasi-deserts of the prairie and clumps of trees—in a word, across the pampas."

"Our guides told us that we were close to a mine rich in magnetic iron. 'I can see that,' said the boss, 'but I'd much

---

[63] The original text emphasizes the first two letters of *résonnes* [sound] to emphasize its phonetic kinship with *raisonnes* [reason], in recognition of the double meaning of *mines*, which can signify "looks" as well as "mines"—a theme picked up by Castagnat.

rather we were near an asbestos mine, which wouldn't make us lose our bearings—no pun intended. Now, if we can't get out of the magic circle of the mine of magnetic iron, my lads, make no mistake about it, we're all f...' And he sketched an expressive gesture which only served to punctuate what he said and make it more energetic. The gesture wasn't pretty, but he was upset.

"We were in the middle of an endless grassland; we marched all day and much of the night, but we didn't emerge from the magic circle.

"Early the next morning, the leader of the expedition, who was a sly dog all the same, in accord with the three guides, told us that we mustn't lark about—no one had any desire to—and had to march straight ahead, without ever deviating to the left or the right, in order to get out of the infernal circle of the mine of magnetic iron and the endless pampas, as large as a sea of burned hay, and that, to keep us in a straight line, we were going to light fires every five hundred meters, putting the grass in heaps so that the fires wouldn't spread.

"By dusk we were exhausted. We'd made the fires, and when darkness fell, we could see them, dying but still distinct, forming an immense circle, in which we were enclosed.

"'There's not only an infernal circle of iron,' said the boss, 'but of fire—the result of an optical illusion, frequent in these grasslands, desolate solitudes without end. This time, my lads, we're well and truly f...'

"Three days running we began the fires in a straight line, and three days running we enclosed ourselves in the same magic circle of iron and the optical illusion.

"Then gripped by despair, we sat down to die, and one of us, thinking about his sweet fiancée, wept so much that he put out the fire—the half-fire—with his tears..."

The train was still rolling along; we were not only long past the Pas de Lanciers tunnel but had gone around the Étang de Berre, and no one had noticed, so engrossed were we all in that deceptive contest of man against the succession of magic circles—that of magnetic iron, that of fire, that of optical illusion, and the bated breath of our own oppression.

Finally, the ever-valiant Marius was the first to break the solemn silence. "And how did you get out of it, my old Boucairol, since here you are, alive?"

"It's quite simple. On the fourth day, the boss had an idea of genius. He had us build a huge circle of fire around us, and by nightfall, having tried to make a circle, we'd made a straight line and got out of the magic circle, and our compasses were working again…but eleven of us had died *en route*…"

Such a prodigy leaving us all open-mouthed, the narrator went on, by way of conclusion: "Optics, my lads, always optical effects, which claim to many victims in the desert…"

"And even in Marseilles."

"How's that?"

"The Mirage!"[64]

And we all shared in a in loud burst of laughter, which, emerging from the windows of the restaurant car, shook the Camargue and the Crau so mightily that in Saintes they thought it was an earthquake.

XI. Strange deaths. The surprising revelations of explorers.
A month underground. The strange practices of yogis.

As we were in the vicinity of Tarascon, it was decided, so as not to waste time, that the floor should then be given to Castebide to tell a good one.

"Needless to say, the ambient air ought to inspire you, old chap."

"One will do one's best," Castebide replied, simply, and began as follows:

"It was in the days when I took up residence in India, after serving in the navy, as a teacher of Belgian, Swiss and Javanese, which I knew perfectly—not to mention the French of

---

[64] The Mirage, in Istres, is one of Marseilles' leading hotels.

our beautiful southern dialect—five languages in all, to which I didn't take long to add Luxembourgian, with the result that I rapidly acquired a brilliant clientele of pupils. All the young Englishwomen and sons of Rajahs came to take lessons from me, or I went to their homes.

"One day, an Indian prince invited me to witness a very curious ceremony in his kingdom. It was a matter of seeing two priests buried alive—two yogis, who would be taken out again a month later, still alive.

"On the appointed day, their companions put them to sleep with ordinary magnetic passes, then they were put into two coffins in the depths of two tombs; the stones were re-place placed, sealing them, and they were covered with a foot of earth. The location was sown with wheat—which, it ought to be said, was watered religiously every day—and a month later, to the day, the wheat was harvested, yellow and fully ripe; the earth was removed, the tombstones lifted, the two yogis taken out of their coffins—and after they were put on a table, stark naked, and rubbed energetically all over their bodies with perfumed aromatic oils, the high priest commenced the rhythmic traction of the sleepers' tongues, one after the other, to the accompaniment of strange chanting. After twenty-two or twenty-three minutes, the worthy yogis slowly opened their eyes again and gradually returned to life. A great religious miracle had just been accomplished in India, and the entire population, delirious with fanaticism and drunk with joy, went to spread the good news in the streets of the town, along the roads, and through the neighboring villages, all the way to the interior of the Himalayan mountains, with lightning rapidity.

"Six months later, I was invited by another Indian prince to a ceremony of the same sort, and hastened to make my way there, accompanied by a comrade from France, who had been a magnetizer-masseur for some years in Paris before setting himself up as a photographer in Japan. He cultivated sensitive plates after having had an excessively sensitive soul, and fleeing the banks of the Adour following a great heartache.

"My poor friend—who had long been familiar with all the secrets of magnetism— had no sooner seen what was going on than he demanded to be buried alongside the lone yogi who had been put to sleep. In response to the prince's pleas, and in spite of mine, the priests spoke to him for a long time—but as, unlike me, he didn't speak six languages, the poor fellow misunderstood their final instructions....

"After a month, he was disinterred with the other yogi. The latter was recalled to life, following the rhythmic traction of the tongue. As for my unfortunate friend, he was quite dead, and as even beginning not to smell very good."

"Explain to us how these damned yogis can remain asleep underground like that for a month," said Marius.

"It's quite simple; once laid in the coffin, they active a spring by pressing a switch; a side-wall opens into the subterranean tunnel by means which they return to their convent, their *bonzery*. After a month, on the morning of the day that their tomb is to be opened, they come to lie down in their coffin again; the trick is complete, the great miracle of yogic resurrection is accomplished, and the people are content! Unfortunately, my photographer—who, unlike me, didn't know six languages..."

"You've already said that."

"...Didn't quite understand the explanations of the monks of Cakya-Mouni,[65] and he couldn't find the release switch. Then again, you see, in spite of the prince's request, the latter forgot about him and didn't go to look for him because they weren't sorry, all things considered, to demonstrate that a westerner, a European—a dirty red devil, in their eyes—couldn't suddenly become saintly enough, just like that, to live for a month underground without dying, like a true yogi."

The train rolled on, and it was agreed that we would take a rest after that curious narration regarding the religious cus-

---

[65] Cakya-Mouni was the most significant incarnation of the Buddha; Vibert uses the same appellation elsewhere.

toms of India—when the terrible Boucairol junior, a professor of criminology in Marseilles asked for the floor.

"It's understood that you'll be the last—the *brush*, as the omnibus-conductors of Paris say—for we're all getting off at Avignon, and we mustn't abuse our host's patience between here and there."

I made a gesture of protest.

XII. Strange deaths. The surprising revelations of explorers. On the banks of the Nile. The art of making three thousand livres a year. Conclusion.

So Boucairol junior, professor of criminology in Marseilles, began:

"Many years ago, I left to take a little pleasure-trip in Upper Egypt with a friend. We had just left the celebrated island of Philae, with its imperishable monuments, and were getting ready to undertake a serious lion-hunt the following day..."

"Like Tartarin?"

"No, old chap, since we were in Upper Egypt, not in Algeria...but I'll continue without paying any heed to your bad jokes. As we were not leaving until the following morning to plunge into the desert in search of its king, it was decided that we would take two Fellahs and a boat and go do a little flamingo-hunting on the Nile."

"How can one kill such lovely animals?"

"I don't like them myself, those long-legged animals, because they have a northern name: fleming. Yes, old chap, I hunt them.

"We had already been sailing for three hours on the Nile, as blue as the sky of that beautiful land, when my clumsy pal, standing up in the boat, fired a rifle-shot that procured him a recoil. He tried to regain his balance but, *splash!*—he was in the water. We tried to rescue him, but *splash!* again, and there we were, all in the soup with the boat capsized.

"'Quickly—swim to the river bank,' shouted our two Fellahs, in bad English. 'for the crocodiles won't take long to cut us in two and swallow us like common slices of roast beef.'

"Right away, we cleaved the waves, then *bang!* A scream—one of the Fellahs had just been caught by a crocodile. Then *bang!* again; another scream, even louder than the first. This time, it was my friend who's been swallowed by a huge crocodile, almost as big as a whale.

"It was impossible to rescue them; we were swimming flat out. Suddenly, I felt something caress the big toe on my left foot—O matchless surprise, it was a crocodile that had missed me, but had carried off a corn in its teeth. What a pedicure, lads!"

"You're joking!"

"Not on your life! We landed—the second or last Fellah, as you wish, and yours truly—on the river-bank. When I had dried off a little and recovered my emotions, I started weeping like a calf, thinking about the sad death of my old comrade—but the Fellah very judiciously remarked that that wouldn't get us anywhere, and that we'd do better to hide, in order to shoot the two crocodiles, which would obviously come back after their meal to have a nap on the sand and digest it. It would be easy to kill them at point-blank range, to avenge our companions.

"'But our cartridges are wet,' I said.

"'We'll kill them with knife-thrusts, then,'—and he pulled out his long *navaja*, victoriously.

"Indeed, we hid behind a clump of esparto-grass, and five minutes later, the two crocodiles came to lie down on the sand to digest their meal and go to sleep.

"Suddenly, I was seized by horror. My friend's body was molded in its entirely through the skin of the horrible saurian—and an idea of genius crossed my mind, giving me truly superhuman courage. While the Fellah launched himself upon the other sleeping crocodile, and ripped its belly open with a clean stroke of his knife, I hurled myself upon the one that was as fat as a whale, seized its two jaws violently and, sticking my head into its gaping maw, called loudly to me friend: 'Come on, my old mate—get out, quickly!'"

A loud burst of laughter interrupted the narrator, and everyone said, in chorus: "But that's a famous monologue that you're reciting there, you old joker!"

"I believe so—I'm the one who adapted the true adventure for narration."

"Did you make much from it?"

"Yes, enough—three thousand francs a year, as when one breeds rabbits."

"For a long time?"

"For a week."

This time, we all nearly died laughing, confronted with so much innocent wit.

By the time Boucairol junior had received everyone's congratulations, we were about to arrive at Avignon. All the members of the Club Nautico-Agricole de la Colonisation Pratique de Marseille bade me a touching farewell, making me promise to come back soon to eat another bouillabaisse at Vincent Roubien's, along the coast road, with the sea, so blue and so beautiful, at our feet.

To summarize the two days, Marius said, tenderly: "I think that we've just competed with the famous Thousand and One Nights, and if Monsieur Vibert consents to believe us, he'll find a fine theme for a fairy-tale on his return to the capital."

And everyone agreed, warmly.

I don't know whether I'll ever write the fairy-tale, but what I do know is that I came back very cheerfully from my terrible political campaign to defend the Republic of Algeria from all the reactionaries, and that I shall never forget the friendly welcome of my friends in Marseilles.

The next day, I was in Paris, and no one could believe that I hadn't left my bones in the hands of the Anti-Semites.

Unexpected Deaths

Bizarre explosions. Strange Deaths.
How one how spends one's life to die blown up!

Jean Richepin, who is a neighbor of mine and who wrote a curious volume in his youth entitled *Morts bizarres*, forgot all those produced by explosions, which are even more bizarre, and it is that lacuna that I want to fill, in part, today. I don't mean, of course, all those that occur in factories by virtue of the explosion of steam-engines, but those that have a truly unexpected and stranger character.

For many years, with Durand-Claye and Francisque Sarcey,[66] I conducted a vigorous campaign in favor of mains drainage, and, after many obstacles, I finally have the pleasure of saying that we succeeded, overcoming all the difficulties. Since then, the admirable final stage of the main drainage system has been inaugurated—if there were a *d* at the end of *finaux* it would render my thought entirely apt[67]—by the five kilometer tunnel that passes under the mountain of Auteuil, between Poissy, Meulan and Pontoise, a marvel of modern subterranean construction.

On the same subject, more than a year ago, I said:

"The General Council of Seine-et-Oise is actively concerned, and rightly so, with conditions of hygiene in the

---

[66] Alfred Durand-Claye (1841-1888) was he chief engineer in charge of sanitary provision in Paris; Francisque Sarcey (1827-1899) was a journalist nowadays best known for his drama criticism. Vibert is not exaggerating the fervor of this battle in the least; the companies responsible for emptying the cesspools of Paris had become highly significant capitalist enterprises, which fought tooth and nail against the introduction of modern sanitation.

[67] The effect would be to change *finaux* [final] into *finaud* [sly].

département. Well-informed people also add that this year, several localized epidemics of measles, smallpox and typhoid fever have recently proved the desirability and the necessity of taking energetic measures to combat these contagious diseases.

"To this deplorable state of affairs there is but one sole remedy: main drainage, with sewage farms, in order not to poison the Seine. Physicians know this; the engineers are ready to go, but the Syndicate of Parisian Landowners does not want to transform the installations, and is supported and encouraged by the cesspool-emptiers. One has the shameful and lamentable spectacle of seeing a great city like Paris and two départements subjected, mercilessly and without defense, to the invasion of all kinds of epidemics, because a handful of fat capitalist cesspool-emptiers don't want mains drainage. Once again, it is shameful, and dangerous for the Seine and for Seine-et-Oise. I don't care whether the cesspool-emptiers lose their money, but only that we become healthy, like all the capitals of Europe, by means of the broad, entire, absolute and immediate application of mains drainage, leading to sewage-farms. That is the only means of purifying the Seine and avoiding epidemics. There lies salvation; there should be no hesitation, and it's necessary to break the self-interested resistance of the dishonest cesspool-emptiers without delay."

By a cruel and fatal coincidence, I had scarcely finished writing those lines when I was proved only too correct; in a fit of madness, a formidable explosion of the deleterious gases in a drainage-ditch at 127 Rue de l'Université blew up the stone cover of the ditch, which was in the courtyard. The concierge, an old man of sixty, and his grand-daughter Marcelle were on top of it at the time; both precipitated to a depth of four meters, they were immediately killed and asphyxiated by the brutal fall and the noxious gases—a death as atrocious as it was unexpected!

Fortunately, mains drainage will prevent all such catastrophes, and I am proud to have made a significant contribution to it.

In this subject area, I could multiply to infinity examples of extraordinary deaths by explosion. Not long ago, workmen were sitting quietly eating their lunch on a gas-pipe in a railway station; the sun and the contact of all those warm bodies caused the gas to expand, and there as a sudden terrible explosion. One of the workmen was thrown into the air, uttering one last cry of anguish and agony. He fell back, and was hurriedly lifted up; he was dead. Seated directly over a plug, it had pierced his body from below and emerged from within like a machine-gun bullet.

Now, here we are in a telegraph office with pneumatic apparatus; in Paris, dispatches are being sent in little metal boxes through subterranean tubes with a thunderous force of several atmospheres, to arrive with a dull thud at the destination office.

An employee is standing in the foreground; he has forgotten to close the receptive apparatus; the dispatch arrives and *bang!*, with one bound the little box is in the unfortunate man's belly, perforates it, knocks him over and goes right through him. He has died without even saying *oof!*

Would you care to look at this magic lantern? It's beautiful, but the operator has a canister of gas next to him, compressed to several atmospheres. *Bang!* It explodes, and before the terrified audience, there goes the magic lantern into the air, along with the operator—killed instantly—in bloody shreds.

We're in the Bois de Boulogne at dusk; amorous couples are circulating on bicycles. Here's a ravishing girl in a figure-hugging costume, steering her bicycle with the aid of its acetylene lamp, as bright as a star; it's Venus illuminating the other Venus that it's guiding. But look out—*bang!* The lamp explodes and the poor little thing, not quite dead, is lying on her side, her head bloody, leaning sadly on a broken wheel.

But to judge by that account, you say, one might blow up at any time! But of course—certainly!

I knew two good bourgeois in the Marais who never set foot on a railway train for fear of being blow up, but one had a soda-water machine enclosed in a finely-woven rush basket, in order to make his own soda-water at the table, and the other had a well-known apparatus with two receptacles for making coffee, also at the table. Well, both of them were blown up, along with their apparatus, although neither died.

"I beg your pardon, but do people often get blown up at the Bourse?"

"Yes, and at the Bullier[68] too, but they don't always die. That's why I shan't talk about them today.

---

[68] The Bal Bullier was one of the most popular dance-halls in Paris. In both the instances cited in this brief exchange "blown up" is intended be construed metaphorically.

How People Die in America

I. The death-penalty in the United States.
A great murderous people.
Twice executed alive. A long martyrdom. Horrible details.

My political friends in the United States and Canada—
the Fenians, the knights of labor, black people and the socialists...true socialists—are sometimes generous enough to remember that I've had a fair amount to do with electricity in
my time, and that I've always defended the negroes; and that's
why, from time to time, they send me documents of the greatest interest.

They often enclose revelations that I can't set before the
eyes of my readers, for fear of compromising the sacred cause
of human emancipation, but today[69] I received from one of
these kind folk a letter so curious that I couldn't resist the
temptation to publish it.

Moreover, my own information and personal enquiries
permit me to affirm that it constitutes nothing but an expression of the exact truth. I shall pass over the customary compliments and get to the essential part:

"Perhaps I shall find in you, my dear sir, who are one of
the staunchest defenders of the claims of socialists and black
people in America, a man courageous enough to expose the
facts that I shall relate to you—in fact, I have no doubt about
it.

"I am not a black man, but a man of color, of mixed race,
born in the United States. For ten years I have been a school-
teacher in a large town not far from New York. Married with
children, I have spent my life very quietly, between my duties
as a teacher and my family duties, with no other ambition.

---

[69] The author inserts a footnote: "Some time in 1893, if I remember
rightly."

"One day, a twelve-year-old child who was in my class suddenly disappeared.

"As I was known to have advanced socialist opinions, was reputed to be affiliated to secret societies, and had the misfortune—unpardonable here, in the land of liberty—to be colored, I was soon accused of having murdered the child. The population wanted to lynch me; saved by the police, I was tried and condemned to death—without any evidence, since I'm innocent.

"When the sentence was pronounced I heard a terrible scream in the hall, followed by a forceful exclamation: 'I'll save you!' It was my valiant wife, a pure-blooded black woman, who was being thrown out by the police.

"Alas! That condemnation to death was nothing, merely the commencement of my long martyrdom, for I was, like all those condemned to death in the United States nowadays, *to be executed and martyrized alive twice over*, and it's truly miraculous that I have come back from it.

"Taken back to my cell after the condemnation, I was informed, a few days later, that I was to be executed, in accordance with the new fashion, by electricity.

"I would much rather have been hanged, for my studies had led me to the invincible conclusion that one must take a long time to die, if one dies at all—and the horrors of the dissection-theater, with regard to a body paralyzed but alive, made me shiver in advance.

"One morning, therefore, I was led to the execution-chamber, installed in and attached to the electric chair with the metal helmet on my head. You know what it's like—illustration has popularized that savage form of execution; you know, so I shall skip the details.

"The current was switched on. After violent convulsions, I remained inert in the chair. I was dead—at least the torturer-physicians said so. But no, I was alive, fully alive, but in a state of anesthetic insensibility, and I could hear perfectly what the physicians around me were saying. I even heard it with the acuity of perception that arsenic poisoning, for instance, produces. Except that I couldn't move.

"Having examined me thoroughly, the physicians had me detached by their assistants, and one of them said: 'Take the body to the theater; we're going to dissect it.'

"And another hastened to add: 'That's the most prudent thing to do, for experience has already demonstrated that *an autopsy is a necessary complement to electrocution*; without that, one never knows whether these scoundrels (sic) are good and dead!'

"You can imagine, my dear sir, that all this caused a sentiment of indescribable terror to grow within me. I had always been brave, but this time, it must be said, the awareness of my impotence in the face of the investigative scalpel froze the blood in my veins.

"A few moments later, stripped of my clothing, I was laid on a large slab, surrounded by the traditional little gutters, and a bucket on legs to receive my blood and entrails. Although my eyes were closed, I was able to take an exact account of my situation; I knew exactly where I was, and I confess that I had never experienced such anguish in my life.

"The physicians conferred; first they would examine the nervous system of the arms. I felt cold steel digging into my flesh, and they butchered me alive in that fashion for some time. I screamed desperately—but internally, alas; they heard nothing. It was perhaps as well, all things considered, for otherwise, they would have finished me off immediately!

"Finally, I lost consciousness—or, rather, my mental self lost perception of things under the intensity of the pain.

"When I came round—after how long, I don't know—I heard that the physicians had finished examining the nerves of my poor arm. 'Let's examine the arteries now.'

"'No, that's unnecessary,' said another—and I experienced a surge of joy, for I felt that once the arteries were cut, that would be death. So strongly does one hold on to life, even when one is officially dead. It's crazy and stupid, Monsieur, what I tell you there, but I have suffered so much!

"The one who seemed to be in charge of the company of official executioners and reputable scientists went on: 'We'll open his kidneys, but let's start with the abdomen.'

"You're not unaware that in the United States, although we have good dentists and passable veterinary surgeons, the physicians are all ignorant, and, apart from kidneys, no knowing of their art.

"I felt the chill of the scalpel again, passing over my abdomen, and I said to myself: 'This time, it's finished,' while enveloping my wife and children with an immense hug. It's extraordinary how rapidly thought moves at such moments, condensing ideas into a flash of time.

"By virtue of a singular phenomenon, however, I suddenly felt the steel, instead of penetrating my skin, escape from the operator's hands, and I heard all the physicians utter a cry of amazement: 'He's white!'

"Later, I understood the meaning of that exclamation. It was just that, under the intensity of the mental and physical tortures I had just endured, my hair and beard had suddenly turned white.

"Then there was a great hubbub in the theater. Through the partly-open door, I heard my wife's voice, who was claiming my cadaver insistently, and a good deal of movement outside. The excitement was in a neighboring building.

"At this unexpected turn of events, the physicians all abandoned me and one of them said to my wife in a brutal tone: "Take this carrion and scram—leave us in peace.'

"With one bound, like a panther, my wife lifted me on to her shoulders and threw me into a carriage outside, where my children were.

"Ten minutes later, not in my own home but that of steadfast friends, my wife deposited me on a bed, bandaged the wounds on my arm, put a dressing on my abdomen—which was only scratched—and blew forcefully into my mouth. Only a few minutes had gone by when, thanks to that artificial respiration, I opened my eyes again. I had come back to life—truly. I was saved.

"We made haste to flee the country; I'm sending you this letter from South America, and I have a strong desire to go to Africa, into the midst of black people, my ancestors—for I think those worthy people are a little less cruel than white men.

"It is therefore quite certain, and I affirm strongly, that all those condemned to death in the United States are executed twice over, alive—once by the electricity and second time by the autopsy. *That is the only means of obtaining a true cadaver*, our physician torturers say.

Great scientists in your country, like Messieurs d'Arsonval, François Biraud and Lacassagne,[70] have already recognized that there is something inhuman in that double martyrdom of a poor creature, alive an helpless.

"Monsieur d'Arsonval has declared that there is only an apparent death after electrocution, and that the stricken individual can be recalled to life by the same procedures that are applied to a person fallen into water.

"And what is horrible is that the physicians of the United States know this full well, and that it is to occasion death that they proceed to the autopsy and butcher living people!

"That's more than enough, my dear Monsieur. I'm safe and I'm very happy, as are all my family—only, make these horrors of American pseudoscience known in Europe; perhaps you will be able to stop many murders, as monstrous as they are juridical, and will usefully serve the cause of humanity!"

I have nothing to add to this long epistle, except that these horrible scenes are repeated every day in the United States, at each new execution, and that it is perhaps time that the Americans brought a little more humanity and circumspection into their method of killing criminals.

---

[70] Jacques-Arsène d'Arsonval (1851-1940) was a significant pioneer of electrophysiology, while Alexandre Lacassagne (1843-1940) was a criminologist who opposed the theories of Cesare Lombroso, insisting that criminality was the product of social conditions rather than heredity.

It is infamous, and it must be said that if it were to cease, it would only be to the honor of the human race to which we belong.

II. Body-snatchers in the United States. Various syndicates.
Necropolis-burglars. Macabre details. Most horrible!

It is very evident that the Anglo-Saxon peoples are infinitely more practical than those of the Latin races, and for a long time they have been able, very pragmatically, to find a capital to exploit in the dead as well as in the living. Everyone remembers the story of the English exploiting Egyptian mummies on a massive scale, making fertilizer out of them after selling the bandages at a good price for various purposes.

Well, for some years, a gang of burglars in the United States—a perfectly-organized syndicate, a formidable Trust, as they call it over there—has been constituted for stealing from cemeteries the princes of finance, railways, wheat or used fat, billionaires or merely millionaires a few hundred times over.

When a Gould, a Mackay, a World, a Rockefeller a Carnegie or one of his family members dies, the syndicate of necropolis-burglars, which has usually bribed the wardens in advance, takes possession of the cadaver, puts it in a safe and secret place, and has it published in the newspapers that it is at the disposal of the family, in exchange for one or two million dollars—five or six million francs—according to the fortune and grief of the people who have to be made to pay up.

It cannot be said that these thieves are often arrested by the police; they take all possible precautions and are able avenge themselves on the dead or the living if one lays a hand on them.

A superb discovery was made, however which drew admiration from Parisians among the great works of the Exposition, along the railway circling Paris, etc. I mean reinforced concrete—and, immediately, with the eye-blink promptitude that distinguishes them, the architects and entrepreneurs of

Yankee buildings formed a second syndicate for digging profound ditches and filling them with reinforced concrete, along with a coffin placed in the center. The whole thing is covered by a wall or a beam, as you please, of reinforced concrete several meters thick, with the result that the billionaires of the United States, having their tombs constructed in advance before their very eyed, said to themselves: 'This time, the burglars are sunk and we can rest in peace in our ultimate sleep.

It did no good, for chemists and diamond-cutters immediately formed a third syndicate, immediately known throughout the United States as the syndicate of perforators, who, by cleverly combining explosive powders and diamond-tipped steel drill-bits, did indeed succeed in perforating reinforced concrete tombs and stealing coffins triple-clad in lead, oak, jacaranda and other precious woods.

Then the situation became critical, and there was an instant of stupor throughout the starry Republic, before this Homeric duel of billionaires defending their dead skin and necropolis-burglars.

Truly, no one knew any longer what measures to take to escape the rapacity of these people, when a temporary solution—you will soon see why I say *temporary*—was finally furnished by a conference of legal experts, journalists and undertakers convened for that purpose. They found, very judiciously and conclusively, that burglars did not want these unfortunate cadavers, and that it was simply a matter of reaching an understanding with them regarding the tax that one needed to pay them, at every burial of an important person known for his large fortune. That is somewhat reminiscent of the customs of Greek brigands, great lords of the mountains, to whom it was necessary to pay for an escort in order not to be robbed— but the idea seemed excellent. It was put into practice and for some time, it was thought that the issue had been resolved.

The rapacity of competition had been forgotten, however, and a fourth syndicate—or, if you prefer, a second one of body-snatchers—was formed and resumed the operations of the first on its own account. The latter, I must say, behaved very correctly and loyally; they undertook to defend the target tombs themselves, by means of a guard on each one. These guard were killed, stabbed on the spot, and the petty but lucrative commerce of the necropolis-burglars continued apace.

What could be done? This second stupor was of short duration.

It was then that the truly supple, inventive and marvelous cleverness of those good Yankees burst forth. A fifth syndicate was immediately formed: that of the hirers and sellers of cadavers. It was very simple, and this is how the said syndicate worked: a billionaire dies; his family has him put in a triply-reinforced coffin of wood, lead, etc., and keeps him at home; at the same time, it hires by the month, like a simple carriage, or buys outright, the anonymous cadaver of some poor devil from one hospital or another, or from a poor family who has given it up it for twenty-five dollars. The syndicate puts it n the tomb, and the trick is worked. The cadaver-thieves don't take it, because it's a fake, and is worthless to them.

There was no hesitation over calling this last syndicate a stroke of genius. On reflection, however, it has proved even more inconvenient. Although the necropolis-burglars have been thoroughly vanquished, residences need to be guarded by a numerous, reliable and faithful domestic staff.

This sounds like a hoax, and yet it is an absolutely true page of history. One can also imagine a sixth syndicate, that of constructors of strong-boxes for coffins or cadavers, which would simplify many things and give great security to families.

Then again, one wonders whether the law and the police will not end up intervening; whether the coffins, put in the cellar, might not end up ruining the fine wines; and finally, when the dead have been accumulated thus within the family, what a nuisance they will be when moving house....

So, I have modestly proposed another solution by cablegram, which is simply to cremate the bodies; that way, there's

nothing more to fear from body-snatchers and other necropolis-burglars.

Yes, but the Americans don't like hat.

What, then? If this goes on, this large question will
threaten to impassion the United States as much as the Dreyfus affair did here, and that's no understatement.

Sleep peacefully; after the next sensational theft of this
kind accomplished in a New World necropolis, I'll keep you
up to date with all the details. Most horrible!

*Author's note: Still on the same subject, and to demonstrate
how this poignant preoccupation threatens to enter definitively
into Yankee custom, the* Aurore *of February 17, 1900 published the following item:*

*"A few months ago, Mademoiselle Martel, the daughter
of a rich American businessman, died in the Dominican convent at Sèvres. Her father had her buried in the town cemetery, and then left for America again. He came back last Tues-
day, after having rendered his soul to God, with the following
apparatus:*

*"His body had been deposited in a series of coffins, the
total weight of which was more than fifteen hundred kilos. The
mortal remains of Monsieur Martel had first been surrounded
by the regulation mixture, then placed in an oak coffin several
centimeters thick. Then came an envelope of lead three milli-
meters thick, then another oak coffin five centimeters thick, the
whole bolted and riveted together, alarmingly.*

*"It required fifteen men to place this monument on the
hearse, which buckled under the weight, and when it arrived
at the cemetery, the burial had to be poisoned; the grave was
too small!*

"Only the Americans have such ideas and coffins."

Finally, for its part, the earnest Gazette Maritime *of July
15 of the same year published the following information:*

*"A curious lawsuit has been brought against the Atlas
Navigation Company by the family of the late A. J. Wormser, a*

rich New York merchant who recently died at sea aboard the steamship Allegheny of that line, forty-eight hours before arriving in Jamaica, coming from New York. His mortal remains were immediately immersed, on the captain's orders, contrary to the opinion of the physician accompanying the defunct and who thought that the body could be suitably conserved until reaching port, given the quantity of ice and pharmaceutical products aboard. The malady was not contagious.

"The majority of the New York newspapers have begun discussing this affair passionately, and it is also preoccupying the American public greatly, for it raises a question of principle that worries many Americans, who desire a determination of the rights of a passenger to be transported to his destination alive or dead, once having paid for his ticket.

"Some companies—the American Line among others—inform their passengers that their steamships always keep ad hoc barrels and the antiseptics necessary to conserve cadavers until they reach their destination. Other companies—including the large German company, the Hamburg-American Line—are even more obliging, and advise their clients that they can carry their coffins, as well as their baggage, without charge.

"American law is mute on the matter, but the Treasury Minister recently decided that cadavers conserved in barrels must be admitted duty-free.

"A law dating from 1882, moreover, which has never been repealed, obliges captains of ships or consigners to declare within forty-eight hours of arrival, and to notify the authorities of any death that has occurred in the course of a voyage—and to pay a fee of ten dollars for each one."

As can be seen, this concern to conserve one's skin after death, protected from the physical voracity of fish and the moral—or, rather, immoral—voracity of burglars, has become a national obsession in the United States.

III. What purpose cold may serve.
The latest new form of execution.
Painless execution. The Iced Club.

I shall begin by posing a prejudicial question. Like my father, I have always strongly demanded the abolition of the death penalty; in consequence, I am not about to defend one form of execution over another—I find them all odious and vile—but simply intend, as a faithful historian of my era, to expose *the latest thing*.

Needless to say, it is inevitably American.

So, a handful of exceedingly rich American capitalists, with the Exposition in mind, have just built and equipped a colossal factory outside Paris, thirty or forty minutes from the fortifications, for the mass production of ice by the usual methods of chemical refrigeration. Naturally, I shall say no more, in order not to raise superfluous protests from these honest businessmen.

In any case, I would find it difficult to say any more, for I have been refused entry at the factory gate; it appears that there are glacial secrets inside. One of my friends, however, more fortunate, has been able to visit it, and has even been allowed into a refrigeration chamber, in which he was enclosed while it was chilled, for a few moments. One reaches incredibly low temperatures by this means, and finds oneself going numb painlessly. One descends insensibly into Nirvana, as the Indians say, without suffering; it is evident that this is entirely ideal.

"A few seconds more," said my friend, "and, without being able to protest, without pain, very gently, I felt that I was going to croak."

"Just so," said the American engineers, with that gross thick laughter that harmonizes so well with the length of their feet. "Precisely—but we were there to stop the thrust of the liberating piston in time."

"What do you mean?"

"It all depends on how your mother-in-law treats you."

Immediately, my friend understood that these American had already been corrupted by the literature of our music halls. This rather frivolous conversation notwithstanding, as they were only too happy to have a Parisian journalist that they thought influential at their disposal, they vouchsafed the following curious revelations, between glasses of iced champagne, and as my friend was somewhat chilled by them himself, I hasten to transcribe here the aforementioned sensational revelations.

"You see, Monsieur, we've come to spend a million dollars or two here, setting up an artificial ice factory, with the 1900 Exposition in mind. That's what the public will see, but for us it's a mere bagatelle, and our real, hidden, unknown goal is a higher one; it's humanitarian. We're citizens of free America, but we're also gentlemen, all members of the celebrated Iced Club of Indianapolis.[71]

"If we refused entry to our factory to your colleague, it's because he supports the abolition of the death-penalty. It can't be abolished, especially in the land of the immortal Lynch!"

"Why not lynx?"

"Because we're respectful of orthography...but don't interrupt. We'll go on. Hanging is sometimes slow, if not licentious, and clubs have even been founded back home of those hanged by persuasion and for fun.

"The garrotte is a cruel torture, only good for Spaniards; the guillotine is old-hat, and as for our electrocution, it only gives lamentable results, without even ensuring the death of the *patient.* O sweet euphemism!

"That's why we've come to Paris with a superior humanitarian goal."

"I don't understand."

---

[71] I have translated *Club des refroidis* slightly oddly, in order to conserve something of the double meaning by which *refroidi* can also mean "murdered." Cool Club and Chilled Club would, in any case, give the wrong impression in the context of modern slang.

"It's quite simple, though. We, the members of the Iced Club of Indianapolis, will ask the President of the Republic, and the French parliament, if necessary, for the exclusive monopoly on all capital punishments in France, by rapid painless freezing."

"But then, just now, when you shut me in your freezing chamber..."

"Exactly—it was to have, in case of need, your deposition of satisfaction at the enquiry as to the *commodo vel incommodo*.[72]

"That's horrible!"

"No, practical! You're not unaware that we Americans are the finest dentists in the world?"

"Yes indeed."

"Well, just as we extract teeth painlessly, by means of cold, we want to extract life in the same way, by means of cold, without any pain for the wretches condemned to death. We're benefactors of humankind; we remember Lafayette and, out of gratitude, for love of France, we want to endow her, in the name of humanity, with this process of *frigorifico-execution*."

"It's genius!"

"No, it's good, it's kind, it's humane, it's proper and it's practical. The cadaver, emerging from the cold chamber after a few minutes, as stiff as an iron bar, is very easy to bury. As a method, it's obvious that, from all points of view—sentimental and practical—it's far superior to electrocution, which has given us so much trouble."

Then they set about swilling champagne in honor of Lafayette, the Iced Club, frigorifico-execution, and the 1900 Exposition—and the next morning, the American engineers and my poor friend were as drunk as skunks.

That's why he was only able to confide these astonishing revelations to me a few days later. He'd eaten too much salmon, as the Americans say.

---

[72] Literally, advantageous or disadvantageous

Pointed Insurance

The flashguard.
From the Prussian helmet to the Colonial helmet.
A surprising new invention.

My old and excellent colleague de Parville offered the following curious statistics in the *Débats* the other day, regarding people killed every year by thunder and lightning—by heavenly fire, as our forefathers used to say:

"Between 1835 and 1895, lightning killed 6198 people in France! And that is a minimum. It is only since 1863 that the statistic of victims of heavenly fire has been calculated by the Ministry of Justice; it is the gendarmes who are responsible for enquiries and the courts of appeal that centralize the results. In general, lightning kills between 80 and 150 people a year on French territory. The figure is very variable from year to year: only 51 in 1860, 156 in 1868, 94 in 1876, 106 in 1877. The maximum years were 1892 (187), 1874 (178), 1884 (174), 1868 (156) and 1893 (155); they correspond to hot, dry summers.

"The distribution of lightning-strikes is far from being regular; there are lightning-rich areas just as there are regions prone to hail. In some countries, it almost never thunders; in others, it thunders constantly. Mountainous regions are the worst afflicted. In the *département* of the Seine, one in 92,000 inhabitants is struck by lightning; in the Channel region, one in 29,414; in Morbihan, one in 18,600; in Lozère, one in 1362; in the lower Alps, one in 1454, etc. The victims of lightning are classified in the following order: under trees; in open country while holding metallic objects, carts, scythes or animals; in isolated houses, farm buildings or sheep-folds; in churches, especially while ringing bells during a storm; in railway buildings; in cities."

Confronted by such figures, a man with a heart cannot remain indifferent, so, when my initial emotion had calmed down somewhat, I immediately thought of seeking a means to avoid such an accumulation of celestial—but nevertheless sad—murders in the future. That's what I've come up with, and am submitting very humbly to my readers. Without losing a minute, I got busy, and I've already taken out patents in the Republic of San Marino, Andorra, Monaco and *chez Mélénick*. This is what's involved.

I thought—quite rightly, I believe—that as soon as houses and public buildings had lightning-conductors, there was no reason why humans, natural individuals, shouldn't also have them. I've even been astonished that until now, there have been none at all—like lightning-conductors elsewhere. For stormy weather, therefore, I've invented a portable lightning-conductor, which I call a *flashguard*, and which screws on to the top of a hat.

"But then one would resemble a Prussian helmet-wearer, or a colonist wearing a colonial helmet."

Momentarily, yes, but where'd the harm in that? I shall continue my demonstration: the weather looks threatening; I have my apparatus on me; I take it out of its case; I fix the point on my hat and I let about two meters of conducive wire trail be behind me, which is attached to it in such a manner as to conduct the lightning to the ground whenever it falls upon the little pointed rod that I have put on my pate.

Now, for elegant ladies who don't want to drag two meters of wire behind them, there's another arrangement. The wire plunges into a bottle full of water, which they have hidden in their pocket. When the lighting falls upon the little point that they have fixed above the sinciput, pop!—the electricity is lost in the water in the bottle, and, by the same token, when they get home, they have an excellent electrified water, cleansed of microbes, and it also saves buying a bottle of soda-water.

I think that my invention, thus contrived, is simple, cheap and easy to use, especially when traveling. And there's scarcely any need to add that I would be only too happy if, as a new benefactor of humankind, I were able to abolish deaths caused by lightning, as if by waving a magic wand, just as the immortal Pasteur—with all due respect to Raspail, his great forerunner[73]—abolished death from rabies…well, nearly.

In the spring of 1899, I think, in a series of lectures at La Bodinière on "The Theater of Nature" I revealed to amazed Parisians that in New York, in summer, to avoid sunburn, straw hats are put on the heads of all the horses, piercing two holes to let the ears through. I am glad to see that my campaign of popularization has borne fruit, for now all the horses of launderers, milkmen, butchers, cesspool-emptiers, etc., wear traditional straw hats on their heads, thanks to the sage and kindly intervention of the Society for the Protection of Animals.

In view of that, I have similarly applied my flashguard to the heads of horses and horned animals during the recent big storms, except that, as I had not taken into account the fact that quadrupeds as horizontal rather than perpendicular—which distinguishes them from bipeds, except for the horizontal ones—and the flashguard only protects a circumference double its radius or its height, as you please, it followed that when lightning fell on a cow equipped with my apparatus, the cow was well-protected, but its tail was burned.

One cannot think of everything at first. So, either quadrupeds require points that are much longer, or it is necessary to teach them, like wise dogs, to sit on their rear feet in stormy weather, in order to obtain temporarily-perpendicular quadrupeds akin to humans.

In any case, that is my invention, and I declare that I am proud of it. From one on, I shall put flashguards at the disposal of my readers at a price of ten francs, twelve francs thirty-five

---

[73] François-Vincent Raspail (1794-1878) is best known for pioneering cell theory, but is here being cited for his support of antisepsis.

if nickeled, two francs more for quadrupeds because of the length of the stem, as I have explained above.

Finally, I also have flashguards for poultry, at the modest price of one franc eighty-five. I do not sell them for ducks, which are always in the water, the best of preservatives.

Now, as they say, let the band play on!

Embalmers

I. Mummies.
An unusual industrial crisis in the land of the pharaohs.
Proposed solutions.

The *Journal des Artistes*, which used to be a conscientious and beautiful art review in the time of Arsène Houssaye, and was founded in Prairial of year III—hats off—has just published, in a technical work on colors intended for painters, the following excessively brief note on the color *mummy*:

"If the Egyptian government continues not only the export of mummies but that of the debris of mummies, it is probable that within a few years, the supplies of conscientious manufacturers will be completely exhausted, and it will be necessary to think of either synthesizing the color in question, as is already practiced on a large scale, or of doing without it. And as it is necessary to choose the lesser of two evils, I deem that latter eventuality is still the best solution, for mummy will not leave a great void in the painter's palette. Indeed, the color derived from the crushing of Egyptian mummies steeped in various sorts of resin and bitumen produces a brown tint reminiscent of, but less beautiful than, Judean bitumen, and possesses the same faults in both oils and water-colors.

"The crushing of mummies must be very difficult to perfect, for, whatever care is invested in its purification, tiny pieces of fabric, bone, flesh, hair, etc., are inevitably left behind, which pass under the muller or the pestle without breaking up completely."

Thus, that poor color *mummy*, which has given us joy for so many years in the somber paintings of Ribot or the studies of Goya, is bound to disappear in a short time, if well-informed individuals can be believed.

Something is already being done—but obviously not enough—and we ought to investigate the practical means of fighting such a catastrophe.

For my part, I feel strongly that I am not at all in the mood to accept the *fait accompli*, for, at the end of the day, let's not lose sight of the fact that great artists, who will no longer have the color mummy to hand—or, rather, on their palette—will not be able to produce paintings as dark and dramatic as those representing negroes fighting in the dark in the depths of a cave.

Then, in sum, as everyone in the world is descended from Father Adam and Mother Eve, according to the popular formula—which means that everyone is related to everyone else, more closely than we imagine, to every individual, all the way back to the word's beginning—it is quite certain that we can recognize in the celebrated color mummy, the ground-up bones, the crushed hair, the pulverized teeth and the muscles, reduced to dust, of our ancestors.

That thought makes a little shiver run along the spine—a *petite mort*, as the divine Marquis put it—and it's not funny to think that it will be necessary to renounce that macabre joy forever, especially if one is an aesthete.

That is why I have sought to discover whether there is any way to remedy a state of affairs as lamentable as it is disastrous—and, if I'm not mistaken, after long sleepless nights and no less laborious meditation, I think I've finally found the sole solution capable of simultaneously preserving the interests of the very specialized industry of mummy-color manufacturers, the needs of painters and the quasi-superstitious and fetishistic aspect of the passionately interesting question.

As I didn't want to overlook anything by neglect, I began by carrying out a long and scrupulous investigation among the interested—and, in consequence, competent—parties. First I interviewed the mummy-color manufacturers in Egypt itself.

We disembarked on the bank of the Nile; I hired a crocodile as my stenographer, and everyone replied to me, tearfully: "We're doomed, Monsieur; the stock of mummies will soon be exhausted; it real is a disappearing industry, which it will be necessary to add to your volume on dying industries. But it's the fault of the English."

"How's that?"

"Certainly. If, before the widespread industrial usage of mummy-color, those mercantile profaners the English had not sold our sacred mummies at a knock-down price to make fertilizer—fertilizer, you understand, filthy manure—we wouldn't be in this mess. We'd still have a stock of mummies capable of feeding us for more than fifty years."

"But it seems to me that in the matter of profanation, you yourselves..."

"Oh, Monsieur, how can you say that? Our mummies, transformed into color, destined to be immortalized on the canvases of painters, in masterpieces immortal in themselves, fulfilling a quasi-divine role and the highest and most noble of missions!"

That's obvious.

Then I consulted all the artists of Europe and the Sandwich Islands—which cost me a long and perilous voyage—and they replied: "What do you want to do about it? We can't invent mummies; we'll have recourse, with our ordinary manufacturers, to artificial mummy-color, thanks to the judicious employment of by-products of coal."

Well, that makes me indignant, and ought not to be the case—I say that loudly, in the name of the superior interests of art. I've found two solutions, or temporary and the other absolute, and those are the two solutions that I'm going to expose respectfully to the eyes and the intellect of eminent artists, members of the Institut, who do me the honor of reading me hebdomadally, if you'll pardon the neologism.[74]

So, the transitory and temporary solution, the modest palliative, consists of replacing the exhausted Egyptian mum-

---

[74] Actually, *hebdomadairement* [hebdomadally] does exist in French, and did not need inventing; its English equivalent is even less common—most people are quite content to say "weekly."

mies by those of the necropolises of South America: Incas, the Indians of Peru, Yucatan, etc.

They are by no means as good quality—as resinous and bituminous—as those of Egypt; they are thinner, if I might put it thus, and paler, which will bring about a minor revolution in the somber aspect of our artists, but, according to my calculations, there will be enough or seven years, eleven months, thirteen days and nine minutes, which is surely not to be disdained.

After that, we arrive at the serious and definitive means, and I'm counting on those years to prepare public opinion for the resurrection of this useful industry—I'm talking about the art of mummifying one's nearest and dearest, when they have kicked the bucket. It's much more chic than amusing oneself by losing everything in that Satanic cremation.

We'll begin by mummifying the poor devils who die in hospitals and similar institutions, and as they will have the right, while alive, to sell their mummified carcasses to industrial mummy-manufacturers, that will provide a means, as simple as it is ingenious, of leaving a little money to their widows and orphans.

Insurance companies will even be able to take charge, very honestly, of various contracts, operations and plans of that sort.

It must not be forgotten that mummies, like Bordeaux wines, gain considerably in aging, so one will be able to stipulate that the price will not be touched by the children until they come of age, and, as a result, they will acquire a more considerable sum.

I'm sketching all this rapidly, but it's obvious that there could be a whole series of interesting consequences for the poor therein.

The proof that I believe in the efficacy of my system is that I declare here and now that I am ready to sell my own carcass, and that of my concierge, to a responsible mummy-manufacturer, if I can get a good price.

Finally, according one's convictions, one could sell one's mummy to be used in religious paintings or freethinkers' paintings; some might reserve it for landscapes, others for generic paintings.

In truth. I tell you this: it would be simultaneously charming, lucrative and practical, and it really is the only solution to the imminent disappearance of ancient mummies from the land of the Pharaohs.

Author's note: I am told that missionaries are now in the process of mummifying more than two million Chinese cadavers. Always practical, those people!

II. A lucrative trade. American embalmers.
A new industry open to feminine activity.
The joy of families.

We know that there is, at the present time, a large number of embalmers and entrepreneurial funeral directors in the United States, because, being more liberal than us, the Yankees have not wanted to reserve the exclusive monopoly of that fine trade to Catholic councils of manufacturers, and the industry in question is absolutely free on the other side of the Atlantic—even for the Portuguese, who usually prefer more cheerful occupations.

At the end of the day, though, all tastes are innate, and on that subject, I find in the trade journals of the funeral business the following curious information:

"A friendly practitioner, Madame Myrtle Hamon, certified by the Embalming College of Massachusetts, announces to the public of Ottawa, by means of the newspapers, that she will take responsibility for funerals and the embalming of bodies at reasonable prices.

"Another embalmeress,[75] who has undertaken specialist studies in Paris, Berlin and New York, established herself a few years ago in the last-named city, and it is well-known that her enterprise is now worth several million dollars."

There, in fact, is a whole vast and charming horizon open to our young women, once qualified as physicians, pharmacists or herbalists, cannot find a clientele sufficient for them to earn their living. Not to mention that with the ingenuity of the French character, it will be easy for them to perfect and extend a profession, probably exercised with a certain dullness and manifest lack of grace by American demoiselles.

For a start, our young embalmeresses will be able to meditate in the crypts of the Tour de Saint-Michel, Bordeaux and in the famous underground Campo Santos located in caverns in Italy, which have skillfully conserved for centuries, visibly fresh, all the Maccabees. It's necessary to run a duster over them from time to time, because of the inevitable accumulation of dust, and sometime to add a little make-up, to put a soupcon of rice-powder on their cheeks, but that's all.

By that means that they will extract from Mother Nature, in the name of practical science, her secrets of indefinite conservation, unknown even to Madame Vachon. It's even probable that these discoveries will not be without a certain spice. What do you think, my geological chemist friends?

Eventually, they will be able to extend their precious industry to all fauna and embalm domestic animals—the lapdogs that society ladies adore so jealously.

I know that there are taxidermists, even female ones, but us the word is coarse, brutal and discourteous, as Mademoiselle Clairon or Mademoiselle Mars[76]—I don't know which,

---

[75] French routinely distinguishes between male and female followers of the same profession, as with *embaumeur* and *embaumeuse*, but English rarely does—even "actress" is nowadays falling out of usage—so I have been forced to improvise.

[76] Claire Léris (1723-1803), alias Mademoiselle Clairon, was the most famous tragedienne of her era, while Anne Boutet (1779-1847), alias Mademoiselle Mars, was the most famous comedienne of hers.

exactly—observed, by comparison with the lovely and graceful vocable *embalmeresses...*

Embalmeresses! The mere evocation of the word makes me salivate, and involuntarily, it seems that I am breathing is the sweetest and most paradisal odors.

Then again, in addition to all the cherished domestic animals, what a vast field will open up to embalmeresses from the moment that Egyptian customs are finally re-established here, after three thousand years of yearning, and one can fortunately keep one's dear departed at home, under glass, in one's drawing-room, and even move them from room to room, like a simple Chouberski,[77] in order to have them permanently before one's eyes.

Oh, simply thinking of that touching idea makes my eyes moist with tears, and I can distinctly hear my pen sobbing like a big turkey.

Yes, this will provide very sweet consolations for us in the future; I don't want to draw out here, to preserve the sensitivity of our readers, the list of all those who will have recourse to embalmeresses and their artifices, as conservative as they are magical.

I don't want to talk about the weeping mother who would love to keep her dear little child, dead in infancy, under the globe of her old family clock. I don't want to talk about the gentle bride who will want to conserve her beloved in this way, in order to have the frequent pleasure of dyeing, grooming and perfuming his beautiful silky beard. No, for I feel emotion overwhelming me—but at least it will be permissible to pay a just homage of admiration, an equitable tribute or gratitude, to the son-in-law who weeps like a calf every morning on kissing the cheeks of his old stuffed—sorry, embalmed—mother-in-law, and putting her in a place of honor in his drawing-room before going to his study...

No matter that she might be getting slightly fat, and overly desiccated, thanks to the embedderess—no, the embalme-

---

[77] A kind of portable gas-heater.

144

ress; that model son-in-law will easily imagine, that he has, like the ancients, conserved in his home his household gods!

These are scenes so touching that my impotent pen refuses to describe and retrace them, I shall not persist.

If, however, I had the good fortune to possess a son, I would want to give him in holy matrimony to a young and poetic embalmeress. It seems to me that she would embalm our entire existence, the entire interior of our home—and how very genteel I would then be, and how affectionate toward her! There would, admittedly, be a slightly sly sentiment of thrift on my part in that, for after my death. I'm sure that she would take personal responsibility for embalming her dear late father-in-law.

A wonderful trade, eh?—and so nice and easy!

THE MYSTERIOUS FLUID

Proving that the Planet Mars Is Inhabited

Curious demonstrations.
The same origin of language as on Earth.
What conclusion can be drawn?

For some time, the scientific world has known about the famous canals of Mars, so regular and so curious in their almost-geometrical forms in the astral province that has been named Libya, which the well-known hemisphere of the planet presents to us in Observatories.

We know that it also possesses an atmosphere, and that there is probably good weather on the surface when it is a little less confused and ruddy. Astronomers, always a little scatterbrained—hence the verb referring to the aiming of their telescopes[78]—would love to see the canals as immense signals that the inhabitants are sending to those of the Earth, and, in the reddish vapor, the revelation of immense fires, lit in order to speak to us by means of conventional signs, somewhat akin to the Saint-Jean fires[79] on the summits of high mountains, reviewed and corrected by a Martial (or Martial?) Chappe.

So long as we do not possess sufficiently powerful telescopes, we are obliged to leave the matter there and remain in the vague domain of conjecture. However, from the day when

---

[78] In French, *braquer*—which has no obvious connection with *braque* [scatterbrained].
[79] Fires traditionally lit in some parts of France in celebration of the saint's day (June 24).

one can see the moon at sixty kilometers and other worlds in the same proportions, astronomers will take heart and the project of establishing communication with the inhabitants of Mars taken up and seriously studied by a group of Russian scientists.

They would begin by undertaking an attentive study of the planet, and, on days when there is good weather on the surface, acquiring the conviction that the Martians are definitely signaling to us by means of large fires that form designs between two canals.

That was an important point to establish.[80] Mars was inhabited, and even inhabited by highly civilized people who, in possession of very powerful telescopes, could probably see what was happening on Earth as if they were standing at a window looking out into their garden.

Armed with that conviction, the Russian astronomers, with admirable devotion, began by gathering the necessary funds, with the aid of a vast national subscription, and as soon as they had the indispensable sums, left to establish themselves in the middle of the Gobi, or Shamo, desert in northern Tibet and China, in the very heart of Asia. There are plateaux there 3300 kilometers long and 7000 broad, where the air is very cold and pure. That is all they would need to enter into direct communication, if possible with the inhabitants of Mars.

Once installed in double-walled wooden barracks, in order not to suffer from the cold, and with all their instruments in place, the Russian astronomers, ever admirable for courage and determination, had six thousand ones of kerosene sent from Baku, which naturally required a delay of several months.

But they had their plan, fully matured, and during that time they had bands of cheaply-hired Mongol nomads dig trenches several kilometers long in the earth where the frozen

---

[80] Vibert continues to vacillate between future and past tenses, quite uncertain as to how to frame this conjectural essay; for the sake of tidiness, I shall stick to the past tense from now on.

ground was hard but watertight—whereas, in the sand, the liquid would have seeped away, and it would have been necessary to render it impermeable with some sort of solid coating. It was a gigantic task, but after seventeen months, everything was finished and the ten thousand tons of kerosene were awaiting deployment.

It was no longer necessary to wait for a day when a serene atmosphere was visible on the surface of Mars to attempt to enter into communication therewith—but would the individuals out there take note of their appeal? A cruel enigma.

As you will already have guessed, our Russian scientists had traced a word with the aid of the trenches, over an extent of more than a hundred kilometers.

Thus, on a lovely clear night, cold and starry, at a given signal, the Mongols immediately filled al the trenches with kerosene, and, at another signal, set fire to it.

The moment was solemn. One could have heard the emotion-stirred heartbeats of the twenty-three astronomers gathered there from a kilometer away.

As every eventuality had been anticipated, three of them rose up into the air to an altitude of six hundred meters in a tethered balloon.

The effect was marvelous, and in large printed letters a hundred kilometers long, an immense, bright, luminous word—HELLO—conveyed the first greeting from the inhabitants of the Earth to those of Mars. It was probably the first attempt of this sort, at least in our own solar system, since the world became a world.[81]

A magnanimous spectacle, calculated to fill such men with emotion. The fire, cleverly maintained in the trenches by the Mongols under the direction of the astronomers—who multiplied their efforts during the night, racing hither and yon

---

[81] Vibert inserts a footnote here to explain that his Russian scientists had chosen a French word (*bonjour*) because it seemed preferable to use the scientific and literary language most familiar throughout the world—but the English would undoubtedly have contested that claim, so the argument applies just as well to the translation.

on their bicycles and also giving orders by telephone—lasted until morning, until the dawn; and in order to make it even more visible, filings were thrown into the flaming liquid that gave it all the colors of the rainbow in succession, according to the compound thrown or the by-products of the coal mixed with the kerosene.

The effect was striking, grandiose, superhuman—universal in the most sublime sense of the word—and far outshone the spectacle of the electrical luminous advertisements in the Place de l'Opéra and the great boulevards.

Finally, daylight arrived and the colossal *hello* that the genius of humankind might perhaps have hurled through space, on the invisible wings of the mysterious fluid named electricity, to another world was gradually extinguished.

Then a problem arose. Unless the Martians already had something ready, they would be slow to respond, if they had read and understood us. The delay, of perhaps six months, would be long, cruel and anxious for our scientists.

On the other hand, perhaps, by means of powerful and improved methods, the Martians would be able to reply more rapidly...

II. Further demonstrations.
The same origin of language as on Earth.
Certain proofs.

Needless to say, in spite of the phlegmatic temperament typical of Russian scientists, the little company waited with feverish impatience during the months that followed, their eyes always aimed, during the cruelly cold and harsh nights of Pamir, on Libya, the famous astral province of the grand canals of Mars.

They devoted themselves assiduously to all sorts of sports, reading and work, and completed astronomical calculations that represented a decade's work, but the waiting was no less painful.

The big question was whether the inhabitants of Mars—
for them, there was no doubt that Mars was inhabited—had
read and understood the word launched across space in luminous form.

Assuming that it had been read and understood, three
hypotheses then presented themselves to the complex minds of
the Russian scientists. Either they had already tried to send
signals themselves, and would be able to resume doing so in a
matter of hours or days, or they would simply undertake a few
large-scale excavations, like us—in which case it was necessary not to expect a reply for six whole months. Some, however, opined in favor of a shorter interval, making the observation that they were dealing with very advanced, civilized
people possessed of powerful means of execution, as their
giant canals seemed to suggest, and that one could therefore
hope to have a response before so much time had elapsed.

The time went by, therefore, in feverish anticipation, the
days dragging lamentably.

In the end, it was the last group who were right; four
months later, almost to the night—O truly marvelous and superhuman prodigy!—the inhabitants of Mars sent a response...but let us proceed in an orderly manner, and not let
ourselves be troubled by the profound emotion that still grips
us by the throat as we inscribe these lines.

So, one beautiful night, they began to distinguish, vaguely at first and then clearly, a red light and then a huge confla-
gration on the surface of Mars.

All their telescopes were aimed as if they wanted to rape
the sky. The moment was solemn and unforgettable. Finally,
one astronomer suddenly shouted; "It's definitely in the province of the grand canals—it's definitely Libya."

Gradually, the light became more precise, and our scientists, more dead than alive, no longer feeling their hearts beating, were able clearly to distinguish signs on the Martian surface that they made haste to copy.

That as all, and the following night, nothing remained.
As no one understood them, the mysterious signs were sent to

the Academy of Letters in St. Petersburg—which, in its turn, was quick to send them to all the Academies in Europe.

It was our Académie des Inscriptions et Belles-Lettres that had the great honor of finding the key and translating the four previously-mysterious and untranslatable signs. One of its members, a distinguished scientist, remarked very judiciously that it was simply a matter of Hebrew words from which the accents and diacritical signs had been removed, as in primitive Hebrew.

The signs meant:

HEU, HEU

KHEU, KHEU

Which is to say: *thank you, thank you*—which meant that the Martians were thanking us and bidding us welcome—and finally: *yes, yes*, or, if you want it more precisely, *that is so, that is so*—which, to their minds, must signify: "We are people like you and Mars is inhabited, as Earth is."

The conversation continued thus for nearly two years, and to speed things up, the Russian astronomers began conversing on the sands in Hebrew, the words being shorter than in French.

By this means, they asked the Martians whether they had known that the Earth was inhabited for a long time, and they replied, always after four months or so: *Lo*—"no." The diacritical mark that ought to have been at the head of the first letter was still omitted.

When they were asked whether they fought against one another, making war, they very wisely replied: *Shalom*—which is to say, "peace,",or "greetings," thus giving an important lesson in civilization and humanity to the still-inferior and half-savage peoples of Earth.

I have no room here to report all the conversations—luminous, it must be said—exchanged between the astronomers of Earth and Mars, but I nevertheless want to extract the two great results obtained in such a striking manner:

Firstly, that Mars in inhabited, like the Earth.

Secondly, that a language is spoken there that is very similar to Hebrew, and, and that, in consequence, a unity of language, with respect to origin, exists not only on Earth, as my father has peremptorily and victoriously demonstrated in his works, but probably also on the surfaces of all other inhabited worlds.

That's something; admit that science gives considerable enjoyment to those who devote themselves to it without afterthought.

When will a marriage take place between an inhabitant of Earth and a pretty Martian, thanks to the intermediary of an electric current?

One should never despair of anything, and in the next chapter I shall explain how I myself have in my possession a very nice photograph, surely a good resemblance, of a young and charming Martian woman!

III. How photography came to be possible
between Mars and Earth.
A portrait of a pretty Martian woman. Curious details.

Thanks to the long and persist campaign of the Russian mission, regular communication between the two planets had already existed for nearly two years, and there was no longer any communication with Mars except by the simplified intermediary of the Hebrew language—without diacritical marks, as I have already remarked—when the hazards of a mission enabled me to meet the Russian scientists on the very field of their endeavors.

They knew that I already had an interest in long-distance photography, and how I had had occasion to inform Edison on the subject. They were also not unaware of my profound conviction that electricity, in its triple form of light, heat and fluid, invisible and imponderable, was really the sole and unique agent of all the forces in the universe.

So, suddenly, very amiably, they asked me point-blank: "Would you like to attempt long-distance photography with Mars?"

"Yes—but it would require a fixed point, clearly determined. How could we inform the inhabitants of Mars?"

"Nothing simpler; it will take some time. But leave it to us; we'll take charge of everything and inform you when you have nothing to do but operate—which is to say, to make the attempt."

What was said as done, and those indefatigable scientists began a conversation on the subject with the Martians. Finally, a few months later, they told me that everything was ready, and that they had made the necessary arrangements with their colleagues on the other planet.

As soon as the latter had a fine night, they inscribed their colossal word:

KHEU

Yes, that's so.

A young Martian woman stood in the exact center of the immense fiery letter, in the location of the diacritical sign marked by a dot in the letter's "belly"—with the result that it was possible to fix and restrict my point of observation. If electricity really reaches us through space in the form of dark light, only becoming visible on contact with our atmosphere, there was no reason why my experiment should not succeed. Sat least they sought by that means to give me a confidence that they certainly did not have themselves—but that did not prevent me from having great anxieties and finding myself in a state of perplexity that is very difficult to describe.

For my part, however, while they were discussing and "negotiating" my procedure with the Martians, I had not been wasting my time. Thanks to some exceedingly rich personal friends in the Ukraine, who put unlimited credit at my disposal, I was able to order the immediate construction in several huge pieces, perfectly cast and welded together by blow-torch, of a giant Crookes tube, according to Röntgen's design, inside which the Arc de Triomphe cold have danced.

In order for it not to break under the pressure of atmospheric weight—although it is less heavy at those high altitudes—I had it surrounded by a powerful iron armature, and eventually, by means of a series of machines representing a force of more than seven thousand five hundred horse-power, I succeeded—after great efforts—in evacuating it completely, or very nearly so.

From then on I was ready, and had nothing more to do but operate it, following the now-well-known Röntgen method, to be able to collect, if possible, the X-rays—which is to say, the invisible fluid—that ought to transmit the images from Mars to me.

That same night, in clear weather, Mars showed us at the end of our telescopes the colossal KHEU without the central point. I took more than ten successive proofs with different lengths of pose, according to rigorous preliminary astronomical measurements, which permitted me, with an extremely exact precision—produced chronometrically, but by means of a powerful steam-engine—to take account of the various motions of the two planets during the procedure and maintain a consistent relationship. My apparatus was thus always on the central axis of the visual ray, maintaining parallax between the center of my apparatus and the center of the luminous letter traced in the immense steppes of Libya—the province of the grand canals of Mars, as you will not have forgotten.

These calculations had taken me months, with the assiduous collaboration of three astronomers that I had summoned from France. I thought, therefore, that I had taken all humanly possible precautions, and had thought of everything—but my anxiety was nevertheless great.

I shall pass over in silence the days of labor and anxiety that followed.

O miracle, O matchless joy, I definitely had an image—but it was a dot, and it was necessary to magnify it several million times.

Two problems arose then, cruel and obsessive:

Would I be able to obtain that insensate magnification; and, in obtaining it, would not all the details of the photograph be spoiled—blurred or obliterated?

I was very familiar with star-charts—quite clear, it's true—but no similar operation had ever been attempted.

Again, I shall pass over in silence the long and delicate successive operations, to which my collaborators and I had to devote ourselves for more than a year. All that I can say is that the success was complete, and that when all the magnifying operations were complete, exactly at the central point of the first of the Hebrew letters, where the diacritical mark should have been, the delightful head of a young Martian appeared, as beautiful as the Venus de Milo and Venus-Aphrodite put together.

That supernatural stellar photograph, that planetary portrait, I will be happy to show to anyone who manifests the desire to see it.

If it should happen one day that someone asks for the hand of that young beauty, however, I shall not take any responsibility for it, and will simply send them to the Russian astronomers who enabled me to realize this marvel!

Author's Note: Since I wrote this succinct and faithful account, scientific discoveries and the progress of science have given me abundant support and helped, in a way, to popularize my initial work.

To cite only the principle examples, in the month of June 1900, Monsieur Mercier[82] has undertaken a dogged campaign to initiate regular communication between Mars and Earth. Again, at the end of the same year, the scientific journals published the following note:

---

[82] The person is question is identified in most contemporary and retrospective reports as "A. Mercier" of the French Astronomical Society; his proposal apparently made news by virtue of its blatant eccentricity, in suggesting the use the Eiffel Tower as a billboard and that signals might be projected on to the Moon.

"There is talk of a new instrument, the telephot, which will permit sight at very long distances.[83] *A newspaper set on a pedestal-lectern, sat up at a specific height in Paris, might be read in Tours by an individual finished with the new apparatus. A photograph could be taken at that distance. The distance between Tours and Paris is approximately sixty leagues."*

Then again, at the plenary session of the Institut on October 25, 1900, Madame Cognet[84] *was solemnly thanked for the 100,000-franc prize that she offered to the inventor of interplanetary communications.*

Finally, on December 27 of the same year, Ch. Malato[85] *took note of the great scientific movement that had finally taken shape, following my articles, in favor of the research to be carried out in order to institute communication with Mars*

Let all these friends, known and unknown, receive my sincere thanks here. I am only too glad and proud to have had the good fortune to be able to provoke this great scientific movement.

That said, here is my excellent colleague's note:

"It was a long time ago that truly scientific minds repudiated the old fable of life solely limited to our infinitesimal globe. It is only poor people irremediably brutalized by belief in the mystery of the holy trinity who still consider the sidereal

---

[83] Image-projection devices were frequently discussed under his label (*telephote* in French) in the late 19th century; there is an elaborate description of a hypothetical telephot in Comte Didier de Chousy's *Ignis* (1883) which is available in a Black Coat Press translation (ISBN 9781934543887).

[84] I have left this name as it is given in the original, as it is presumably copied from another source, but the prize in question was actually endowed by Clara Guzman in honor of her son, who had been a great admirer of Camille Flammarion. Interestingly, communication with Mars was excluded from the qualification for the prize, as it was held to be too easy. The prize was eventually awarded in 1969 to the crew of *Apollo 11*.

[85] Charles Malato (1857-1938).

worlds as poor lamps it for our convenience by Father Sa-
baoth.

  "Since spectral analysis has demonstrated the analogy of
constitution of these worlds, with one another and with ours,
their habitability is no longer envisaged as a dream. It would
be an insult to readers of the Aurore *to set out to demonstrate*
at length that organic life, a product of the combinations of
matter, may be manifest everywhere that matter exists.

  "We are not unaware that Mars and the other planets of
our solar system once drifted, confused with the elements
forming our Earth in the state of incandescent dust, through
the infinity of space. Thus far, everything has confirmed Lap-
lace's hypothesis. Then these swirling masses of dust sepa-
rated out, condensing to form the worlds that gradually solidi-
fied and cooled, continuing, under the double action of centri-
fugal and centripetal force, to gravitate around the solar nuc-
leus.

  "Mars, being smaller than our globe, consequently
cooled more rapidly; life must have appeared there sooner; its
humankind must therefore be more advanced than ours. Is it
necessary to recall the famous rectilinear canals that seem to
be the work of conscious design, with the intention of connect-
ing up the planet's seas?

  "For more than a quarter of a century, intermittent ap-
pearances of lights on the Martian surface have encouraged
the thought that we are in the presence of appeals made to the
terrestrial world by beings probably more powerful than we
are. On December 8, 1900—a date which, if the fact is con-
firmed, will remain immortal in the annals of science—the
astronomer Douglas,[86] *who is no novice, recorded a signal at*
Flagstaff Observatory in the United States, of which there can
be no mistake: a series of fiery straight lines several hundred

---

[86] Soon after making this mistake, Andrew Ellicott Douglas (1867-
1962) fell out with his boss, Percival Lowell, and William Henry
Pickering (whose name is misrendered here as Perkering) when he
called the Martian canals into question. He went on to found the
science of dendrochronology.

158

kilometers long. These lights, having been suddenly lit up, shone for about an hour and ten minutes, and then were extinguished as quickly as they had been lit.

"Now, nature never proceeds in this manner; it is therefore not absurd to suppose that we are in the presence of an appeal issued by 'brothers in space.'

"Monsieur Douglas' observation has been announced at the central bureau of Kiel by Monsieur Perkering, the director of Harvard University Observatory, a scientist of the first rank; the astronomical publications Nature, *in London, and* Astronomische Nachrichten *have reported it."*

It would seem that, in the presence of this fact, the most important to be produced in the history of humankind, and which ought to be the glory of our concluding century, the entire press ought only to have uttered a cry of enthusiasm. One could have understood the most extreme excitement or scientific reputation. Well, nothing! With a few proximal exceptions, there have only been articles by ignorant jokers: military brigandage, militaresque clownishness and the affectations of renowned whores—that is what is most likely to excite the enthusiasm of our contemporaries.

Brave Martians, you are ahead of time! Try again in a few centuries; perhaps humankind will be capable of understanding you. One argument that I have not seen advertised anywhere in favor of the luminous signal is this: the aforementioned signal lasted one hour ten minutes. Now, taking account of the time taken by the light to reach the Earth, that time represents an exact division of the Martian day, one local hour, if you wish.

Since then, it has been observed that it was simply a matter of the Martian dusk, when the sun setting at its horizon gilds or inflames the summits of its high mountains, but this research is no less interesting and worthy of being encouraged.

It would, however, be unpardonable if I were not also to report here, in spite of the length of this note, the following lines by Tapernoux, of June 15, 1900, which prove that every day, a new discovery arrives to confirm my own works:

"Monsieur and Madame Curie, while studying pitch-blende—one of the minerals from which uranium is extracted—at the laboratory of the École Municipale de Physique et Chimie Industrielle, have observed that some specimens are more active than uranium itself. From this they conclude, very logically, that a third radioactive substance gave its properties to the studied mineral. They have isolated this substance, by means of a series of procedures, and obtained a new metal, polonium, a near relative of bismuth in its analytical characteristics, but which emits Becquerel rays four hundred times as active as those of uranium.

"This was a superb result, but our chemists have not stopped there. Long and patient research has allowed them to discover a fourth metal, nine hundred times more active than uranium, to which they have given the well-merited name of radium.

"Radium is very similar to barium from a chemical viewpoint. It emits Becquerel rays that permit the production of good photographic prints after a pose of half a minute, as a result of which it is possible to obtain radiographs—those beautiful images of skeletons—without Crookes tubes.

"The rays admitted by radium are powerful enough to render barium platino-cyanide fluorescent—a property associated with the strongest does of X-rays.

"For centuries, people imagined that only light perceptible to their eyes existed. Crooke and Röntgen probed to them that in a vacuum, an electrical spark gives birth to luminous rays ungraspable by sight, able to pass through certain reputedly opaque bodies, permitting the projection of the silhouette of a human skeleton in spite of the flesh covering it.

"Monsieur and Madame Curie offer the scientific world a substance that possesses these properties in itself and permanently. X-rays have revolutionized optics. To what will the Becquerel rays of radium lead?"

There is nothing to do but wait, confidently.

A Monster Telescope

In America. How the planet Eros is inhabited. A funny story.

The Yankees have no suspicion of it, but as they have probably not yet attained the same degree of civilization as old Europe, funny stories sometimes happen there; it's the most recent of those that I'm going to tell my readers today, with the intention of giving them a good laugh.

The rich and powerful university of Harvard in the United States has just constructed, with all the desirable care, a telescope 162 feet long and a thirteen-inch aperture—in the starry republic everything is done on a vast scale, and it's because it's starry that it devotes such vast sums to studying its heavenly sisters.

As if its pretty girls were insufficient!

This telescope, the exact name of which is a photohelio-graph, set up horizontally, was created and built, at enormous cost, with the express purpose of photographing the planet Eros—a pretty name for a planet![87]

Everything had been anticipated with minute and—let's say this loudly—truly scientific care. The image of Eros was to be captured by a mirror, while a clockwork mechanism of the greatest precision was to compensate for the inevitable displacement resulting from the motion of the Earth.

All that was well-planned, wasn't it?

The great day—or, rather, the great night—of the inauguration arrived; the astronomical scientists attacked to the celebrated university of Harvard took aim and started their

---

[87] The minor plant Eros had been discovered in 1898 and caused much excitement by virtue of the near approach of its orbit to that of Earth; a worldwide project was organized to measure its parallax during its opposition of 1900-01.

machine, beautiful, polished and functioning like a chronometer. They took several pictures, or photographs, of Eros, which posed obligingly, like a good little girl, as it passed in front of the telescope that was impatient to capture its charms.

In spite of the impatience of the honorable scientists, it was necessary to wait several more days for the prints to be developed and to obtain an appropriate result.

Everything worked out admirably and demonstrated—O prodigy!—that the planet Eros was inhabited, for one very large animal and one much smaller could be distinguished there, very visibly and very distinctly. Even more curiously, the two animals were found in every image, but in very different poses.

The larger of the two animals, a trifle blurred but four-footed, inevitably rendered our astronomers rather pensive; some affirmed that it proved the youth of Eros—ever young, like its name—and that these enormous beasts must be colossal cousins of our primitive mastodons.

Finally, it was decided to take further photographs of Eros, but the weather was bad, the nights dark and cloudy. They had to be patient for a few more days. Finally, they were able to catch Eros in the semicircle again and obtain new prints of supreme quality. As for the two giant animals, there was no more trace of them than in the palm of my hand.

One of the astronomers, however, remarked very judiciously that it would be wise, with the much-improved methods they possessed, to magnify the prints considerably. They set to work right away, and soon found themselves confronted by new and immense prints on which at least half a dozen tiny insects could be distinctly seen.

A further prodigy; they ran to find the university's entomologists, one of whom declared that they must be mosquitoes, which tended to demonstrate that Eros possessed an atmosphere, but as one of them seemed to be jumping rather than flying he called them, in Latin, *the jumping mosquitoes of Eros*. Another scientist, attempting to determine their sex, lost his sight in the process.

Finally, as the matter created an enormous stir throughout the scientific worlds of the two Americas, an old professor of physics, who was very skeptical and only believed in the experimental method, secretly devoted himself to a scrupulous investigation, and did not take long to demonstrate peremptorily that a kitten had slipped into the photoheliograph on the evening of the first operation in pursuit of a mouse, and that it was simply them that had been mistaken for inhabitants of Eros, distant cousins of mastodons or mammonths.

There remained the jumping mosquitoes, however, but with a supplementary enquiry and further prints, much enlarged, the same scientists did not take long to demonstrate that it was simply a matter of fleas left behind by the cat.

Far from declaring himself satisfied, however, another zoologist—an entomologist who was the nephew of the one who had lost his sight—continued his micrographic studies of the prints of Eros and succeeded in proving that there were two distinct varieties of insects there. That was the day when science finally discovered that the parasite known by the vulgar name of flea is not the same in cats as in mice.

Which proves that scientists never waste their time!

But that did not prevent the photoheliographic telescope of the celebrated university of Harvard from turning the scientific world of the starry Republic upside-down for some time. Admit that there was cause enough—but the idea that Eros might perhaps be uninhabited leaves me distinctly melancholy...

Solar Eclipse

*In America. Among the superstitious blacks
and the double-dealing whites.
Curious memories.*

A few years ago—I'd rather not be more exact in order not to cause trouble for anyone—I found myself in America at the time of a famous eclipse of the sun, central and therefore almost total.

It is well-known that in the southern states of the United States—including New Orleans, Georgia and the Floridas—the black element is very numerous, and that the descendants of Ham are not far from ten million strong.

One evening a few days before the eclipse, among educated and enlightened friends, we were talking about popular superstitions, and my friends affirmed that all the excesses provoked by the ignorance of yesteryear did not appear to recur any longer.

"And why, if you please," I continued, "should the legendary follies—or, rather, the crimes—of the year one thousand, when the end of the world was supposed to arrive, not be reproduced? Humankind is more advanced, you say? For an affranchised elite, certainly, the observation is true, but in the masses, you may be certain that as long as priests dominate the minds of women and children, all superstition will be perpetuated intact, which renders all crimes possible in a moment of panic. And don't lose sight of the fact that some will commit those crimes in the ferocious naivety of their ignorance, while others will be glad to profit from the opportunity to find a pretext therein to satisfy their petty vengeances."

"This time," exclaimed a fat sugar-cane planter, "I believe you're right, and that you're speaking from experience."

Another interlocutor, however—a bad-tempered little Englishman—said: "As for the blacks, all excesses are certainly to be dreaded, for those people are savages, after all, but I'll wager that there wouldn't be any excesses committed by whites, by the Europeans whose sons we are…"

"Then again," interjected a gentleman who was an important person in the administration, "I give you my guarantee that all precautions will be taken: all the police, armed forces and volunteers convened and deployed—and at the first sign of trouble…" He made an energetic gesture to indicate that the perpetrators would be immediately hanged, long and short.

"Yes, lynch-law elevated to the rank of a social institution," I said, laughing.

The worthy functionary shrugged his shoulders, with more-than-contestable politeness, and turned toward me. "A Parisian negrophile is a dreamer who knows nothing about this country; the blacks are not human, they can be machine-gunned *en masse*…"

Calmly, as everyone awaited my response curiously, I replied: "Permit me, Monsieur, not to reply here and now. You know that I do not allow anyone to insult a man in front of me; a black man is my equal and we shall continue this conversation on another terrain, whenever you wish. For the moment, though, on the eve of the total solar eclipse that is about to occur, I will say in front of all of the numerous intelligent people in this club who are listening to me, that there will be crimes committed by the blacks—always as a result of the superstitious education given to them by their priests—which will be *sincere and naïve* crimes, if I might be permitted those qualifications, while the whites will only commit cowardly ones to profit from the impunity of the moment."

I thought for a moment that those worthy folk were going to lynch me on the spot.

"You're too negrophilic—that's an infamy; you're slandering your race. You're insulting us. How can you place civilized people beneath savages? You're mad…"

Etc., etc.

I allowed the storm to pass and the threatening fists raised against me to fall back, an, after an imperious gesture

165

from the functionary, was finally able to resume speaking. Knowing the Yankee mind, I said: "Please calm down, Messieurs. Let's not argue—let's make a bet…"

"That's it! Let's make a bet. But what are you putting up?"

"Listen, Messieurs, I'm poor, but I'm so certain of winning that I'll stake anything you wish. Make a list; I give you my word."

Soon, the list came back to me with the names of my adversaries and the stakes adjacent to their names. They had taken pity on me; they had only wagered $4500 against me.

I had them, I tell you. The evening passed cordially, swilling champagne, and a jury of honor was appointed to judge the outcome, if necessary.

"As for your police," I said to the functionary, "they'll be overwhelmed and will get cold feet, just like the blacks and the poor people."

"We'll see, all right?"

Three days later, at the appointed time, like a well-brought-up person, the famous total solar eclipse took place, and everyone thought it was the end of the world.

The police and the army were the first to panic, and were unable to do anything.

A certain number of black men killed their wives and children to prevent their suffering and then killed themselves, in the naïve belief that the world was ending. But a no less equal number of white men, Europeans or native-born Yankees, hastened to loot and pillage, to set fire to their enemies' houses, and, under the pretext of humanity, to send their mothers-in-law *ad patres*.[88] I put mothers-in-law in the plural, because many of them had been married several times, and were only too happy to liquidated at a stroke "all those old

---

[88] Literally, "to their ancestors"—i.e., they murdered them.

boilers," as one of them—a heating-engineer[89] by trade—put it.

That as the only bet I ever made and won in my life—and was never paid, anyway, for reasons that are too complicated to go into here.

---

[89] The French *fumiste* [heating engineer] is also a slang term for a fraud.

Divine Prescience

New explanations. Physics and Chemistry.
Marvelous voyages undertaken in a cataleptic state.

Some time ago, at a friend's house, I encountered an Indian priest of the religion of Cakya-Mouni, superb and imposing with his great white beard. After the usually introductions, I did not take long to perceive that I was in the presence of a truly superior human being.

"In Europe," I told him, "you are reputed to be thaumaturges who seek to take advantage of the credulity of crowds."

"That's easy to say, but take note that, although I don't defend the frauds and charlatans in one religion more than another, it's necessary to avow that it would be appropriate to understand us before throwing stones at us."

"That's true. Admit, though, that all your pretensions of esotericism are only designed to throw dust in the eyes of naïve individuals."

"Not at all; our esotericism is simply the representation of a scientific patrimony, so well-informed that it would be unjust to confuse with your Medieval alchemy—which nevertheless contained, along with the mystical follies inherent in the times, a sort of embryo of modern physical and chemical sciences.[90]

---

[90] Vibert inserts a long footnote, which cannot be moved to the end of the chapter, where there is an even longer one: "This is so true that, at least two years after writing this story, I found a further proof in the following letter, published in the July 8 issue of the *Aurore:*
We have received this very interesting letter from Mulhouse, which our readers will find it fruitful to read:
Mulhouse, July 5, 1900
To the Editor of L'Aurore,

"That's possible, but I'd like to have an example, all the same."

I read in your July 4 number an article regarding the transformation of phosphorus into arsenic, which M. Fittica claims to have achieved. This fact, if true, would indeed be of the highest importance, but thus far, unfortunately, nothing seems to confirm it. It is sufficient, for a chemist with access to a laboratory, to read M. Fittica's original memoir attentively to become skeptical. His demonstrations are not at all rigorous. Clemens Winchler, one of the foremost German chemists, has demonstrated that commercial phosphorus contains arsenic, and that the method employed by M. Fittica for the alleged transformation of phosphorus into arsenic only furnishes the quantity that was originally contained therein. For my part, I am occupied in verifying M. Fittica's experiments, and thus far nothing leads me to give them credence. I believe that the artificial production of arsenic will join in well-deserved forgetfulness M. Strindberg's synthesis of iodine and M. Emmens' transformation of silver into gold.

It is annoying that work so poorly executed is published, for it can only bring science into discredit. I will also add that, in principle, the transformation of one simple substance into another does not seem to me to be impossible; I am not, therefore, rising against M. Fittica in horror on the basis of a preconceived and dogmatic idea. I merely claim that he experiments do not prove anything and that those of Winchler nullify them completely.

Accept, Monsieur the Editor, the assurance of my distinguished consideration.

E. NOELTING

Director of the Mulhouse School of Chemistry.

Naturally, I have not given my opinion of this fraud, so well-judged above; I am content to observe it."

The references in the letter are to the German chemists Friedrich Fittica (1850-1912) and Clemens Winkler (1838-1904); to the celebrated Swedish playwright August Strindberg, who took a break from literary work to conduct experiments in chemistry and occult science during the 1890s; and to Stephen H. Emmens, who published *Argentaurana* in 1897, claiming to have discovered a new element of which gold and silver were derivatives; his claim to have made a considerable quantity of gold from Mexican silver dollars and sold it to the US Mint made headlines in 1899.

And, with the ice broken, the conversation continued in this fashion, touching on numerous topics of more-or-less transcendent psychology. That was how, in threading the needle, we ended up talking about divine prescience."

"A neat trick which you'd have a hard time explaining to me," I said to him, laughing.

Calm and smiling, he replied: "Nothing easier, my dear Monsieur."

"Well now, if you understood our Parisian argot…"

"Go on."

"I'd tell you that you're backing me into a corner. How can God, if he exists, see everything in the past and the future, throughout the infinity of worlds? Can you explain that to me in other terms than blind faith, scientifically?"

"Of course."

The ladies, keenly interested, had gathered around us, and when the priest of Cakya-Mouni resumed in these terms, one could have heard a fly in flight in the large drawing-room in my friend's house in the Place des Vosges.

"I say that God always sees the entire past and the entire future, not because he is God, but simply because he has advanced knowledge of the physical sciences…"

"You're making fun of us."

"That's not in my character," the priest went on, with a genuine sentiment of sadness and mild reproach, which hurt me. "Look, I who am speaking, who am not God but only one of his most humble servants, can show you the past and enable you see the future, at will…"

These words were spoken so naturally and confidently that a little frisson ran over the shoulders of the pretty women who were there, attentive and charmed.

"And you can go as far back into the past as forward into the future?" a young blonde, who appeared to come from Germany, hazarded to ask. "You can show us what was happening on Earth a thousand or two thousand years ago?"

I can show you what was happening on Earth, lovely lady, a hundred thousand years ago, or a hundred billion…"

This time, there was a moment of amazement in the drawing-room, and anyone able to read what was in those ardently eyes fixed on the old man's noble face would have seen very clearly what everyone was thinking.

The man's mad.

He divined that, and continued, smiling: "Listen to me, ye of little faith, not religiously, but only scientifically. You all know that light takes a certain time to travel through space, and that merely traveling the radius of our telescopic horizon takes it 1,503,000 years, according to the calculation of Prince Grigori Stourdza[91] himself."

"That's perfectly accurate."

"We can go much further by means of thought than our telescopic radius, but let's stick to those fifteen hundred thousand years. If I want to enable you to see the St. Bartholomew's Day massacre, the death of Cakya-Mouni, or Zoroaster or Jesus Christ, a feast in Babylon, Adam and Eve's breakfast or the latter's conversation with the serpent, a very simple calculation as to the duration of the progress of light tells me to which star I need to transport you in order to arrive half an hour before the sight of the event in question, which will unfold in our visual field."

"Superb—but how are you going to take us there?"

"I shall put you to sleep, and only transport your spirit there."

"And it will be able to see?"

"Perfectly, for a spirit does not have our physical imperfections, and sees clearly, because nothing is lost in the infinity of time and space! Stand at that well-lit window, lovely lady, and through that window, in five hundred billion trillion years, at any point whatsoever in the infinity of space, a man as knowledgeable as I am in the sciences called esoteric, because they are not widespread, will be able to contemplate you in the full glow of your youth and radiant beauty..."

---

[91] The mysterious Stourdza had published *Les Lois fondamentales de l'univers* in 1891.

We all uttered an exclamation of surprise and admiration. Recovering from my amazement, however, I said: "So much for the past—but what about the future?"

"That takes longer, but is just as simple. It's sufficient to be a good chemist and to follow by means of calculation the necessary, inevitable and ineluctable transformations of bodies and atoms to know at what point the Earth, the world, or the universe will be in five hundred billion centuries. It's merely a question of knowing and applying chemical formulae."

"I'd like to make one of those voyages into the past with you, if you'll put me to sleep."

"Tomorrow, at my house, at two o'clock."

The following day, I was at his house at ten to two, and at ten past two, transported to another world, according to my desire, I saw Adam and Eve in the Earthly paradise, just as I see my concierge bringing up my mail every morning.

When we arrived at the famous scene of our poor grandmother's seduction by the serpent, however, my spirit uttered a strident cry, and I said to the old priest of Cakya-Mouni: "Look—I understand now why Eve succumbed. The serpent has feet resembling legs and forearms. It's not like today's serpents—as my father has always written and affirmed, for the last thirty years, according o the explanation of the texts themselves."

"Obviously. It's an illustration of one of the celebrated and curious laws of transformism."

Beside myself, my spirit could not help saying: "It's wonderful how travel forms youth; now I understand divine prescience of the original sin. It's true that travel isn't yet at everyone's disposal, but every day, the progress of science is destroying the supernatural and the marvelous, by explaining very simply...."

"When I woke up and found myself in the modest drawing-room in the priest of Cakya-Mouni's house, after the thanks and congratulations customary in such circumstances, I couldn't help thinking: *That's nothing; if I could inaugurate these voyages for the Exposition, it would steal the show and make a huge fortune!*

Author's note: From one viewpoint, it is clear that in the recent past, wireless telegraphy, combined with Röntgen, have proved my old Indian priest absolutely right, and that explain the astonishing experiment that he carried out before me and on me.

Thus, on April 22, 1901 I received the following telegram from Nice:

"Experiments with wireless telegraph are continuing apace; at Biot they have been crowned with the greatest success.

"Among the trials bearing on the very fact of the transmission, it is necessary to highlight those concerning its speed, which have given a result of 605 words an hour. Verse, not prose, was transmitted in this experiment.

"In addition, it has been possible to obtain the conviction of the possibility of a double transmission from the same point, at the same time, via the same antenna, by means of two transmitters. Similar experiments at sea will be carried out in the next few days. A cruiser put at the disposal of the commission has just arrived at Villefranche.

"In respect of the possible interception of a dispatch, something to be expected of the experiments currently being made, have no doubt on that subject. A dispatch transmitted from Biot to Calvi has been intercepted at Villefranche in every detail, with perfect clarity—which did not prevent it from reaching Calvi is a similar condition."

And on July 22 of the same year, the following dispatch was sent to us from Brussels:

"The Madrid correspondent of the Étoile Belge has telegraphed to his newspaper that he had interviewed a member of the technical commission who has carried out experiments

in wireless telegraphy using the system of the Spaniard Major Cervera.[92] *The major has telegraphed faultlessly between Tarifa and Ceuta. He will telegraph imminently from Barcelona to the Balearic Islands.*

"Major Cervera offers his personal assurance that he will be able to telegraph from Spain to America.

"Near Alicante, Major Servera has detonated mines at a distance, still wirelessly. He thinks that he will be able to provoke the explosion of the powder-magazine of a warship at a distance."

That is conclusive enough for me to abstain from insisting unduly on the importance of these experiments, far surpassed today by the latest results obtained in this field of research.

---

[92] Julio Cervera Baviera was sent by the Spanish army to visit Guglielmo Marconi in 1899 and study his experiments; he subsequently develop a wireless telegraphy system of his own, which was adopted in Spain.

The Universal Soul

The two fluids: the soul and electricity.
The soul, the intellectual fluid.
Electricity, the material fluid. The two motors of the world.

For twenty years I have demonstrated peremptorily, in hundreds if not thousands of articles, that electricity, in its three forms of imponderable fluid, light and heat, is the unique agent of the universe—cold heat and black light in the void of space, only becoming manifest on contact with our atmosphere.

Today, I want to demonstrate that the other fluid, the one we call the soul, the intellectual or intelligent fluid, as you wish, similarly resides in a general state, distributed throughout the universe.

To make my idea more easily comprehensible, I will say that it is not a matter of admiring the intelligence of humans, dogs, elephants or ants, but simply affirming loudly that intelligence is distributed everywhere in the universe, in a fluid state, just like electricity, and that specific circumstance are sufficient to bring it into evidence and register its manifestations.

Just as electricity, fluid in the two forms of light and heat, is only manifest on contact with our atmosphere, so the soul-fluid, distributed in the world, is only manifest when it enters into a living body, when resides there and is, so to speak, condensed there.

This is so true that not only can I give numerous examples of it, but can even undertake to provoke external manifestations of this soul-fluid at will, in various beings that have been supposed until now to be entirely devoid of it.

Two examples, from among a hundred, that I have taken from contemporary newspapers, will, I think, clarify my demonstration:

"Numerous complaints of cheating have been made in London and Antwerp against a female snake-charmer named Zulema Kerdy, who arrived in Paris a few days ago, where she has been hired by an impresario.

"An instruction was given to Monsieur Hamard, the deputy head of the Sûreté, who went to see the charmer at a house in the Rue de Trévise. Zulema was in bed. When M. Hamard made the purpose of his visit known, she whistled softly, and several snakes of menacing appearance emerged from beneath her bolster.

"She said to M. Hamard: 'If you come any closer you'll be bitten, for I shall launch these snakes against you, which are only obedient to me. Their bite causes immediate death.

"Fearlessly, the policeman replied to the charmer that her threats would not prevent him from carrying out his orders, and that in making threats she was risking forced labor. Zulema yielded to this reasoning, and rang a bell. A domestic appeared, whom she ordered to shut the snakes up in a basket. When that was done, she got dressed and meekly followed M. Hamard, who took her to headquarters in custody."

Here, therefore, is a woman who has been able to awaken the dormant universal soul in the bodies of her snakes, and to condense it there after a fashion. But is not the example of the savant seals recently exhibited on the stage of the Casino de Paris even more conclusive? Has not the voice of the worthy animals' tamer and friend awakened their dormant intelligence and condensed the intellectual fluid marvelously?

Thus, I am not exaggerating in saying that I can provoke manifestations of the soul-fluid at will, exactly like the electrical fluid. It is sufficient, for that, to give me any living creature whatsoever, and I will succeed so well in causing the universal soul to spring forth, if I might put it thus, that everyone will be obliged to recognize that I am telling the truth.

It must be admitted, however, that petty-minded individuals with chagrined minds will probably say that it is pure pantheism that I am in the process of setting before them. To which I reply, firstly, that I can't help that; and secondly, that all my life I have been an admirer and passionate lover of beautiful, good and great Nature, the source of all poetry, without knowing whether or not I was practicing pantheism.

In my youth, magnetically drawn to philosophy, I devoured and meditated upon Spinoza, Schelling and Hegel, but I confess that I never understood their concepts of materialist or idealist pantheism. "Everything in God" or "God in everything" seemed to me to be equally vacuous formulae. Those men were never anything but dreamers; they never took account of tangible realities, which experimental science alone can reveal to us, gradually.

Thus, whether I am practicing pantheism or not, I don't know, but what I do know is that electricity is the unique motor of the universe in its three forms: fluid, heat and light. What I also know is that I can provoke at will manifestations of the soul-fluid, or intelligence, as you please, among the most obscure creatures. That is sufficient for me, for I believe that this double deposition will be extremely fecund from the viewpoint of the future development of all the sciences, whether they are purely experimental or moral, in the false meaning that has been given to that qualification. Everything must, in fact, be rational, experimental and demonstrated in the scientific realm.

Now, people of good faith, who follow my work with too much benevolence, say to me: "You've arrived at the conclusion that one can condense and awaken the intelligence-fluid, the universal soul, at will in living creatures, in any fauna—that's fine. However, you don't believe yourself in the principle of life in the infinitely small; there, you see only chemical combinations re-entering the domain of electricity and heat. How do you sort that out?"

"I don't sort it out; I observe, that's all, in advance of any explanation."

"Haven't you tried to provoke external manifestations of the universal soul, the intelligence-fluid, in flora and in the geological or mineralogical realm?"

"No, because I don't believe in chimeras."

"Trees and plants, however, seek the light and seem to love the sun; how do we know that they don't suffer and think as we do, but in a more obscure fashion?"

"I don't think so, and, to tell the truth, I don't know anything about it. As for seeking light, that's included in the ordinary phenomena if light- and heat-electricity."

For now, I think I've explained clearly enough the nature of the electricity-heat-light-fluid, the unique motor of the universe, and the soul-fluid, the motor of all the actions of animate beings. I'll leave it at that.

Whether infinitely small creatures participate in both, which I'm not far from believing, is possible, but we shall see in future, if the discoveries of science permit it. Until then, let us reserve our conclusions with regard to the role of the two fluids in the microbial realm.

Why I Don't Like Traveling

Why the Earth is too small. Of air and space.
The necessity of sometimes leaving one's village.

I recently ran into Gontran. You don't know Gontran, one of my old friends, a young English multimillionaire? No? Well, listen to this conversation and you'll make his acquaintance.

So, I ran into him at the Exposition, in the process yawning as if he might dislocate his jaw.

"How are you?"

"Extremely bored?"

"Why don't you travel a little, to get a change of scene?"

"Oh, no!"

"I thought you like traveling?"

"I'd adore it if it were possible, but alas, it's not—and in spite of all modern discoveries, no one has yet found a means of traveling, other than in thought or in dream…as I do. That's why I've devoted myself to spiritualism."

"I don't understand. If I'm not mistaken, you've gone around the world several times—and you don't like traveling?"

Seeing my bewilderment, Gontran went on in a calm and sober tone: "Come on, my poor friend—let's be serious. Let's speak little and say much, as an old cousin of mine says. I could have believed that I liked what people call traveling, over land and sea, when I was fifteen, but now?

"Yes, I've been around the world five or six times, but afterwards, it's always the same. With steam and electricity, the Earth is as large as one's hand nowadays. I'm stifling here; I need air, space—I want to get away from it.

"Not only doesn't it amuse me to stroll around this grain of sand—me, a poor human microbe—but, at my age, I blush

179

as I set forth on what petty humans call great voyages. Poor fellows! To me, it seems that I'm always on a carousel of wooden horses, and I repeat, at my age, that makes me ashamed."

"You're joking!"

"Never."

"The Earth is too small for you, then?"

"For traveling, yes. Come on, you're a serious chap yourself, thoughtful and intelligent. Well, you'll understand without difficulty why I get bored on Earth, why I have a yearning for movement, space, open sky…truly open, between worlds!

"Why, when everyone knows that there are billions of worlds, billions of leagues apart in space, can't I go there, my fortune notwithstanding? I have no idea what's happening there, and you want me to amuse myself?

"We've photographed and catalogued more than thirty million stars, and I can't visit any of them. How is it that I can't even visit the kindred worlds of our own solar system, and it's even forbidden for me to drop in on the moon, which is on our very doorstep?—which I consider as the dressing-room of my bedroom, so to speak."

And as I displayed my astonishment with an interrogative stare, he went on vehemently, carried away, and truly handsome: "And you want me to amuse myself trailing miserably around the carousel of wooden horses that is the Earth! No, it's you who are making fun of me, and you're too intelligent not to share my opinion, deep down. What—travel over this heap of mud, to see why? Water, earth, mountains, trees, houses. And what then? Nothing—always the same thing, always the carousel going round and round, nothing new. It's only at the Museum that I can imagine that there were once a few differences, with other animals—but the vague impression scarcely last a quarter of an hour.

"What I thirst for is new worlds, lost in the infinity of space. There, there must be novelties, and beings perhaps less bestial than my co-citizens and yours. You see, my poor old chap, I feel that I'm dying of boredom, and that I shall go to my grave in consequence—for the so-called occult sciences, alas, have only given me the illusions of dreams and mirages.

"A pleasure-balloon bound for Mars, Jupiter and Saturn, please—and I'll give you my millions. Let's go colonize the stars, somewhere far away—it doesn't matter where; in other solar systems—but let's get away from Earth, where I'm stifling and have no space."

I could see well enough that Gontran's illness was profound, and as he perceived my dolor, he declared slowly, with false cheerfulness: "Come on, let's go—we'll watch bayaderes dancing in Benares, and then we'll go have a cup of tea with a friend in Yokohama."

"No," I said, sadly, in my turn. "You've convinced me; I no longer like traveling, at least on Earth."

And we stayed there, run aground like two old wrecks, on the terrace of a café, while the slow dull music of a belly-dance, performed by a suave Oriental from Ménilmontant, resounded behind us.

Oh yes, the Earth really is too small now—and who will finally find the means of permitting us to take a little excursion to neighboring worlds? That inventor will be blessed, and will make a great deal of money, because there are many people like Gontran and your humble servant, who no longer like to travel because the Earth is so small.

It really will be time, after the Exposition, to find something else and enable us to get off this eternal terrestrial carousel of wooden horses, no bigger than one's hand and, at the end of the day, too banal—especially when one feels that there would be so much to see, to learn and admire amid the thirty million stars that surround us.

Don't I have good reason not to like traveling anymore?

The Lightning Soul

*A new, simple and easy means of traveling the world,
without fatigue, without expense and without wasting time.*

I'm well aware that above title is a trifle over-long, but I think it's necessary to explain the purpose of what follows.

My readers will doubtless remember the article in why I explained that, alongside the electricity-fluid, the unique agent of the universe, an intelligence-fluid exists, which is found in a more-or-less latent state in all the living and animate creatures on the world's surface. They will also remember the more recent one in which I explained why and how, with steam and electricity in their multiple applications, the Earth has become so small that I no longer like traveling and that my sole ambition henceforth is to be able to roam freely from one world to another, amid the sixty million worlds that surround us—to begin with.

I had reached that point when, after long research, I was finally led to make a decisive discovery which, I dare say, will turn the world upside down and render it smaller than the Place de la Concorde, if you absolutely have to have a comparison. In brief, this is what it comprises, and how I have finally been able to realize the scientific dream of my life.

For I long time I was convinced that the intelligence-fluid would be revealed and treated like the electricity-fluid; once I had been convinced of that by the series of curious examples that I gave of the universal soul, I told myself that it ought not to be impossible, not to resuscitate the dead—for the intimate and still unknown link that constitutes life is then broken—but simply to be able to change the temporary domiciles of souls, the parcels of universal intelligence that constitute human personality.

Then I remembered the reciprocal and instantaneous transmission of two dispatches over the same wire, in opposite directions—between Paris and Marseilles, for example—and I told myself that with a little drive and will-power, I ought to be able to obtain a similar result with the intelligence-fluid that animates all human beings.

I've tried, and succeeded twenty times, a hundred times over, in the most various circumstances. Today, there is no longer any doubt; I'm sure of myself, and at the disposal of all my co-citizens to enable them to travel instantaneously through all the countries in the world—on condition, of course, that I have correspondents who will accept my tariffs.[93]

For example: you want to go to Peking immediately, for a week. Out there, I have an honorable mandarin who is at my disposal, for a determined price. Naturally, I take a 20% commission for myself, and, for a fee of 4000 francs for a week, on a signal from my will, you find yourself in Peking in the skin of the mandarin, whose soul passes into your body in Paris.

Naturally, you would not want to spend a week in the skin of a badly brought-up person, so I am in the process of ensuring that I have correspondents everywhere belonging to the best society. As it is necessary that your body should not be subject to any deterioration during our absence, I shall have them design a very strict contract concerning the use of beverages and other pleasures. Above all, this will be useful, not to say indispensable, for married clients; it is important that the temporary tenant should not lead a dissolute life with your carcass during his brief occupation.

---

[93] This notion, with several of the details extrapolated here, is recapitulated in the future history mapped out by Gaston de Pawlowski in the book translated as *Journey to the Land of the Fourth Dimension*, q.v.

To this effect, I have even constituted a parallel insurance company, which should further augment my modest income.

Where bachelors are concerned, it is evident that some of these difficulties disappear, and that the majority of these precautions are superfluous.

I can also effect temporary exchanges of soul-fluid between individuals of different sexes, but the operation is more delicate and I'm always afraid that one of the tenants might damage the temporary envelope, which obliges me to make a very scrupulous inventory of intimate places. That's the nub of the question; I don't think it's necessary to say any more.

Now, the applications of my discovery are as numerous as they are fecund. When the two contracting parties both want to be displaced in opposite directions at the same time, between Paris and Yokohama, or San Francisco, for example, I simply take my 20% and the right of insurance, in case of reciprocal deterioration, according to the general tariff that I've set up, and the journey then becomes almost trivial, so far as my two clients are concerned.

I can organize journeys of this sort to the ends of the earth, for a month or only an hour—and it's utterly charming to be able to spend a mere hour, after lunch or a aperitif time, in Japan!

Similarly, for the purpose of studying mores, I can send scientists, artists, explorers or simple curiosity-seekers into the body of a beggar, a bonze, a savage, a monk or a Hottentot princess, in order that my clients can carry out studies of the highest interest, thanks to my various combinations.

I think that it would be quite puerile to insist on the full importance of such an application of twentieth-century science. The consequences would not be long delayed in manifesting their fecundity in all branches of human activity. From the moment I succeeded in mobilizing the intelligence-fluid in the same way as the electricity-fluid, there was no limit to my discoveries, and I hope that I will soon be able to exchange soul-fluids with the inhabitants of other worlds.

Then, finally, I shall be able to travel freely, at my whim, through the infinity of worlds.

In the meantime, I can see only one shadow over my happiness and my joy in having rendered such a great service to humankind. I mean the terrible hatred that omnibuses, ferryboats, railways and steamships will infallibly avow against me, since I'm delivering a mortal blow to their tortoise-paced industry. The blow is all the more terrible because I can establish tariffs that will defy all competition, given that I am eliminating the time and dispensing with the fatigue of traveling, and that everyone, in future, will employ my system—for I shall have branches all over the world. All men and women will be subscribers, with their pass books, and the time is not far off when I shall be able to effect these temporary transmutations of intelligence-fluid on a massive scale, for the price of a simple ticket.

Whatever is said, let no one fear for me. I'm brave and well-armed, and I laugh at the impotent hatred and rage of all the transport companies in the entire world!

Interastral Telegraphy

A new application of wireless telegraphy.
How to communicate with all the stars.
Decisive and conclusive experiments.

Recently, I read a note in the majority of the scientific journals conceived very much in these terms:

"Experiments in wireless telegraphy are being multiplied and extended. They have been carried out between the port of Cuxhaven and the island of Heligoland, Sixty-two kilometers separate these two stations, and the communications were made in perfect conditions of precision. Wireless telegraphy has ceased to be a subject of scientific curiosity; it exists, and we can be certain that it development will be rapid.

"Already, in England, a Post Office commission that has been studying the question for several months has delivered a report in which it concludes in favor of the adoption of the Marconi system by the English postal authorities. There is no need to stress the importance of this news. Its confirmation will be neither more nor less than the commencement of a revolution in the telegraphic system of the world."

I beg you to believe that I bring no authorial pretension or inventorial jealousy to this matter, but when I had finished reading that item I could not help smiling in pity.

Poor folk! They're still at a distance of sixty-two kilometers, while it's been a long time since I not only achieved interplanetary telegraphy by interastral telegraphy, between the thirty million worlds catalogued by Janssen[94] and the eighty

---

[94] This is probably be an invention; the most recent star-catalogue published when Vibert wrote this story was the second Washington catalogue compiled by J. R. Eastman; I cannot find evidence of any

million other worlds that, being too distant, have not yet been revealed by photography, either because their light has not reached us yet or for some other cause.

Since the day when, thanks to my profound knowledge of the electrical fluid I was able to enter into sustained communication with the inhabitants of the planet Mars, as I have described here, by means of fire—which is to say, visible electricity—and photography—which is to say, light or invisible electricity—the problem was mentally resolved, so far as I was concerned. All that remained was fining the material application, and with patience, tenacity and—ought I admit?—a great deal of fumbling, I finally arrived at a victorious solution to the problem.

What was to be determined, first of all, was whether the star-worlds were inhabited, and whether it was possible to understand their languages, which were probably very varied.

There remained that matter of entering into communication with their inhabitants by wireless telegraphy, which was mathematically possible, in my view—but how could I alert them?

It was then that I reasoned, very simply, as follows:

I ought to find myself facing one of three alternatives. Either the stars are too old, dead or uninhabited—one day, I shall explain how a star dies—or, according to the theory of Fontenelle, who believed, quite rightly, in the plurality of worlds, a large number of star-worlds are inhabited, but the inhabitants are in a savage state and would have no suspicion of my attempts to contact them, or, finally, the stars are inhabited by people as civilized as us. In the last-cited case, there was a good chance that, their already being in possession of electric telegraphy apparatus perhaps much more powerful than ours, my provocative dispatches would encounter their receivers and would be recorded as a result.

---

involvement in a recent catalogue by anyone named Janssen or Jansen.

Fortified by these ideas and hopes, I therefore embarked calmly on that course, naturally making use of wireless telegraphy and sending, if I might put it thus, a collective dispatch to the hundred and twenty million star-worlds immediately surrounding us, in what might be called the suburbs of Earth, within a few billion trillion quadrillion leagues.

I waited with a combination of confidence, impatience and tranquility, and while I waited in that very particular state of mind—which is incomprehensible to anyone who has never sent dispatches that far—I made calculations and told myself that even with my electric fluid, which moved rapidly, there were definitely large numbers of stars too distant for any communication, from which I would not receive a response within seventy-five years. I was even getting ready to make my will in order to implore my notary's successors to record the replies after my death, when I reflected that I still had time to think about it.

Then the terrible idea occurred to me, with the nagging pan of a dagger slowly tickling my heart, that I would never be able to establish a direct service of balloons or interplanetary ten-centime tramways. And that realization caused me veritable sadness.

Soon, however, replies began to arrive in quantity; I had not been mistaken. The problem of long-distance telegraphy, through the spaces of infinity, was resolved; millions of star-worlds were inhabited and civilized, like the Earth; and—an important and curious point—with a profound knowledge of Hebrew, I succeeded with relative ease in translating and understanding all the dispatches, written in the most various languages and with the most bizarre characters, conventional or otherwise.

There is, I think, no need to insist on the importance of my discovery. At the present moment, I have not yet opened all my replies, with the aid of my seventy-one secretaries, to whom I have given a key to decipher them; I can say, however, that I already have correspondents in seventeen million, eight hundred and twenty-nine thousand, four hundred and seven planets, stars or worlds as unfamiliar to date as the telegraph service.

I really did say 17,829,407 *worlds*, and I believe that, on that account, without flattering myself, I have outdone Mougeot,[95] who has not yet succeeded in corresponding with anyone beyond the Earth except St. Anthony of Padua, and Swedenborg himself is conclusively buried all the way to the hilt.

Now, in order to undertake further studies and pay my secretaries, I have opened a telegraph office for anyone who wants to send interastral dispatches, in the hope of re-establishing contact with their mother-in-law or someone they love.

I have a list of stars and correspondents and, until further notice, I have established a uniform tariff. It's a thousand francs a letter; when there's an acute or grave accent, or a period, it's twelve francs a letter; a diacresis or circumflex accent costs thirteen francs with the letter; finally, a cedilla is valued at fifteen francs, given the difficulty of certain interastral punctuations and accentuations.

I don't know if the clientele will flood in, but, in spite of the relatively high process—which is hardly anything, if one takes account of the distances, and which our general expenses prevent me from lowering for the moment—either I'm much mistaken or it seems to me that I'm finally on the verge of making a fortune, while having accomplished it by means of one of the greatest scientific discoveries of the beginning of the 20th century.

---

[95] An artist who signed himself E. Mougeot produced several images of saints in the early 1900s, but I cannot find any record of his being in communication with any of them.

What's the Point?

The death of the Sun.
The impossibility of communication between the stars.
The negligibility of glory before time and space.
The uselessness of writing.

I recently found myself at the banquet of a literary society, infiltrated by a number of funeral directors, at which a writer made the following very judicious speech over dessert, which I made an effort to learn by heart, and which I am reproducing here with almost total fidelity:

"Ladies and dear colleagues.

"It is with tears in my voice that I come to say my farewells to you, so permit me modestly to propose a toast: put out the torches! But I perceive that there's nothing here but electricity, so I shall call: put out the bulbs.

"Don't worry, I'm always brief; you won't have time to put earplugs in.

"As we're all old friends here and I've been taking part in your fraternal love-feasts for twenty years, I owe you an explanation of the reasons for this retirement, as premature as it is unexpected. It will be brief, simple and clear.

"All today's scientists agree in affirming that that the sun will soon die. Some say in three hundred million years, others affirm that it will only happen in three hundred billion years, but that slight difference of opinion is of no importance. The brutal fact remains; the sun is going to die tomorrow—for three hundred billion years is tomorrow, by comparison with eternity.

"On the other hand, our excellent and illustrious friend Janssen has already catalogued, labeled and baptized—the dear chap—more than thirty million stars, and by his own admission, there are still more than a hundred and twenty million that are still hanging around, waiting in the vertiginous plains

190

of infinity for an opportunity to pass before an astronomer's objective lens.

"Apart from the suns and a few worlds perhaps reverted to infancy because they are too old, it is evident that all these worlds are inhabited, and yet, in the present state of science, we have not yet found a means of communicating with them. Thus far, as I have recounted here myself, I have scarcely been able to exchange a few brief sentences with the inhabitants of Mars and photograph a young Martian woman.

"From these two observations, it follows clearly that it is utterly useless to write, since we have the certainty that our works cannot endure either in time or in space, and the only thing that could incite me to continue writing is the possibility of telegraphing my works to all the worlds—but in a broader sense that the one attached to that banal phrase on the Earth.[96]

"As this is not the case, however, what is three hundred billion years? Scarcely a token gesture sketched in time.

"What are a hundred and twenty million stars—or five hundred billion, if you wish? A few grains of dust, almost invisible in the dark void, the impalpable waves of the boundless infinity of space.

"Given that, at least until further notice, my thought cannot endure either in time or in space, what point is there in continuing to accumulate an immense quotidian labor, as I have been doing for thirty years?

"Charron said: *what do I know?*—and that was also the opinion of his friend Montaigne.[97] For myself, more modestly, I say: *What's the point?*

"And that is why, from now on, my resolution is irrevocable. I shall retire from the field—to Courcelles!

---

[96] Because the French *monde* means "social stratum" as well as "world," *tous les mondes* [all the worlds], in the context of literary marketing conventionally implies "all sections of society."

[97] It was Michel de Montaigne (1533-1592) who made "Que sais-je?" into a celebrated motto; Pierre Charron (1541-1603) merely took over responsibility for his intellectual heritage after his death.

"With the mind thus freed of any sickening preoccupation, abrupt or creeping, however, before retiring forever to the wilderness out there beyond the Place Monceau, I want to tell you that I shall still remain in your midst, a dependable, active, virile and devoted member, for as long as possible.

"And now, ladies and dear colleagues, my dear friends, I raise my glass and drink to the old French gaiety, to *joie de vivre*, to all that is good on the earth: to liberty, love, justice and friendship!"

Indeed, the colleague who, while still relatively young, declares in such a casual manner that he is renouncing the ephemeral glory of a day, the notoriety, the celebrity and the posterity, because, in his thirst for the ideal and the absolute, he feels, he *sees* that eternity is escaping him, appears to me to be a profound philosopher.

It is necessary to see things from on high to reason with that freedom of mind, that amiable grace, to be moved in that manner, without having vertigo, in the very ambience of the redoubtable problems that will always pose themselves to the interrogative and curious mind of every thinking being in time and space!

In addition, here is a spiritual lesson in transcendental philosophy, which ought not to be entirely lost on the funeral directors who heard it.

Similis similibus curantor.

Unless you prefer: *contraria contrariis.*[98]

Personally, it's all the same to me—and that, quite simply, is my conclusion.

---

[98] When the former of these two contrasted phrases ("like to cure like") was advanced in the early 19th century as the fundamental principle of homeopathy, the latter ("contrast [against] contrariety") was suggested, tongue-in-cheek, as the tacit principle of classical medicine.

Assured Survival

I. The soul-ticket. Means of conserving the will.
A psychological colombarium.
A new branch of the science of electricity.

I have already explained here, in detail and peremptorily, that what we call the soul is nothing, in essence, but a fluid akin to electricity, and how it will be possible to do away with traveling in the future, when one will be able to hire the body of an individual for a day or two and install one's own soul—which is to say, one's own individuality—by cable in a foreign carcass, in exchange for a modest remuneration.

Those are givens, and I shall not return to them. Having perfected my system, however, and thus being able to perceive what will happen in future, I think I can be sure that I have finally resolved the problem of survival, which is so irritating and, at the same time, so flattering—especially for those who have lots of money and are annoyed at having to quit so soon what is only a vale of tears for those who haven't a sou.

All spiritualists and all spiritual people admit that the soul, that imponderable fluid, is immortal and survives our bodies, just like the electrical fluid, which is the very agent of the universe.

Now, this is what I have imagined in order to give pleasure to rich people and the curious, and, fundamentally, what I shall be able to realize scientifically. In the dreams of their profligate imagination, our forefathers desired it before me, for, all things considered, it's nothing more than a new and tangible form of the legend of Faust. As a clientele, I'm certain to have that of all the rich people who are afraid of dying, and all curious individuals who would like to know what will happen on earth in a hundred, two hundred, five hundred years or more—for the soul-fluid is something that can be conserved, and does not decompose in bottles.

193

So, a great nobleman says to me: "I'd like to come back to the earth in a hundred and fifty-one years"—the exact figure doesn't matter.

I reply: "This is the tariff: a thousand francs a year. First give me a hundred and fifty-one thousand francs."

Then, by an entirely new scientific procedure that I shall leave in my will to the Académie des Sciences, but which I shall be permitted to keep secret for the time being, in order not to deprive me of my means of existence, I shall commence by removing, very gently, without any danger, a portion of his soul-fluid—which will, in any case, renew itself very quickly—and I shall store it, condense it and conserve it, if I might put it thus, in an *ad hoc* flask.

I shall conserve souls thus, as life, voices and movements are literally conserved today by cinematographs, phonographs and thaumatropes.[99]

Needless to say, all this will be done seriously and appropriately, and when a joint stock company has been set up to construct a palatial building, I shall arrange all the souls in a psychological colombarium.[100]

When that is done, I shall give my client a receipt—a futuristic birth-certificate, if you wish—which I shall call a soul-ticket; which, in order that it will not be lost, will be deposited in the office of a notary who will have a special section in his minutes for this kind of operation.

Now it remains for me to explain the purely material side of the operation. It's quite simple.

I shall return to the example of my client, who has deposited his soul-fluid in my psychological columbarium and has given me a hundred and fifty-one thousand francs.

---

[99] A thaumatrope is an optical instrument for illustrating the persistence of vision, by means of which two rapidly alternating images seem to fuse into one.

[100] The substitution of an *o* for the more usual *u* in *columbarium* emphasizes the reference to a dovecot (i.e., a set of pigeon-holes), but the Latin *columbarium* was a metaphorical adaptation of the term to a vault with recesses in which cinerary urns were placed.

First I keep half for myself and the expenses of the upkeep and supervision of the columbarium. Of the other half, half of that—which is to say, a quarter—will be given to the notary for the conservation of the soul-ticket in his archives. The other quarter is deposited in the Banque de France, with the natural compounding of interest—which will be a tidy sum in a hundred and fifty-one years. On that day, the titular notary then in charge will easily be able to find parents who will surrender the body of their child for that tidy sum, for they will be enriched in their turn by the procedure, of which I alone know the secret, but which I shall bequeath to the Académie des Sciences. My client's soul-fluid will be decanted into the body of the young child, and my client will return to the world, with his soul and his personality, after a hundred and fifty-one years.

Note that, if he wishes, he will be able to stipulate a preference for being the tenant of a man fifteen, twenty or thirty years of age, in which case the contract will be made directly, the notary offering the sum.

The problem of survival is, therefore, victorious resolved, in a very simple fashion, very easy to carry out. Understandably, however, it will always be expensive, and only within the range of very rich people, for it will be necessary for my client—still following the same example—to deposit a sum of money in the Banque de France on his own account, at compound interest, which he will be able to access after a hundred and fifty-one years, when he returns to the earth. Someone who only wants to return after a hundred and fifty-one years, though, given the compounding of interest, will not have to lay out a very considerable sum.

I'm aware of the objections. Firstly, of course, it will require new legislation to permit the Banque de France and notaries to engage in operations of this kind; secondly, who can tell whether there might not be upheavals during such a long lapse of time, and whether banks and notaries will still exist? Obviously, that's only human, but with all those *ifs* and *buts* one would never achieve anything great, and would always remained encrusted in routine.

Admit, though, what a joy there would be in being able to return at will to the earth, after a century, or two, or ten, in feeling oneself again. What a joy for the curious, for the scientists who would observe the progress of humankind, what intoxication!

But that's not all, and I shall indicate in the next chapter the fecund consequences that will inevitably stem from my discovery.

II. Different means of transmission. A new honeymoon. Various schemes within the range of rich people.

I have said that it will require new legislation to authorize notaries and the Banque de France to do what it necessary to fulfill the indispensable formalities; that's understood—but taking responsibility for all this material red-tape cuisine, if I might put it thus, would surely require great establishments analogous to our present-day life-insurance companies, which could offer you the most varied and interesting schemes.

I don't want to cite them all, but, for example, rich men who do not care about the expense, and who are happy at home, could arrange to include their wives in the scheme, in such a manner as to return to earth at exactly the same time, after two or three centuries; and those who are extremely rich will be able to commission the company specifically to have their wife-soul reincarnated in a younger body. Those who fancy a change, by paying a further price for the expenses of the correspondence, would be able to have the ineffable joy of comparing different carnal envelopes and ensuring the survival of their spouse, at a fixed date, in a black, Japanese or Chinese woman.

It goes without saying, of course, that, should the occasion arise, one would be able to offer the same truly regal gallantry to one's mistress, if one had the misfortune still to be a bachelor.

It seems to me that there's no need to go on; the benevolent reader will have understood me without it being spelled out, and there's no doubt that the establishment in question would be able to offer its clientele the choice—if, again, I might put it this way—of schemes infinitely more seductive than those presently imagined even in New York.

It now remains to elucidate a very serious point, with regard to which I humbly confess, in spite of all my research, that I have not yet settled—although I may say, at present, that everything seems to permit me to hope for a happy solution.

The point is, in fact, grave, delicate and interesting. This is what it amounts to: can a man, if he wishes, retain his soul-fluid in his way in order to be reincarnated and live again in a woman's body, and a woman in the body of a man? It's obvious that this would be infinitely more interesting, from points of view as varied as they are different. Suppose momentarily that a man of Zola's stripe were to find himself thus returned in the body of a woman. The great psychologist, having analyzed the sentiments of man, would be able to analyze those of woman—after a certain lapse of time, it's true—with equal sincerity and self-knowledge...which is invaluable if one wants to write pages on our poor humanity that are sincere and truly lived.

Once again, however, I repeat, I am continuing my research and I have not despaired in the least of vanquishing this difficulty. It would not generate a true Androgyne, since the phenomenon would only be produced in time, successively not simultaneously, and in the long term—but what a world of marvelous speculations for a thinker, a philosopher, an attentive and resourceful observer. How interesting it would be, for instance, to know from experience to which sex it is more *amusing* to belong, during the divine moment in which two souls exchange a supreme kiss!

I don't want to deflower the subject; nevertheless, it might be permissible for me to observe that, if I arrive at this superb and definitive result, my discovery will be perfect...and when I say that, it's not out of a sentiment of misplaced pride, but simply because I believe, with a very clear and precise consciousness, that in recent years I have taken a huge step forward in this interesting field of the physical and natural sciences concerned with the two mysterious agents, still misunderstood at present, but which rule the universe nevertheless: the material-electrical fluid and the soul-electrical fluid—which is to say, the moral fluid.

That is the future, and I shall be happy and proud if I have been able to cast a little light on the ardent and passionate researches of science in this respect.

The Chemical Life of the Future

I. How everything will be sold in bottles or in powder form. The simplification of existence. A few curious examples.

I have already observed more than once that there is nothing that stimulates the bee that we almost all have, more or less dormant, in our bonnets like an *Exposition Universelle*. It's a stimulant almost as powerful for the minds of inventors, researchers and discoverers as a great cataclysm or a great national crisis—a war, for example.

I recently found myself at the Exposition with one of these birds, which are less rare than one might imagine, and as we were dining peacefully on the terrace of one of the restaurants in the Trocadero, vaguely watching the fireworks at the Château d'Eau through the fumes of our cigars, my companion broke the silence.

"Will you go to see the next Exposition in eleven years, in the Bois de Boulogne?"

"They say there won't be another one."

"Yes there will, for there will be new needs and new ambitions to satisfy after that time. But that's not the question...don't interrupt me. The other evening, I was at your lecture on the Exposition. You explain magisterially how it is based on genuinely new elements, on a framework of iron and wood—rejuvenated—on reinforced concrete, the patisserie for making all these palaces with a little plaster and stucco, and, finally, electricity..."

"You flatter me."

"Not at all. You've made a host of true and curious observations—but in eleven years, my dear chap, the *Exposition Universelle du Bois de Boulogne* will be even newer, because it will be primarily chemical."

"What do you mean?"

199

"It's quite simple. You've told me a hundred times that you consider electricity to be the unique agent of the universe, and I'm in absolute agreement with you. Have no doubt about it. But there are chemical transformations as well, often by means of electricity: chemistry is the great science of the future, you see."

"Perfectly, but I don't quite see…"

It's very simple. You'll admit its considerable progress eleven years from now, or twelve if you wish?"

"How could I not?"

"Then we're in agreement. By that time, life will be singularly simplified, thanks to recent chemical discoveries, and that will be the whole of the scientific progress that the Exposition's mission will be to show us—we know this already—or, rather, to gather before our eyes in an admirable and dazzling synthesis. Is that clear?"

"Very nearly. Examples?"

"Examples? There's a swarm of them. There won't be any more need for combustibles, stoves in winter or ice for refreshment in summer, because, either in bottles or in powder form, warmth, cold, wind, air, etc., etc., will be on sale whenever you want at your local grocer's shop."

"Perfect."

"Wait, that's not all. He will also sell you light and darkness in equally small volume, weighing very little and easy to slip into your pocket, for use according to the needs of the moment—which will be infinitely convenient.

"Thus one can be scornful of the sun, day and night, the seasons, the poles and tropics alike, and everywhere on Earth will be a veritable paradise, thanks to my bottled warmth and cold. That's nothing, though, to the services that light and darkness will provide. Thus, if I lose my wallet on the stairs at night, I take two drops of light from my bottle and there it is, found again.

"In a railway train or on an omnibus, I catch sight of a delightful young woman who makes me go weak at the knees. *Pop!* I spread two drops of darkness around us, and silently, as a man of the world, I steal a kiss without anyone having seen anything.

"I think that the chemical life of the future, thus comprised, will certainly not lack charm, and that's why I'm convinced that its simultaneous synthesis and analysis will have a great success at the next Exposition Universelle de Bois de Boulogne. Are you beginning to be persuaded?"

"Entirely?"

"Good. Well, since that's the case, I take you fully into my confidence. I'll admit to you that I've sworn to keep my secret to myself, but you've wormed it out of me."

"You're too kind."

"Not at all, that's you. I'll go on. Thus far, I've only talked about warmth, cold, air, wind, light, darkness, etc.— which is to say, all the ambiences in which we move around. That will undoubtedly be a great revolution in itself, but since you want to listen, I'll explain to you what the chemical life will be in direct relation to the human body, by the time of the next Exposition. It's absolutely marvelous, as you'll see!"

"I don't doubt it."

Eleven o'clock was chiming at the Palais de la Femme, however, and the Château d'Eau was about to put an end to its incandescent nocturnal marvels.

"It's late, and I want to listen to you with jealous attention. How about dinner tomorrow, here, at the same time?"

"Agreed."

And my brave interlocutor wandered off, after shaking my hand, as if subjugated by his intense interior vision, still murmuring, as he went downstairs: "Chemical life—that's the future!"

II. After the external world, the body.
The nourishment of the future.
A curious transformation.

The next day, he continued in these terms:

"I've just revealed that warmth, cold, light and darkness will soon be sold in bottles, as well as void, compressed air and wind. That's it for the external world, for the ambiences that surround us. Today, I'll say something about the direct transformations that the chemistry of tomorrow will impose, first on our nourishment, and then on our bodies.

"When the alchemists were always talking about the unity of matter, pearls made of hardened light and morning dew changed into crystal and diamond by salamanders, sylphs and gnomes, their poetic divagations weren't as extravagant as all that, all things considered.

"You're familiar with Darwin's theory of transformation, and, without wanting to agree with him completely, we can take It for granted that it won't take long to *get going*, as the Canadians say, and take a giant step forward—and it's chemistry that will enable that.

"Anyway, these idea aren't new: *nil novi sub sole*;[101] and it's with reason that, again into the mouth of an alchemist, the amiable fantasist Anatole France puts these words:

"'Man's teeth are a sign of his ferocity. When we are able to nourish ourselves properly, those teeth with give way to some ornament similar to the pearls of salamanders. Then it will be inconceivable that a lover will any longer be able to see canine teeth in his mistress's mouth without horror and disgust.'"[102]

"That's curious," I said. "If my memory serves me right, about thirty-five or forty years ago, a literary colleague of my father's under the Empire, the Vicomte de Maricourt—the grandson of one of the three *valets de chambre* who followed Louis XVI to the scaffold, Baron Hue, I believe—published a prophetic pamphlet on the same subject."[103]

---

[101] [There is] nothing new under the sun.

[102] The quotation is from *La Rôtisserie de la reine Pédauque* (1892; tr. as *At the Sign of the Reine Pedauque*).

[103] René du Mesnil de Maricourt (1829-1893), the grandson of Louis XVI's most devoted courtier, Baron François Hue, published the item

He went on: "Today, however, thanks to the incessant progress of chemistry, all that is becoming more precise, and yesterday's dreams will not be long delayed in becoming today's tangible reality.

"Soon, chemistry, in the matter of alimentation, will no longer be the monopoly of preserves—which are manufactured, as everyone knows, with by-products of coal—but will become common usage in everyday life.

"As we know the chemical make-up of all the solid substances, organic or vegetable—meat, fruit and vegetables—that we absorb, the day is not far off when that abundant and cumbersome cuisine will be replaced by one pill that we swallow in the morning for breakfast and one in the evening for dinner. We will still be able to keep beverages and liquids, temporarily, but truly refined, distinguished and *elegant* minds—to use the fashionable term—will not take long to replace them, gradually, with the inhalation of perfumes."

"The most fortunate and fecund transformations will be immediately produced in the world, but as I don't want to write a whole book on that subject, I shall content myself with briefly identifying the most important, sure that my benevolent readers will be able to deduce the others for themselves, if I ever write it.

"To begin with, first in line, it is appropriate to place the economy of time and money, which will be so colossal that the social question will be resolved completely, at a stroke.

"With heat, light, cold, void, etc., sold in bottles or in powder form, according to circumstances, there will be no more stoves, lamps or freezers, but only very simple apparatus, even simpler than an electric light-bulb. But it's in the matter of bodily nourishment, most of all, that the economy will be admirable and he transformations over the next century or two incalculable.

---

of futuristic fiction in question, *La Commune en l'an 2073*, in 1874. As its title implies, its primary purpose is political.

"In the same way that we will no longer have any need of coal for heating, no longer having the need to nourish ourselves with anything but two or three pills comprised of all the chemical products that we absorb so grossly and bestially today, in the form of meat or vegetables, we shall no longer kill animals in order to eat them and will cease to be the murderers of our inferior brothers. It will be a Golden Age, ameliorating mores.

"All today's merchants of comestibles—grocers, butchers, pork-butchers, fruiterers, tripe-sellers, greengrocers, dairymen, restaurateurs, café-owners, etc., etc.—will have disappeared, giving way to the shops of alimentary chemists, who will be obliged to pass examinations, like pharmacists, in order that there should be no fraud in the good quality of nutritive pills.

"It's unnecessary, though, to grieve too much over those poor people without employment, firstly because the transformations will be accomplished in successive stages, and secondly because the majority will be able to make use of their aptitudes in other branches of human activity. Thus, the grocers will be able to go into politics or literature spiced with licentiousness, butchers into the army, pork-butchers into medicine, lemonade-makers into the ranks of sappers and firemen, etc., etc.

"But where the consequences will be truly admirable and strange, according to Darwin's theories, will be in the human body. However, I can see that the subject will take me much longer, for it still requires a few brief developments—and that will be for the next dinner."

III. Consequences for the human body.
The modification of organs.
The ideal age of humankind.

On the same terrace of the same restaurant in the Trocadero, at the same time on the third evening, when our dinner was over, my terrible interlocutor picked up the thread of his story, just at the point where he had left it the previous evening, as in a tale in the Thousand and One Nights.

"You'll think, my dear friend, that I'm taking a long time, but I assure you that I'll have finished by the time you've finished your cigar.

"So, after the ambiences, we've seen how the nourishment of the human body, in the form of pills and a pinch of powder, will become purely chemical. That's a given, to which we have no need to return."

"Of course."

"Yes, but one last point remains to which I ought to draw your attention, in order to see whether, in this matter too, you think as I do."

"Go on."

"It's quite simple. If you admit, as I do, that the future of humankind, for a host of economic and other reasons, which we have no ne to revisit here, will necessarily reside in the chemical nourishment of human beings, it is also necessary to admit, as a logical and inevitable consequence, that the said nourishment will lead to profound modifications of the human body."

"Really?"

"What do you mean, really? Definitely—you're not unaware that when an organ is no longer used, it gradually atrophies, and may even end up disappearing completely. Thus, the most eminent scientists have affirmed for a long time that the spleen is merely a witness, today useless and idle, of unknown ancestral functions. Well, follow my reasoning..."

"Of course; I'm drinking in your words."

"Thus, with the chemical nourishment of the future, not only we have no need of the cow's belly, as the peasant's say, but the stomach itself. People in need might perhaps be able to sell their stomachs to tanners, leather-manufacturers if you prefer, to make purses or handbags for ladies..."

Then, lowering his voice, my poor friend, carried away by his subject, suddenly said to me: "And then, what will be the tangible triumph of transformism, of the Darwinian method? It's quite evident that the greater part of our intestines, without employment, will inevitably lose length. There will be a simplification of the human machine, and as we are talking as men, let me add that you, who have defended mains drainage all your life, will be well satisfied."

"How's that?"

"Why, naturally, with chemical nourishment in the form of the infinitesimal pills dear to homeopaths, it's clear that it will put a final end to cesspool-emptiers…"

"That's true." And, on thinking about that aspect of the question, I let out a burst of laughter that almost turned into a veritable attack of nerves.

Meanwhile, still calm and placid, continuing the implacable development of his ideas, the inventor added: "Dead ducks, so to speak! And see how, immediately, at a stroke, human life will be purified, magnified and ennobled. From the moment when there is no more heavy and solid nourishment, and chemistry and perfumes provide everything, not only will there be no more stomach- and belly-aches, but no more gout, and almost no more need for sleep, for of all the other fatigues, it's the table that kills people and forces them to send half their lives in that temporary and tyrannical death called sleep.

"It will be possible to bring the greatest works of the mind to a final period, without being troubled three times a day by the cruel *ditto*, no wordplay intended. That won't prevent people from resting, but you'll see thinkers, artists and lovers entirely given to their dreams of glory, happiness or quasi-divine pleasure, no longer tormented by that vile and cowardly despot that our ancestors called Master Gaster.

"Has nature delivered a light and discreet warning? *Pop!* One pill, rapidly absorbed, and the machine is working admirably again. Which means that there will no longer be any locomotive or chronometer comparable to the human machine, redesigned, corrected and, above all, simplified by the wise application of triumphant chemistry to human nourishment.

"The heart and the brain—which is to say, thought and flame—will remain, but all the interior tripe from the esophagus to the rectum will gradually disappear, according to the immortal theory of the great Lamarck, Darwin's veritable French St. Jean-Baptiste. One may say that human beings, thus purified and simplified, will be akin to earthly angels, and will leave the mistake of the Paradise lost with Adam and Eve far behind them.

"It is necessary, in any case, only to see symbols in the naïve tales of theogony, and it will really be the advent of Paradise Regained, and of the Antichrist—which is to say, of stomach-ache and diarrhea forever vanquished by the new chemical life...not to mention that it will prolong the life of the Earth itself, too populated to be able to nourish all its children."[104]

"I admit that this new explanation of times to come opens new horizons to me, and gives me a better understanding of a host of points that have been obscure until now in my mind."

"Say that this future will be tomorrow, for we are about to enter it. Say that you're convinced."

"I am."

"Good—and in 1911, at the next Exposition, in the Bois de Boulogne, I shall invite you to dinner at the chemical restaurant that will be located to the left of the balloon boarding-platform. There will no longer be any table or crockery, but only sofas, incense-burners and exquisite music. There you are—the restaurant of the future! Long live the chemical life!"

"And in the meantime, another glass of champagne?"

"I won't refuse."

Author's note: "Curiously enough, Monsieur J. Holt Schooling has just published an article in The Cosmopolitan *in which the following conclusions seem to give abundant reason*

---

[104] The author inserts a footnote here that I have moved a short distance to the end of the chapter.

to my visionary inventor of the Exposition.[105] *Judge for your-selves, since he affirms that:*

"'Firstly, that the rate of increase of the world's popula-tion leapt from 5.5 million in 1800 to 62.5 million in 1890, which is doubtless a record; secondly, in all the great Aryan nations, that rate of increase is decreasing rapidly[106]*; thirdly, the Teutons (the United States, United Kingdom and Germanic races) are increasing much faster than the Latin races, of which they are already almost double; fourthly, Belgium leads the way with 572 inhabitants per square mile, and Russia is last with 15.'*

"M. Schooling considers that the Earth will be 'full' when it has a thousand inhabitants per square mile. 'If,' he says, 'we apply to the increasing world population the rate of increase obtained during the 19th century—which is to say, 1% per year—we obtain the following results:

Year	Millions of people	Number of people per square mile
1900	1.600	31
2000	4.328	83
2100	17.706	225
2200	31.662	609
2250	52.073	1001

---

[105] "When Will the Earth be Full?" in the July 1901 issue. What fol-lows is not a quotation but a summary; the tables are accurate but the five-point digest of the argument simplifies a discourse that is far more elaborate.

[106] Although this point may seem contradictory to the others in the context of this summary, Schooling's article does call attention to the deceleration of the rate of population increase in several European nations, especially France. Vibert was not the only Frenchman note of that statistic, but he went into the matter in sufficient depth to pro-duce his own analysis of *La Dépopulation de France* in 1903.

"'As there are 52 million square miles of land, the world will be "full" when we have a population of 52 billion individuals-which is to say, in 2250. We have, therefore, another 350 years to wait."

Life Does Not Exist

The infinitely small, rods in blood and rotifers. Dust of life.
Life is a myth. The triumph of chemistry.

Recently, a young and illustrious physician, specializing in the applications, as various as they are infinite, of electricity to therapeutics—and perhaps a closer friend because of that, because he knows about my profound faith in electricity from the viewpoint of my own work—spend a tranquil evening at my home, between a cigar and a cup of tea (in the plural, of course).

We had a few other good friends there, belonging to the most various intellectual professions, but—an important point of contact—all resolute partisans of the experimental and purely scientific method.

Addressing my friend between two puffs of smoke, I said: "Well, you've been appointed director of a laboratory of electricity applied to microbiology; you've got everything you wished for—congratulations all round. Before going home, however, tell us something about what led you to your relentless study of microbes and the infinitely small—in broad terms, of course. Has your sagacious, probing, inquisitive and often divinatory mind led you toward the unknown, or simply put you on the track of great scientific discoveries destined to change the world?"

"Since you pose the question so clearly, I'll reply in the same way: I don't know whether I shall change the world, but certainly, without false modesty, I believe that I'm on the track of two observations—or, as you generously put it, two discoveries—whose consequences will not fail to render great services.

"The first is likely to relieve human suffering in large measure, since it proves that the majority of diseases are caused and propagated by microbes, and that the majority of these tiny animals can be destroyed by electricity in determined conditions that are unfortunately still unclear. From the moment when we set forth upon the fecund path of the manipulation of static electricity, however, it's only a matter of time.

"That the everyday application of the therapeutics in question will soon become prolific, I am convinced, but I'm in haste to arrive at the second, purely scientific—or rather philosophical—observation...if only to make you jump..."

"That might be difficult."

"Well, I've arrived in the course of my relentless study of the infinitely small at the profound conviction that life does not exist.[107] No, life at the bottom of the scale of beings does not exist, and we are merely victims of an illusion that will dissipate as our means of investigation grow more powerful on a daily basis..."

"As it happens, that's what I've always said and thought myself, based only on reasoning and logic."

"Here, of course, I can't enter into great detail, which would only bore you, but take a drop of blood and look at it under a microscope. Before your eyes the rods,[108] the micro-

---

[107] This assertion may seem odd, but it must be remembered that Vibert was writing at a time when it was still widely assumed that there was some crucial kind of "vital spirit" or "vital spark" differentiating living matter from inert matter, and it is the non-existence of that independent spark of life that the microbiologist is really proclaiming. Nowadays, of course (whether we believe it or not) we are well used to the notion that life is merely a complex chemical phenomenon without any quasi-magical vitalistic supplement, and that the judgment in question applies to us as well as to single-celled creatures of various sorts.

[108] The term *bâtonnets*, which I have translated literally as "rods," is nowadays applied to rod-like bacteria, but the microscopes of 1900 had considerable difficulty distinguishing bacteria. The objects seen in blood to which the speaker is referring, as he implies himself, are more likely to have been blood cells and platelets (and are highly unlikely to have been dividing at all).

211

bes, infinitely small creatures, are incessantly dividing and being born, infinitely. They are what were once called, without really knowing what was meant, *hematics* and *leucocytes*. Are they alive? There's good reason to think not.

"And the gelatinous bodies, that entire immense family of rotifers, representing the third order of the class of *Rotators*, which you allow to become desiccated inert and dead in the dust on some staple at the bottom of your drawer, and which your great-grand-nephews will be able to reanimate centuries later and bring back to *apparent* life by moistening them—is that really life?"

"No, a thousand times no—life does not exist, and is only a deceptive myth, a charming but false illusion, at least among the lowest fauna on the scale of beings."

"But what, then, is that appearance of life?"

"Oh, it's quite simple, and brings us back as ever to the great unique motor of the universe—which is to say, electricity, in one of its three forms, which is heat. Now, all chemical reactions produce heat. When you watch, amazed, the infinite and infinitely rapid births of microbes and resurrections of rotifers, you aren't witnessing manifestations of animal life, but simply chemical reactions.

"No, my friends, once more, believe me…"

And in a grave and solemn voice that I did not recognize, suddenly transfigured by the superior faith in science, intangible and immortal when it is experimental and based on the certainty of observed facts, he slowly let fall these words: "*Life does not exist; only chemistry exists.*"

An involuntary frisson ran through the assembly and we all had the sensation that we were dead. Suddenly, however, his wife clapped him on the shoulder.

"It's nearly two o'clock in the morning; we have to go home."

"Is that life?"[109]

"I'm only talking about microbes, the infinitely small…"

"But not large animals," his wife interjected, with a burst of laughter—and the couple left, he grave and she the image of life, young and ardent.

We remained thoughtful for some time before our cold tea, murmuring mechanically, without understanding the fateful words: "Life doesn't exist; it's only a dream; chemistry alone is a fecund reality."

O science, that is surely one of your *coups de théâtre*, and yet it must be true, and my friend is quite right. Fortunately, we belong to the category of large animals, as my friend's wife said.

What, after all, do we possess? In any case, it's so short that the question isn't worth discussing, for, in the infinity of time and space, our life is as short as the *chemical manifestation* of a microbe. How, then, can we know whether life is a myth or a reality?

---

[109] This is one of the points at which the text seems slightly confused, perhaps because at least one line, and possibly more, has been omitted by the printer.

The Art of Dressing Oneself with Clouds

An azure-colored mantle.
Hydrogen coats and oxygen trousers. Electric hats.
Solidified gases. Curious applications of toilette.

For a long time—since childhood, in fact—I was always surprised to read or hear that God appeared to Adam and Eve or Moses dressed in clouds, and all the fairy tales of the Middle Ages seemed hyperbolic when they represented fairies in beautiful azure robes.

I confess, to my shame, that I didn't understand very well.

As I grew up, however, I leaned that we are able to see, or at least conceive of, all substances in three states: solid, liquid and gas. Theoretically, the good Lord's robe of clouds and the azure mantles of fairies began to appear slightly less exaggerated to me.

Finally, the Eiffel Tower arrived, then the experiments of Cailletet,[110] who, with his long tubes and high atmospheric pressures, succeeded in liquefying gases. This time I understood entirely, and resolved firmly to take another look at the problem, for my own benefit. With the obstinacy of a Breton—I was born in Paris, near the Louvre and the Palais-Royal, not far from the Gare Montparnasse, which leads to Brittany, which is therefore its suburb—I told myself that I would succeed in solidifying gases, and, in consequence, dressing myself like God the Father and the fairies.

Determination was not sufficient, though; I needed to find a practical means of getting there, and it was with the

---

[110] Louis-Paul Cailletet (1832-1913) was one of two physicists who succeeded independently in liquefying oxygen in 1877 (the other was Raoul Pictet).

discovery, or rather the invention, of my monster cannon on hydraulic rails, with a tunnel several kilometers long, through a mountain, serving as a barrel, that I contrived the practical application of my idea.

Before firing a shot to set my cart in motion with vertiginous rapidity, I blocked the opening of the exit with an enormous screw-threaded and armored disk and filled he tunnel with some sort of gas.

The first few times, I said to myself: "I'm going to blow up the mountain under force of the pressure," but bah!—my tunnel-cannon was well-constructed, as I've explained in a special chapter, and perfectly resistant to everything.

Then, I only had to unscrew the disk at the opening to find behind it, in a beautifully thick solid layer, the different gases that I had submitted to that preparatory system. Thus, the coat that I am wearing is made of woven hydrogen, perfectly dry, clean and flexible; my trousers are made of oxygen, sewn by machine; and my waistcoat is made of nitrogen, embroidered from the inside by means of a spindle. As for my wife's azure dress, it's made of watered and spun carbon dioxide, but won't asphyxiate anyone, nor even its wearer. To make the gases pass not merely into the liquid, but the solid state, it was sufficient to generate a high enough pressure, which, on this occasion, my cannon furnished victoriously.

I really ran into trouble, though, when I was stubborn enough to try to make myself a hat out of electricity. That was hard, but I succeeded all the same, and this is how I went about it:

I began, one stormy evening, by filling my cannon with compressed nitrogen, with the aid of a powerful mechanical pump, like those producing compressed air for tramways, after which I gradually removed the oxygen by means of chemical reactions that it would take too long to explain here in detail, with the result that my tunnel-cannon was no longer filled by anything but electricity As that was almost a vacuum, I loaded it fully, and finally found, as thick as a Breton housewife's buckwheat pancake, a great roundel of the celebrated fluid, finally solidified. Here, look at it and touch it, see how admirably soft and supple it is. Well, my hat puts all the panamas in the world in the shade, for it's made of braided electricity!

This walking-stick is simply made of hydrocarbon, which is neither the cousin nor the neighbor of diamond. As for my gloves, they're much rarer, for I made them with a little-known atmospheric gas, argon, and I was only able to make them because my hand isn't very large. I would never have found the material necessary for the gross and heavy hand of an Auvergnat.

I know that my discovery is not yet known, and will disconcert many people; it is, however, curious and real—and how singular! Thus, last summer, one of my friends, whom I had dressed in this fashion, visited my power station; he was clumsy enough to bring the tip of his umbrella into contact with a dynamo, and was immediately surrounded by a thick cloud. We thought he had been killed and rushed to his aid; there was absolutely nothing wrong with him, but the electricity had returned all the substances to a gaseous state, and when the cloud dispersed he was as naked as a worm, which was a considerable temporary inconvenience.

It is evident that a similar accident might happen to you in stormy weather, if lightning struck you, or fell nearby, but that is so rare, and it is, on the other hand, so nice to dress like God and the fairies.

Now, for incredulous individuals, I am at their disposal in the boutique that I have just opened at the Exposition, near the Château d'Eau[111]—but I ought to warn them that, until further notice, the solidification and weaving of gases is very expensive; I can't deliver a pair of trousers in woven oxygen for less than thirty thousand francs, or a chiné[112] nitrogen coat for less than sixty thousand.

---

[111] The author inserts a footnote: "Since the closing of the Exposition, I have moved my shop next door to my factory in the Rue Mouffetard, for the sake of economy."

[112] Chiné is a fabric, but the word's literal meaning is "clouded."

However, I sell hand-stitched Robespierre waistcoats in potassium picrate[113] cheaply, at only fifteen thousand francs.

Think about it!

---

[113] Picrates explode when struck.

Metempsychosis

An irrefutable demonstration.
Olympe Audouard and the horse that could write.
Amazing experiments.

Thirty years ago, before and after the war, I was well-acquainted with an exceptionally charming and kind woman of letters, Olympe Audouard.[114] We met at Dentu's, if I remember correctly, where I had gone to settle an old account relating to *Edmond Reille*, my father's first book, which first appeared in 1856—not exactly yesterday.

Young in appearance, with the visible residue of an incontestable beauty, Olympe Audouard—who ran *Le Papillon* from a little ground-floor entresol in the Rue Saint-Roch, if my memory can be trusted—was in the second half of her life. She was always sad, and had thrown herself body and soul, with the unreflective and spontaneous fervor of a woman, into the study of the occult sciences and he brutalizing commerce of table-turning.

Why had that beautiful intelligence sunk so low? Because the poor woman had lost—in Marseilles, I think—her only child of ten or twelve, and had never been reconciled to it. After that cruel separation, she only had one goal: to enter into communication with her child and to know the whereabouts of his soul, and even his entire personality. She had consulted all the somnambulists in France and caused large quan-

---

[114] Olympe Audouard (1832-1890) was a successful writer and editor, who founded the *Revue cosmopolite* as well as the humorously-inclined *Le Papillon*. Only one of her numerous books touches on the occult, but she was and still is famous for her pioneering militant feminism—an aspect of her achievement that Vibert (whose strident egalitarianism does not seem to extend to women) fails to mention.

tities of tables to turn, but until then, her son had never made any response. Meanwhile, time was passing.

As she spoke to me often about her preoccupations and hopes, I always sought, with infinite precaution, to dissuade her, as one would have done for a sick mother or big sister.

"Shut up, shut up," she replied, suddenly nervous. "If I didn't believe profoundly in metempsychosis, if I didn't believe that I'd find my son again one day, I feel that I'd go mad." She began to weep silently, and then went on: "It's because I know that metempsychosis exists that I have more difficulty in entering into communication with him; otherwise, he'd be a pure spirit, and would have replied a long time ago, given my all-powerful will, through the intermediary of a table or a medium."

Then the conversation lapsed sadly, for I could hardly clarify that maternal anguish, that obstinate—and, in a sense, voluntary—blindness.

Soon, however, in circumstances as strange as they were unexpected, we were to have proof of the reality of metempsychosis, and that confirmation at least soothed the final years of her life.

Almost immediately after the war, Olympe Audouard numbered among her friends a Russian prince, a worthy fellow, very rich, but a gambler and card-player, who was bound to ruin himself before long at racecourses and casinos, not to mention the wings of small theaters, where he found pink and peevish little animals that cost him even more than horses. One day, he found himself three-quarters ruined, with considerable debts that he could not pay. A single word, and his family would have come to his aid, but a residue of shame prevented him from saying anything, and he calmly blew out his brains.

The stupid death of that worthy fellow, almost a child, hit Olympe very hard, and revived her maternal grief. So, as it was the beginning of summer she went to send a few months in the country, not to escape that grief but to nourish it at her ease.

219

"You'll come to see me, won't you?"

"Certainly."

And a fortnight later, at half past one Paris time, I disembarked at her house. She had rented a kind of old manor, flanked by a farm, which did not lack a certain cachet, and which, with its large graveled courtyard and its green lawns, was genuinely lovely.

When I had given her the news from Paris, she said: "By the way, that poor prince, with his fatal passions and tragic death, must have passed into the body of a creature inferior to humans. You laugh, but I have an intuition and am certain of it. He's not like my poor soon, so noble and intelligent in spite of his youth…" And she lost herself in further reveries.

We ate lunch cheerfully, however, and during dessert she showed me he prince's last letter. It was a series of broad angular strokes, straight and emphatic, which would have revealed a plebeian origin had it not been a matter of a Russian prince.

"A nobleman of the Middles Ages," I said, laughing.

"That may be—but his handwriting is very curious…"

And we went out of the front door, to take coffee in the shade of the château, in front of the large graveled courtyard.

I was calmly smoking a cigar and she a Levantine cigarette, in the state of bliss that follows a good lunch, when a young colt, escaped from the farm, came toward us, gamboling like a kitten. The farmer's granddaughter ran after it to catch it by its halter, and as soon as she was within voice range she shouted: "Don't be afraid—he won't harm you. He's so cunning that he's coming to demand sugar from you, the brigand."

"Let him," said Olympe, very amused—and she held out a large sugar-lump, which the horse swallowed daintily. He came to me, and had another lump, and we were laughing heartily at the juvenile grace of the colt when, suddenly taking three steps back, it began to draw in the gravel with the hoof of its left foot.

That went on for a full minute, and all three of us, including the farm-girl, were astonished. Then he stopped and fled like an arrow in the direction of the farm.

We bounded to the streaks, and read quite clearly, in large angular letters, solid and emphatic: *Bonjour, Olympe.*

"The prince's writing!" we exclaimed, both at the same time.

"And the prince was left-handed, so the colt wrote it with his left foot. There's the proof of metempsychosis..." And she fainted into my arms.

The poor woman, afflicted with a cerebral fever, remained between life and death for three months, and during that interval the farmer sold the horse.

When she returned to life, that event, strangely enough, consoled poor Olympe Audouard somewhat. From that day on, she no longer had any doubt as to the fortunate fate of her son. As for me, that was the day when the grave question of metempsychosis began to interest me.

All in all, when one has been a Russian prince, it must be rather humiliating to pass into the body of a horse, even if it races and costs a million, like those for which Monsieur Edmond Blanc[115] pays so readily.

Poor Olympe, he would have forgiven her a great deal, for she loved him dearly.

---

[115] Edmond Blanc (1856-1920) was the foremost French owner and breeder of racehorses of his era; he founded Saint-Cloud racecourse.

The Conquest of the Void

Assault on the Himalayas. Getting rid of a balloon.
The victorious deep-sea diver.

People are always talking about the conquest of the air;
it's a bad joke, a noxious legend, which it's time to destroy.
It's really the conquest of the void that ought to be in question,
since everybody knows, the celebrated experiments of Gay-
Lussac notwithstanding,[116] that above 7000 meters—21,000
feet, if you prefer—one kicks the bucket for lack of breathable
air.

Humans have, until now, consoled themselves for the
fact that one cannot rise up to 8000 meters in the atmosphere,
or descend to the same depth in a watertight electric submarine vessel, but that one cannot explore the whole of the Earth
because it is too high, that one cannot even climb Mount
Everest, or Gauri-Sankar, at the summit of the Himalayan
chain, because it is 8840 meters high. One cannot breathe
there; blood comes out of one's ears and pores. That's simply
too *ridiculous*, as the Duchess d'Urzé said on learning of the
death of General Boulanger. I shan't mention the numerous
peaks that are between 7000 and 9000 meters—Chamalari, for
example—but it's certain that until now, nature seems to have
said to humans, with respect to the *abode of the snows*, as the
Indians say: you shall go no higher than 7000 meters and the
superior regions of the Himalayas will always remain mysterious and inviolate regions, so far as you are concerned.

---

[116] The physicist Joseph-Louis Gay-Lussac made a famous balloon
ascent in 1804 with Jean-Baptiste Biot, in order to measure the temperature and humidity of the atmosphere at various altitudes; they
succeeded in taking measurements all the way up to 6400 meters.

Oh yes, it's ridiculous, and even humiliating, for savant humankind.

In the meantime, a rich and powerful rajah of the region, who had heard talk of my work on electricity and the upper atmosphere, and who was no miser, appealed to me to solve the problem, offering me as much gold as I wished to find the answer. As you can imagine, I set off for India right away.

When I arrived in the foothills of the Himalayas, the rajah showed me, with a despairing gesture, a superb tethered balloon, which could not go up as high as it might because humans lose consciousness at an altitude of 7000 meters, if not 6000.

Without any hesitation, I replied: "Get rid of that balloon, my prince, give me unlimited credit, and in six months, we'll be organizing caravans with the agencies to the summit of Chamalari, 9000 meters above the Indian Ocean. It's as good as done...but let's not get ahead of ourselves."

The rajah was so content with this formal promise, however, that, knowing that I was from Paris and not Marseilles, he immediately put the sash of the Order of the Coral Elephant around my neck.

Still in a rush, utilizing a waterfall with a force of 11,731 horse-power, I established a powerful machine for storing ultra-compressed air in a valley at an altitude of 6800 meters, and I sent to Paris for an assortment of diving-suits of various sizes and models.

Once in possession of these vestments, as heavy as they were inelegant, I said to the rajah: "The problem is solved, my prince. Tomorrow we're going to swill champagne on the highest summit in the Himalayas, at 9000 meters."

He was bowled over, but bravely promised to go with me, along with his first minister, his silversmith, his favorite wife and three of his children.

On the morning of the next day, having slept in my compressed-air factory, which was fitted out like a palace, and to which one gained access by means of a funicular railway made of galvanized camel-skin—another of my inventions—

we each put on a diving-suit of the appropriate size, with a gutta-percha tube behind linked to the factory, which would furnish us with the air necessary to live at great heights. A telephonic wire also ran along the tube, linking our mouths to the factory.

Gravely, slowly and heavily, we set out, and began to climb the eternally white and previously inviolate summit.

At first, each thrust of the piston sending us air produced a certain trepidation, like the vent d'Autan[117] in Toulouse, but the favorite wife soon declared that it provoked a charming sensation, and we all started to laugh inside our mica helmets—mica being lighter, though less transparent, than glass. As we couldn't hear through the diving-suits, though, especially because of the lack of air in those high regions, we chatted by writing our impressions on the paper of our note-pads.

After a few hours of slow ascent, we reached half way; as I had lined the diving-suits with fur and herring-skin, no one as suffering from the cold.

Having made good use of our ice-axes, we reached the summit of Chamalari, and were able to swill champagne through an *ad hoc* tube.

A week later we recommenced the expedition, with numerous diving-suited porters, and when we arrived at the summit we built a vast wooden hall in a matter of hours, with all the cracks perfectly sealed, and a wide *ad hoc* tube coming from the factory. With a barometer attached to the wall to measure the pressure, we filled the room with air, which permitted us to take off our dining-suits and like down on the spot, having had a veritable feast and made the customary speeches.

The rajah wept with joy and pride for his reign, science, progress, his estates and his august family.

Today, the problem is solved. I have conquered—or, rather, vanquished—the void, which is better than conquering

---

[117] The *vent d'Autan*, a south or south-westerly wind affecting the south of France, is said to drive people mad.

the air. My deep-sea divers are in the process of establishing a funicular all the way to the summit, where I shall furnish several rooms with compressed air, and people will even be able to go there without diving-suits, in chambers of compressed air replacing the carriages of the funicular.

From up there, at an altitude of 9000 meters, on a sunny day, one enjoys a spectacle unique in all the world, and one is tranquil in the midst of the eternal snows; the silence there is absolute. It's very cold, though, and the sun is no brighter than here, the ambient atmosphere being in default as a transmitter. Curiously enough, it's like the so-called midnight sun of Lapland.

To conclude, I'm glad to inform my readers that I've already organized caravans from at a price of twenty thousand francs, one class only, there and back, starting from the foot of the obelisk in the Place de la Concorde, from the first of next year. People who want to travel directly will find tickets given them the right of ascent and three glasses of champagne, at a single price of 1000 francs, on sale every day at my compressed air factory. No reduction for military personnel!

Let no one be mistaken; it will be the fashionable excursion of tomorrow for truly chic people.

Fireworks

The trials and tribulations of an inventor. A strange concept,

An inventor among my friends has had the generosity for many years to keep me informed of his research projects, his endeavors and his experiments, and I think the time has come, with his permission, to impart them to my readers.

For a long time, he was haunted by the original idea of making fireworks in broad daylight: not luminous fireworks, like those fired in the evening—which would be absurd, since they would inevitably by eclipsed by the sunlight—but fireworks comprised of darkness and shadow, to slice through the light as classical fireworks slice through the night.

"I know," he told me, "that at first glance, the idea seems extravagant, and everyone that I have ever talked to about it has treated me as a madman, but I don't allow myself to be discouraged by so little. From the moment when it become possible to pierce the night with a thousand fires, a thousand lights, with the rockets and sunbursts of ordinary fireworks, it was possible to invert the proposition and pierce the midday sky with rockets, skybursts, flowers and decorative motifs made of night and darkness—which is to say, of shadow and blackness. Two facts led me to formulate this strange reasoning, and, if you'll permit it, I'll tell you about them."

"Please do."

"The first was, for me, a sudden revelation: I'm referring to the luminous fountains that date, as you know, from the great Exposition of 1889, at least in Paris. There, I observed the strange and truly marvelous phenomenon that each droplet of water, for an appreciable length of time, stored light and kept it captive, even as it fell back. That was the flash of enlightenment for me, and I said to myself: *since water is capable of storing light like that, I need to find another substance*

226

to retain and store night in the same way, darkness in broad
daylight, and the problem of my fireworks made of darkness at
noon is solved.

"Yes, but where and how was I to find that substance,
that liquid, or that gas? If it firmed a solid body, it would be
brightened itself at the surface, and my objective would not be
attained, while I dreamed of an immense bouquet of flowers of
darkness in the noonday sky, very black, standing out vigo-
rously in the atmosphere, and yet as if diaphanous, truly giving the impression of a bouquet of void....

"That void I have found—and it was your own works on
electricity only changing into light and heat in the environment of our atmosphere that were, for me, the second flash of
enlightenment...."

"You're very kind. You've found it, then?"

"Theoretically, yes. Given that light is only manifest in
our atmosphere, it was sufficient for me to find a means of
making void for all my bouquets, skybursts, rockets, mounted
pieces, and so on...and then I would have my fireworks of
darkness at noon. That would be wonderful...."

And, pursuing the vision he had glimpsed and caressed
or so many years into space, his eyes fixed, my poor inventor
was genuinely transfigured. I was simultaneously seized by
admiration and terror before the power of the idea, even
though it seemed extravagant to other people, and I felt something akin to remorse, and a great heartache, on thinking that
my own research on electricity, as the unique agent of the universe, had been the determining cause of his own experiments.

Suddenly, however, emerging from the ecstasy into
which he had plunged for a few moments, he let himself fall
back heavily into a squat armchair, exhausted and broken, his
convulsive face expressing the most horrible suffering, and,
thumping the table mightily with his fist, he cried out in a dull
and hoarse voice:

"Yes, certainly, I have it, I see it—the discovery unique
in all the world—but how can the void be enclosed as a drop

227

of water encloses light? Yes, in what can that void be enclosed and captured, rendering it obscure by isolating it from the ambient milieu that transforms electricity into light? You're right, though—the Röntgen rays are there to prove it. But the void escapes me; I can't domesticate it to my will. How can the pretty flowers of darkness that haunt my thoughts be rendered tangible and visible, as if palpable, to the eyes of everyone?"

That effort had worn him out. I made him take a cordial and tried to make him smoke a good cigar, to alter the course of his ideas; it was wasted effort, and my poor friend returned to his laboratory, his mind tormented by the incessant obsession of his discovery.

No matter; if, one day, he ever manages to give us fireworks made of darkness and shadow in the luminous and clear midday sky—nothing is impossible to science—I promise to let you know and to invite you all to the first great public performance.

Scientific Consequences of Röntgen Rays

I. Practical applications. Long-distance photography.
The marvelous probabilities of tomorrow
with regard to electricity.

Open letter to M. Edison, Commander of the New York
Legion of Honor, U.S.A.

Monsieur,

It is more than probable that you do not remember me, a
poor devil of a Parisian journalist; I have, however, had the
good fortune of meeting you several times, during our last
Exposition Universelle in 1889, and I retain the fondest memories of your face—a trifle fleshy, as befits a man and a Yankee of our age, but deliberate—and that is why I am taking the
great liberty today of writing to you directly, not to give you
advice—far from me to be so audacious—but simply to make
a humble request, in the name of the interests of science,
which we must both love with an equal passion, if not equal
good fortune with regard to my modest personality.

That said, I shall get to the point.

You cannot have failed to carry out numerous and various experiments with the famous Röntgen rays—X-rays, ca-
thode rays black light, as you please—and cannot have been
unaware, having taken immediate account of it with that
American eye which distinguishes your compatriots and is far
superior to that of an eagle, that you are in confrontation with
a purely electrical phenomenon: a new and certain manifestation of electricity.

So, since we are certainly in agreement on that point, and
I have no need to wait for a cablegram on your part to confirm
it, I shall continue with my demonstration.

Since light, heat and electricity are merely, at one and the
same time, a triple and unique phenomenon; since light is

merely tangible electricity and since electricity is merely invisible light—invisible, at least to our feeble organs—and since it has now been clearly demonstrated, thanks to Röntgen's admirable discovery, that one can obtain photographs with black or invisible light—which is to say, with electricity—do you not think that this suddenly raises up a vast field of research, doubtless hypothetical at first, but surely fecund thereafter, for the sagacious mind of an inventor like yourself? Do you not have the gift of double vision in the superior sense—which is to say, the almost divinatory power of foresight, of deducing rigorously the logical connections between facts, experiments and ideas.

Are you not strong, since success has given you a self-confidence that has nothing to do with pride when it rests on a past like yours, overflowing with glorious labor? Do me the honor, then, of bearing with me for five minutes, and I hope that I shall have the good fortune, however imperfect my language might be in expressing the highest hopes of science, to share with you those exact hopes, as well as my ideas.

Since light is unnecessary for photography, and Röntgen radiation—which is to say, an electric current of a particular and still ill-defined order—is sufficient, why do you not search for a means of taking photographs at a great distance, with the aid of the transmission of these mysterious rays, these currents which we employ today without knowing it?

Can you, the king of electricians, see yourself maneuvering your electro-photographic apparatus in New York and photographing, here in Paris, the President of the Republic, across the Atlantic Ocean.

What an inauguration and what a consecration! Immediately, I would demand for you the Cross of the *Grand Officier de la Légion d'honneur*, and I believe that you would have deserved it thoroughly.

Can you see the operator cabling the traditional *don't move* and pressing the switch or button, *snapping* his client at a distance of two thousand leagues?

Why not?

People will decry it as a dream, a utopia, a fantasy; let them say what they want, dear master, and search on, search forever—you have no lack of staying-power.

I shall go even further; I have the profound conviction that the discovery of Röntgen rays will lead, logically and inevitably, to that of long-distance photography, or electricity would no longer be electricity, and that is not possible.

And on this slope, sometimes deceptive but always consoling, which is leading us to the clear vision of victorious and liberating science, permit me not to stop again and to believe in the omnipotence of your tenacious genius in research, and let me hope that after having found he means of photographing individuals across the sea at 5000 leagues, you will also find them means of enabling us to see, of showing us their smiling and living faces.

Permit the belief that one day, you will finally be able to set us before the magic mirror and allow us to converse with our American brothers, whose tangible and real image will be reflected before our eyes.

Before realizing the second part of this program, however, try to realize the first—which is to say, long-distance photography, across the oceans. Either I am much mistaken, or the Röntgen rays ought, by logical deduction from the facts, lead you to the realization of that great scientific hypothesis; but I want to believe that this hypothesis will soon become, thanks to you, tomorrow's fecund reality, and that is why a modest economist is permitting himself to address this open letter to you.

If my belief in you is excessive, forgive me, for that is my excuse, and your self-respect ought not to be offended.

Yours, etc.

Author's note: Since this was written, my experiments with regard to Mars have victoriously demonstrated that these hopes will indeed be tomorrow's fecund reality.

II. A fantastic application. The electric soul. Why not?

I believe that I have explained abundantly here, and to some extent elsewhere in the press, over the last twenty-five years, that light, heat and electricity are a triple and unique phenomenon revealed in different forms, according to the milieu, the ambiances, in which it is required to manifest itself.

The Röntgen, X- or dark rays, the polarization of light, the luminous fountains whose droplets capture and store light, the aerophiles[118] that reveal to us the almost complete darkness at 70 degrees of frost at an altitude of 15,000 meters and prove to us that in the void of space there is neither light nor heat but only the dark and cold electric fluid, which only becomes warming and luminous on contact with air, appear to form a bundle of such striking proofs in favor of my theory that it seems to me to be absolutely needless to insist on it further.

Moreover, it's no longer general data about which I want to talk today, but about an entirely new and perhaps possible application of the marvelous discovery of Röntgen rays, which are surely a most palpable demonstration of the universal existence of electricity, as the unique agent of the universe and the absolute absence of tangible light and heat outside our atmosphere. And yet they exist, that light and that heat; they are transmitted to us by the sun, but invisible and impalpable, since, a few kilometers above our heads, there is darkness and intense cold—probably 282 degrees below zero, according to the most rigorous calculations.[119] We are, therefore, once more—as ever—confronted by electricity, and it is conclusively demonstrated this time that light, heat and electricity, in

---

[118] The French *aérophile* and the English "aerophile" were both used in the 19th century to signify a lover of ballooning, but Vibert seems to be using the word to refer to measuring devices rather than individuals, no human having got anywhere near an altitude of 15,000 meters in 1901.

[119] Vibert is presumably referring to "absolute zero", which is actually -273°C

our atmosphere, are merely three different manifestations of the same unique and mysterious fluid.

Thus, I had made my scientific calculations when I had the good fortune, a few months ago, of forming a close friendship with and illustrious scientist in the retinue of Li-Hung-Chang,[120] while the celebrated ambassador was in Paris.

Naturally, we touched, somewhat at hazard, on all sorts of subjects in our intimate conversations on what I shall call the transcendental philosophy of the sciences, and I had already had the opportunity to explain enthusiastically to the young but illustrious mandarin my theories of electricity as the unique agent of the universe, and tell him that electricity appeared to play a considerable role in epidemics, about its terrible influence on microbes, that a storm had been able to make cholera disappear from Paris as if by magic some fifty years before and that, finally, that even chemical reactions, which always produce heat, are probably electrical phenomena and that life itself—especially the infinitely small—seemed to be a series of chemical transformations operated under the influence of the currents of the mysterious and imponderable fluid.

At that time, I confess, I did not think that Monsieur Gréard[121] would give me full support and approve my theories so clearly at the Sorbonne, in the presence of the President of the Republic, by pronouncing the following words:

"Where untested and incomplete speculation once described the multiplicity and apparent incoherence of the phenomena of nature, modern science discovers a little more every day of the unity of the principle of life; it is heading toward those summits of which d'Alembert spoke, from which

---

[120] Li-Hung-Chang (Li Hong Zhang in modern orthography) was a leading statesman and diplomat of the Qing Empire. His reputation in China is equivocal, to say the least, as he lost all his military engagements with foreign powers and helped put a stop to the Boxer rebellion—for which reason he was and is far more highly esteemed in the West. He toured Europe and the USA in 1896.

[121] The famous educator Octave Gréard (1828-1904).

the universe would appear to humankind as a single point and a unique verity."

That is quite clear, and I shall refrain from adding a single word to the affirmation of the eminent Academician, for fear of weakening its impact with unnecessary commentary.

In our quotidian conversations, however, my Chinaman always came back to his unique preoccupation: the suppression of distance.

"Yes, we have the telegraph, the telephone, we have ships that travel much more rapidly, quadruple-expansion steam-engines, perhaps a direct road from Paris to Peking, across Europe and Asia, I hear, but the journey will still be long." And he added, sadly: "What point is there in deluding myself? Once I've gone, you won't ever come to see me in China."

"Perhaps," I told him.

"How?"

"It's quite simple. A week ago, we spent all day talking about Röntgen rays, didn't we?"

"Indeed."

"Well, given that those rays are certainly electrical…"

"Agreed."

"Perhaps they will succeed in discovering in the human brain that which we call the soul—the principle of intellectual life, which must also be a fluid, forming part of the great mysterious whole of the universe—and making contact with it. Are you following me?"

"Avidly."

"Suppose that we succeed, with the aid of Röntgen rays, is finally knowing what the soul is—the mind, the intellectual fluid of human beings. There is no reason why we cannot then succeed in its scientific domestication—if I might put it thus—and sending it wherever we wish, with the aid of transmitting wires."

"But then one would die."

"No, for the operation would take place very rapidly, and the suspension of life would be imperceptible; the heart wouldn't have time to stop."

"I no longer understand."

"That would be the rapid resolution—or, rather, the suppression—of journeys, since my soul could be in Peking instantly, in your family."

"How?"

"Suppose the achievement were realized; in consequence, agencies would be founded in all the great cities of the world for hiring bodies to souls wanting to travel rapidly. You want to arrive right away in Peking or Japan; you get in touch with an agency, and immediately, for a day, a week, a fortnight at the most, it puts your brain in communication with the brain of some poor devil in China or Japan by electric cable, and you immediately exchange your souls, you electrical fluids, and you enter into the body you have hired for a determined time. There are many poor people who would be happy to earn a living that way, by hiring out their body temporarily to lodge the soul of someone who needs to travel rapidly— without losing a minute, one may say—from one end of the world to the other."

"But if he's a drunkard he will damage my body in the interim."

"No, for very strict contracts will be signed; payment will only be made after each party has been reintegrated with his personal envelope. Then again, my dear chap, you can always have the individual lodged in your skin monitored; there would be expert surveys, if necessary, like those for apartments."

"Your idea is, in truth, very seductive."

"Isn't it?"

"But all the same, if you're young, handsome and distinguished, and your soul is lodged for a month in the skin of some street-porter, that would be disagreeable."

"It's a petty inconvenience, and one could always have a photograph of one's own body about one's person by way of compensation. You see, though, that when we are firmly convinced that our soul, our intelligence, is only a form of fluid—which we shall discovered with the aid of Röntgen rays—and that one can send it across the world by means of wires or electric cables, changing residences, which is to say bodies, at will, it's obvious that the question of distance will be suppressed and solved at the same time."

"But it will be very expensive."

"Why? There are so many idlers who would be happy to hire out their bodies in order to live and do nothing—and then there's competition, my dear chap."

"That's true—you've thought of everything." And the young Chinese mandarin fell into my arms, weeping with joy. "I'll tell the Emperor about your idea, when I return to China."

Since then I haven't heard any further mention of him. Is he an ingrate, or has he lost faith in my idea?

Author's note: We have seen that I was eventually victorious, and how I resolved the great problem practically by means of my "soul-ticket" system.

SCIENTIFIC APPLICATIONS

Modern Ballistics

I. A monster cannon. A new means of defense.
On the coasts and at the frontier.
A surprising discovery.

Every time there is a war on the surface of the globe which makes a noise and enthralls public opinion, you can be sure and certain that a quantity of more-or-less practical inventions will immediately surge forth, and even more chimerical projects.

Those who are unfortunately old enough to have witnessed the war of 1870 will remember how, every day, two or three inventors and fifty lunatics presented themselves at the Ministry of War in order to identify a means of immediately reducing the Prussians to dust. On an smaller scale, obviously—the war being distant and not affecting us directly—recent events in South Africa have produced the same effect, and I want to relate here a conversation I had with a very serious inventor who has submitted a new project for a monster cannon, which, I confess, I found very seductive.

After the preliminary compliments, my engineer-inventor continued in these terms:

"You're not up to date, you say, with the curious and complex problems of ballistics; permit me not to believe that—and in any case, your work in astronomy and cosmogony has prepared you admirably to listen to me and understand me…"

I only had to bow as a gesture of protest. He continued:

"You're not unaware that in recent years, without going back to the Greek kalends, ballistics as it has been understood since remotest antiquity no longer exists. That's easy to understand; take the slingshot of the primitive inhabitants of the Balearic Islands, the boomerang of the Australian savage—when there still were any—the ballista of the ancients and even flintlock rifles; there was nothing there but problems of ballistics, that's agreed. On the day, however, when rifled barrels, smokeless gunpowder and high explosives were invented, one after another, a host of new problems arose, of force, resistance, the expansion of gases, etc., which brought physics, chemistry and dynamics directly into play. Dynamite put cracks everywhere in its scientific domain, even the exact sciences sometimes being powerless to give us all the required formulae immediately."

"That's very true."

You see, don't you, that it will not be long, in the current state of science, before shells can no longer be loaded with explosives, in case they burst. I'm not concerned here with material considerations of enormous expense—for the cost of a cannon shot is insane—but the impossibility of going any further, of making larger machines that fire heavier loads over greater distances. The last word of modern artillery seems to have been said, for the time being."

"That's my opinion."

"Yes, but like any inventor, I was—and this will make you laugh—haunted by two ideas: firstly, of finding cannons much more murderous, for I think that's the best way of avoiding war…"

"How right you are, and how I share your opinion. The greatest philanthropist of all, who would merit a massive golden statue, would be the man who can find a means of annihilating an army in five minutes, for that would render war virtually impossible…"

"Obviously. My second idea was to serve my country usefully. Well, Monsieur, after long research, not only in ballistics but most of all in problems of motion and force, such as statics and dynamics, in association with physics and chemistry, display them to us, I have succeeded in inventing a cannon much more powerful than all known cannons, which can rain death upon an army or a fleet ten leagues out at sea.

"Then you've also obtained long ranges?"

"Yes, Monsieur."

"You can send a cannonball enclosing an enormous mass of dynamite or some other high explosive forty kilometers?"

"Ten thousand kilograms, if you wish."

"What is the length of your canon, then?"

"Between five hundred meters and twelve kilometers—it depends."

And as I started in surprise, looking at him in bewilderment, he slowly deposited his cigar in a little Japanese ash-tray and put his hand on the table.

"I'm not mad. Listen to me, and you'll understand. I've just told you, though, that it was necessary for me to find a means of vanquishing all the difficulties of force, resistance, gas expansion etc. Well, I shall construct my cannons in the Pyrenees, the Alps, and on the heights of Ingouville to defend Le Havre. First, I make a long tunnel under the mountain, directed toward the frontier or the sea; I line it with a triple layer of mortar and millstone grit, itself lined with strong hoops of cast steel, and in the interior, I place a series of enormous thick hoops, riveted and welded together, also in cast steel. That is my canon, and its strength of resistance is such that I can load it with any charge I wish. It can't explode, or the mountain would explode with it."

"I'm beginning to understand—but how do you launch the cannonball?"

"Pardon me; I no longer have a cannonball but a small cart which is closely fitted to the rifled tube, all the way through, with the exactitude of a clockwork mechanism."

"But how can you obtain enough velocity without heating up your cannonball-cart in its long trajectory through your cannon—five hundred meters to twelve kilometers, you say?"

"It's quite simple. You're familiar with the principle of the hydraulic railway train, moved along the rails by water; its theoretical velocity is almost unlimited, because the force of resistance is almost nullified. Well, my cart is based on that principle, except that I shall replace the water with refined neatsfoot oil, and with my charge I thus obtain an enormous velocity and force, since, as I have had the honor of telling you, I can launch ten thousand kilograms of high explosive forty kilometers out to sea, from Le Havre, for instance."

"That's admirable."

"Wait—that's not all. To increase the velocity and initial force of my projectile further, to diminish the resistance in the barrel of my monster cannon, I create a vacuum by means of very powerful machines, the tube being sealed—and it opens automatically at the moment when the shot is fired. I believe I've thought of everything, you see, inasmuch as is humanly possible. I shall attempt to improve it even further."

"And you expect to build many of these?"

"I'd like to begin with our great ports."

"An excellent idea—but what do you think each cannon shot will cost?"

"That depends on the length of the installation. Let's say, if you wish, in round figures, between 325,000 and 775,000 francs."

And as I seemed a trifle alarmed, my knowledgeable and amiable inventor judiciously made the remark that one must never be niggardly in matters of national defense.

II. The Klondyke.
A practical means of sending supplies by means of artillery. A marvelous application of ballistics.

On Monday March 28, 1898—let's be precise—all the newspapers published the following fallacious information without turning a hair:

"Yesterday, at midnight, the members of the Varicle[122] expedition left for America from the Gare Saint-Lazare by the transatlantic train, bound for the Klondyke. Monsieur Varicle is taking an aerostat constructed by Monsieur Mallet,[123] which is named *Paris-Alaska*. The explorers will depart from Juneau for the mining center by means of this aerostat, which they can steer at will into the eye of the wind. They will send news by means of carrier pigeons that have been acclimated in Juneau for two months."

There is no need to add that these people were hoaxers, and that nothing more has been heard of them since.

Fortunately, I have had an infinitely simpler and more practical idea for renewing the supplies of the unfortunate gold-seekers, and as I'm not asking anyone for anything, I want to offer it to my contemporaries immediately.

Follow my reasoning carefully; it's as simple as any, and, I think, a work of genius.

From the port of Juneau, where on disembarks, to the center of the gold-bearing deposits of the Klondyke—which is to say, the very capital, Dawson City—is twenty or thirty days' march, depending on the weather. It's between six and seven degrees—let's say seven, if you want to be specific—which is only 175 ordinary leagues, which isn't a matter of drinking the sea, but only of sucking the ice, generally speaking—and crossing it!

On the other hand, it's necessary not to lose sight of the fact that there are always more than thirteen degrees Centigrade of frost in that Satanic region from the first of Septem-

---

[122] The leader of the "expedition" in question was, indeed, a dentist named Anthony Varicle, who really did make an (unsuccessful) attempt to use balloons to supply the Klondyke miners—but he did not set off from the Gare Saint-Lazare, being already resident in the Yukon.
[123] Maurice Mallet was one of the leading French airship-constructors; the company he founded in 1896 still exists, somewhat transfigured, as Zodiac Aerospace. He was not involved in Varicle's scheme.

ber to the thirty-first of May, when it's not even longer. In January 1896, for example, lovers of cold measured 56.5 degrees below zero—congratulations! We can, therefore, always count during those nine months of an average of more than twenty degrees of frost.

This is where I shall invoke the intervention of modern artillery.

First, I take long-range canons that kindly send their cannonballs four leagues, which is sixteen kilometers; then I load them—by the breech, naturally—replacing steel cannonballs with balls of butter, cheese, grease and lard, in the middle of which I have wrapped meat, wine and liqueurs, which are less apt to freeze at low temperatures. To avoid my cannonballs being broken as they fall, I enclose them in a lattice of galvanized iron wire, very neat and elegant, as one might say of a hairnet. Then, the point of arrival having been determined by tests, I have them received in vast *ad hoc* nets suspended above the ground on poles, and filled with bran, so that the balls of butter, grease, etc will be received very gently, as if in cotton, and won't break when they fall. In any case, the metallic lattice is there to prevent that. As the materials are not as heavy as steel cannonballs, it's certain that I shall gain more distance.

Finally in addition to these liquid and congealed materials, I shall have tins of conserves made in the form of conical bullets, and will thus easily send the majority of Potin's products.[124] That's clear, as an old communard said.

Now, I divide my 175 leagues by four and I find that I'll requires slightly more than 43 stations between Juneau and Dawson City to supply all of the Klondyke, for, as soon as a foodball falls into the bran, it will be resent to the next post by the cannon, and so on. At each station, it will be soaked in frozen seal-oil to avoid friction and heating.

---

[124] Félix Potin was France's largest mass-distribution retailer in the 1890s.

As you see, I've thought of all the most important points, but that's not all—and this is where I'm truly superior to Varicle, because I'm borrowing the practical element from his project.

Once again, follow my reasoning closely—it's marvelous.

At every station, I set up a tethered balloon at an altitude of five hundred meters, and I put my cannon, solidly, fixed, in the gondola of the balloon; then, at that elevation, the trajectory *falling* rather than *descending*—it's all there—I obtain double the distance, and I only need 22 stations to resupply the Klondyke at will, in the long interval of nine months of the year.

This time, I believe that my demonstration, entirely luminous, will have converted my contemporaries. I ask nothing for myself, but I think that a joint-stock company with a capital of 25 million could easily look it in the face and realize dividends of 17.75% from the first year onwards. It would be salvation for the unfortunate gold-seekers.

Oh, if, all the same, very modestly, I do ask something for myself I request the title of *benefactor of humankind*.

III. A Voyage to the Moon. An astronomer in a cassock. Childhood memories.

To Émile Zola
My dear colleague,
since you are a journalist,
My dear fellow-member,
since we both belong to the Societé des Gens de Lettres,
My dear friend,
since we both have the same ideas about justice,
My dear Master,
for I admire your courage and your great talent,

Last year, toward the end of July, the newspapers published the following note, in the wake of a communication by our excellent friend and collaborator Alexandre Geoffroy,[125] well known in the word of engraving for his erudition, as sure as it is varied:

"In the church at Médan, near Verneuil (Seine-et-Oise), there is a stone baptismal font, octagonal in form, on one side of which is engraved a long inscription in French verse, containing the complete history, not only of the vessel that bears it, but also the church in which it is now set. The font, which, judging by the design of the moldings with which it is decorated, appears to date from the thirteenth century, originally belonged to the church of St. Paul in Paris, from which it was transported to Médan in 1494 by Henri Perdrier, the lord of the manor and founder of the church. That is what the inscription tells us.

"Here is the text, as reproduced by our colleague Alexandre Geoffroy:[126]

> At this font were once baptized
> Numerous dukes and kings,
> Princes, Comtes, Barons, Prelates
> And other men of all estates;
> And in order that it should be known
> They made use of it in the royal
> Parish of St. Paul in Paris,
> Where kings once resided;
> Among other honorably baptized
> Herein were notably
> The wise king Charles the Fifth
> And his son who came after him
> The beloved Charles the Wise
> Sixth of that calm name.

---

[125] The historian Charles-Alexandre Geoffroy de Grandmaison (1858-1931)

[126] The verse is, of course, in Medieval French; it is carefully rhymed, but its scansion is uncertain. As it is the meaning that is important (where it is clear—the chronological element is peculiar) I have made no attempt to reproduce the rhyme-scheme.

Now, was the aforesaid font
Transported, I declare,
By the lord of the manor in the fourth year
Called the fourth—fourteenth,
His soul in paradise reposed.
Henry Perdrier was his name.
God grant him grace.
Here the lord began,
After a short time
To rebuild this church
Which was in a poor state
Such, that, as I hear,
It was nearly a hundred years
Since mass had been sung in it
So poorly was it attended
Now it is so well-procured
That it has a parish priest
And a large flock.
God multiplies its wealth
And we must say our prayers
That Perdriers and Perdrières,
To Paradise, free of cares
Might go—and me too!

Well, as the little village of Médan is the very one where
you have spent your holidays since the war, and as I spent the
first fifteen years of my childhood in Verneuil-sur-Seine, in
the beautiful canton of Poissy, where there is another marvelous church, certain details of which date back to St. Louis, I
resolved today to distract you from the melancholies of exile
by telling you about an eccentric who lived in the village some
thirty-five or thirty-six years ago, under the Empire, exercising
there the modest profession of incumbent.

This worthy curé, tall, thin and sturdy, his beard and hair
a dull red-blond, was very poor, but proud in his poverty, with
a terrible accent. He was Alsatian, and never called my father

245

anything other than *Monsieur Vipère*—and he called me, familiarly, *Baul*.

One day, the local bigwigs, like Baroche, who was the Lord Chancellor and lived in Jusier, near Meulan, got the Empress to give him a cassock—but he was still just as poor.

It's true that the benefits weren't rich in Médan at that time, but this man, who was no one-sou fanatic, said his mass in front of a single choir-boy and had almost as much faith as us—which is to say, none at all—had a vice that swallowed up his meager emoluments. Yes, he was an astronomer, and his money went on buying instruments that were, alas, insufficient to extinguish his thirst for science.

He was crazy about the Moon; he loved it; he was scientifically enamored of it—and as I see that this love is shared by the great majority of Frenchmen, for every Sunday they do me the honor of listening to me passionately at La Bodinière when I talk about the lunar voyages of Cyrano de Bergerac or Edgar Poe's Dutch cobbler, I dare to hope that you would not want to make an exception of yourself by not sharing this universal sympathy for our genteel astral neighbor. Selenite studies are very much in fashion just now, at any rate, like those concerning the planet Mars.[127]

So, for years he had been calculating the effort necessary to overcome the resistance of the air and terrestrial attraction, and he had succeeded in discovering the exact formula for the cannon that he would need to send a cannonball to the moon.

His despair was in not having the money necessary to construct the cannon of his dreams—which were doubtless somewhat chimerical.

He said that by enclosing within a hollow cannonball another, similarly hollow cannonball, made of cast iron in order that it would not break on falling on the moon, one would be able to send a message to the inhabitants of the

---

[127] The author inserts a footnote: "The author will already have realized that this was written during the Dreyfus affair, when Zola was in London."

moon—if there are any— securely screwed within that central bullet, and thus provoke a response by the same means…all the more so because, on the Moon, the resistance of lunar attraction would be six times less to overcome. He had all the calculations to demonstrate how the lunar cannonball could return to us.

The poor man lived in his starry dream: a dream that filled his life. When he told me all about it for hours on end, when I was only ten years old—he liked *M. Baul Vipère* very much—I listened to him with a gentle a tender compassion, and it did not fail to charm my imagination.

In fact, was it as insane as all that? Recently, an English scientist determined that the Earth weighs 120 thousand trillion quintals, which would require a 10,000 horse-powers steam engine working for 70 billion years, which would consume 80,000 billion quintals of carbon, which would require 200 hundred billion wagons, to transport it. That's surely comparable to the equally ridiculous dream that amused the poor rural curé of establishing a postal service between the Earth and the moon with the aid of cannonballs.

And speaking of post, he received an astronomical journal, and for two or three months in succession, the post office made the mistake of sending it to my father, who received a great many periodicals. I ought to make honorable amends for my mischief; I had put all the numbers to one side and, the following year, on fixed days, with a new stamp stuck over the old one, I sent him his journal. The unfortunate fellow, so strong in astronomy—for he was truly outstanding on his favorite hobby-horse—was never able to understand why, for three months, his journal arrived exactly a year after it had been posted.

What was his name? I've forgotten. When did he die? I don't know. I've written several times to the mayor of Médan, enclosing return postage, but I'm still waiting, from which I conclude that the unfortunate mayor doesn't know how to read or write, even to spell out the manual of simple and honest civility.

But that's all right; the rude and unpolished face of that old Alsatian curé and passionate astronomer remains engraved on my memory, and I've often thought about him during melancholy moments of remembrance of early childhood.

So, when you return to Médan, my dear Master and friend, talk to the old folk then; it will amuse you, and they'll certainly be more loquacious than Monsieur le Maire.

Your very devoted,
Paul Vibert

P.S. At the last minute I received a belated letter from the mayor of Médan, which tells me that the brave Alsatian curé was named Maupert, that he stayed in Médan for twelve years and that he left in 1872 for Saint-Denis, where he has since died. That is the precision of my authentic story of the astronomer curé. Better late than never.

New Houses

I. When land becomes expensive. The telescopic house.
How necessity renders landlords ingenious.

All those who are familiar with New York and the famous southern sector of Manhattan Island, where the world of that most active of cities' commercial and financial dealings is concentrated, have conserved the intense visual image of its tall buildings.

Who does not remember the palatial Masonic Hall, so high and narrow that it is reminiscent of a vast red-brick column,[128] and that other palace with twenty stories, similarly in brick, but stouter, as vast as a citadel, which is simply the offices of the Equitable, one of the big U.S. life insurance companies, which has the particularity, interesting for us to know, that the director's son is the sponsor and organizer of French lecture-tours through the great Republic-when he has time!

So, it is difficult to construct more elevated buildings, and yet the land that is in short supply there is selling for as much as six thousand francs a square meter.

In Paris, where the City does not permit such high buildings, land sometimes sells for more than three thousand francs a square meter, and also has places where space is lacking, on the eve of the Exposition.

Well, to remedy this inconvenience, in Paris, London and New York, bold architects and engineers have thought of building fourteen-storey houses in Paris, seven above ground and seven below, and forty-story houses in New York, twenty above ground and twenty below. Given the present progress of science, nothing is simpler.

---

[128] The building is still there, at 71 West 23rd Street, but it no longer seems vast.

Thus, with respect to elevators, so costly to install, whether they be electric or hydraulic, everything is resolved with a simple system of counterweights, and when one goes up, the other goes down—it works automatically.

The question of lighting for the subterranean floors is entirely resolved with electricity, and even with acetylene. As for the view, I'm aware of the objection. It's simply a matter of combining the system of the *camera obscura* with that of the spy-holes found in all the windows of Belgian houses. All the way to the seventh underground floor, with a simple *ad hoc* reflector, everyone can see quite clearly what is happening, and who is passing by, in the street.

Now if this system, already put into practice a long time ago in the City of London for two subterranean floors, will be useful to landlords, it will be no less so to the public. Those who like noise, movement and dust will continue to live in the stories above ground, but the others—and they are numerous—will live on the lower floors: the amorous, young married couples, in order to spend their honeymoon in devout meditation, far from noise and the indiscreet and profane eyes of the indifferent; scientists and writers, in order to work without being incessantly disturbed. And these men of science and labor will have no need to consult their electric clocks or hear them chime; by darting a glance at the reflector they will see a swarm of joyful young women filling the street, laughing and chattering; they will even be able to press a button and hear them, with their microphones, and then they will say to themselves: why, it's midday, the time when the little seamstresses leave their workshops and go to lunch. Later, seeing the cafes fill up, they will say to themselves: why, it's absinthe time, six o'clock...and so on.

But that's not all. It's obvious that the system will also render the greatest service to physicians, always on the lookout to satisfy the latest fantasies of their patients. Those who desire a cure of air and natural light we go to live five or six stories above ground, but those who need calm and rest for their nerves—and they are numerous—will live seven floors underground; thus, both will be promptly put on their feet again.

I might be mistaken, but it seems to me that this system of housing, which I shall gladly call telescopic, half above and half below the ground, is bound to render great service to all classes of society.

"But," the enemies of all progress will say, "people will become anemic living underground like that."

To that it's easy to reply, firstly that those floors will always be inundated with light, thanks to an abundant distribution of electricity, and secondly, that there are many workers, busy individuals, in a great city like Paris or London, who only go home to sleep, and it won't make much difference to them.

"But what about Sunday?"

"Well, on Sunday, they can go out for a walk, and those who stay at home to rest will enjoy perfect tranquility.

Now, it's obvious that it's always necessary to be honest, and I'm in favor of telling the truth. Those who live on the fifth, sixth and seventh floors underground ought to go out go out occasionally, for I know an eccentric in London, a former champagne-merchant retired from business, who had kept his shop in the city near Pater Street, and who had his apartment there. He only had two underground floors, but it's only fair to add that he never went out. Well, after six months, as it was more-or-less poorly lit, his superb red hair and magnificent flavescent beard, under the inevitable influence of discoloration and anemia, had become reminiscent of *barbe de capucin*—the salad vegetable that's grown in barrels in cellars.[129] But he was an eccentric, and I persist in believing that fourteen-story houses, half of which are underground, will have a great and legitimate success during next year's Exposition Universelle.

---

[129] The vegetable thus forced is chicory.

Author's note: This chapter was, of course, written in 1899, and I ought to admit that, with their stick-in-the-mud attitude, my compatriots did not, alas, prove me right. But what do you expect? One day or another, it will become imperative, and it will probably be for the next exposition. It's necessary to console oneself for the indifference and ingratitude of one's contemporaries—but don't push me too far, or I'll take my invention abroad!

II. Houses in flesh and bone.
Jonah's whale and the elephant in the Place de la Bastille.
The influence of violet light on animals.
A new and curious application.

As the most idiotic legends of all cosmologies always had a rationale of some sort to begin with, I confess that in my youth the filthy adventure of Jonah—one of the twelve minor Jewish prophets, if I'm not mistaken—had the ability to interest me very keenly.

To me, with the evocative power of a childish imagination, it seemed that the more-or-less legendary story in question, which, it's said, dated back to the ninth century before Christ, happened only yesterday, and, while closing my eyes, I loved to relive in thought the time spent by that brave man in the stomach—for the belly seemed impossible to me—of the great marine mammal: the whale, to call it by its name. But that's enough; I'll go on.

Was he comfortable? Could he sit down? Didn't he feel ill? Could he breathe and see clearly through the esophageal tube? So many questions, which interested me keenly. It's true that, fundamentally, it was all very speculative and just for fun, for my parents had brought me up too well for me to believe in all that nonsense; but still, it was, for my young imagination, a motive for cerebral sport that was not without charm.

Later, I always regretted arriving in the world too late to have been able to see the great white(?) elephant of the Place de la Bastille. When it was demolished, thousands of rats emerged, which escaped and spread throughout Paris, which proves that it too was inhabited inside, just like Jonah's whale.

For a long time, all these ideas had been running confusedly around my brain, muffled by time, that great thinner, as Émile Girardin[130] said, if I'm not mistaken, when a series of discoveries, events or petty facts arrived to galvanize those old memories and give me hope that we might finally arrive at a solution and possess a house of flesh and bone.

The concept is audacious; can it be realized?

Now, quite sincerely, I'm beginning to believe so, although there's obviously a lot still to do in that regard.

It's quite evident that there can never be any question of possessing a vast apartment, but merely a small residence, warm and comfortable, since it will change location at will and humans will have thus resolved the problem of the portable house and outdone the snail and the whelk as well as the tortoise.

Anyway, listen to me for two minutes and you'll see whether my project can be easily realized. It's obvious that if I want to travel on land, I'll establish my little residence in the stomach of an elephant, where there is space, and not in the belly, which would be absurd, since there's nothing there but the interminable corridors of the intestines and bowels, while I'll establish it in the stomach of a whale if I want to undertake a sea voyage. In that case, I'd possess a little submarine of flesh and bone, just like good old Jonah—see the Bible, page, etc. It's as simple as that.

I hear the benevolent reader stopping me at this point with a triumphant and authoritarian gesture and saying to me: "Pardon me, I don't see how you will have the wherewithal to take up residence in these animals, even narrowly, especially if you have a family, with our wife and mother-in-law, not to mention the kids."

---

[130] The politician Émile Girardin (1802-1881); I can find no record of the quotation in question.

Don't be so impatient; I've resolved the difficulty, and it's exactly that of which I'm so proud. First of all, by way of preparation, I submit my young elephant, in a glass-stable, or my young whale, in a pool-aquarium, to the well-known influence of violent radiation, and after six months I possess a pachyderm or a whale five or six times as large as their ordinary peers, which will ensure that I immediately have in their stomach a small residence into which an entire family will fit comfortably. But I understand that it would be disagreeable to live and sleep all in the same room, and if you have a mother-in-law who absolutely has to have a drawing-room, I also have a solution for that—two equally elegant solutions, in fact.

I can revive the celebrated procedure of the king rat, the prosthetic graft, and in two elephants or whales together, and then, when the graft has been made, I only have to make a small communicating incision—and, as I have, of course, used animals subjected to the action of violet rays, I will then be in possession of a truly comfortable little apartment.

The second procedure is equally simple, for it even does away with the aforementioned prosthetic graft; it is sufficient to select from the animals the young phenomena, Siamese twins, in conventional parlance, that are occasionally encountered; then, communication via the membrane between the two stomachs is not difficult to establish, very reminiscent of the famous bellows that links the carriages of express trains.

Finally, for the benefit of ladies, I will say that all *eaux de toilette* and others will be naturally evacuated via the pylorus into the intestines—and that ingenious application of mains drainage even had the advantage of nourishing the animal, which no longer has any need to eat by means of its mouth, and thus leaves you a stomach that is free and tidy.

It is very easy to tame it by striking it, and it will let you enter and leave at will via the esophagus, by opening its pretty pink mouth, which is like the antechamber of your apartment, prior to the corridor of the esophagus. With the two united or Siamese animals you even have the possibility of having two entrances, one for the master and one for the servants! Isn't that practical and marvelous?

With the result that you can rapidly, without expense, in total security, in the warm and with no fear of draughts, travel the earth over land and sea.

That, then, is the house of flesh and bone of which I dream and which I am in the process of realizing. At this moment I am raising two Siamese-twin elephants in my stable-hothouse with violet glass. I hope that they will soon be half as large as Notre-Dame, or the Opéra. Then there will be room in their two stomachs, and before setting off to go around the world, I shall invite you to the inauguration, the ball and the house-warming party in by apartment of flesh and bone. To avoid crowding, though, especially in the corridor of the esophagus, I will invite you in series.

My elephants, well-dressed, will delicately seize my guests with their trunks and introduce them of their own accord into the antechamber—which is to say, into their pretty pink young pachydermal mouths, lit for the occasion by small electric lamps.

You will see that it's a charming effect; one might believe that one were in a fairy grotto made of coral.

Ladies who are afraid will remain at the door, and the elephant-houses will play dominoes with them.

Now, let anyone say that my idea is not a stroke of genius. Yes, let someone say that to my face.

As I'm generous and want to profit all rich people by researching a new means of locomotion, original and unpublished, I haven't taken out a patent. But I have a park of young Siamese-twin elephants in the Upper Ubangi, and an aquarium of young Siamese-twin whales in the Kerguelen Isles, and I am at the disposal of all persons who need information as to the price of purchase, the upkeep of the animals, etc., only too happy to have been able to create, invent, realize and—who knows?—perhaps one day to popularize and vulgarize, portative houses of flesh and bone that walk of their own accord.

You only have to ask!

255

The Danger of Certain Mineral Waters

A curious example. How an American woman was saved.

For she's made of stone
(popular song)

Two years ago, on returning from my electoral campaign in Algiers, as I was exhausted and dead on my feet, I decided to take a few days rest in the Midi, and one morning, in company with my wife, I visited the famous Pont du Gard.

By a happy chance, at the very foot of the celebrated Roman aqueduct, we had the good fortune to meet one of my old Yankee friends, who, knowing that I was in Africa, was tranquilly touring the Midi while awaiting my return to Paris.

After the initial effusions, we began a serious examination of the bridge and—something worthy of note—the dog from the nearby restaurant, without being invited and without knowing us, benevolently came to serve as our guide and show us the famous upper passage, with the sole objective of dragging us thereafter into his master's establishment.

I salute in passing the memory of that admirable-trained tracker dog, which lacked nothing but speech.

Thus, we had started out along the ancient superior channel, which gave passage to the waters and were remarking, with cries of both surprise and admiration, how the slow work of the waters had partly blocked and obstructed the large square channel, to the point of hardly leaving room for a man to pass, and how the deposits of phosphate stone,[131] a material

---

[131] In fact, and as the text subsequently confirms, the deposits that have almost completely blocked the channel in the uppermost of the Pont du Gard's three levels over the centuries are mostly calcium carbonate.

as geological as it was solid, had remained there, intact and indestructible, for many centuries.

My young American friend felt, scraped and even licked these sedimentary deposits with a sort of feverish precipitation, his eyes haggard, and we all stopped anxiously to stare at him, with the same thought: he's mad!

He was joking, to some extent. He was no longer paying attention to us. Suddenly, he stood up straight, radiant with joy, as if transfigured, and shouted in a fit of delirious satisfaction that is impossible to describe: "Saved! She's saved!"

And without saying any more, he ran like a madman down the little crumbling stone stairway that led to the famous aqueduct, at the risk of broken bones, and disappeared in the direction of the railway station, which was ten minutes away.

When we arrived at the aforementioned station, we learned that he had jumped on to a train that was just leaving, and had shouted to a porter: "Tell my friends that I'm going straight back to America and that I'll write to them from New York."

It was Wednesday; I thought that he would be unable to leave from Le Havre until Saturday, unless he went via England—but that would not have gained him much time, and I told myself that it would be a good three weeks, perhaps a month, to wait before having news of him.

What a cruel wait—as cruel as it as enigmatic! My young friend was thoughtful, serious and intelligent, and yet he had seemed to us to all to be quite mad during that unforgettable morning spent in the narrow channel of the Pont du Gard.

Finally, six days later, I received the following curious letter from him:

Milwaukee (Wisconsin)
U.S.A. June 13, 1898.
My dear friend,
Madame Vibert, on seeing me run to the Pont du Gard station, must have taken me for a madman. Fortunately, it was

not so—only that the sight of those deposits of chalk in the narrow channel of the Pont du Gard had been a sudden revelation for me.

You know that our water is often poor in the United States. We don't always have Chamberland filters to hand,[132] or the rubber is sometimes worn, and we drink water that contains a solution of calcareous matter in large concentration.

Now, you know my profound affection for my poor mother, who has been afflicted for many years by a mysterious and incurable malady that is manifest in intolerable stomach aches and, curiously, by an abnormal increase in weight entirely out of proportion to her modest plumpness. Can you imagine that my mother presently weighs 391 kilos—yes, you read that correctly; three hundred and ninety-one kilos, not counting fractions.

On seeing the calcareous deposits on the Pont du Gard I said to myself: "That's it! Thanks to our bad water, my mother must have stone—which is to say, calcareous deposits—lining her stomach and intestine." All the more so because I remember hearing her say on several occasions, while smiling sadly: "My dear Will, I have, as you say in that horrible Paris argot, a *wooden mouth*, although I haven't *eaten to much salmon*. I haven't been feasting at all."

Alas, it wasn't a wooden mouth but a stony one that she had.

Now that I know what's wrong with her, and I know why she is so heavy that she can no longer weak, or even stand up, I'm full of hope. I've spoken to the physicians about solvents, but they told me that the remedy was worse than the disease, producing ulcers, and for the moment we're sticking to methodical but violent massage, in the firm hope of succeeding in

---

[132] The microbiologist Charles Chamberland (1852-1908) invented a porcelain filter in 1884, sometimes co-credited to Louis Pasteur, whose pores were smaller than bacteria, and which could therefore filter infectious organisms out of water.

breaking up the layers of chalk lining the interior of her body, and ending up unblocking her digestive conduits entirely.

I'll keep you up to date.

>Yours,
>Will

I still remained quite perplexed, and anxious for my poor friend—and even more so for his mother—in the face of the announcement of this news and the strange malady. Seven more weeks had passed when I received the following missive:

Victory, my dear friend—my worthy mother is saved, cured, as alert and frisky as her daughters, and this is how: the expected break-up did not happen, and Röntgen rays had not revealed any cracks in the stone tubes inside her when I persuaded her, recently, to take a ride into the country in a large carriage, with my sisters, in order to distract her a little. On a hillside road, the horses became alarmed and bolted. My mother, my three sisters, Kate, Maud and Rita, whom you know well, the carriage, the two horses and the coachman tumbled down the slope from top to bottom.

What a mess, my friend! Kate had a broken leg, but it has been set, and my mother was saved—doubly saved. Can you imagine that, during her fall, all the calcareous substances that were obstructing her stomach and intestines were broken up, and with the aid of two or three good doses of medicine,[133] she had evacuated all the pieces in five days.

A week ago my mother still weight 397 kilos; today, she weighs 49.5—yes, you heard me right; less than a hundred

---

[133] At the end of the 19th century, the word "medicine" and its French equivalent were often used, much as "physick" had earlier been employed, as a euphemism for "laxative," laxatives being among the most popular quack medicines—perhaps the only ones, barring the placebo effect, that occasionally did more good than harm. They featured in a lot of jokes, tall stories and urban legends.

pounds. She is supple, agile, can ride a horse or a bicycle, and looks like her daughters' older sister.

Needless to say, we are eternally grateful to you and your wife, for it was you who revealed all to me, by showing me the calcareous deposits on the Pont du Gard. But what a curious malady, all the same, old chap—and how necessary it is to pay attention to the mineral waters that are mistakenly drunk across the United Sates.

> Ever yours,
> Will

I immediately cabled him:

Congratulations; we all embrace you effusively. Put groundsel cataplasms on Kate's leg. Your thanks ought to be addressed to the dog at the Pont du Gard restaurant, which was our cicerone, and I have passed them on by telephone.

Antique Pronunciation

I. How the Egyptians pronounced the letter u.
Ou as old as the world.
How the pyramids furnished me with irrefutable proof.

I was still very young when the Comte de Pistois, an old
friend of Balzac, Hetzel, the Comte de Grammont and the entire Republican Movement of the day, under the Empire, came
one day to introduce the Marquis de la Lance—who had just
published a sixty-copy edition of a fat volume entitled *Mes
petits papiers*—to my father.[134]

What became of writers like the Marquis de Belloy,[135]
and other secretaries of Balzac whom my father knew? I have
no idea. All dead, without a doubt, so long and short at the
same time is a period of thirty-five to forty years in this base
world.

Still, while yet a child, I read the various chapters of *Mes
petits papiers*, written in a somewhat disconnected fashion
with ken interest, and there was one in particular that made an
impact on my inquisitive mind, avid for learning—as one
sometimes is at ten years of age, when one has been brought
up in a purely intellectual environment.

*How was the letter u pronounced in antiquity, admitting
that it existed?* On that theme, passionate for a philologist, the

---

[134] The publisher P.-J. Hetzel was a well-known Republican, but the
reference to "the Comte" de Grammont is presumably to Henri Del-
mas de Grammont (1830-1892), mistakenly awarded the title by virtue of confusion with the 17th century Comte de Grammont whose
supposed memoires were written by Antoine Hamilton. The Comte
de Pistois and the Marquis de la Lance remain elusive, although there
is an Italian title Conde di Pistoia, whose name might be rendered in
the former style in French.

[135] The Marquis Auguste de Belloy (1815-1871) had, indeed, died
long before this story was written.

Marquis de la Lance had written a short but substantial essay, and, without bothering overmuch as to whether *U* really existed or not, after having noted that it was not officially introduced into typography until 1629, by the Strasbourg printer Zeitner,[136] he examined the old *v*-vowel and *v*-consonant of our Middle Ages and antiquity, and boldly concluded that antiquity had only ever known the pronunciation *ou*, and that *u* was, in consequence, quite recent, and did not, in fact, go back any further than the beginning of the seventeenth century.

Although some claim that the Greeks pronounced their *upsilon i*, like our *y*—the *i-grec*—many think that they pronounced it *ou*, like the Latins. Elsewhere, the Germans pronounce *ou*, the English *ou* and *iou*, so it seemed quite likely that *u* was a modern invention and very French.[137]

I confess that all this seemed curious and conclusive, and when, much later, I was able to establish myself that *ou* existed even in the Scandinavian countries, that it was never pronounced there in any other way than the Latin, and profound study had revealed to me that *ou* really was the only Latin pronunciation, according to the law of the twelve tables,[138] the case seemed to be made.

---

[136] The Strasbourg printer named Zeitner who invented the capital U and J in 1629 did so because he could not concern himself solely with Latin texts, in which they had previously been rendered I and V, being forced to contend with vernacular languages.

[137] It is worth noting that the contemporary controversy regarding the pronunciation of the Latin letter in question is reflected *en passant* in a mock-scholarly essay by Alphonse Allais' protégé Gabriel de Lautrec, which Lautrec reprinted in his collection *Poèmes en prose* (1898). A translation can be found in the Black Coat Press sampler of Lautrec's work, *The Vengeance of the Oval Portrait*, q.v. By "pronouncing *u*," as opposed to "pronouncing *ou*," Vibert is, of course, referring to the guttural pronunciation found in English words such as *but* and *gun*, as opposed to the pronunciation featured in *mute* and *dune*, so his comment about the German and English languages is disingenuous.

[138] *Lex Duodecimum Tabularum* was the founding document of Roman law.

I was still avid, however, to support my conviction with new proofs when the opportunity arose—but the current of life bore me away and I had not given the problem any thought for some time, when I has suddenly able, only a few years ago, to resolve it in an absolutely conclusive and definitive fashion.

The event was so unexpected and extraordinary, in certain respects, that I resolved to tell the story here, briefly.

All though overly dramatic from the political point of view, my journey to Algeria had given me a desire to spend some time in Egypt. I was finally able to do that, and the memory, still sharp, on my cousin Alphonse Hardon, the great engineer who actually built the Suez canal,[139] under de Lesseps' orders, caused me to be welcomed with open arms and opened all doors to me—even those most securely closed, including those to the great pyramids.

With great generosity, the Khedive advised me to dress as an Arab in order not to excites the susceptibilities—still a trifle fanatical—of the local inhabitants. He provided me with a reliable escort, drawn from among his own servants, and it was thus that I had the favor, unique in the world, not only of climbing the great pyramids but also of visiting the interior in detail, including the most insensate depths of that of Cheops.

It was there that I found, in the dust on the ground, human footprints several thousand years old, and I was able to collect enough grains of wheat dating back to the ancient kings of Memphis to sow a whole small field and eat excellent bread the following year. My only regret was not having been able to eat it with the arch-millenary mammonth-meat on the Siberian coast, as I have related in another chapter.

Soon, however, another discovery, more extraordinary still, brought my joy to its culmination—and truly, as I tell the story now, I remember as if I were there the hectic emotion that it caused me at the time.

---

[139] This is a trifle exaggerated; Alphonse Hardon did work for de Lesseps on the Suez canal, but his job was a routine matter of hiring of native laborers.

By means of a host of tortuous, bizarre, steep paths, which forced us to draw a map as we advanced into the entrails of the megalithic monster in order not to be lost forever, lacking air, stifling and badly lit, we had descended much lower than ground level inside the great pyramid of Cheops. My companions, visibly weary—as I was—were beginning to manifest sentiments of terror in spite of the Khedive's formal orders to protect me and follow me everywhere, even into the bosom of Hell.

Finally, we arrived at the bottom of a little circular room in the form of a cheese-cover, and in front of us, at our feet, on low pedestals of porphyry, were four sarcophagi: those of two important individuals and two children doubtless about ten years old.

I shall not go into detail regarding the religious precautions with which I opened the two larger ones, the first of which enclosed the mummy of a man and the other the mummy of a woman, whom I recognized immediately as a king and queen by the admirably conserved attributions painted on the sarcophagi.

When I opened the two small ones, with even more emotion, I found myself facing two superb mummies of ten-year-old girls—the royal couple's children—each holding in her arms...guess what? I'll give you any number...a superb Egyptian doll, as well-dressed as their little owners, in clothes that were doubtless very *passé*—no pun intended—but still intact.

It was the first time that anyone had made a similar discovery in an Egyptian tomb. Tears ran silently down my cheeks—tears of joy and amazement—and, in truth, the mean of my escort were as emotional as I was.

I stood there stupidly, dumbstruck, not daring to violate that youth interrupted by death thousands of years before, that infancy that I found frozen in its hieratic play. It was mad and sublime, and those two mummies of little girls made a much deeper impression on me than those of their parents, because, even seen through the profound darkness of time and space, the death of a child is always infinitely poignant.

How long did I stay like that? I have no idea. My men were no longer afraid, because, little by little, they had divined something of the sentiments, simultaneously tumultuous and superior, that had taken possession of my soul and which, in a certain measure—the measure of their restricted intellectual culture—they shared, so much does the grandeur of circumstance raise men up.

For myself, I no longer felt the choking atmosphere, nor the intense heat; I was dominated by a world of thoughts, which were all colliding with one another at the same time within my brain, and I scarcely suspected, as I stood dumbfounded before the sarcophagi of those two little queens, holding their cherished dolls in their mummified arms, that I was on the threshold of one of the most curious philological discoveries of the end of the last century....

II. How the Egyptians pronounced the letter u.
Ou as old as the world.
A stupefying demonstration.

After a long silence devoted to the quasi-religious contemplation of the children, I made an effort to pull myself together, as if I were demerging from a dream, and, slowly kneeling down beside the sarcophagus of one of the little princesses, with infinite precaution, I picked up the beautiful doll that she had been holding her arms, clutched to her heart for thousands of years, like a good mummy.

The doll was fully-dressed and well-conserved, with eyes of jade and precious stones replacing the enamel.

Suddenly, my inquisitive gaze was attracted by two little cords hanging down between the legs, and I had the sudden vision that I was confronted by an Egyptian doll that was designed to close its eyes at will, or to speak.

I examined the eyes attentively; they were fixed, but large beads of sweat were falling from my forehead on to its impassive face and, shaking off the multi-millenary dust, appeared to render it a life that it had never had, with a sort of enigmatic smile.

There was no more doubt about it; I really was holding a talking doll from the time of the Pharaohs, and I confess that I could hear the beating of my own heat, so intense was my poignant emotion becoming.

Finally, I slowly tugged on one of the cords, which seemed solid but somewhat frayed by time. It broke in my hand. I made a knot, but it broke again.

Having stood up again, I stayed there for some time with the doll in my hands, letting my tears flow—tears of blood and despair, this time.

My men, overwhelmed, dared not say a word. Finally, the very excess of despair provoked a salutary reaction; I was ashamed of my moment of weakness and, sitting down on a block of porphyry that separated the sarcophagi, I began slowly undressing the doll.

O prodigy! The fabric was not yet crumbling into lint, with the result that, after having taken off its dress and bouffant trousers, like those still worn by the Arab women of today, I discovered intact, high up between the legs, two little metal hooks—probably made of bronze or brass—which ought to have retained the two cords.

Without delay, I deposited my doll in the arms of its little mother and, seizing the hem of the burnoose sworn by one of my fellahs, I cut off a long strip with my knife, following the weave of the cloth.

I unpicked the weave feverishly, and rebraided the thread two or three times, in order to have two improvised strings, which I attached to the two little hooks.

My impatience was extreme; and, strangely enough—a mystery of the human heart—instead of pulling the string immediately, I dressed the doll with the same precaution as before. To act otherwise would have seemed both a violation and a profanation.

As I have already said, environments, circumstances and contacts sometimes abruptly elevate and develop the intelligence and hidden qualities of individuals. It must be said that the coarse and primitive men surrounding me were as keenly interested, as firmly gripped and almost as emotional as me, if that were possible.

Finally, I slowly pulled one of the strings, and—O miracle!—the doll spoke, and I heard, or thought I heard, in old Egyptian: *iri haru nofir*. Word for word, than means: *iri*, time, *haru*, day, *nofir*, good—which actually means: *have a nice day*, and corresponds roughly to our *bonjour*. But I pulled a second time, more slowly, and, forewarned, I distinctly heard: *iri harou nofir*.

What! The letter *u* already pronounced *ou*, in diphthong, among the Egyptians of Pharaonic times! But then, in that palpable testimony, I had a demonstration of the greatest philological discovery of modern times!

I was dazzled, I admit, and rapidly lifted my gourd of *eau-de-vie* to my lips to avoid falling ill in the sudden commotion.

With easily-understandable anxiety, I tugged the second string, and the doll responded clearly: *Anougit harou—k*, instead of *Anugit haru—k*. There was a hard *h* in the word *harou*, so the whole probably signifies, word for word: *Anougit*, rub, *harou—k*, your face, and seems to correspond to a primitive method of greeting, which was no longer in use, at least currently, in early Egypt. The constructor of the doll had thus tried to contrive something already archaic, in his own time, that form of greeting would have been easy to render and imitate. For myself, I only saw one thing, which was that, for the second time, the doll had revealed to me clearly that *u* was pronounced *ou* by the Egyptians, which I had never suspected, personally. This time, however, I was finally in possession of a material and indisputable proof.

In order that this story should not go on too long, I shall just say that I had the same difficulties and the same emotions with the doll of the second mummified little princess in the second sarcophagus, but that I succeeded in overcoming them with equal good fortune. This time, however, one of my companions, overcome by the passionate interest of the discovery, which he felt confusedly to be of capital importance, and who was *Hadj*, like all Arabs who have been to Mecca, plucked a piece of the camel-hair cord holding his turban around his head, which simplified my task considerably.

When I pulled the first cord thus reconstituted, the second doll said: *Ia atfou-I rempit nofrit*—which means *daddy*, or *father*, if you prefer—and not *Ia atfu-i*. When I pulled the second camel-hair cord, it responded *Ia maouit-i*—*mommy*, or *mother*—not *Ia maut-i* or *mut*. That, again, was clear and conclusive: the letter *u* had definitely been replaced by the diphthong *ou*. I was definitively enlightened, and thus, by the greatest stroke of luck, had just had the good fortune to settle once and for all a philological issue that has divided linguists into two camps for centuries.

As I was satisfied, I carefully reclosed the sarcophagi, after having replaced the two dolls, the unwitting clarifiers of a transhuman mystery of pronunciation, in the arms of their little princesses and owners, who had lain there for thousands of years in their eternal hieratic sleep. We all went out of the great pyramid, each of us lost, on his own account, in an abysm of reflections—for, without having understood the scientific aspect of my discovery, all my men had been struck and stirred by the truly tragic grandeur of that unforgettable scene.

Shortly afterwards, I hastened to draw up a report of the double exemplar, which I sent to the Khedive via my cousin, and also to the Académie des Inscriptions et Belles Lettres.

But hazard plays a large role in life, doesn't it? And that's why I've taken the trouble to relate here, simply and without embellishment, the various and sometimes poignant details of this discovery, of capital importance from the viewpoint of comparative philology.

Author's note: Later, I was to find another talking doll in another sarcophagus, this time talking Hebrew—which proves that it only goes back to the time of the captivity. On pulling the first string, it said Baroukh attar—bless you—*instead of*

Barukh atta, *and on pulling the second cord, it pronounced* Adounai Imma khem—the Lord be with you—*and not* Adonai Imma khem, *which victoriously corroborates my first discovery and demonstrates once more that the Hebrews, like the Egyptians, always pronounced ou, being ignorant of u. After that, it was only natural that Greek, Latin, Sanskrit and all the wrongly so-called Indo-European languages, which descend word-for-word from Hebrew, were ignorant of* u, *as my father and I had always argued, before the fortunate material demonstration that I had finally succeeded in making, as you have just seen.*

A Tragic Story

The anguish of oblivion. The obsession with survival.
The eternal dolor of creative impotence.

Recently, all the newspapers, under the heading of legal proceedings, recounted the story of a poor old painter who had bequeathed an income to his six mistresses, and everyone gloated over it.

For myself, I know of nothing more poignant than this story, and I was absolutely bowled over by it for an entire week. I will also quote the following passage from the *Aurore*, which clearly exposes the drama of the tormented soul in question:

"The painter Goubot,[140] who passed away one evening in 1897 in the middle of a theatrical performance in Liège, was said to have a tidy fortune, relatives—who were not visible in his paintings—and exactly half a dozen mistresses. He sometimes spaced out these *distractions*, but sometimes maintained two in parallel. He even had the whim, a few years ago, of having four of them in harness. He excused himself, moreover, in very civil terms, in his will—or rather wills, for he made five of them, but not in favor of his relatives; it's well-known that he couldn't abide them.

"Goubot did not hesitate. He disposed of his house and his movable property in favor, firstly, of the Oeuvre de l'hospitalité de nuit, the Societé philanthropique[141] and the City of Paris, then in favor of his mistresses. In 1892—the era

---

[140] Gallica currently produces only one reference to a painter named Goubot active in the relevant period, whose name was Claude, not Jean. How fast notoriety fades!

[141] Both of these charitable institutions had been founded in the 18th century; the former pioneered night shelters for the homeless.

of his luxurious four-in-hand—he wrote (these are the excuses mentioned above) after having mentioned the four beneficiaries in his will: 'Now, I beg these ladies to forgive me. This is my excuse: I always wanted a child. That's why I switched. My heart bid you adieu and wishes you good health and happiness. Don't be too angry with old Jean, who loved you. Give him your regrets. Farewell.'

"Death not arriving yet, Goubot took two more mistresses, and, of course, did not forget these latecomers in his subsequent dispositions. In 1894, therefore, he wrote: 'I give to the mesdames et mesdemoiselles whose names follow, the following sums, thanking them for their favors. None of them has been good enough to become my wife, and none is pregnant at this point in time. All have tried to tame me. Of them, however, I have only good memories, and wish to render their lives easier and avoid their falling into poverty:

"'To Madame A, Faubourg Saint-Martin, I leave an annual income of 500 francs.

"'To Madame B, Rue des Martyrs, an annual income of 1200 francs.

"'To Mademoiselle C, Rue de Dunkerque, an annual income of 800 francs.

"'To Mademoiselle D, Rue Dautancourt, an annual income of 1200 francs.

"'To Madame E, divorced, Faubourg Poissonnière, an annual income of 1000 francs.

"'Madame F, Rue Rochechouart, is to have an annual income of 500 francs, but without access to the capital; she is too stupid to hold on to it.

"'I beg these ladies and demoiselles to receive the expression of all my regrets at not having had children with them. That was what I always wanted. God has not granted my wishes.'

"Take note also of this clause in the artist's final will: 'As I desire that everyone should retain a good memory of me, I beg my executor to give all my tenants, *except for the coal-merchant*, six months free rent on my behalf.'"

Naturally, the Oeuvre de l'hospitalité de nuit, the Societé philanthropique and the city of Paris, on whom that man had heaped his benefits, attacked the will as immoral, but, quite rightly, the court upheld it, in view of the fact that it had been made in a spirit of benevolence.

All the petty chroniclers have embroidered the above, pouring out their joyous hearts, into pornography. Well, I tell them quite frankly that they are wrong, and have not understood the intimate drama that has ravaged the brain, the heart, the soul and the intelligence of this artist throughout his life.

Yes, he was a painter, but he wanted his name to survive him, and his work to be continued. He dreamed of a son greater and more powerful than himself, to carry forward the conquest of the ideal. And that dreamed-of child soon became the obsession of his entire life, of every minute of that life.

You can laugh and you can cry: "The man had a ball! He had six mistresses!" No, he didn't have a ball; for him, those women were only the instrument, the living mold into which he wanted to pour his image, to create a son, an heir, a successor, a continuer of his work. And he dream was always disappointed.

Well, short-sighted people, I do not hesitate to declare here that I take my hat off, respectfully, to the simple evocation of this lamentable memorial, this martyr soul, to the memory of a man who suffered so much and wept so frequently over his impotence all his life. Personally, I think that it is impossible to witness a spectacle more poignant, a calvary more dolorous, for can you not feel, as I do, that heart bleeding throughout its life and lamenting in the arid desert of impotence, death and oblivion?

Yesterday I read these emotional and true lines by Mirbeau, on the subject of *Fécondité*:

"He offers nature, not as a sacrifice but as a joy, the effort of his body and soul, lives, creates, acts, finally, in beauty and simplicity.... And that is the insemination of the earth and a woman; it is the harvest. It is nature increasingly submissive, sterility banished from the soil and humankind, and richness coming, flowing from the two primal sources, the fecund woman the virgin earth, in a communion of love..."[142]

I said to myself, it's fortunate that Goubot died two years ago, for if he had been given Zola's epic in honor of maternity and the fecund and triumphant family to read, it would have been a fate worse than death for him, a new cruel martyrdom...

That is why Émile Zola's work *Fécondité* is admirable and superhuman, why it is like the joyous *hosanna* of life, and the most eloquent appeal to the virile virtues that it is possible to address to a people on the brink of an abyss, who are going to die! That is also why, far from mocking, joking or sniggering stupidly at the dolorous life of Goubot, at the horrible and secret drama of his heart, at the long heartbreak of his soul, revealed to the world by his wills, I weep with him retrospectively and understand at a stroke all that he must have suffered.

That man a libertine? Get away—a lamentable victim of destiny, who had too much heart and honey, since he held his duty to humanity so high!

It does not astonish me that the snobs jeer and laugh; they are neither worthy nor capable of understanding that inextinguishable, insatiable and immortal thirst for paternity that make a man the equal of the gods!

---

[142] This (perfectly accurate) quotation is from Octave Mirbeau's rave review of Émile Zola's *Fécondité* (1899; tr. as *Fruitfulness*), which appeared in the November 29, 1899 issue of *L'Aurore*.

A Christmas Story

Christmas in Brittany. The Valley of Jehosophat.
Supreme coquetry.

As I do every year, I had gone to pass the second fortnight of December in Brittany, not far from Huelgoat and
Locmaria, at the home of my old childhood friend Baron de
Poullaouen,[143] who lived there in seclusion, in the old and
modest château, quasi-feudal but half-ruined, of his ancestors.

He had found a means of chipping away at his still-
adequate maternal inheritance by attempting to devote himself
to the exploitation of the local lead and silver mines, which
had become too poor and too waterlogged to be able to render
a profit, with the result that he became increasingly self-
absorbed was reputed in the region to be a great eccentric.

At the precise moment when I reached his house that
Christmas, about seven years ago he might have been thirty-
four or thirty-five years old. Tall, upright and well-built, with
an admirable fan-shaped black beard, he had the air of majesty
of an Assyrian emperor, and was genuinely very handsome—a
beauty that was both gentle and masculine, which subjugated
all those who were close to him. And yet, it was said in the
locality that he did not wish to marry, that he considered himself too poor to ask for the hand of a noble and rich daughter
of Brittany, and too proud to ask for any other. Then again, it
was known, or believed, that he had religious sentiments of an
exalted mysticism, and did not much like hunting and his
dogs.

It is true that the Montagnes Noires and the Monts
d'Arrée had no secrets for him, and that he waited impatiently

---

[143] There is a commune called Poullaouen in Finistère, in Brittany,
near to the other places named, but it never had a Baron.

for my arrival every winter in order to hunt the last few foxes and wild boars that were there, which might have be left over from the time of the Druids.

Thus, we were coming back, in very harsh weather—quite rare in Brittany—from a long hunting expedition, in pitch darkness, even though it was not yet six o'clock, on the twenty-fourth of December, firmly decided to have at the château, not a good Christmas but simply a good dinner.

We went back into the château, and after freshening up a little, we were comfortably installed at table beside an immense fireplace, in which enormous logs—Yule logs—were burning gaily, along with the village curé, who was still a good trencherman in spite of his sixty years, and two or three young sons of the neighboring chatelaines, all friends of the Baron de Poullaouen.

Needless to say, the meal was cheerful, and over coffee, while smoking a pipe or an excellent cigar, each of us undertook to tell a little Christmas story. In a land of tradition and religious superstition like Brittany, from Druid times to the present day, there has been no lack of Christmas stories, and any peasant will be able to tell you three or four, each more authentic and terrifying than the last—for there is no one like the inhabitants of that land of heightened religiosity for always seeing life in its most saddest and tragic aspects, both at the same time.

By degrees, as always happens between more or less learned men—and my friend was very learned—the conversation touched all subjects, and ended up becoming both mystical and metaphysical.

"Now," said the Baron de Poullaouen, who was somewhat overexcited, although he had drunk less than anyone else—but he was thinking of the anniversary of the death of his mother, who had left him, still young, ten year earlier, who had died on the twenty-third—"I don't ask for the opinion of my Parisian friend"—he pointed at me—"who is a miscreant, but yours, Abbé. Do you really believe in the general resurrection of all humankind at the end of time?"

"Well, since we are informed to that effect by holy scripture...."

"You're answering like a Norman, Abbé. Do you really believe it, in your heart and your conscience?"

"I do believe it."

"And you believe in the reunion of all humankind in the Valley of Jehosophat?"

"Certainly."

"But there won't be enough room on the banks of the Cedron to contain everyone, will there?"

"Perhaps it's figurative, and it would certainly be a miracle," the Abbé opined, with an appearance of conviction, "but I believe it, for it is a great consolation for we poor mortals to be able to tell ourselves that we shall be able to find there all those we have loved on this earth of tears..."

"That's exactly what I often tell myself," the Baron de Poullaouen replied, his eyes glued to the ceiling, in the vague and lost tone of a man pursuing a distant dream while wide awake...

"Come on, Abbé," I said, filling his glass to the brim with fine champagne—but as eleven o'clock chimed, the curé took his leave in order to supervise the preparations for midnight mass. The friends left, but, as it had been snowing for half an hour, the shivering Baron declared that he would not go to church but would stay by the fire to keep me company, while waiting the return of his servants—for whom he would provide the traditional Christmas goodwill offering of cooked meat washed down with a few mugs of cider.

And tranquilly, having taken up his pipe again, as I had mine, with his feet in front of a fine bright fire, while the snow was falling in gusts outside and our dogs, huddling around the ancestral andirons for warmth, offered their crouched backs as warm footstools, we continued the interrupted conversation.

"So, you heard the curé's opinion: he believes in a general resurrection in the Valley of Jehosophat."

"It's amusing—only, in order to recognize one another, it will be necessary to make sure one has all one's bits and pieces."

"You're always joking."

"Not at all—personally, I find it very poetic."

"That's a concession, but if one is resurrected, it will presumably be as one was at the moment of one's death?"

"Evidently."

"That's what I tell myself—so, when you have lost your wife, your lover or your fiancée in the full glow of her beauty, having died young, and if you meet her again, having died old, being ugly, shriveled and decrepit, she won't recognize you, and will turn away from you for all eternity..."

"It's probable."

The Baron went pale, becoming as white as a sheet—except that his eyes were shining feverishly.

Suddenly, I exclaimed: "You've been in love, then?"

"Yes," he murmured, "and my fiancée, a pure daughter of Armorica, as beautiful as the ancient Druid priestesses, with the hair and the golden sickle, was taken from me by the pitiless phthisis...."

I understood my friend's immense grief, and kept quiet—alas, that was and will be the eternal regret of my life...

"Yes," he murmured, in a whisper, "I will remain worthy of her"—and he fell back, collapsing in his armchair, his head slumped on his breast, as if lost in thought.

Suddenly, the bell in the village church of Poullaouen began to ring, just as half past midnight chimed on the large wall-cock in the dining-room—but the noise arrived muffled, as if from a great distance, through the thickly-falling snow.

Suddenly, at the same moment, as the sounds died away in the opaque space, a squall shook the entire château violently, causing the flame of the large lamp suspended above the old oak table to flicker, and even curving the flames in the hearth. The dogs, getting up on their forefeet, set back their heads and howled fatally, just as I saw the Baron de Poullaouen lift the stone of his ring swiftly to his lips...

I launched myself forwards.

Not a word, not a sign, not a movement; the poison in the ring was instantaneous.

My poor dear friend would finally be able meet his fiancée in all the glory of his incomparable statuesque beauty, in the Valley of Jehosophat, on the day of the Last Judgment.

And half an hour later, the old village curé came to say the prayers customary in Brittany over the body of a dead man.

"Well, Abbé," I said, with a sob in my voice, "we've killed him—you with your mysticism and I with my skepticism and joking,"

"That's true," murmured the poor old curé, weeping.

And involuntarily, but very quietly, I could not help thinking: *All the same, for a man in love, my poor friend had a hard comedown.*

Why People Go Mad

I. The imbroglio of the moment. Theaters and railways.
Why there are so many lunatics in the asylums.
The radical remedy.

Today I want to tell you the terrible story of one of my friends, a poor fellow who was interned last week—which is today, buried alive in a madhouse for good, which is a hundred times sadder than brutal death.

Never having left his province, which was in the median region of France, his schooling complete and finding himself an orphan in possession of a fairly tidy fortune, he decided to take up residence in Paris, to follow a course in diplomatic studies at the École and pursue research in the libraries on the inventor of the macaroni-mold, who was an Auvergnat, not an Italian. He saw that, rightly, as a patriotic goal, and expected to spend four or five years in Paris, waiting for and eventually reaching the age of thirty, when he would consider marrying.

His first visit was to me, and he found me in the process of writing my ninety-first article to prove to my stubborn contemporaries that the twentieth century would begin at midnight on the first of January 1900, the nineteenth expiring on the thirty-first of December 1899 and not on the first of January 1901, as a pack of cretinous poseurs claim, without knowing why.[144]

After have read my article he exclaimed: "But what you say here is obvious."

---

[144] As Vibert's delusion still seems to be common, it is probably worth reminding the reader that the contemporaries in question were absolutely right and presumably knew exactly why, being able to count.

"It is obvious...but that doesn't prevent it being necessary to write it, to demonstrate it to a mass of people who deny the daylight."

And he left, thoughtfully. The next day he came to see me again after coming out of the Institut, where he had heard a long and exhausting dissertation, badly read with a strong German or Alsatian accent on "Aberrations of the notion of time in the Middle Ages in the monastic mind"—which imagined that it was possible to stop its march by means of spells and incantations. He was so deep in thought that his state of mind was beginning to disturb me.

I did not know how to react, and he told me himself: "Fortunately, we're not so stupid today."

"Who knows?"

Seeing that this perfectly natural reaction on my part had disturbed him, I offered him a half-pint of beer—my means did not permit me to offer him a whole pint—and he left, telling me that he intended to spend the afternoon of the following day at the Théâtre-Français, at the performance of *Le Malade imaginaire ou la joie des médecins*, a well-known repertory piece.[145]

The day after the next, which was a Monday, he came into my apartment like a gust of wind and said: "A curious discovery, my dear chap—at home, morning finishes at noon, in accordance with the dictionary. Here, matinées[146] last until seven o'clock at night in the theaters every Sunday and Thursday, and I've been invited to *matinées* in society. How amusing that is."

"Yes," I said, mechanically—and I had no more news of him for three months.

One day, he wrote to me: "Come to see me, I'm laid up in bed, having received a sword-thrust in my ribs. I was in-

---

[145] Molière's farcical study of hypochondria.

[146] The French *matinée* means "morning," the deceptive theatrical meaning having been derived to distinguish early performances from evening performances.

vited to lunch by friends and arrived at four o'clock. They
were bad-tempered, having been drinking beer after coffee
while waiting for me. I timidly observed that, until seven in
the evening, morning had not yet elapsed. The husband, a colonel, told me that I was mocking him; it was necessary to
fight a duel. Does morning last until seven o'clock or not? I'm
perplexed."

I flew round to see him, cared for him, did my best to
console him, and made him understand that it was necessary
not to confuse theatrical *matinées* with astronomical ones.

Some time thereafter he was obliged to return to his homeland several times over, to see his sick mother, and when he
said to a railway employee: "I don't want to leave in the morning, but only in the evening," the employee replied: "Of
course—there's a train at one forty-five in the evening."

He arrived tranquilly at the station after spending the
evening with a friend, and there was no train. He quarreled
with the employees, who threw him out, and he came to wake
me up at three o'clock in the morning to ask my opinion of a
matter he could no longer understand, since for him, the evening began at six o'clock.

"No," I told him, "on the railways, evening begins at
noon, in broad daylight; you see, it's necessary not to confuse
railway time with astronomical time."

"Nor with theatrical time," he replied, bitterly, and left,
mortally saddened, to catch his train.

When he arrived, his mother was dead, and after having
buried her, the lawyer summoned him to hear his mother's
will read—she had left him her entire fortune—at *two p.m.*[147]

Two p.m.? Was that morning, afternoon or evening?
Yes, but was it morning as the theaters understand it, evening
as the railways understand it, or afternoon as the world under-
stands it—or might it be something else entirely? And he
emitted a burst of strident and terrible laughter, which made

---

[147] I have been obliged to improvise here, as there is no English
equivalent of the French *relevée*.

the lawyer and his clerks tremble, and cried: "That's clear! No notary—the monks of the Middle Ages were right; every day the theatres stop the progress of the sun, but the railways thumb their noses at them, at noon!"

He was mad—irremediably mad—and that's why I was obliged to take my poor friend to a asylum last week. And that, finally revealed, is the reason why there are so many madmen in lunatic asylums.

Is there a radical remedy for this lamentable state of affairs?

There are two.

Firstly, bring together all the theaters and railway companies, to figure out whether afternoon is still afternoon, or whether it ought to become morning for the convenience of the former or evening for the pleasure of the latter. They could easily come to an agreement and have morning A and morning B for the theaters, and evening A for the railways and evening B for everyone else.

Then, as it's quite certain, on his occasion, that the theaters and the railways are the only guilty parties, with their baroque manner of dividing time, force them to maintain the lunatic asylums at their expense. That would lighten the budget by as much.

Finally, the ministerial officers should be forced to pay for the poor lunatics to have treats every Sunday and Thursday, to teach them a lesson for having complicated the question with their *p.m.*s. All the more so as that is what caused my poor friend's cup— sorry, I mean brain—to overflow.

II. From Paris to the Antipodes.
The deepest artesian well in the world.
Is it necessary to go up or down? A cruel enigma.

Everyone knows the legendary story of the poor old scientist who, wanting to measure the time of vision, stood at his window, then went downstairs four at a time and went out into the street to see whether he could still see himself. He invented a rapid stairway, then slid down a pole like firemen, and was still disappointed in his calculations, for he never arrived quickly enough to see himself.

He wasted half his life in that sterile effort, and ended up dying utterly mad.

Well, the story I want to tell you today is even sadder and much stranger, for he adventure happened, not to one of my friends, but to a man in whom I ended up being very interested. The unfortunate lunatic was an erudite man, a scientist of the first rank in some disciplines, and utterly inoffensive, but he had the most curious kind of madness and the strangest to study: he belonged to the category of inventors.

Thus, one morning, let's say ten years ago, a man presented himself at my home and asked to see me. Let's say, for the sake of the story, that his name was Jean Dascare, with no *particule*, and say no more about it, for you'll understand the sense of delicacy with respect to his memory that forbids me to reveal his real name.

Not being a government minister, either past or future, being too Republican, I'm not in the habit of demanding that those who ask to see me make an appointment, I had him introduced immediately and the following brief dialogue was not long delayed in taking place between us:

"My God, Monsieur, I beg our pardon for introducing myself personally, but here's my card, and as I've heard talk of your father's and your own works and I know you don't believe at all in the Earth's central fire, and have always demonstrated conclusively that it could not exist, I've come both to submit my plan to you and ask your advice."

"It's true," I said, "that I don't believe in the possibility of the central fire; if it existed it would have blown us all up like rabbits a long time ago—or, rather, the Earth would no longer exist."

"Obviously."

"But go on—what's this about?"

"It's quite simple. We're at the end of 1889; the Exposition is about to close. I have eleven years before me. I want to prepare a very extraordinary attraction for the next Exposition, which will open the next century in 1900."

"A noble ambition!"

"Isn't it, Monsieur? I'm rich—I've earned a few million, thanks to my previous inventions—and I count on easily finding ten backers among my friends, and even among speculators enticed by my idea, by its boldness and novelty. In a word, I want to dig an artesian well, but a very deep one, which will traverse the Earth from one side to the other and terminate"—and the tapped my parquet with his foot—"down there, at the Antipodean island."

As one grows old one gets used to hearing and seeing all sorts of things, but I could not help starting in surprise.

"I see that you take me for a madman. I expected that."

"Not at all, but I confess that astonishment...."

"Let me continue. I've drawn up all my plans and estimates; from the moment you guarantee that there is no central fire, I'm sure of success. The well will be vast and broad, with a landing and a large hall every six hundred meters. A hydraulic apparatus will be installed in each of these halls to send an elevator down a further six hundred meters, and so on. It's as simple as day. The hole is circular, vast—no broken drills, as in the boring of artesian wells. I've taken all my measures, made all my calculations; we'll come out exactly on the Antipodean island south-west of New Zealand. It's only a question of time and money, and I swear to you that it will be ready by 1900."

He left, but came back to see me frequently, and that devil of a man was so convincing, so well-armed, from the scientific point of view, that he ended up extracting a promise from me that I would accept the honorary presidency of the enterprise.

Two years passed thus in preparations; he had a colossal factory installed at the gates of Paris, near the fortifications, and the work of *piercing the globe*, as he liked to call it, would soon beg. He was always inviting me to come along and strike the first ceremonious blow of the pick. Then, one morning, he came into my apartment like a gust of wind, his eyes bulging, and collapsed in an armchair.

"Oh, my friend, I'm ruined."

"How's that?"

"It's quite simple—your advice, quickly. I drill all the way to the center of the Earth, and we're still going down, and I can send down my hammer-drills at will, like hydraulic force, through pipes."

"Obviously."

"Yes, but afterwards, in the second part of the drilling toward the Antipodes, am I still going down?"

"No, you're going up again."

Then, exploding in a surge of despair: "That's what I've just told myself—but then my equipment is no longer going down; I'll need power-pumps, and I'll never obtain the necessary force."

"That's true—but pierce the well from the two ends; with your exact calculations, the two shafts will surely meet in the center of the Earth."

"Yes, but I don't have enough time. I'll never be able transport the equipment and install a factory on the Antipodean island." But, suddenly getting up, and striking his forehead like Galileo uttering *E pur si muovo!* he declared: "Yes, you're right, science backs you up, but I no longer understand. Listen, I want to *go down* to the Antipodes, I don't want to *go up*…to go up, when one is digging a well, although one's still going down…you're the one who's mad…you…"

"No, my poor friend, when one is traversing the Earth with a well, from the center onwards, one is going up."

He looked at me for a moment, giggling, his eyes haggard—and fled.

After that day he abandoned his factory, and spent his millions having demonstrative spheres constructed and perforated, in order to see whether he would be *going down* or *going up* in these miniature wells.

"But what about gravity?"

"In this case, gravity is meaningless. Why would there be any at the center?"

In the end, eight mortal years passed thus; then, suddenly, he had a glimmer of reason and came to find me to tell me that he had finally understood the cruel enigma, and that he would install a factory on the Antipodean island, as well as the one in Paris, in order to *go down* from both ends simultaneously.

"That's the practical solution," I told him.

"I know that, and when it's finished, I'll put a man at the center of the well and the Earth, to prove that he can't fall in either direction, which will be all the more convincing, as he's in empty space. Look, it's not us, my dear friend, but science that is mad. The problem is insoluble."

"A cruel enigma."

And he left. The next day, I received a letter from him informing me that, having lost eight years and not being able to be ready for 1900, in twenty-seven months, he was blowing his brains out, leaving it to someone else to find the solution.

And now, dear readers, that I have exposed the problem that cost that poor fellow his life, above all, don't try to tackle it yourselves. Don't ever think about it, for I wouldn't want to have another death on my conscience.

The Flowery Way

To replace the tunnel under and the bridge over the Channel.
A new means of crossing with dry feet. The Victoria regia.

Everyone knows that the English, in their timid and slightly puerile chauvinism, don't want to let us dig a tunnel under the Channel or erect a bridge above its waters—not even a boat-bridge—for they claim that they don't want to get angry about it.

Well, I—a modest economist—have the great pretention and legitimate pride of having found the solution, and being able to indicate the means of uniting ourselves with our good friends the English, of offering them a fraternal hand, without causing them the slightest umbrage—and that is what I have the honor of briefly setting before you. That said, I think it useless to insist on the eminently practical and civilizing side of my enterprise, which I will even permit myself to describe as august and serene.

Everyone who has traveled in South America is familiar with the *Victoria regia*,[148] a phenomenal plant found on the river Amazon, which belongs to the great family of *Nymphaeaceae*. Its leaves, pellate in form, rounded and flat like a table with raised borders, attain truly extraordinary dimensions, being several meters in diameter. Dark green above and reddish below, they are equipped with stout ribs that form a kind of framework, like a powerful bone-structure.

When they are still young, these leaves are rolled up and supported by thick peduncles, which are elongated according to the often-considerable depth of the waters in which the plant grows.

---

[148] The plant in question is now known as *Victoria amazonica.*

287

In reality, this plant is an immense nenuphar lily with co-lossal leaves and flowers. The latter are no less than thirty to thirty-five centimeters in diameter, with dark red sepals, white exterior petals diminishing in breadth toward the center and becoming carmine red. When they are in full bloom, the sta-mens are displayed in the center, where they form a lovely red and yellow crown.

These flowers only last for two or three days and only bloom at night, with the result that, in order to admire them, it is necessary to equip oneself with the red glass lanterns used by photographers, or their light and luminous friends the trop-ical fireflies, which are large flying insects as bright as ligh-thouses.

Their scent is that of magnolia and the fruits are very large; the plant sinks into the water to ripen its seeds.

Now you will understand why my system is not only practical but also full of a delicate attention for our excellent neighbors: the genus *Victoria*, created by Lindsay, has been dedicated to the queen of England. The *Victoria regia*, royal Victoria, had been named *Nymphaea Victoria* by the Danish botanist Schumacker,[149] but it is appropriate to conserve the former name, especially if I can obtain my concession.

At the present moment, this marvelous plant, which is no longer cultivated by the City of Paris's horticulturalist in the Parc des Princes, can easily be grown in a vast artificially-heated aquarium. It is sufficient to maintain the water in the basin at a temperature between twenty and thirty degrees cen-tigrade, according to the phase of the vegetation.

Now, for those who had not been to see the *Victoria re-gia* on the Amazon, its place of origin, or in the hothouses of some great lord, I will remind them that they have seen and admired it unwittingly at the *Nouveau Cirque*, in an aquatic

---

[149] I can find no evidence of this, or of any Danish botanist called Schumacker; John Lindsay's specimens had been provided by Robert Schomburgk, and it is possible that Vibert is misremembering what he had read.

ballet in which each of the leaves supported a pretty young dancer—but then they were made of zinc! The illusion was, however, complete. Nevertheless, the leaves were so vast that many spectators, without suspecting the fidelity of the reproduction, simply thought that they were in Marseilles!

Well, the matter now seems simple and luminous. From Calais to Dover, I sow, plant or transplant—that remains to be decided—seeds, roots or cuttings—that also remains to be decided—of *Victoria regia* in the bed of the Channel, in such a way as to have a beautiful double row of parallel leaves, two for pedestrians going to England and two or pedestrians returning to France. In order that the plant may live at its normal temperature, I warm the sea water at intervals by means of powerful electric heaters; it's as simple as that.

And in order not to cause umbrage to England, I establish a system that could scythe down all my leaves at a single stroke, the electric switch of which would always be in the hands of her most gracious majesty. It appears that she has, in any case, decided to set up a special corps of reapers, in case of diplomatic difficulties. So there is nothing to fear for modest Albion!

That's my plan; I think it's simply a stroke of genius. I've mentioned that the immense leaves, several meters n diameter, have raised borders. One will therefore be certain of never getting one's feet wet, which will permit the Prince of Wales to come and visit us frequently, in slippers.[150]

I might be mistaken, but it seems to me in this way, that I would have done much more for world peace than the Hague Conference.[151]

---

[150] The author inserts a footnote: "Thus far, alas, I do not know Edward's inclinations with regard to my project."

[151] The first Hague Peace Conference of 1899, summoned by Tsar Nicholas II and Queen Wilhelmina of the Netherlands, to which 26 nations sent delegates, inevitably foundered on the rock of irreconcilable international differences, thus setting a precedent that remains inviolate to this day, but it did establish the Hague Tribunal.

As soon as the trial run has been a great success—which is not in doubt—I expect to set up a company with a capital of 1,500 million, as for Panama, to install a road of flowers from Le Havre to New York, across the Atlantic Ocean.

What would be very expensive, I don't deny, would be to heat the ocean over such a great extent, but a crossing thus contrived would be charming, and would avoid sea-sickness. For good walkers it would be a delightful stroll, and for others, I've thought of everything. Firstly, at intervals, there would be vast hotel-café-restaurant ships anchored in place, in which one would find all the comfort desirable or drinking, sleeping, eating and relaxing. The final perfection—which seems to me to be destined for the greatest success—is that two rows of *Victoria regia* leaves will be covered with light battens, to permit cyclists to cross the Atlantic.

If this progresses as I have every reason to suppose, judging by the enthusiasm of the select few individuals who know about my projects, my first action, to inaugurate this highway, as magisterial as it is poetic, which will outshine the Milky Way itself in the imagination of feeble mortals, will be to organize an international cycle race from Le Havre to New York along my flowery track, my perfumed and intoxicating road across the ocean.

All right!

The Suppression of Train Stops in Big Cities

Circular moving stations. No more loss of time.
Future communications with the planets.

A long time has already passed since the Americans invented the excellent formula: *Time is Money*—and as more time passes, the more modern society is obliged to recognize that, in every country in the world, it is only too true.

You have trains today that travel, nominally, at a hundred or a hundred and twenty kilometers per hour; that's doubtless very nice, but as they lose an enormous amount of time stopping in stations and taking on heaps of more-or-less clumsy clients, the result is that one only travels, in effect, at half that speed—which is to say, at sixty kilometers per hour.

It is obvious that this custom, worthy of a festive tortoise, will become increasingly disastrous for people in a hurry, and that is why serious thought must be given to no longer stopping trains in stations, or, at least, only slowing them down to twenty kilometers per hour, which would already be a notable progress. Anyway, to explain the matter briefly, I have only to quote the following lines of Dr. Héricourt[152] on the new and ingenious application of moving walkways to railways. Fortunately, this is a doctor who doesn't waste his patients' time; with him, they wouldn't have time to get rheumatism.

"Five years ago, an engineer of bridges and highways, Monsieur J. Thévenet Le Boul, proposed and elegant, if not

---

[152] I cannot identify Dr. Héricourt any more accurately, nor the M. Perry subsequently cited, but Jean-Marie Thévenet Le Boul's idea of moving platforms was widely-reported and much-discussed at the time, although nothing came of it.

very practical, solution to this problem, consisting of making trains circulate continuously alongside rotating platforms.

"This system is essentially different from so-called rolling platforms, with which everyone is now familiar, having seen them in action at the Exposition. For such rolling walkways to achieve the velocity of railway trains would, in fact, require a series of successive walkways, which is economically inadmissible.

"In Monsieur Thévenet Le Boul's system, on the contrary, the trains are only accessible at determined stations, but they retain a constant speed that can be as high as twelve, fifteen or twenty kilometers per hour, and the travelers board it by means of a unique maneuver, simple and free of danger.

"This faculty of boarding a moving train is assured by rotating embarkation-decks formed by platforms propelled around their center by a movement such that the sped at their circumference is equal to that of the train, which passes around approximately three-quarters of their perimeter.

"The public board these platforms at the central region, whose speed is, of course, considerably reduced. If the radius of the central gap were, for example, four meters, and the total radius twenty meters, the train moving at twelve kilometers per hour, the travelers would only have to confront, at the center of the embarkation-deck, a velocity of 0.66 meters per second—which is to say, half walking speed.

"One sees, therefore, that a traveler, even if his use of his legs is slightly impaired, can easily get on to such a rotating platform and head toward the exterior edge, where he will then have a velocity equal to the train. He can then climb aboard the latter without experiencing any appreciable reaction, as easily as one moves long a compartment of a moving train.

"The descent from the train will be effected with the same facility, by the inverse maneuver, the traveler having at his disposal, to quit his compartment, all the time during which his carriage remains in contact with the platform of the station at which he wants to get off."

Monsieur Perry has conceived a more comfortable and practical plan:

"Of course, with trains composed of ordinary carriages, only able to follow very broad curves, platforms of small radius could not be used, and those envisaged by Monsieur Perry would be no less than 150 meters in diameter. To achieve a speed of 12.8 kilometers per hour at the open edge, the central stairway of such a platform would have to effect its revolution in 134 seconds. The time left for travelers to board or descend would be sixty seconds—a broadly sufficient time in these conditions—and prominently-placed indicator-boards would indicate the time still available for that operation: fifty, forty, thirty, twenty, ten seconds. At the signal zero a barrier would close the extremity of the corridor, the traveler would see the train draw away, and would wait for the next train. The train door could, in any case, be opened and closed automatically at the initial contact with the rotating platform and at the moment when the train quits it."

It is evident that with this further improved system it would soon be possible, by increasing the number and the successive speeds of the circular sections of the rotating platform, to embark at forty, fifty or perhaps even eighty kilometers per hour. That would be ideal.

In the future, however—distant, if you wish—I dare to hope for even better. As I have demonstrated a thousand times, it is certain that our planetary system, and the entire universe, is ruled and governed by a single force: electricity. Well, on the day when we have absolute mastery of the mysterious fluid, there is nothing to say that we will not be able to bring the planets—those that are our neighbors—closer together, and succeed in bringing them into virtual contact, at a distance of exactly one centimeter.

In order that there should be no friction or impact, the two planets that want to come together, brushing without colliding, would each have prepared a vast plain—an immense, perfectly flat hippodrome able to contain two or three million travelers and tourists—and at the moment when the two planetary hippodromes pass alongside one another the travelers would pass from one platform to the other. It would be as simple as daylight

"But you're forgetting that these planets move at three or four hundred thousand kilometers a second."

"I'm not forgetting anything; from the moment that they'll both have identical speeds, one won't feel a thing. It's the story of the candle whose flame is motionless in the most violent tempest, aboard the gondola of a free-moving balloon that is following the wind at a hundred kilometers an hour."

"That's true-but where will you find the station-maters and signalmen for these interplanetary pleasure-trips?"

"In our Observatories, of course; they will be put in communication by a serious transmitter cable with poles converted into immense domesticated dynamos. One flick of the manipulator's—or manometricist's, if you prefer—switch, and according to the impulsion of the fluids, the worlds will draw closer or further apart at will.

When the next voyage takes place, I intend to organize a performance by Sarah Bernhardt on the planet Mars; there'll be money to be made. But then, there's no time to lose—before she gets too old.

"Unless you can clap the two of them together."

"Don't discourage the tenacious researchers and audacious inventors like that!"

The Art of Killing People

Tomorrow's war. No noise and much light.
Toward universal peace by means of science.

Following in the noble tradition of my father, I have always energetically demanded the abolition of the death penalty, and I consider war as the most ignoble and cowardly of murders unless its sole objective is the defense of the borders of the soil of the fatherland.

That is why, every time someone tells me that a new, reliable, powerful and rapid means of killing men *en masse* has been discovered, I jump for joy.

That joy seems cruel and paradoxical to imbeciles, and yet, it is science alone that will one day triumph over the passions of headstrong tyrants, in rendering war impossible by virtue of the exorbitant power of its means of destruction. Whether one likes it or not, nothing is truer or more certain.

So, true or false, I am happy to acquaint my readers today with two new inventions in the art of killing the poor fellows whom the ambition or dementia of kings and emperors send to be butchered, with great efficiency.

The first of these inventions, which is no more than an improved catapult, and is somewhat reminiscent of the circular rotating platforms about which I talked in the last chapter, is designed to kill noiselessly. Unfortunately, it's American, like the second, and that's what makes me slightly suspicious.

In any case, here are the essential details, according to my colleague Gautier:[153]

"Imagine a large disk 1.56 meters in diameter, weighing 225 kilograms and rotating, under the action of an electric

---

[153] Presumably Émile Gautier, the editor of *La Science Française*, a diehard promoter and occasional writer of future war fiction.

motor, at the vertiginous speed of two hundred rotations per second. The projectiles are arranged, one after another, in a groove excavated in the perimeter of the disk and things are arranged in such a way that they can, at a given moment, be released automatically. Being no longer retained in any way, they would yield to centrifugal force, which would give them an initial velocity of 610 meters per second, with a range of over three kilometers.

"It is, as one can see, as simple as saying hello.

"This is not a new invention in the true sense of the word. It is, rather, an exhumation, a resurrection, and the holy King David would tell you that it was a machine of the same sort, although more rudimentary and on a smaller scale, that he employed, with the collaboration of the same centrifugal force, to relieve Goliath of his appetite for bread. The only essential difference is that, in Biblical times, it was called a sling.

"One could launch a projectile at each half-rotation of the disk, which is two projectiles per rotation: four hundred per second; *twenty four thousand a minute*. But the inventor is not as ambitious as that; he will be content with only one projectile every four rotations, which would still permit him to hurl upon the enemy in a single minute three thousand small explosive shells 7.5 centimeters in diameter and forty centimeters long—a veritable whirlwind of gunfire, a continuous rain of iron or steel.

"'But,' you might say, 'don't the Bange, Krupp, Armstrong, Canet, Schneider, Maxim and Hotchkiss cannons, etc., all those 'Long Toms' and 'pompoms' that are performing marvels in the Transvaal and in China, satisfy our present needs much better? What point is there in resuscitating these ridiculous machines that one had thought to be abandoned for good as old junk?'

"A complete error! Cannons of bronze or steel, whatever kind of explosive one employs to charge them, make a lot of noise—far too much noise. They are cumbersome, dangerous to handle, and excessively expensive into the bargain.

"With a rotatory catapult with an automatic release-mechanism, the projectile duly launched at the psychological moment will fly 'sweetly,' without shock, din or any noise at all, to fall on the backs of the enemy, who will have no suspicion of it until the downpour begins. Not to mention that you have a summary, rustic artillery exempt from recoil, presenting as small a vulnerable surface as possible, easy for any common-or-garden locksmith to set up effectively in a matter of hours, no matter where, able to go almost anywhere, over mountains and through valleys, to be mounted in a battery as easily at the summit of a steep crag or the steeple of a bell-tower as in the depths of a ravine or the roof of a house.

"Which cannot help but be rather interesting, and if the trials to which Monsieur James Judge's catapult have, it appears, already been submitted have really given the results that have been advertised, one wonders why John Bull has not already expedited a few dozen of these new engines to South Africa, where the need for something 'marvelous' is beginning to make itself felt.

"Ten years ago an American answering, if my memory serves me right, to the name of Hicks had already given birth—on paper, at least—to an analogous project. Our own Turpin, for his part, dreamed of a rotating artillery, silent and centrifugal, which he has been unable to perfect, although he has not yet definitively abandoned it. Finally, we have Monsieur Zalinski's pneumatic cannon, a kind of giant pea-shooter that sends enormous parcels of dynamite two or three thousand meters without shock or detonation."[154]

In fact, the worthy Turpin has talked to me about his projects of that sort, and I don't believe that he has abandoned it at all—on the contrary.

---

[154] I have not been able to find any further data on James Judge or Mr. Hicks, who are understandably immune to Google searches, but Eugène Turpin (1848-1927) remains famous and Edmund Zalinski (1849-1909) actually managed so set up the Pneumatic Dynamite Gun Company to manufacture and market his device, although not many were sold.

Now let us pass on to the second invention, similarly American. I mean the 'flash-bombs'[155] that are destined to complement the first very advantageously.

Here is the scant information that the journals specializing in the subject have given:

"The American navy, finding the electric searchlights employed by ships for nocturnal reconnaissance to be inadequate, have tried to supplement them with the employment of so-called flash-bombs. They are filled with a gas which catches fire when the bomb explodes and produces a very bright light, which illuminates a vast area. In recent experiments, cannons of ten to fifteen centimeters have been used to launch these flash-bombs, and the results have been excellent."

The American program thus appears clearly: to kill their adversaries without noise while inundating them with light so that they are dazzled. I will say that it is simple and in good taste, like everything that comes to us from the United States.

But that's not all, fortunately, and now that the way is open, one may hope that inventors will work wonders. Thus, one thing following another, there is already talk of improvements and new applications capable of astonishing the world.

With an easily-understandable humanitarian objective, whose lofty ambition will be obvious to everyone, an American dentist has proposed to load flash-bombs with nitrous oxide as well, in order that enemies can be illuminated, stupefied, put to sleep and killed painlessly. There, truly, is generosity.

A celebrated Portuguese engineer also proposes equipping flash-bombs with an exhilarating gas—because, he says, still with a superior humanitarian objective and to respond to

---

[155] I have translated *bombes d'éclairage* as "flash-bombs" to emphasize that the term "flares" had not yet been devised, although that is, of course, what is being described. Edward Wilson Very (1847-1910) was working for the U.S. Navy at the time on the development of his hand-held flare-gun.

the idea of Christian charity, he wants to make his enemies die laughing on the battlefield.

Finally, the last news I have is that one of the acolytes of Max Régis; in a truly nationalistic and patriotic spirit, has invented bombs full of itching powder. It's evident that, in combination with Drumont's hair-shirts, they could work marvels.

At any rate, all the scientist are working hard to render what impossible by virtue of the very power of its means of destruction, and that's why I believe that it will disappear one day, in spite of the ferocious passions of kings and emperors.

The Disappearance of a River

Everyone is asking where the Meuse has gone.
Fishy coal-heavers.
Terrible anguish in the kingdom of Belgium.

The fatherland of Cléo de Mérode[156] is literally in tears. It has suddenly lost its superb shared river. I say *shared* because it runs through both France and Belgium.

Thus, one fine day—which is a manner of speaking, because it was actually dull—the Meuse disappeared entirely in the vicinity of Liège, with all its inhabitants, or very nearly, known in the Belgian language as *poissons*.

Initially a trifle shocked by the news, the riverside burgomasters promised an honest recompense, and then a regal one, to anyone who could bring back, or at least provide news, of the vagabond river.

Bad jokers—who are found in all countries, even in Leopold's fatherland, you know—affirm that the Meuse, weary of lying in since the beginning of the world, had wanted, not to get out of, but to vanish from its bed. But the anxiety increased with every passing day; the anguish in Liège was horrible, and, as people were even beginning to talk about it here, from Asnières-les-Bains to Montrouge, I hastened to leap on a train in order to go to Liège to consult my friend, the celebrated Nautilus, the man most familiar with the secrets of the

---

[156] The famous dancer Cléo (i.e., Cleopatra) de Mérode was actually born in Paris to an Austrian father, but her family name was Belgian in origin, and she became permanently and disastrously linked with that country when King Leopold fell in love with her after seeing her dance in 1896, occasioning gossip that ruined her reputation (his was already irreparable).

300

Meuse, given that the rascal has been living with it on the most intimate terms for many years.

I had the right idea; I was awaiting my visit, and without hesitation, he replied to me incontinently with a little technico-lachrymose discourse that lasted three hours forty-seven minutes. As I had taken a phonograph with me, I shall make haste to transcribe the most salient passage here:

"Five years ago, some work on the port of Jemmeppe having been required, the harbor wall was raised by placing new coping-stones on top of the old ones. Presently, the last-placed ones are at flotation-level and need to be raised again next year.

"The port of Tilleur, which was constructed in 1883, will also have to be raised; the materials have been ordered and some have already been delivered.

Finally, which is more serious, the barrage at Jemmeppe has sunk between thirty or thirty-five centimeters. The result is highly prejudicial to navigation, for the purpose of the barrage is to keep the water at a certain level, so as to maintain it 2.10 meters above the sill of the lock at Chockier. The level can no longer be maintained and this year—which was, parenthetically, rather dry—boats loaded to 1.90 meters, the regulation load, are only able to go through the said lock with the greatest difficulty.

"Thus, between the eleventh and twelfth of September, the tug *Télémaque I*, hauling a train of four barges loaded to 1.80 meters, was held up for an entire day at Chockier. It was necessary to spend four hours casting off one of the barges that had stuck on the dill of the lock.

"On the second day, the twelfth of September, the tug *Ernest* was stuck there or a day with its train for the same reason. The Alliance I was held up there from four o'clock on the thirteenth until noon the following day.

"On the twenty-sixth of September, the *Ernest*, bringing three iron-boats upriver, the *Rodolphe*, the *Polua* and the *Trois Soeurs* from Disery were obliged to spend a day there, and on the eighth of October, the same tug, with another train, had to spend a day and a half there, always for the same causes: low water, boat resting on the sill, which they were unable to get over.

"On the other hand, on the seventh of September, Monsieur de Lamine's *Croix Rouge,* pulled by the *Alliance 3*, was beached in the cutting for more than two hours."

"Enough, enough," I said. "My brain's full."

But he still went on, and the phonograph recorded with deplorable stubbornness.

When he had finished, worn out, gesturing like a dying man, Nautilus virtually threw himself at my feet, moaning: "I beg you, my French colleague—Parisian, and therefore magnanimous—will you lend me your reels?"

"What?"

"Yes—your phonograph reels."

"Of course."

He wrapped them carefully in silk paper—the seventeen of them that he had filled with his harangue, and launched himself feverishly through the streets of the city, taking them to the celebrated Liège newspaper, the *Express.*

During his absence, his son—a distinguished young man of fourteen springs, plus one summer—arrived red-faced and out of breath. While he was still on the stairway he shouted to me: "There's news, Monsieur, come and see, quickly!" And he led me to the bed of the Meuse.

On the way, he explained to me how, with his friends, he had noticed rather large and dangerous cracks in the idle of the river bed, how they had pooled their savings to buy some stout thread more than six hundred meters long, fitted with hooks and stones to take them down, and how, with a thousand precautions, lying prone on planks laid across them, in order not to fall into the cracks, they had succeeded in catching fish as black as ink, seemingly rolled in charcoal.

We ran, and when we arrived at the place I was amazed; those fish were an utter revelation to me; they had come from the bottom of a mine, but, as they had not been there long, they were not yet blind but only myopic—as I was able to

302

ascertain by putting my spectacles on their heads and offering them worms, which they could see very well and made every effort to grab.

It was a flash of enlightenment for me, and when Nautilus arrived I shouted; "I see what's happened. We're not dealing with a flight or an escapade on the Meuse's part but a suicide. It's thrown itself down a mine-shaft."

Nautilus, astounded, could only say: "That's also my opinion."

I returned to Paris. According to the latest news, the Meuse seems to want to return gradually to its bed, but there is still no news of the mines. Have their inhabitants, which are generally called *mineurs* in the Belgian language,[157] as you know, been saved, or have they been devoured by pike? We still don't know, and the anguishing wait is horrible.

I'll telegraph Nautilus again.

---

[157] The French *mineur* means "minor" as well as "miner."

A Philanthropic Employment and Matrimonial Agency

Love illuminating young blind people.
A matrimonial employment agency.
A nice theme for a clock.

I had just finished breakfast when one of my old friends, who has the good fortune to possess excellent health and an annual income of hundred thousand francs—which isn't bad—plus an excellent heart—which is worthless from a practical viewpoint—suddenly arrived at my apartment.

The following dialogue soon took place between us.

"My dear chap, I want to tell you about a philanthropic idea that I believe to be wonderful—so, without even waiting for your opinion, I've already distributed the circulars and set things in motion. You'll see..."

"Take this cup of coffee in the meantime, and light this cigar. I'm listening."

"Of course. I know what you think—you have a horror of employment agencies, don't you?"

"Absolutely. They're infamous institutions that exploit the poor, and I would like to see them replaced, everywhere and forever—in every city and every trade—by bodies made up of the workers themselves, syndicates that would place their members honestly and gratuitously, including those belonging to a trade without being part of the syndicate. That's my opinion."

"That's fine—but you also have, if I'm not mistaken a holy horror of matrimonial agencies..."

"I believe so. There we're confronted by pure and simple swindling, in all its moral—or, rather immoral—forms, for nine times out of ten the individual doesn't even exist, or the one to whom you are introduced is only a fake hired by the hour or the job, and the worthy fellow is done out of the money he is naïve enough to allow to be extorted from him by the fallacious promise of a young lady with a stainless reputation and a good dowry. Anyway, in most cases that victim is no more honest than the thief, and every time I read about one of these preposterous stories unfolding before a tribunal, it seems to me that I'm watching a drama performed at the Palais-Royal."

"Thank you. Well, listen to me carefully." And, emphasizing his words carefully, he went on: "I'm founding an employment agency that will also be a matrimonial agency…"

I didn't let him finish. Bounding to my feet I said: "You're mad."

"No."

"Then you're making fun of me."

"Not at all."

"But it's idiotic and monstrous."

"Neither one nor the other, but please, listen to me for five minutes…"

"What will your poor mother say? What a comedown, what dishonor…"

"Will you listen to me," he said, authoritatively. Soon, when we were both calmer, he continued: "My project is quite simple, and if it wasn't me who had conceived it, invented it, created it, got it going and caressed it lovingly, like a child, I'd permit myself to consider it sublime.

"You know that once, for some years, we went out together almost every evening…"

"Let's not go back to the Deluge, I beg you—you're reminding me that we're getting old…"

"That's true; still, you can't have failed to notice—especially you, such a lover of Beauty…"

"You flatter me."

"Will you shut up? …Failed to notice how many perfectly honest, good, well brought-up young ladies there are, meekly playing *Cloches de monastère*,[158] even having a certain dowry and yet coiffing Saint Catherine, because they're horribly ugly, which isn't permissible. No one wants to buy such old scrap at any price."

"You're cruel."

"I'm quite simply an impartial observer—and these poor creatures are reduced in consequence to pickling themselves in bigotry and ending their lives in the monotonous and sterile company of their cat and their parrot."

"The picture is accurate."

"Isn't it? And yet, these young women have treasures of generosity, devotion and love in the depths of their heart. But all that must remain uncultivated, like a field over which the fecund plow has never passed, which has never been watered by the benevolent morning dew."

"Oh, shut up, or I'll start crying. I'm beginning to get maudlin."

"Always joking...but follow my argument to the end. Now, while these poor girls are running to seed, while these sad flowers are drying out, there are thousands of blind men in the world who will never know the joys of the family, because they can't get married, because no mother wants to hand over her daughter to them. And in the meantime, how their hearts also suffer, these poor orphans of nature, cheated, but forbidden to see it, like simple pachyderms.

"Every time I see a wedding in a church and hear the organ playing during the mass a whole poem of love and despair, for whoever is able understand music, I'm not deceived—it's because it's being played by an organist who is a bachelor, and blind!"

"You're mad."

---

[158] There is a musical piece with this title, but Vibert is, of course, speaking metaphorically, as in the conventional phrase "coiffing Sainte Catherine," whose implication is identical.

"No, my dear chap; I observe, I understand and, most of all, I sympathize with the dolors of my peers, their hidden despairs..."

"Brave heart," I said, sincerely moved.

"Well, you see, there it is—my work in its entirety, resplendent with philanthropy and tender charity. Do you understand now?"

"Not at all."

"But yes. I've founded an employment bureau doubled with a matrimonial agency, as I said. In the employment agency I only enroll ugly demoiselles who desire to marry, as well as blind persons of the stronger sex—and I marry them off. A blind man has no need for his wife to be beautiful, but simply that she be good and devoted, with the result that I succeed in finding reciprocal employment for all the ugly women and all the poor blind men, and making them happy.

"Exceptionally, when the circumstances present themselves, I also marry young blind women with crippled, deformed or misshapen men who are very happy to find a little indulgence for their infirmity in their wife's extinct gaze.

"Well, is my project humanitarian enough, my incredulous friend? *Love illuminating young blind people*, eh? What a beautiful subject for a clock of the last century!"

"That's true, and you're a generous fellow; not only are you doing great work for the cause of human solidarity, exquisite and full of touching poetry, but you've also found the paradoxical means of creating an honest employment agency and a serious matrimonial agency, which puts the lid on it. But it must be expensive."

"No, I'm rich and can bear the expenses of a simple reception-room, a servant and a book-keeper."

"Found a limited company—I'll buy a hundred shares; it would be a good...deed.[159] Make that a hundred and one."

---

[159] The French *action* signifies "share [in a joint-stock company]" as well as "deed."

"No, I want to keep all the honor and losses of my idea for myself, jealously. Except, as I like you very much, I promise that you shall be the godfather of the first child of the first couple of an ugly woman and a blind man that I marry in this fashion, if the families don't object. That will make you happy…"

"Agreed."

And I shook his hand with unfeigned emotion. What a nice theme for a clock! But my friend had already made that remark, and my amiable female readers, although very emotional and even more touched, will not have forgotten it. I'll stop there!

SF & FANTASY

Guy d'Armen. *Doc Ardan: The City of Gold and Lepers*
G.-J. Arnaud. *The Ice Company*
Cyprien Bérard. *The Vampire Lord Ruthwen*
Aloysius Bertrand. *Gaspard de la Nuit*
Richard Bessière. *The Gardens of the Apocalypse*
Albert Bleunard. *Ever Smaller*
Félix Bodin. *The Novel of the Future*
André Caroff. *The Terror of Madame Atomos; Miss Atomos*
Didier de Chousy. *Ignis*
Captain Danrit. *Undersea Odyssey*
C. I. Defontenay. *Star (Psi Cassiopeia)*
Charles Derennes. *The People of the Pole*
Georges Dodds (anthologist). *The Missing Link*
Harry Dickson. *The Heir of Dracula*
Jules Dornay. *Lord Ruthven Begins*
Sâr Dubnotal *vs. Jack the Ripper*
Alexandre Dumas. *The Return of Lord Ruthven*
J.-C. Dunyach. *The Night Orchid; The Thieves of Silence*
Henri Duvernois. *The Man Who Found Himself*
Achille Eyraud. *Voyage to Venus*
Henri Falk. *The Age of Lead*
Paul Féval. *Anne of the Isles; Knightshade; Revenants; Vampire City; The Vampire Countess; The Wandering Jew's Daughter*
Paul Féval, *fils. Felifax, the Tiger-Man*
Charles de Fieux. *Lamékis*
Arnould Galopin. *Doctor Omega*
G.L. Gick. *Harry Dickson and the Werewolf of Rutherford Grange*
Nathalie Henneberg. *The Green Gods*
V. Hugo, P. Foucher & P. Meurice. *The Hunchback of Notre-Dame*
Michel Jeury. *Chronolysis*
Octave Joncquel & Theo Varlet. *The Martian Epic*
Gérard Klein. *The Mote in Time's Eye*
Jean de La Hire. *Enter the Nyctalope; The Nyctalope on Mars; The Nyctalope vs. Lucifer*
André Laurie. *Spiridon*
Gabriel de Lautrec. *The Vengeance of the Oval Portrait*
Georges Le Faure & Henri de Graffigny. *The Extraordinary Adventures of a Russian Scientist Across the Solar System* (2 vols.)
Gustave Le Rouge. *The Vampires of Mars*

Jules Lermina. *Mysteryville; Panic in Paris; To-Ho and the Gold Destroyers; The Secret of Zippelius*
Jean-Marc & Randy Lofficier. *Edgar Allan Poe on Mars; The Katrina Protocol; Pacifica; Robonocchio; Tales of the Shadowmen 1-7*
Xavier Mauméjean. *The League of Heroes*
John-Antoine Nau. *Enemy Force*
Marie Nizet. *Captain Vampire*
C. Nodier, A. Beraud & Toussaint-Merle. *Frankenstein*
Henri de Parville. *An Inhabitant of the Planet Mars*
J. Polidori, C. Nodier, E. Scribe. *Lord Ruthven the Vampire*
P.-A. Ponson du Terrail. *The Vampire and the Devil's Son*
Maurice Renard. *The Blue Peril; Doctor Lerne; The Doctored Man; A Man Among the Microbes; The Master of Light*
Albert Robida. *The Adventures of Saturnin Farandoul; The Clock of the Centuries; Chalet in the Sky*
J.-H. Rosny Aîné. *Helgvor of the Blue River; The Givreuse Enigma; The Mysterious Force; The Navigators of Space; Vamireh; The World of the Variants; The Young Vampire*
Han Ryner. *The Superhumans*
Brian Stableford. *The New Faust at the Tragicomique; The Empire of the Necromancers (The Shadow of Frankenstein; Frankenstein and the Vampire Countess; Frankenstein in London); Sherlock Holmes & The Vampires of Eternity; The Stones of Camelot; The Wayward Muse.* (anthologist) *The Germans on Venus; News from the Moon; The Supreme Progress; The World Above the World*
Jacques Spitz. *The Eye of Purgatory*
Kurt Steiner. *Ortog*
Eugène Thébault. *Radio-Terror*
Paul Vibert. *The Mysterious Fluid*
Villiers de l'Isle-Adam. *The Scaffold; The Vampire Soul*
Philippe Ward. *Artahe*
Philippe Ward & Sylvie Miller. *The Song of Montségur*

MYSTERIES & THRILLERS

M. Allain & P. Souvestre. *The Daughter of Fantômas*
A. Anicet-Bourgeois, Lucien Dabril. *Rocambole*
A. Bisson & G. Livet. *Nick Carter vs. Fantômas*
V. Darlay & H. de Gorsse. *Lupin vs. Holmes: The Stage Play*

Paul Féval. *Gentlemen of the Night; John Devil; The Black Coats ('Salem Street; The Invisible Weapon; The Parisian Jungle; The Companions of the Treasure; Heart of Steel; The Cadet Gang)*
Emile Gaboriau. *Monsieur Lecoq*
Steve Leadley. *Sherlock Holmes: The Circle of Blood*
Maurice Leblanc. *Arsène Lupin vs. Countess Cagliostro; Lupin vs. Holmes (The Blonde Phantom; The Hollow Needle)*
Gaston Leroux. *Chéri-Bibi; The Phantom of the Opera; Rouletabille & the Mystery of the Yellow Room*
William Patrick Maynard. *The Terror of Fu Manchu*
Frank J. Morlock. *Sherlock Holmes: The Grand Horizontals*
P. de Wattyne & Y. Walter. *Sherlock Holmes vs. Fantômas*
David White. *Fantômas in America*

SCREENPLAYS

Mike Baron. *The Iron Triangle*
Emma Bull & Will Shetterly. *Nightspeeder; War for the Oaks*
Gerry Conway & Roy Thomas. *Doc Dynamo*
Steve Englehart. *Majorca*
James Hudnall. *The Devastator*
Jean-Marc & Randy Lofficier. *Royal Flush*
J.-M. & R. Lofficier & Marc Agapit. *Despair*
Andrew Paquette. *Peripheral Vision*
R. Thomas, J. Hendler & L. Sprague de Camp. *Rivers of Time*

NON-FICTION

Stephen R. Bissette. *Blur 1-5; Green Mountain Cinema 1; Teen Angels & New Mutants*
Win Scott Eckert. *Crossovers* (2 vols.)
Jean-Marc & Randy Lofficier. *Shadowmen* (2 vols.)
Randy Lofficier. *Over Here*

ART BOOKS

Jean-Pierre Normand. *Science Fiction Illustrations*
Raven Okeefe. *Raven's L'il Critters*
Randy Lofficier & Raven OKeefe. *If Your Possum Go Daylight...*
Daniele Serra. *Illusions*

HEXAGON COMICS

Franco Frescura & Luciano Bernasconi. *Wampus*
Franco Frescura & Giorgio Trevisan. *CLASH*
L. Bernasconi, J.-M. Lofficier & Juan Roncagliolo Berger. *Phenix*
Claude Legrand, J.-M. Lofficier & L. Bernasconi. *Kabur*
Franco Oneta. *Zembla*
L. Buffolente, Lofficier & J.-J. Dzialowski. *Strangers: Homicron*
Danilo Grossi. *Strangers: Jaydee*
Claude Legrand & Luciano Bernasconi. *Strangers: Starlock*